Praise for the Mrs. Murphy Series

TAIL GAIT

"[Brown] successfully weaves mystery, history, real estate and romance into her latest novel. The blend is unusual but gripping, and combined with bipedal and quadrupedal characters who constitute old friends, it shines as imaginative and educational entertainment."
—*Richmond Times-Dispatch*

"A cute premise . . . [with] a clever plot twist."
—*RT Book Reviews*

NINE LIVES TO DIE

"Murder and mayhem are the order of the day in best-seller Brown's well-plotted 22nd Mrs. Murphy mystery. . . . Brown's idyllic world, with its Christian values, talking animals, and sympathetic middle-aged pet owners, has understandably struck a chord with many readers."
—*Publishers Weekly*

"Rita Mae Brown, along with . . . Sneaky Pie, have made Harry Haristeen and her feline companion, Mrs. Murphy, household names."
—*Library Journal*

THE LITTER OF THE LAW

"Will appeal to all cozy mystery fans, especially animal lovers."
—*Fresh Fiction*

SNEAKY PIE FOR PRESIDENT

"A deft combination of entertainment and education, Brown's latest will resonate with anyone concerned about the future of the nation—and the world."
—*Richmond Times-Dispatch*

"There are many election-related books you could choose to help you endure the final months of the presidential race, from desk-pounding policy proposals to thick, shelf-crushing biographies.
Or, you could turn to Sneaky Pie."
—NPR

THE BIG CAT NAP

"[A] charming and enchanting mystery that affirms the Crozet cozies remain fun tales as Harry and her Puss 'n Cahoots squad investigate the homicides. . . . Fans will appreciate this engaging anthropomorphic whodunit."
—*Futures Mystery Anthology Magazine*

"Top honors go to the author's love for her beloved Virginia countryside and for her animal characters, who as usual steal the show."
—*Kirkus Reviews*

"A welcome return to cozy form . . . Amusing exchanges among the cats and dog and their commentary on the humans around them will please series fans."
—*Publishers Weekly*

HISS OF DEATH

"[Rita Mae] Brown ratchets up the tension in a conclusion that brings Harry, the killer, both cats, the dog and two horses into the final showdown. Brown . . . reunites the reader with beloved characters, supplies a wealth of local color and creates a killer whose identity and crimes are shocking (in one case, particularly so)."

—*Richmond Times-Dispatch*

"As explained on the book's cover, it takes a cat to write the *purr*-fect mystery. Indeed . . . With a baffling mystery at hand (or paw), it might just prove to be one of [Harry's] most perplexing cases."

—*Tucson Citizen*

"Brown sensitively depicts Harry's cancer treatment as the paw-biting action . . . builds to the revelation of a surprising killer."

—*Publishers Weekly*

CAT OF THE CENTURY

"[Rita Mae Brown's] animals are as witty as ever."

—*Kirkus Reviews*

"There are plenty of suspects with motives in a well-constructed cozy that readers will enjoy in this one sitting read."

—*The Mystery Gazette*

"The mystery part of *Cat of the Century* is quite good. The clues are there but the reader is still left guessing."

—*Jandy's Reading Room*

SANTA CLAWED

"Fun and satisfying . . . an essential purchase for all mystery collections."—*Booklist*

"[A] whodunit . . . that fans of the furry detectives and their two-legged pals will appreciate."
—*Publishers Weekly*

"Fearless feline and clever canine sleuths."
—*Kirkus Reviews*

"For all mystery collections and essential for series fans."
—*Library Journal*

"Captivating . . . will keep readers guessing whodunit to the very end. A delightful Christmas present indeed."
—*The Free Lance Star*

"Anyone who's a sucker for talking animals or who simply enjoys fantasizing about the thoughts running through a beloved pet's brain will find heaps of guilty pleasure in Brown's latest addition to the Mrs. Murphy series."—*Rocky Mountain News*

"The animals once again provide . . . the best comic moments."
—*Alfred Hitchcock's Mystery Magazine*

"[A] satisfying whodunit with a wealth of Virginia color. And, as always, the real fun comes from Tee Tucker, Mrs. Murphy and Pewter. . . . In *Santa Clawed*, they're the true Christmas angels."
—*Richmond Times-Dispatch*

THE PURRFECT MURDER

"Brown provides a perfect diversion for a cold night, complete with a cat or a dog on your lap."
—*Richmond Times-Dispatch*

"Veteran readers . . .
will not be disappointed in this outing."
—*Winston-Salem Journal*

"The well-paced plot builds to an unpredictable and complex conclusion."
—*Publishers Weekly*

"The pets steal the limelight . . .
[and] offer pleasure to fans of animal sleuths."
—*Kirkus Reviews*

"The plot moves easily and those non-humans who speak to each other, if not to their people, are a real pleasure and well worth one's time."
—*iloveamystery.com*

PUSS 'N CAHOOTS

"Such a delight to read."
—*Albuquerque Journal*

"The novel's tight pacing, combined with intriguing local color, make this mystery a blue-ribbon winner."
—*Publishers Weekly*

"This clever mystery strikes a comfortable balance between suspense and silliness."
—*Booklist*

"Fans of the cunning animal sleuths will enjoy their antics and the spot-on descriptions of the horse-show circuit."
—*Kirkus Reviews*

"[Rita Mae Brown has] readers guessing whodunit until the very end."
—*The Free Lance Star*

SOUR PUSS

"*Sour Puss* makes for a sweet read. . . . Brown has a devilish sense of humor."
—*The Free Lance Star*

"One of my all-time favorite cozy series . . . This series is just plain charming."
—*The Kingston Observer*

"[The authors] have once again pounced upon just the right ideas to keep this delightful mystery series as fresh as catnip in spring. . . . These are books written about and for animal lovers. . . . One of the best books in a good series, *Sour Puss* should leave fans purring."
—*Winston-Salem Journal*

"A captivating look at grape growing and the passionate dedication it requires."
—*Publishers Weekly*

"This venerable mystery series has been on a good run of late. Brown does everything right here. . . . Wine fanciers or not, readers will happily toast the animal-loving author for creating this robust and flavorful tale."
—*Booklist*

CAT'S EYEWITNESS

"Thirteen is good luck for the writing team of Rita Mae Brown and her cat Sneaky Pie—and for their many fans. The Browns know how to keep a mystery series fresh and fun."
—*Winston-Salem Journal*

"This mystery, more than the others, has depth—more character development, a more intricate plot, greater exploration of the big topics. I give it nine out of ten stars."
—*Chicago Free Press*

"This book could not have arrived at a better time, the day before a snowstorm, so I had the perfect excuse to curl up by the fire and devour *Cat's Eyewitness* virtually at a sitting. . . . Entertaining, just the thing for a snowy afternoon . . . well worth reading."
—*The Roanoke Times*

"It is always a pleasure to read a book starring Harry and Mrs. Murphy but *Cat's Eyewitness* is particularly good. . . . Rita Mae Brown delights her fans with this fantastic feline mystery."
—*Midwest Book Review*

"It's terrific like all those that preceded it. . . . Brew the tea, get cozy, and enjoy. This series is altogether delightful."
—*The Kingston Observer*

"Frothy mayhem."
—*Omaha Sunday World-Herald*

"[An] irresistible mix of talking animals and a baffling murder or two . . . the animals' wry observations on human nature and beliefs amuse as ever."
—*Publishers Weekly*

"Delightful . . . Grade A."
—*Deadly Pleasures Mystery Magazine*

WHISKER OF EVIL

"A page-turner . . . A welcome sign of early spring is the latest sprightly Mrs. Murphy mystery. . . . There's plenty of fresh material to keep readers entertained. For one thing, the mystery is a real puzzler, with some subtle clues and credible false leads. . . . [They] have done it again. Give them a toast with a sprig of catnip."
—*Winston-Salem Journal*

"Rita Mae Brown and Sneaky Pie Brown fans will gladly settle in for a good long read and a well-spun yarn while Harry and her cronies get to the bottom of the mystery. . . . The series is worthy of attention."
—*Wichita Falls Times Record News*

"Another winsome tale of endearing talking animals and fallible, occasionally homicidal humans."
—*Publishers Weekly*

"The gang from Crozet, Virginia, is back in a book that really advances the lives of the characters. . . . Readers of this series will be interested in the developments, and will anxiously be awaiting the next installment, as is this reader."
—*Deadly Pleasures Mystery Magazine*

"An intriguing new adventure . . . suspenseful . . . Brown comes into her own here; never has she seemed more comfortable with her characters."
—*Booklist*

"Another fabulous tale . . . wonderful . . . The book is delightful and vastly entertaining with a tightly created mystery."
—*Old Book Barn Gazette*

"Undoubtedly one of the best books of the Mrs. Murphy series . . . a satisfying read."
—*Florence Times Daily*

BOOKS BY RITA MAE BROWN & SNEAKY PIE BROWN

Wish You Were Here
Rest in Pieces
Murder at Monticello
Pay Dirt
Murder, She Meowed
Murder on the Prowl
Cat on the Scent
Sneaky Pie's Cookbook for Mystery Lovers
Pawing Through the Past
Claws and Effect
Catch as Cat Can
The Tail of the Tip-Off
Whisker of Evil
Cat's Eyewitness
Sour Puss
Puss 'N Cahoots
The Purrfect Murder
Santa Clawed
Cat of the Century
Hiss of Death
The Big Cat Nap
Sneaky Pie for President
The Litter of the Law
Nine Lives to Die
Tail Gait
Tall Tail
A Hiss Before Dying

BOOKS BY RITA MAE BROWN FEATURING "SISTER" JANE ARNOLD

Outfoxed
Hotspur
Full Cry
The Hunt Ball
The Hounds and the Fury
The Tell-Tale Horse
Hounded to Death
Fox Tracks
Let Sleeping Dogs Lie

THE MAGS ROGERS BOOKS

Murder Unleashed
A Nose for Justice

BOOKS BY RITA MAE BROWN

Animal Magnetism: My Life with Creatures Great and Small
The Hand that Cradles the Rock
Songs to a Handsome Woman
The Plain Brown Rapper
Rubyfruit Jungle
In Her Day
Six of One
Southern Discomfort
Sudden Death
High Hearts
Started from Scratch: A Different Kind of Writer's Manual
Bingo
Venus Envy
Dolley: A Novel of Dolley Madison in Love and War
Riding Shotgun
Rita Will: Memoir of a Literary Rabble-Rouser
Loose Lips
Alma Mater
Sand Castle
Cakewalk

1550 E. College Ave.
309-452-7475
Your cashier was CHEC 504

DASANI WATER	3.59 B
TAX	0.04
**** BALANCE	3.63

Normal IL 61761
MASTERCARD Purchase
************5959 - C
REF#: 09082Z TOTAL: 3.63
AID: A0000000041010
TC: A2F9DDB81DDDFD32

MASTERCARD	3.63
CHANGE	0.00

TOTAL NUMBER OF ITEMS SOLD = 1
08/03/21 03:53pm 347 504 97 999999504

THANK YOU FOR SHOPPING KROGER
Now Hiring - Apply Today!
jobs.kroger.com
www.kroger.com

Tall Tail

A MRS. MURPHY MYSTERY

RITA MAE BROWN
& SNEAKY PIE BROWN

ILLUSTRATED BY MICHAEL GELLATLY

BANTAM BOOKS • NEW YORK

2017 Bantam Books Mass Market Edition

Published in the United States by Bantam Books, an imprint of Random House, a division of Penguin Random House LLC, New York.

BANTAM BOOKS and the HOUSE colophon are registered trademarks of Penguin Random House LLC.

Originally published in hardcover in the United States by Bantam Books, an imprint of Random House, a division of Penguin Random House LLC, in 2016.

This book contains an excerpt from the forthcoming book *A Hiss Before Dying* by Rita Mae Brown. This excerpt has been set for this edition only and may not reflect the final content of the forthcoming edition.

ISBN 978-0-553-39248-7
Ebook ISBN 978-0-553-39247-0

Cover design: Beverly Leung
Cover illustration: Beverly Leung, with images © Shutterstock/eva_mask (cat outline and sky), Sarawut Chamsaeng (tree), Klagyivik Viktor (grass)

Printed in the United States of America

randomhousebooks.com

987654321

Bantam Books mass market edition: May 2017

For Ruth Dalsky, my old polo teammate.
She never let me down on the pitch
and she doesn’t in life, either.

The Cast of Characters

The Present

Mary Minor Haristeen, "Harry"—A Smith graduate in art history, she wound up back in Crozet, Virginia, where she runs the family farm. Her two cats and dog are her constant companions.

Pharamond Haristeen, DVM, "Fair"—Harry's husband is an equine vet specializing in reproduction. He has long ago given up keeping up with his wife. She sometimes mystifies him, but he loves her.

Susan Tucker—Harry's friend from cradle days. They tease, bicker, and prod each other along. They are good at handling each other.

Ned Tucker—Susan's husband, a lawyer, is now a representative in the House of Delegates.

Governor Samuel Holloway—a World War II naval hero, the former governor, Susan's maternal grandfather, at ninety-six is dying of leukemia. His mind is razor sharp.

Penny Holloway—the governor's wife, Susan's grandmother, struggles to keep everything and everyone on an even keel. She is mostly successful. Like her granddaughter, she is a good golfer.

Millicent Grimstead—Susan's mother, who spends much of her time now at her parents' estate, Big Rawly, to help with her father.

Edward Holloway Cunningham—Susan's cousin is a state senator with a big following. He is now running for a Senate seat in Washington, feeling Richmond is too small for him. He rides on his grandfather's coattails.

Mignon Skipwith—A young writer and researcher, she works with the governor as he writes his autobiography. She is discreet and reliable.

Barbara Leader—A home nurse, Barbara tends to the governor, jollies him along, and gives him his meds as well as restorative bourbon. She was a class behind Harry and Susan at Crozet High. They weren't close, but they all like one another.

The Eighteenth Century

Catherine Schuyler—at twenty, intelligent, levelheaded, and impossibly beautiful, she is learning from her brilliant father about business. She already has a reputation as a leading horsewoman.

John Schuyler—A former major in the Revolutionary War, only a few years older than his smashing wife, he is powerfully built and works hard. As he is from Massachusetts he can miss some of the undercurrents of Virginia society.

Rachel West—Two years younger than her sister, Catherine, she, too, is beautiful but her beauty is softer, sweeter. She's easy to please, ready to help, and possessed of deep moral conviction.

Charles West—Captured by John Schuyler at the Battle of Saratoga, the then nineteen-year-old marched all the way to The Barracks prisoner-of-war camp outside Charlottesville. The second son of a baron in England, he had the good sense to stay in America. Like John, he is dazzled by his wife and knows how lucky he is.

Karl Ix—A Hessian also captured. He and Charles become friends in the camp and continue working together after the war.

Francisco Selisse—A man of middle years, he made a pot of money, first through marriage and then from his own efforts.

Aesthetically attuned, ruthless in business, and hard on his slaves, he is not well liked.

Maureen Selisse—The daughter of a Caribbean banker, she was a great catch for Francisco. Keenly aware of her social position, she is also accustomed to getting her way. While the love has faded for Francisco, she hates that he carries on with a beautiful slave, making little attempt to hide it.

Hiram Meisner—The county constable responsible for catching criminals and runaway slaves. He's not a bad fellow, and does his job without much enthusiasm.

Dennis McComb—As Hiram's assistant, he evidences more enthusiasm. Not bright, he sees the world in black and white.

Ewing Garth, the father of Catherine and Rachel, is a loving man, brilliant in business. He is a creature of his time, but one who can learn. He helped finance the war and hopes the new nation can hold together. A widower, he misses his wife, a true partner.

Bartholomew Graves, an Irishman, was an artillery officer for the British in the war. He, too, was at The Barracks. He escaped to build a new life.

Mary Graves, younger than her husband, is sensible, well-built, adoring, and keeps a happy home for the veteran. They are well suited to each other.

The Slaves: Big Rawly

Aileen (Ailee) has cat's eyes, a voluptuous body, and a joy for life. She loves Moses. Francisco lusts after her, forces himself on her, and beats her if necessary. She avoids him as best she can and refuses to let him dampen her joys.

Moses Durkin works in the stable with his father. His love for Ailee is all-consuming. He wants to protect her, but how?

Sheba is Maureen Selisse's lady-in-waiting. Really, she's Maureen's right hand and she enjoys the power. She'll destroy anyone who stands in her way.

DoRe Durkin, Moses's father, limps from an old fall from a horse. He's worried about Moses, who he fears will do something very foolish.

The Slaves: Cloverfields

Bettina is a cook of fabulous abilities. She's the head woman of the slaves, thanks to her fame, her wisdom, and her wondrous warmth. She also has a beautiful voice. Bettina's view: "I could be a queen in Africa, but I'm not in Africa. I'm here." She made a vow to Isabelle, Ewing's wife, as she died. Bettina vowed to take care of Catherine and Rachel. She has kept her pledge.

Serena is young, learning from Bettina both in the kitchen and out. She has uncommon good sense and will, in the future, wield power among her people.

Jeddie Rice is eighteen, a natural with horses. He loves them. He's been riding, working, and studying bloodlines with Catherine since they were children. Like Serena, Jeddie has all the qualities of someone who will rise, difficult though the world they live in is.

Tulli—A little fellow at the stables who tries hard to learn.

Ralston—Fifteen and thin, he, too, is at the stables. He works hard.

Father Gabe is old, calm, watchful. He accepts Christianity but practices the old religion. Many believe he can conjure spirits. No matter if he can or can't, he is a healer.

Roger is Ewing's house butler, the most powerful position a male slave can have. He has a sure touch with people, black or white.

Weymouth, Roger's son, is in his middle twenties. The hope is he will inherit his father's position someday, but for now he's fine with being second banana. He's a good barber and in truth not very ambitious.

Barker O., powerful, quiet, he drives the majestic coach-in-four. He's known throughout Virginia for his ability.

Bumbee fights with her husband. Finally she moves into the weaving cabin to get away from him and to comfort a lost soul.

Ruth has a two-year-old and a new baby. How she loves any baby, kitten, puppy, and she gets to show this love to save a little life.

The Animals

Mrs. Murphy, Harry's tiger cat, knows she has more brains than her human. She used to try to keep Harry out of trouble. She gave up, knowing all she can do is extricate her human once she's in another mess.

Pewter, a fat gray cat, believes the world began when she entered it. What a diva. But the Queen of All She Surveys does come through in a pinch, although you'll never hear the end of it.

Tee Tucker was bred by Susan Tucker. A tough, resourceful corgi, she knows she has to protect Harry, work with the levelheaded Mrs. Murphy, and endure Pewter.

Owen is Tucker's brother. They adore being with each other. For Tucker it's a relief to sometimes be away from the cats.

Shortro is a young Saddlebred ridden as a hunter.

Tomahawk is Harry's old Thoroughbred hunter who hotly resents being thought old.

The Eighteenth-Century Animals

Piglet is a brave, smart corgi who went through the war and imprisonment with Captain Charles West. He loves living in Virginia with the other animals and people.

Serenissima is Francisco Selisse's fabulous blooded mare whom he sends to Catherine to be bred to her stallion, Reynaldo.

Reynaldo is up-and-coming, with terrific conformation, but hot. Catherine and Jeddie can handle him.

Crown Prince is a younger half brother to Reynaldo. Both are out of Queen Esther, and fortunately, Crown Prince has her temperament.

King David is one of the driving horses. He's heavier built than Reynaldo, and Crown Prince. Solomon is King David's brother. They are a flashy matched pair.

Castor and Pollux are two Percherons who do heavy-duty work. They are such good boys.

Sweet Potato is a saucy pony teaching Tulli to ride.

Martin was Maureen Selisse's mare but winds up in York, Pennsylvania, where Mary Graves spoils him with goodies. He takes care of her.

Tall Tail

1

Tuesday, July 12, 2016

Flaming sword in hand, the Avenging Angel, bestride a monumental tomb, looked over the rolling land toward the Blue Ridge Mountains. His mouth set hard, his eyes piercing, he was not the promise of peace, repose, and eternal joy with the Almighty.

Lying underneath this imposing marble tomb rested the bones of Francisco Selisse, born January 12, 1731. Died September 10, 1784. Historians still puzzle over exactly how he was murdered. Three other people stood in the room when it happened. The stories varied, but no one denied that Francisco had been stabbed to death.

Big Rawly, the plantation on which this sordid event occurred, looked much as it did in 1784. Brick or clapboard, most early Virginia homes resembled one another. In general, the wealthy wanted Georgian homes, but Big Rawly, modeled after a French château, down to the stables and outbuildings, never failed to impress.

Harry had played there as a child with children from the neighboring estate Beau Pre, Big Rawly itself, plus those children whose mothers drove them to the estate. The estate's owners, the Holloways, had children, loved children, and were welcoming to any and all. Susan Tucker, Harry's best friend, was their granddaughter.

Francisco and Maureen Selisse had been childless, and this gaggle of children might have pleased them. Hard to say, for their reputation for ruthlessness endures to this day.

The cemetery in which this imposing tomb commanded center stage was said to be haunted. As a child, Harry had steered clear of the graveyard, and even as an adult that hard-eye stone angel gave her a shiver. Over the centuries, many declared they had seen ghosts here, but with a consideration praiseworthy in the disembodied, the departed never disturbed children.

Now, as an adult, as Harry passed the place, rumbling on the narrow road leading out of Garth Road, she wondered if this consideration would always hold true.

Turning left, heading for Crozet, she noted dark clouds backing up behind the Blue Ridge. Never a good sign. Accompanying her in her old 1978 F-150 sat Mrs. Murphy, the tiger cat, and Pewter, the gray cat. Tucker, a corgi, was also present and always ready to help. The same could not be said of the cats.

They reached another left turn, which wound a few miles down to old Three-Chopt Road, Route 250. Given the threat of a storm, Harry chose this faster route instead of the pleasant drive to Whitehall, where she would also turn left to head home.

Coming at her in the opposite direction, a red Camry flew around a curve up ahead. On such a twisty road, Harry thought it best to be alert. She had stopped, put her left flasher on, when a tremendous clap of thunder startled her and her passengers.

Immediately after, the red Camry swerved straight at them. The car appeared totally out of control. Harry hit the gas, and the vehicle missed her truck bed by inches. She quickly surged ahead before turning around in the small Mt. Olivet church parking lot up ahead. Returning to the turnoff, she found the red Camry nosed into the low runoff ditch. Its wheels spun, the motor kept running.

Turning onto Owensville Road, Harry pulled as far as she could off to the side. Closing the door as the first raindrop fell, she ran to the Camry. A middle-aged woman was slumped over the wheel and did not respond to Harry's rapping on the window. Recognizing the driver, Barbara Leader, who had been in the class behind her at high school, Harry rapped louder. "Barbara!"

No response.

Fortunately, the door was not locked. Harry opened it, touched Barbara's shoulder. No response. She took her pulse. No pulse. Barbara's head dropped forward. Seeing the glassy eyes, Harry knew there was no hope.

Racing back to her truck, Harry climbed into the bed

where she kept her tool box, yanked out two flares, and ran back, putting one on each side of the Camry to cover both directions of Garth Road. The flares burned about twenty yards from the beached automobile, giving passing motorists time to slow.

Harry ran back to her truck, hopped in as the rain increased, plucked her cell from the visor where she always tucked it and dialed her friend, her neighbor, and a deputy of the Sheriff's department, Cynthia Cooper.

"Coop. I'm at Garth and Owensville Roads. A car has gone off the road. The driver, Barbara Leader, is dead."

"Be right there."

"Is there any food in the dead lady's car?" Pewter asked.

"Pewter!" The dog's voice carried a reprimand. *"Have some respect."*

"Why? There's no point in it going to waste." The gray cat was nothing if not practical.

Trees began to bend low; small branches flew out of them. The sky turned black with the now hard rain, and Harry could barely see ten feet ahead. She hoped passersby would see the flares and her flashers.

Fortunately, the sudden terrible weather proved a help, keeping more sensible drivers off the road. Within ten minutes, Harry heard the siren, then saw the flashing lights. Heedless of the weather, she jumped out from the driver's seat, hurrying to the squad car.

"Harry, you're soaked."

"It's warm," Harry answered Coop, who wore her slicker.

The slender officer opened the Camry's door, used her flashlight to glance around. She, too, felt for a pulse. Walking to the passenger side, she opened the door. From the glove compartment, she pulled out registration papers, then returned them.

Harry sighed. "Knew her from high school. She became a nurse. I mean, I didn't know her well, but she was a class behind in school, popular. She was home-nursing Susan's grandfather."

Susan Tucker, Harry's closest friend, also knew Barbara. Susan's grandfather Samuel Holloway had been governor of Virginia in the early seventies. Diagnosed with leukemia, he'd ignored it and kept going, but finally the disease and his advanced age were taking their toll. Barbara was at the farm, Big Rawly, Monday through Friday. The nurse's buoyant personality lifted everyone's spirits.

"At least she died quickly." Cooper exhaled. "I suppose that's some consolation."

Saddened to see a longtime acquaintance in such a state, Harry simply shrugged. Yes, a lingering death is painful to watch, but a sudden death, especially when the deceased is young, is a shock.

"I guess you're never too young for a massive heart attack or stroke." Cooper then ordered Harry, "You go on."

"I'll wait with you until the ambulance comes."

"Go. I heard over the radio driving here that the winds will pick up. This is turning into some kind of storm. We'll catch up later and you can give me what details you have."

Back in the truck, Harry cut on the motor. The rumble always sounded glorious to her ears.

"No food?" Pewter pressed.

Harry reached over to pet the fat gray. She kept her flashers on, slowly driving down the road. It took her forever to reach St. Paul's, where she turned right. Moving with care, she noticed cars pulled off to the side of the road, cowed by the inclement weather. Branches flew around, a few landing on the pavement and forcing Harry to drive around them. By the time she reached her farm, she uttered a prayer of thanks. It felt like a miracle that she'd made it.

Cooper was right, this was some kind of storm. The rain dropped like a steel gray curtain, and the wind blew dangerous gusts of sixty miles an hour.

Rolling down her stone-covered farm road, she noticed trees that had fallen in the rain. She pulled the truck in front of the barn, ran in, and opened the outside stall doors, all of which opened onto paddocks. She could barely see the horses, huddled with their backs to the wind. She whistled and they happily trotted in, each horse entering his or her stall. Petting her friends as she moved from stall to stall, she closed those outside doors, then closed the big end doors, leaving them open a crack. It wouldn't be too smart in this situation to allow the interior of the barn to keep a higher pressure than the outside.

The wind screamed. Slipping back outside, she opened the truck door. The cats shot out, flying for the house, nearly colliding as they hit the animal door in the screened porch door.

Lifting out Tucker, Harry, too, bolted for the house. Tucker, even faster, ran ahead.

Once inside, she stripped off the wet clothes, dried herself with a fluffy towel, pulled on dry clothes. She left her soggy garments in the shower. She'd come back to wring them out and take them downstairs to the washer, but right now she was hungry and worried.

The lights flickered and went out. She put down food for the animals and tried calling her husband on the cell, as the power was out. She couldn't get through. Not that she was worried about her six-foot-five-inch husband. The equine veterinarian was equal to just about any task, but she wanted to hear his voice.

The windows rattled. Tucker looked worried.

The cats did, too.

Harry knelt down to pet everyone, in case the violence of the storm frightened them. "We've been through a lot together," she said consolingly.

"Yes, we have," Tucker agreed.

Mrs. Murphy rubbed against Harry's leg. *"Indeed. We have been through a lot together."*

"And most of it was your fault," Pewter firmly stated.

"Pewter, you are so full of it," Mrs. Murphy shot back.

"Buttface," Pewter grumbled.

"Your language has deteriorated," Tucker criticized her.

"You all drive me to it. On my own, I am perfectly well behaved." The gray cat said this, knowing it was a major fib no one within hearing distance would believe.

Standing up, Harry smiled. "What are you two chattering about?" A ferocious gust of wind diverted her attention to the kitchen window. "I can't see a thing."

She opened the refrigerator door. Without its light, she knew where everything was and pulled out a piece of cheese and a Co-Cola. Sitting down, she shoved the cheese in her face, she was so hungry.

"I like cheese, too," Pewter announced.

Harry glanced down at the cat, who put on her best begging face, then looked up again as the windows rattled more. "I wonder if Barbara's ghost will haunt the curve where she went off the road."

"What?" Tucker asked.

Harry shook her head. "It's the Avenging Angel in that boneyard. Makes me think of ghosts. I don't know if I believe in ghosts, but people say animals can see them."

"I don't want to see one," Pewter replied. *"If I see one, I'm going the other way."*

"What if the ghost had tuna?" the dog said.

"Well, that's different," the fat gray cat responded.

"But wouldn't the tuna be ghost food?" Mrs. Murphy tormented Pewter.

"Fish aren't ghosts." Pewter declared this with authority.

"You don't know." Mrs. Murphy licked her front paw. *"Maybe Moby-Dick is out there, scaring everybody."*

"Really, why would anyone write a giant book about a pea-brained whale? If humans intend to write, they should write about cats." Pewter puffed out her cheeks. This was a sore spot for Pewter. She hated Melville's storytelling. When alone, Harry had been known to read to them from *Moby-Dick.*

Now, as the animals bantered back and forth, Harry thought about the tenuousness of life. She'd seen people die. It didn't upset or frighten her. But Barbara Leader wasn't old. Death arrives when He wishes, most generally unannounced. Harry said a prayer for Barbara Leader and then thought again about her spirit. A ghost would not haunt that spot. That was silly.

She said another prayer and then thought that was the end of it.

It wasn't, of course.

2

Tuesday, July 12, 2016

6:30 P.M.

Knowing most everyone in the area, Fair drove down the country roads and cleared debris along the way. Doing so, he also checked on the local horses in pastures and poked down driveways, usually finding the owner clearing mess from the storm. The miracle was no horses had been hurt at any place Fair checked. Cell service fluctuated, meaning the weather fouled a lot of stuff. Whatever this storm was, it wasn't over. He just prayed the strong winds wouldn't return.

Fair finally drove down his own driveway at six-thirty P.M. Drenched, tired, hungry, he walked through the door, lights on, thanks to the generator, a five-thousand-dollar job worth every penny.

"Honey!" Harry turned from the stove to embrace him. "You look like the dogs got at you under the porch."

"*I resent that,*" Tucker grumbled.

"*If you got at anyone under the porch, only their ankles would be bleeding.*" Pewter smirked.

The dog curled her lip. "*You could do better?*"

"*Better! I'd claw their eyes out. Then I'd attack from every direction. They'd be shredded like government documents.*" She puffed up.

"*You could sit on them. That might break a few ribs.*" Tucker reached out a paw to tap her.

Pewter hissed. "*Don't touch me. Don't you dare touch me!*"

"*Oh, shut up,*" said Mrs. Murphy. "*I want to hear what Daddy has to say.*" She leapt onto the counter.

Harry was so relieved her husband was home. "Sit down. I've been waiting for you. Tried to call, but even cell service is out."

"I know." He wearily dropped his large frame onto a chair at the kitchen table.

"Snow peas. Rice and flank steak. Not French cooking but good for you, plus it's all I could find. Today is shopping day and I never made it." She placed the food in front of him, sitting down to eat, too.

The animals' bowls were full, so they didn't bother either of the humans, especially since Harry had sliced up some steak. *Spoiled* doesn't begin to cover it.

"How much damage did you see?" she asked.

He swallowed a big bite of snow peas, which he loved. "Roofs peeled off, especially the standing seam roofs. Just as though a can opener had cut open a side. But only narrow sections. I didn't see one structure without some roof damage. Large branches down. Loblolly pines are uprooted, and here's a strange thing, anytime I passed a creek, downed trees everywhere."

"The creeks must have acted like a wind tunnel," Harry wondered.

"I guess."

"If our cellphones start working again, we can find The Weather Channel."

"Power crews are everywhere. Gotta give it to the utility companies."

"Honey, what we give the utility companies is our money, lots of money." Harry was tough about money and service.

She worked hard for a living, as did her husband, and she expected anyone with whom she did business to do the same. The problem with the utilities and cell servers, Internet stuff, was holding their feet to the fire if they slogged off. If sufficiently disgusted, she cut off the service. She'd been studying ways to generate her own power with old-fashioned farm windmills. A very exciting cube structure using wind was being developed in Akron, Ohio. Once engaged, she stuck to it, and none of her friends doubted she would be the first to generate her own power with the latest affordable technology. Solar panels sounded good, but days and occasionally a week might pass without sunlight, thanks to heavy cloud cover or fog. The surrounding Blue Ridge Mountains had their own weather system. Harry, being born to it, could feel the weather in her bones. Seeing the clouds when they piled up behind the nearby peaks gave her fair warning of a storm. She didn't know how fierce it would be, though.

Fair shoveled the food into his mouth before asking, "Do I need to pump more gas for the generator?"

The farm had two pumps, one for regular gasoline, one for diesel. Most farms had their own pumps. You can't plow, bushhog, or make hay if you have to run to the gas station and keep filling up five-gallon cans.

"No," Harry answered. "Thought I would wait until I told you what happened to me today. It was upsetting."

His demeanor changed to immediate concern. "Honey, what happened? You didn't need to wait."

"Would have spoiled supper. I dropped by Susan's family just for a minute, you know. I gave her grandmother a small gardenia for her garden. She looks great, by the way. No one would ever believe that Penny Holloway is eighty-eight. Just there a minute, then I drove down the drive and turned left onto Garth Road. Black clouds were piling up behind the mountains, so I hurried to get home. Anyway, I no sooner reached the tiny white clapboard church when a raindrop splashed, then another, and then *boom*, rain. Slowed down, put on my turn signal to turn left, and this little red Camry was barreling down Garth Road in the opposite direction. It was Barbara Leader coming and missing me by a hair before going off the road.

"Well, Fair, I rushed over, but there was nothing I could do. She was dead. Coop was there in ten minutes."

"Honey, I'm so sorry." He reached over and took her hand. "What a shock. Barbara, that's a loss. She's one of those people always ready to pitch in, or she was. She was a good cheerleader, too," he reminisced.

"I think she was dead before the car stopped. At least, I hope she was."

"Sounds like a heart attack or stroke. I'm sorry she's gone, but I'm glad you weren't hit."

"*Me, too,*" Pewter agreed.

"You never know." Harry sighed, then glanced out the kitchen window. "More rain. Is it possible?"

"Sure is."

"Let's run over to Cooper's. This will be a long day for her. Lots of accidents, I bet. We can start her generator and put some food in the fridge. We have plenty left."

Once over at Cooper's, Fair carefully walked around the house, checking her old generator, while Harry put covered dishes with a note in the fridge. Just as they were leaving the house, Cooper drove up.

Fair greeted her first as she walked inside.

"Cooper, perfect timing," said Harry. "Your supper is in the fridge."

"God, Harry, thank you. I'm bushed." Cooper headed for the fridge.

Harry pulled out the covered dishes. "Sit down. You sit right down."

Fair, who knew Cooper's kitchen almost as well as his own, pulled out heavy everyday china.

"I could use a special treat," Pewter informed them.

"Top cabinet, lower shelf." Cooper told them what they already knew.

"Cooper, you don't need to feed my animals," said Harry, knowing she occasionally overindulged them.

"Oh, it makes them happy, and me, too." Cooper filled her fork with rice. "Still warm."

"We just came over."

"You cleared my driveway of branches. Wood chips gave you away. Thank you."

"Wasn't too bad." Harry handed Cooper a beer as Fair sat down.

"I should have offered to warm everything up and let you get out of those wet clothes," Harry said.

"Starved. By now I'm half dry."

"A lot of accidents?" Fair asked.

"Some, but not as many as I'd feared. All the stoplights went out, but people are smart. They do the who-came-first routine and that takes care of it. I think most people had the sense to get off the road. Still, that storm hit us fast."

"You know, just before the wind hit, no birds were flying. No deer out in the field. The horses seemed fine. I should have noticed they all faced the same direction. Hindsight makes us all smart."

"Sometimes it does, but most times I kick myself in the butt," said Cooper.

"Oh, let me do that for you," Harry teased her. "That's what friends are for."

The wooden steps reverberated again. Fair rejoined them after double-checking the generator. "You've got an extra five gallons down there."

"Glad I did that. I try to back up everything, but I don't like keeping gasoline in the house."

"I don't, either, but if you think about it, wood near the fireplace isn't always the smartest thing, either," Harry added.

"True, but wood won't explode." Cooper had finished her plate in record time.

Harry uttered those sweetest words. "You're right."

Rain started again, medium not driving.

"Here it comes again." Cooper stared out the window at the downpour. "Rick and I"—she named the sheriff—"had to tell Jordan Leader about Barbara at work. You know, that's the hardest part of the job. His coworkers were wonderful, drove him home. One of them is staying with him."

"No idea what went wrong?"

"Often with sudden death the family requests an autopsy, just a basic autopsy that can be done by a hospital pathologist. He said he wanted one. Said she was the picture of health."

Harry nodded. "Funny, isn't it? People want to know. It makes them feel better somehow."

Fair replied, "It does, but if someone died of a condition that can be inherited or is transmittable, it makes sense. And things like stroke are silent killers. How many times have you heard about someone who just had a complete checkup and they drop dead of a heart attack? I guess it's good to know the exact cause of death."

"Right," Harry concurred. "But it doesn't really change anything."

In this case, it would.

3

Wednesday, July 13, 2016

Sliding sideways, recovering, Harry slowly drove her year-old ATV down the farm road. With two exceptions, the pasture fences remained unbroken. Near the creek that separates Harry's place from Cooper's place, two trees had crashed into the far pastures. Uprooted sycamores, mud clinging to their roots, littered the creek bed. Rumbling to the beaver dam, she cut the motor, swinging her leg over the seat.

Hands on her hips, Tucker by her side, she examined the beaver dam. Part of it, torn away, was already being repaired by the industrious beasts, who paid little attention to Harry. Seeing her over the years, they knew her, of course. She never bothered them, nor did Tucker, with rare exceptions. None of them slapped their tail on the water as warning. Perched on their haunches, they looked at the human for a moment before returning to their task. Intelligent creatures, they retrieved those pieces of wood entangled in roots or hung up behind rocks halfway in the water. Other beavers chewed at saplings farther away from the creek.

"Come on, Tucker." Harry remounted as Tucker jumped onto her lap, muddy paws and all.

Harry considered pawprints her fashion signature.

The ATV had been altered so instead of pushing a little lever for the gas with her right thumb she could twist the right handlebar cover as one would do on a motorcycle. Sure made long trips on the ATV easier. She felt she had better control.

Harry preferred two wheels to four, but covering the kind of terrain she did in various weather conditions, an off-the-road motorcycle wasn't as useful—plus, on a motorcycle she couldn't carry anything. A toolkit affixed to the back of her machine met most needs. Much as Harry loved her old 4x4 truck, this was cheaper on gas and she could wiggle into places forbidden to the truck, unless she wanted to wreck it.

Up the east side of the Blue Ridge they climbed, dodging downed limbs along the way. This side occasionally saw weather fly over it, dipping to the lower land below, which rested at eight hundred feet above sea level. The top of this particular ridge hovered at two thousand five hundred feet, high enough. Humpback Mountain's top stood higher than that. The gap for Interstate 64 neared three thousand feet, and Humpback even stood higher. Along this old path, Harry had cut out turnarounds. Halfway up the mountain stood a sturdy shed. All was in order. The walnut trees were unscathed, but then they were more than a century old, with root systems deep and wide unlike the loblolly pines. Other conifers also stood tall; they, too, were very old. Harry thought some of them might even be virgin trees, along with some old oaks and hickories, impressive.

Most of the damage lay below.

"Okay, sugar, down we go." She turned the ATV around and put it in creep gear to slowly descend.

Once at the bottom, she could view her farm from the back and much of the old Jones place, which Cooper rented. A herd of deer snuck out of the forest, turned to stare at her, then loped toward Cooper's.

Back at the barn, driving in the aisle, the minute Harry turned off the motor, she heard the welcome hum of electricity.

"Thank heavens."

"Imagine life without electricity?" Tucker jumped down. *"Think of all the work, of haying without a tractor. Well, a tractor doesn't use electricity."* The small dog was smart.

"Simon, are you up there?" Harry called up to the hayloft.

No response sent her up the ladder and she spotted him: The possum, awakening, blinked, curled his head tighter to his chest and fell back asleep. Harry then looked up at the barn's cupola. The big owl, Flatface, safe and sound, dozed in her nest.

Harry scrubbed out the water buckets inside each stall, refilled them, then picked out the stalls, since the horses had spent the night inside. She left the outside stall door open so they could come and go at will. Usually in summer they spent the day outside only when it was cooler. As the rain had pounded and the wind wailed, she had allowed each horse to make up his or her own mind. They elected to stay in. The four broodmares contently ate. She hadn't bred any this year. Short of cash, it takes a fair amount of money to raise a horse, then train it. So the girls munched away while her two foxhunters, one a Thoroughbred and one a Saddlebred, played outside, lots of chasing back and forth.

Harry rolled out the wheelbarrow to the manure pile. She covered the big compost heap, cut down six feet into the earth with a tarp so it would degrade faster. Made the best garden mulch ever, which she would deliver to friends. As she and Fair rarely gave dinner parties due to his work schedule, this was her gift, a way of keeping in touch.

After sweeping out the center aisle, she retreated to her tack room, which was invitingly cool. The mercury hovered at seventy-three degrees Fahrenheit, unusual for July.

Picking up the phone, she dialed Susan Tucker's number.

"You okay over there?" Harry asked after Susan answered.

"Yes. What about you?"

"Two trees over fences by the creek. Actually, that's about it."

"Same here. Have you watched the weather?"

"No, I've been out doing chores," said Harry. "When I left, still no power. Thank God for the generator. I rode up to check on the timber, yours and mine. Fine. A few branches down low, but once you climb, fine. If that wasn't the damndest thing. One minute it was calm and the next minute, *Kaboom!*"

"The power came back on about an hour ago, so the first thing I turned to was The Weather Channel. Should be clear until the weekend, then maybe a few pop-up thunderstorms."

Harry filled Susan in on yesterday's sad event.

"Barbara Leader?" Susan repeated.

"Right."

"Oh, dear, she was such a nice person. G-Pop adores her. He needs help in the house now. He refuses to go to hospice."

"This will be hard on your grandfather."

"Barbara could handle him. She'd whisper to him, 'I know you have secrets.' And he'd laugh. He needs to laugh. You've seen him. He's lost so much weight, but he's a real fighter."

Samuel Holloway, a World War II naval hero, became governor of Virginia in the early 1970s, helped in part by his war record and strong leadership qualities. Susan and Harry had both been born in the middle of his gubernatorial term. They had no memory of his years in office.

"Yes, he's a fighter," said Harry. "He was such fun when we were growing up. We were too little to know anything about politics, but he would play with us when he was home. I wonder if elected officials still do that?"

"Harry, of course they do." Susan laughed. "They aren't all egotists and monsters."

"Your cousin weighs in heavily on the egotism scale."

Edward Holloway Cunningham, the son of Susan's aunt, Pauline Cunningham, had a seat in the state Senate. At forty-two, he was readying for a run for senator, the election in the fall. Campaigning never stops in America, and Eddie was coming out swinging.

"I'm not Eddie's biggest fan, but Mother always says, 'Don't hang your dirty laundry on the line,' and I don't. Mom and Aunt Pauline saw a lot of political turmoil growing up."

"They got through it." Harry complimented the two sisters, now in their late sixties.

"One of the good things about sexism is that although I was the granddaughter of a governor, no one expected much of me other than being a good hostess. And here I am married to a state delegate, but in Ned's defense, that came late. He didn't start out to be in politics."

"He's lucky to have you. You handle it well, all those fund-raisers, charity events, dinner parties. You amaze me."

"Harry." Susan felt a rush of gratitude. "What a sweet thing to say. As long as I have my kids, both out in the work world, you, my dog, and golf, always golf, I can keep sane, I think."

"You can. Hey, know what? When I passed the Avenging Angel, he still scares me!"

"Me, too." They both laughed.

4

Monday, September 6, 1784

The setting sun, bisected by a spearlike gray cloud, was turning scarlet. It was 7:30 P.M., shadows lay long on the fields. Most of the forage crops, piled loose onto open wagons, had been stored in a seventy-two-foot-by-forty-eight-foot shed, twenty feet high. Charles West, a former British prisoner of war and self-taught architect, had designed the shed so air would circulate through it. Three inches open between the roof and the side wall allowed air to flow, while the overhang protected the hay from all but the fiercest blowing rain. At the foot of the building, small louvers opened to allow more air inside. In the middle of the sides, two-inch round holes had been drilled out. The hay sat on a solid wooden floor so moisture would not rot the hay on the bottom.

A few hay ricks stood in the fields for cattle and horses to enjoy. The ricks, giant overturned thimbles, shed water. The outermost layer might suffer some, but all an animal had to do was dig in deep and the reward was sweet hay.

John Schuyler was imposing, well over six feet tall, with broad shoulders and heavy muscles. He stood next to his former prisoner Charles West, who was almost as tall, muscled but more slender. West folded his arms across his soaked shirt. They'd worked hard that day. At Charles's feet sat Piglet, his faithful corgi who had gone through the War for Independence with him, as well as imprisonment in two separate camps.

The Barracks was a more-than-two-hundred-acre prisoner-of-war camp. Abutting the back of Ewing Garth's three-thousand-acre estate, The Barracks still hosted remaining Englishmen, Irish and Scots, although not as prisoners. Initially, these men were to be repatriated to the United Kingdom, an agonizingly slow process, as King George and his advisers dragged their feet. Living in makeshift buildings, one by one, the men gave up on returning home. Resourceful, they plied the trade they had learned before soldiering while they lived without rent in the log buildings. Each dreamed of saving enough to buy a patch of land and strike out on his own. The state of Virginia bore them no ill will, and since the state need not pay any expenses, the men were free to squat.

Both John Schuyler and Charles West would call on these highly skilled squatters, from time to time making use of their crafting or iron work, or hiring them for day work on the Ewing estate. Karl Ix, a captured Hessian, became close to Charles and John when building three bridges on Ewing's property. Charles and Karl Ix worked hand in glove, two young men from different backgrounds and countries, who grasped the limitless possibilities in the new nation.

As all three men, John, Charles, and Karl, had married American women, great sweetness was added to the future's limitless possibilities. While still a major in the Continental army, John married first. Perhaps he didn't know the first time he set eyes on Catherine Garth that they would marry, but just about everyone else did. Catherine was wealthy, well schooled, and beautiful. She also brought John and Charles West together. Back when Charles was still a resident of The Barracks, in exchange for extra supplies for his men, he trained John in the ways of a gentleman. Certainly, a lady of Catherine's station couldn't marry a Massachusetts farmer's son like John Schuyler, devoid of refinement, although not of good looks. Charles West, a baron's younger son, would never inherit, but he had all the polish of a titled aristocrat with none of the snobbery. The openness of this New World enchanted Charles even as it sometimes shocked him.

When John Schuyler met Catherine Garth she was eighteen. Now, at twenty, she was even more beautiful, if that was possible. Her younger sister, Rachel, now eighteen, had married last year. While Rachel was a delightful, lovely, extremely pretty young woman, her sister Catherine looked like a goddess. Catherine was also strong-willed and had a head for business. Women's talk and circumscribed lives bored her to bits, although when she had been in the company of the governor's wife or other wives of powerful men, she had banished that boredom. If not intellectually brilliant, however, certainly some of these ladies were shrewd. They well understood how the world worked and were committed to their husbands' ascents.

Unlike Catherine, Rachel was easygoing, tall, shy of argument. She couldn't dissemble. She tried not to wear her heart on her sleeve, but somehow it always showed. Both young women were loving, but Catherine hid this quality. Both sisters shared strong feelings about right from wrong. For all Rachel's sweetness and desire to please, if she felt someone had been wronged or something was shady, she wouldn't budge. Indeed, she would do all she could to help.

Charles West had come to Ewing Garth's for a job when he ran away in deep winter from the prisoner-of-war camp at York, Pennsylvania, where he'd been shifted due to overcrowding at The Barracks. From the start, he was hardly immune to Rachel Ewing's grace, kindness and beauty, but she was sixteen then and he nineteen. He thought her young and sheltered. But the more he saw her, had a conversation here and there, the more he perceived how kind and mature she was. He fell in love. So did she.

Poor Ewing Garth found himself paying for a second wedding extravaganza the year after Catherine's. Those two weddings became the standard for Albemarle County, for all of Virginia, really—and many a father cursed Ewing Garth under his breath for his lavish spending.

Karl Ix also found a handsome girl, a resident of Charlottesville. Her parents were German. She understood his native tongue and she certainly evidenced all the earmarks of a clean, crisp, well-organized personality. Germans helped populate the mid-Atlantic. Karl and Giselle lived on the Garth estate in a small cottage, which she filled with painted furniture, a big wall clock from her parents, and already one son, the spitting image of his father.

Young and in love, all three men watched the red rim of the sun dip below the Blue Ridge Mountains.

Charles felt he would never fully adjust to Virginia weather. "Should cool off now."

Karl felt the same. "If only the wind would pick up."

"Maybe it will be cooler tomorrow," John said. "Summer's at an end. I don't know about you two, but I need a bath and a cool drink." He turned toward his four-over-four farmhouse, built as a wedding present for Catherine by her father.

"We could sit in the icehouse," Charles suggested.

"Have to climb in a big basket and be lowered down and the Mrs. would fuss." Karl laughed.

"You know the Romans knew how to build icehouses and to make sherbet," remarked Charles, educated at Oxford. "Oh, I wish I hadn't mentioned sherbet."

"*Me, too,*" Piglet barked.

"Piglet, you and me, we always agree." John laughed with his booming good humor. "Remember, Charles, we have to go to the Selisses tomorrow early evening?"

"I know," he said, unhappy at the prospect.

"Well, I'm off the hook." Karl slapped his thigh and turned away. "Home to my bride."

"Excellent idea," Charles agreed.

As the men turned to walk to their respective dwellings, they heard Bettina singing. The voice of an angel. Her work as a cook in the Garths' big house was done for the day, and she'd gathered all the children to her front porch. Whenever Bettina sang, a crowd gathered.

A long, long twilight kept the sky clear and dark blue, but when John looked to the big house, he could see some candles shining.

Gathering up papers with her father as he hunkered down at his desk, Catherine remarked, "Father, you aren't thinking of buying into the forge with Francisco, are you?"

"No, no, my dear." Ewing shook his head. "But it will be an important business and we must stay on good terms."

"He's a beast," Catherine sharply replied.

Ewing folded his hands over his linen waistcoat. "His methods are harsh on his estate and in business."

"Harsh. He'd skin a maggot."

Ewing laughed, rose to kiss his daughter on her cheek. "That he would." He paused, pecked her cheek again. "I am awaiting my first grandchild, you know. I assume you'll precede your sister."

"We're trying." Catherine's demeanor softened. Her laugh was like silver.

"How I remember your mother and I praying for our firstborn: you." His eyes brightened as he beheld the evening star out the window. "Venus." Then he looked at her. "You, of course."

"Oh, Father." Catherine playfully pushed him, then left by the back door to walk to her own house.

A whip-poor-will called out. She heard a soft flutter overhead, looked up to see the barn owl and the last of the fireflies. Twinkles and flashes of green and yellow danced over the herringbone brick walkway, above the meadows. If there weren't fireflies in heaven, she didn't want to go.

Even before she reached her clapboard house, John's deep baritone reached her ears. While not musically gifted, the man remembered every hymn he'd ever sung in church. Right now he was mangling "A Mighty Fortress Is Our God."

She opened the door, tiptoeing to the back of the house, where her husband sat in a large tub, scrubbing his back with a long-handled brush. She joined in singing the hymn. He smiled at the duet. Taking the brush, she finished scrubbing his back.

"You sparkle like a firefly," he cooed.

"You flatter me. Come on, haul your carcass out of the water. Let's have a cool drink while we watch the fireflies from the porch."

He grinned as she handed him a towel. "Yes, my darling."

"Just wrap it around you. No one will see you."

"You will."

"That's why I suggested it." She flashed a grin. "Go on. I'll bring two sweet teas, or would you rather have an untea?" She used the expression for unsweetened tea.

John was still learning southern terms. "Un, I think."

Minutes later they sat, watching the blue of the mountains deepening. A light breeze picked up, and lightning bugs were everywhere, squadrons of them now. Bettina's voice, singing in the distance, was joined by others.

"There is no sound like the sound of our people singing. I remember curling in Mother's arms, Rachel in mine, and we'd listen." Catherine meant "our people." Only a churl would say "slave." The etiquette was clear, as was the injustice, which some had spoken of—notably, General Washington and Thomas Jefferson. Catherine, like her generation, didn't think too much about it. They had always known this way of life.

"It's beautiful," said John. "I sometimes think they are closer to God."

"I wonder," she quietly replied. "Before I forget, don't you forget we've got to be dressed and ready to leave at four tomorrow. The Selisses."

"I'll be ready."

Neither could know, could even imagine, that tomorrow would be the beginning of a crime, a horror even, that would silently seep through two hundred and thirty-two years.

5

Friday, July 15, 2016

Both still wearing their golf clothes, Harry and Susan looked at their reflections and took a few moments to preen.

Susan wrinkled her nose. "These shorts are too tight."

Without looking at her friend's navy Bermuda shorts, Harry quipped, "Lose weight."

"I have lost weight."

"Then buy baggy shorts." Harry thought of other golfers at the country club. "You know how they are at Farmington about the dress code. I'm your caddy and I'm wearing this ridiculous lemon-yellow golf shirt with lemon-yellow knee-length skirt to match. I look completely absurd."

"You look like a golfer."

"Exactly," Harry shot back.

Since high school, Harry had caddied for her best friend. Not a golfer herself, she nevertheless had an uncanny ability to read terrain, which she attributed to farming. Dutifully she wore long shorts or a skirt along with golf shoes, so comfortable that she sometimes wore them walking through the pastures.

Harry could pick the right club given the terrain, distance, and wind conditions. And unlike others, she could tolerate Susan's fretting over her game.

Susan teed off at ten in the morning. The soil, soggy from the recent rains, drained as best it could.

As one of the better golfers in the state, Susan often preferred to play alone. She could move faster, study without boring a companion, and she could try to work out a kink or two. She was determined to win the club championship this year. Coming in as runner-up two years in a row wasn't good enough. Practicing hard now, working with the club pro, Susan felt she would be ready when the championship rolled around in September.

Harry decided she would wear the white coat caddies wore during tournaments. That and keeping Susan calm were her only concerns.

Pushing open the door of Over the Moon bookstore, Harry spotted the book display right in front of her. Susan made a beeline for it.

Harry and Susan adored Over the Moon, in part because of the featured books. Of course, they shopped at Barnes & Noble when in Charlottesville, yet something reverberated with them about the small store, with an owner, Anne DeVault, who loved books. Both friends were avid readers, although of quite different books. Susan favored works written by women about women. Harry loved history, any kind of history. She also couldn't resist books that she had to order from Kentucky about various equine bloodlines.

Susan called her a snob. Harry always giggled at that, because when it came to horses, she was. When it came to human bloodlines, she felt they were all besmirched. How many thousands of Virginians claimed to be descended from Pocahontas, known as "Poke"?

"Did you make par today?" Anne asked Susan.

"You know, I shot two over today, but I'm working on it." Susan beamed. "Do you recommend anything?"

"Every book in the store." Anne smiled, left for the back room, returned handing a little book to Harry. "Just for you."

"Why Princess Margaret Will Never Be a Kappa Kappa Gamma," Harry read out loud as she fished in her golf skirt pocket for the modest sum the humorous book cost.

Back in Susan's car, Harry read out loud from her purchase. The two began screaming with laughter as Harry read aloud.

"My God, that's what Mom used to say," Susan howled while still managing to keep the car on the road.

"Oh, here's one. Silverware. I can't read this, you'll have to look at the drawings, but it's about what different patterns reveal about the woman. Counts if it's inherited, even though she didn't pick it. Well, Susan, the whole point of silver and china is they're supposed to be inherited. If you buy something, you don't have any people. Oh, listen to this, and this is true: Georg Jensen silver is expensive and beautiful but suspicious. I'm paraphrasing, but it says the owner of this silver probably has Yankee liberal tendencies."

Susan hooted with laugher. Both she and Harry, drilled from early childhood, never could quite shake the Dixie Dame imprint. "Well, it is kind of true. Meagan Underhill has Georg Jensen."

"She really is a Georg Jensen person," Harry uttered with relish.

"What is there about laughing about yourself and your people? Everyone is related to everyone in the South. Cousins, first, second, third cousins, first cousins once removed, and the dreaded shirttail cousins. You couldn't escape your relatives even if you didn't know them." Susan spoke the God's-honest truth.

"Hang on." Susan was careful backing out of the bookstore, as the parking was quite close.

"Hey, you're going in the wrong direction."

"No. We're going to Mom's. I want to give her that book and I'll buy you another copy."

"Okay." Harry took the cellphone that Susan handed her.

"Call her to say we're coming," said Susan. "You know how she gets."

"Uh-huh." So Harry punched in the numbers. "Mrs. Grimstead." She listened as Millicent Grimstead recognized her voice. "Susan is on her way to see you and she has a present."

"Tell her I'm at Momma's. Come on over here," her modulated, cultured voice replied.

Susan knew her mother deeply felt the decline of her father, Susan's grandfather. She went to Big Rawly every day to help where she could, to keep things as normal as possible.

"Yes, ma'am. We'll see you shortly. Bye-bye." Harry pressed the button. "Go to G-Mom's. She's over there."

"Right-o."

Within ten minutes, they turned right by Beau Pre, then continued down the drive to turn into Big Rawly, the Avenging Angel glaring from the graveyard, as always.

Walking down the grand house's long hall, Harry looked at the paintings of Holloway ancestors, as she had since childhood. The men on the east wall faced their wives on the west wall.

Some of the men had died in wars, a few even suffering heroic deaths. Governor Holloway's great-grandfather died in 1863, standing by his post under heavy artillery fire. His line held because of his steadfastness. Even with his arm blown off, he refused to be carried behind the lines. All the Holloway men had served in our various wars.

As for the women, granted paintings flatter, but they appeared a good-looking lot, the change in fashions apparent. The governor's maternal ancestor from President

Monroe's days wore a daring low-cut bodice, while Sam's grandmother wore a high-necked dress, major pearls encircling her covered throat. The hallway was a journey through time, through fashion, through physical attractions.

Better nomenclature for passing developed. Each portrait carried a story about the person's passing, often relayed by Governor Holloway to Susan and Harry when they were young. Consumption became tuberculosis. Wasting became cancer. Malaise became stroke, blood disorder became leukemia. If anyone remarried, the second spouse hung on the wall to the sunroom, not exactly excluded, but the first spouse got to shine in pride of place.

Harry knew Susan's family history as well as her own. She found history and people fascinating.

In the hall, the governor's office, other rooms, huge glazed pots filled with walking sticks, caught one's eye. Samuel Holloway collected them, and the house bore testimony to this unusual passion, which had started in his childhood. At ninety-six, he probably had more walking sticks than anyone in the state. In his will, he cited his many friends who would receive one when he was gone.

After many kisses and offers for tea or more from Penny Holloway, the governor's wife, the two sat down as bidden in the covered back porch.

Susan's grandmother read aloud from the humorous

book Susan had brought and they all screamed. An attractive young woman ducked her head in the room.

"Mignon, sit down," Penny invited her. "We're having too much fun."

"The governor felt sure you were laughing about him with his wife, his daughter, his granddaughter." Mignon smiled slyly. "How shall I tell him he's not the center of attention?"

They all laughed. "Mignon, do invite him in. He hasn't seen Harry in some time. This, forgive me, is Susan's cradle friend, Mary Minor Haristeen, Harry. We all know one another"—she paused—"too well."

More laughter, and as Mignon disappeared down the center hallway, Penny conspiratorially mentioned, "He doesn't know yet about Barbara Leader. He's so frail and we're trying to keep his spirits up. You do understand."

"Yes, G-Mom." Susan nodded.

"Yes, Mrs. Holloway," Harry added.

They heard the ninety-six-year-old man shuffling toward them, Mignon at his side. Stepping into the room, he burst into that dazzling smile which had long wooed Virginia's voters. "There must be a recess in Heaven." The ladies laughed and then he fixed his gaze on Susan and Harry. "Two good Democrats."

"Oh, Governor, only one," Harry demurred. "I'm not good at anything."

"Nonsense." He glowed. "Penny, my dear, this calls for a celebration." He squinted at the mountains. "The sun's almost over the yardarm."

Within minutes the drink caddy was wheeled out and Governor Holloway mixed drinks for the ladies, whether they wanted them or not.

Susan and Harry waited until after his toast, then sipped a very good Tom Collins. Governor Holloway came from a generation of men that knew how to mix drinks, what to drink when, and how to hold their liquor. Ladies could drink sherry. Men could not. But anyone could drink a Tom Collins on a summer day. The governor drank his regular bourbon.

Mignon sipped her drink, studying the two women just a few years older than her.

Millicent Grimstead told "the girls," as she thought of them, "Daddy's writing his autobiography. Miss Skipworth is helping and Daddy declares she's a whiz at research."

Mignon demurely lowered her head a moment. "The Internet speeds everything up."

"Does, but news can't be weighed. Everything is presented as though it is of critical importance. I believe this harms the political process," the governor pronounced.

"Governor Holloway has such a deep understanding of, I would say, statecraft." Mignon flattered him, but it was true. "This will be a very important book."

"Think I'll call it *Move Over, Jefferson,*" the aging gentleman joked.

"Daddy, how about *Where's the Party?*" Millicent Grimstead joked right back.

"Sugar Pie, I'd be shot on publication day. It's so partisan now, so crude. You can't govern without compromise, and what passes for public servants today are narrow-minded ideologues. There, I've said it." He held up his glass.

The others held up theirs. "Hear, hear."

As Penny leaned toward her daughter, the resemblance between the three generations of women was remarkable. "Sam really must tell his story. The good, the bad, and the ugly, as they say. We all made mistakes, that's human, but we learn from them, and I will brag on my husband. First he served in the war and truly was a hero—"

The governor interrupted her. "Honey, now, there were fourteen million of us in uniform."

"Sam, your ship was torpedoed and sinking, and you, a young JG, leapt into the water and stayed there, swimming to help other men, pulling them to life rafts. You were the last sailor to be hauled onto a life raft."

"Honey, the war was filled with men who died for their comrades. I was lucky. I lived and"—he paused, dropping his voice dramatically—"came home to Virginia and married the prettiest girl in the state."

"Oh, Sam." She blushed.

They married in 1949, raised two daughters, and never stopped loving each other. Harry wondered why some couples draw together and others don't.

Mignon pretended to pout. "He won't tell me those things."

The governor grew serious for a moment, "Ladies, if you've seen war, you don't want to talk about it."

"Daddy, I know that's true because you never talked about it to Pauline and me, but we now have—what?—three generations of men who have never served. That's frightening."

"Yes, it is." His voice deepened. "Getting rid of the draft was a disaster. I learned to trust men I would have never met in any other way and they learned to trust me. I believe, I truly believe, that one of the reasons politicians today don't cooperate together is they don't know one another. I knew smart-mouthed boys from New Jersey and laconic cowboys from Idaho, and if I didn't value them at first I sure learned to value them in good time. Our units weren't integrated by race—that came later in a big way. I think that was a mistake, not preparing us in World War Two. We might have had name calling and fistfights, but we would have worked it out. What came later was a disgrace, and I was part of that disgrace."

A silence enveloped them until Susan Tucker said, "G-Pop, it was a different time. You apologized, you worked hard once you understood. I am proud of you."

His eyes misted, and he leaned toward his granddaughter. "Little Susie, you don't know what that means to me." Then he drew a deep sigh. "You get old. Your mistakes are underlined. You forget that you might have done a bit of good. And I assume no one cares much except for my family, but even you, Precious, when you were in your teens you seemed to me to live in another America."

"G-Pop, I had to learn, too."

Driving back to Harry's farm, where Susan had left her car, Harry said, "You did a wonderful thing. We forget to tell old people, we forget to thank them."

"Back when I was a little brat, all I wanted to do was hide the fact that my grandfather was Governor Samuel Holloway. And now what pains me is when he dies, the damned media will rake it all up again, how he refused to desegregate the schools. How he defied Washington. The man apologized on his eightieth birthday. He apologized for how long it took him to understand, and he did make good on it! My grandfather has worked harder than anyone I know to raise money for scholarships to the University of Virginia and Duke, his two alma maters, for people of color. It took me a long time to see him for what he is: a man of his class, race, education, time, and gender. The new world had to seem like a repudiation of everything he worked for, and I was part of that repudiation."

"We all were, and mostly we were right. Change comes hard. Who knows what we'll bitch and moan about?"

"I already know. You bitch and moan about the weather." Susan laughed.

"Getting back to school desegregation." Harry impishly smiled. "Sure gave us a lot of schools named for saints. Every church in the state fired up their own school."

They both laughed.

Susan then said, "Fortunate we didn't have to go through that. It was mostly over and done by the time we reached high school. But if there had been a school for you and me, a saint's school, it would have been St. Rita's."

"Why is that?" Harry puzzled.

"The saint of impossible causes, and Harry, you are impossible."

6

Thursday, September 9, 1784

Attached to a sash, a long, heavy cloth, six feet by four feet, was being slowly unfurled above the dinner guests. Francisco Selisse had observed such an arrangement in the rice country of South Carolina. Not only did it provide welcoming light breezes, it blew away the flies, which had been exceptionally persistent this summer. Waving the sash was an African American child of nine, dressed in summer livery, trying not to die of boredom.

Servers glided back and forth from the summer kitchen, which, as was the custom in the hot South, was located a distance from the house. This meant the servers had to dash to the kitchen and carry the tureen or cold meats back to the main house. The second their feet touched the doorjamb, door open to the outside, they composed themselves for "the glide" so favored by Francisco and Maureen, his wife.

Details of Caribbean-born Francisco's early life were

sketchy, but pointed to a man who, when young, was on the make. Highly intelligent and ruthless, he had made his way up. Some thought he started as a blackbirder, a slave trader. Others said no, Francisco worked for a series of island bankers, from whom he had gathered much knowledge, as well as his wife, Maureen. She was the daughter of a successful banker in Martinique. She brought with her not only heaving bosoms but a large dowry. Francisco, like most men, was enchanted with both gifts. Maureen, for her part, had learned how to use her breasts to get exactly what she wanted from men, hence the nickname "Nightingale," a euphemism for prostitutes, all of whom knew how to use their bosoms. This was uttered behind her back by other women, including her own slaves, who could imitate her to a T. Never failed to cause eruptions of laughter.

Now forty-seven, Maureen was still lovely of visage, even as she had thickened a bit with age. Like many good-looking women, she hated growing older, working too hard to capture her fleeting youth.

Ewing Garth, ever sensitive to investment, cash as well as credit, trod softly around his neighbor Francisco. The two had made a few profitable investments together over the years. Ewing never invested more than he could afford to lose, and this was a lesson he drove home to Catherine. Ewing considered his dealings with Francisco as keeping harmony. Keeping tolerable relations with other businessmen was a key to Ewing's success. As for Francisco's wife, Maureen, Ewing loathed her. She would flirt, play the coquette, and try to get a rise out of him, literally. A Virginia gentleman knew all the steps of the social minuet, especially those in which a man pretends the lady before him is enchanting, be she seventy, forty, or a ripe twenty. Such flatteries were considered a lady's due. Only a fool would act upon them, but every man had a duty to make a woman feel desirable, delightful, and admired. The reverse of this was every woman was to demure; she had to convey that the gentleman before her was a hero in disguise; and handsome to boot. This was the grease to the social wheels.

Poor Ewing and his wife, Isabelle, practically had to hogtie their daughter Catherine when young to get her to behave in ladylike fashion. Rachel had been easy. Over time, Catherine perceived the value of such behavior. That didn't mean she liked it.

"Ah, Mrs. Selisse, you have outdone yourself." Ewing smiled benevolently. "Your table is as beautiful as the food is superb."

She smiled back, with a flourish of her hand. "A secret from the islands."

Francisco swooped his spoon away from him, bringing the cold potato soup to his mouth. He liked his wife. Maureen helped his business, and he was not insensitive to her dowry, nor the connections she had brought into his life. Keeping a good table never hurt any man in the wider world. Francisco kept to his domain, Maureen kept to hers, and they succeeded.

• • •

At the stables, the carriage horses had been taken from their harnesses, sponged down, and put in a stall out of the lowering sun.

Entrusted with their horses by Catherine, Jeddie Rice performed this service. He allowed Moses Durkin to help him. Moses, twenty-five, ran Francisco's stables under the tutelage of DoRe Durkin, his father, who was slowing down. No one quite knew why, but the father suffered pains deep inside and they moved. No bleeding, no fevers, just strange moving pains that would abate, then return, bringing with them more fatigue. A few of the other servants complained of similar pains, but not much came of it.

Jeddie rode as postillion while Barker O.—no last name, just O.—handled the graceful, immensely expensive open coach-in-four. Driving a coach-in-four was a skill not acquired superficially, and Barker was the best in central Virginia. He had been plied with offers to leave Ewing, offers of money to himself as well as a large sum to Ewing, but Barker loved the Garths' horses. He also believed "Better the devil you know than the devil you don't." He knew his master's ways. He wasn't eager to learn those of a new master. In the back of his mind he heard his mother's whisper: "Never trust a white man. Some you can honor. Some you can even love, but son, never trust one."

• • •

Charles West drove his not-quite-so-expensive but elegant phaeton. Sitting next to her husband, the air brushing her cheeks, hearing the wonderfully musical beat of the two horses, Rachel beamed. Charles could drive just fine. Once at the Selisses, Charles tipped Francisco's people to assist Jeddie, who took charge of the horses.

Visits such as this early evening dinner fueled friendships, business, and, of course, gossip. The ladies might bring a lady-in-waiting, a slave, to help them, and once the white folks gathered for drinks, dinner, and sitting a spell, the slaves could gossip with relish. The men talked about shipping, cargo costs, harvests. The slave gossip was ever so much more exciting. After all, the house ladies changed sheets. They knew just how those sheets were used, including those not of the marriage bed. Who ate what. Who was allergic to what. Who was a hothouse flower. Who was barking mad. Who was fair-minded. Who was kind. Predictions for the future usually accompanied such gossip.

Wiping down one of Ewing's beautiful bays, Barker said to Moses, "Yancy Grant going to run his big horse, Jack Night, down on the levels come fall. Put money on Jack. Longest stride I ever saw, once he gets going."

"He's talking it up." Moses had heard from some other people about Yancy's fine runner. "He'd better run that horse and win 'cause I heard his tobacco crop ain't worth squat."

Focused only on horses, Jeddie flicked a cloth over King David's well-muscled rump, asked, "Why grow 'bacca?"

Barker patted Solomon's neck. "People all over this big world want Virginia 'bacca."

"Yes, I know that, but you get a drought, you get hard rains, there goes the 'bacca," said Moses. He looked at Jeddie, a slight fellow a few years younger than himself.

"Mr. Garth grows it on his North Carolina land," Jeddie remarked. "Risk must be worth it."

"Mr. Garth is plenty smart. Easy to ship out of Carolina. I don't reckon Ewing could ever spend all his money." Moses admired the fancy coach, which two young boys were wiping down, hoping to be rewarded with a bit of change. "That coach could buy a farm, a farm with a couple hundred acres."

"Yes, it could." Barker smiled broadly. After all, he drove that coach and he was a respected man in these parts, slave or no. Everyone knew about Barker O.

The men straightened up as Aileen—Ailee, to most people—flitted by the stable. "Master's had two drinks. He's in a good mood. Missus has snuck three."

Face darkening, Moses pleaded, "Say you've taken the vapors. Don't you stay in the house if they pour more down their throats."

She kissed him on the cheek, her cat eyes sparkling. "Honey, I can't do that, but I'll do my best to disappear into the kitchen and work my fingers to the bone." She laughed, then skipped back to the house.

Moses glanced down at the ground, then up.

Jeddie, not too familiar with the Selisses, asked, "Ugly?"

Moses nodded. "My God, that Selisse woman's hateful mean, but hateful as she is, she doesn't force herself on Ailee."

Barker shook his head. "Nothing you can do, Moses. Only the women can help her and there's but so much they can do."

Moses clenched his teeth. "I can kill the son of a bitch."

Barker walked over, put a huge hand on his shoulder. "Don't talk like that, Moses. That's crazy talk."

The conversation over dessert centered on iron supplies for the foundry.

Francisco sipped a light tea to cleanse his palate after the good wine, plus he enjoyed light teas. "Just about a mile south of Scottsville there's a good landing."

"River's a boon," Ewing mentioned.

The Upper James River flowed by Scottsville, the county seat. From there, one could load about anything to carry down to Richmond and beyond.

"You probably know the James better than we do." Francisco nodded to John.

"The Marquis made us study maps, but Tarleton worked his will before the war shifted to the South, wish we could have gotten him. It's a formidable river."

John quietly spoke, not one to revisit his wartime service.

"We finally got them in the end." Francisco looked up as Ailee swept by.

Maureen observed his lingering look, and a tight smile crossed her lips.

Quick to surmise the situation, Rachel engaged her hostess. "Mrs. Selisse, you know your gowns are the envy of the state. Won't you divulge your seamstress's name?"

Tilting her head, Maureen cooed, "Madame Varnese, Paris. Duchesses, countesses, princesses flock to her. She can enhance any woman, even those not blessed by Nature."

"Not a problem for you, Mrs. Selisse." Rachel beamed at her hostess, who waved her hand as though dismissing the compliment.

Catherine then added, "But it's not just your seamstress. Where do you procure such unique fabrics?"

"Ah, I have an agent in Amsterdam, and I tell you, Italy is much overlooked. Milan alone produces such beautiful fabrics, light as air. But then one must be patient, the Italians are not celebrated for punctuality." On and on she rattled, occasionally catching a glimpse of Ailee. A flash of anger would momentarily appear then be gone. The two visiting sisters kept Maureen talking.

Finally, an hour after sunset, Ewing effusely praised host and hostess. Time to go.

Having been alerted, Jeddie brought out the coach-in-four first, then the phaeton. Barker slipped on his livery, impressive as the driver.

Jeddie whispered to Ewing, "Sir, the two boys there wiped down the coach." He repeated this to Charles.

Both men tipped the boys, then Ewing slipped two dollars in large coins to Moses. Charles followed with a silver dollar, quite generous.

The Selisses lived three miles south and east from Ewing's estate. The same creek bordered part of their lands. If you walked along the creek you'd reach Ewing's or Francisco's estates. For a leisurely walk, the path proved pleasant.

Next to John, Catherine breathed in the night air. "Do you think it's possible to die of boredom?"

"Not until tonight," he replied, and they both laughed.

Behind them, Charles West wore his red-gold hair neatly tied at his nape. The thought of a wig on a night like this made him sweat, but wigs, while always fashionable, were being ignored more and more.

"Such a beautiful night. The stars like portals to heaven, sparkling, inviting us to smile." Charles put the reins in his left hand while placing his arm around his wife's tiny waist.

"Do you think Francisco will offer you a commission? He'll have to build some kind of storage house down on the James?"

"I don't know, but I wouldn't want to work for him.

Besides, Karl and a small group of Lutherans have been talking to me about designing a church west of us, near Wayland's Crossing, at the foot of the mountains right on Three Notch'd Road. I can say I'm engaged in a project."

"Think they'll do it?"

"I do. Few churches west of us, and the ones east are too far to travel unless people want to leave at four in the morning." He changed the subject. "You were so clever."

"Me?"

"You see things I don't, or you see them before I do, and you and Catherine lured Maureen into a fulsome discussion of her wardrobe."

She leaned on him. "Vain."

He teased her. "Aren't all women vain?"

"Men are worse. Think of the pompous fools you knew in uniform."

"Put a little braid on a man, epaulettes on his shoulders, a few shiny buttons, and you're right. Maybe men are as bad as women, but you certainly did keep Maureen busy and puffed up."

"Like a broody hen." Rachel laughed, then added, "Not a happy henhouse."

"Not at all."

It was soon to become desperately unhappy.

7

Saturday, July 16, 2016

"Had she ever mentioned financial problems or domestic troubles? Disagreements with anyone?" Cooper was gently asking questions about Barbara Leader to Penny Holloway and her daughter, Millicent Grimstead, Susan's mother.

"Not a thing," Penny replied. "Barbara never really complained about anything."

The three women sat in the air-conditioned part of the summer porch.

Hearing a noise from the main part of the house, Millicent rose, briefly leaving the room before returning. "Wendell Holmes, trying to get into the garbage."

Wendell Holmes was the Holloway's springer spaniel.

"Good. I was afraid Sam had awakened." Penny lowered her voice. "Deputy, we haven't told Sam anything about Barbara's accident. It will greatly unnerve the governor, he liked her so."

"He hasn't read about the accident or seen a TV report?"

"We've monitored the news," Millicent replied. "Mostly he reads *The Washington Post, The New York Times,* and *The Wall Street Journal*. He watches CNN and sometimes the other channels, but he doesn't have much time for TV. He says if you want to find out about something, you read the newspapers."

"We'll never run out of news." Cooper smiled.

"Deputy, you asked us about complaints, domestic problems. Why?" Penny missed nothing.

"My experience is if a person is upset, they drive badly. Perhaps Barbara was distressed about something. It's curious. She was dead when Harry Haristeen opened the door. It was quick and I hope painless." Cooper tried to be soothing.

"We thought we'd tell Daddy next week," said Millicent. "We told him she'd taken a week off, and since he can be a little forgetful, he was okay. We fibbed and said she'd informed him." She leaned back in the blue-and-white striped chair.

Penny nodded. "Sam becomes attached to people," she said, her voice lovely. "Barbara would jolly him along. She'd ring the ship's bell in his library when it was time to take a pill and she enlivened it with a bit of bourbon. She'd bring him a real drink at five. Funny thing, the young woman working with him on his autobiography is sweet and smart. He likes going back with her in time, but I think he talked to Barbara more. He trusted her, but then she made him feel better. If he was becoming tired, she'd find a way to suggest a nap."

"This is such a loss," Millicent confided.

"Yes, I can understand that," Cooper said sympathetically.

"Leukemia is a cruel disease." Penny folded her hands together. "He's fought it so long. He doesn't get angry or fuss. He doesn't feel sorry for himself."

"Daddy's concern is leaving Mother," said Millicent. "He wants to make sure she's all right. He's organized me, really, to run this big place when he's gone."

"You two made a wonderful life together," Cooper complimented Penny.

She brightened. "We did. We met so many exciting people, people who did things, whether it was in the arts or business or medicine or politics. As you know, politics is bruising, but my Sam would always bounce back no matter what, and he'd be ready for the next problem." She smiled slightly, then added, "A year ago when he received his diagnosis that nothing more could be done, Sam took my hand and said, 'I'm not ready to leave you yet.' Not 'How much time have I got?' Not 'Do you recommend more chemo just to try?' Nothing like that. He never mentions it. Forgive me. I've rattled on and you're here to discuss poor, dear, Barbara."

"Mrs. Holloway, anything you can tell me is helpful. Often a casual remark can help."

Suddenly super-alert, Millicent said, "Barbara died in an accident, right?"

Cooper cleared her throat. "That seems to be the case, but we must always double-check."

8

Saturday, September 11, 1784

As promised at the Friday dinner, DoRe Durkin and his son Moses brought a blooded mare to Catherine. Catherine Garth Schuyler's fame as a successful breeder had spread throughout the mid-Atlantic. Ewing, proud of his daughter's singular achievement, one that no man could subsume, urged Francisco Selisse to deliver his best mare to be bred to Reynaldo, Catherine's powerful yet refined stallion. Catherine adored riding this fierce horse, scaring her father and sometimes even John, for the animal was hotter than a pistol. Yet he loved Catherine and obeyed most times.

Jeddie Rice hurried out of the barn when he heard the open wagon clunking along. The mare, Serenissima, was tied to the back, trotting along.

"She'll live like a queen." Jeddie took the sleek chestnut by her halter, good English leather.

Moses fell in on the other side of the horse while his

father pulled the wagon away from the front of the large stable, large enough for three cupolas and one big weather vane in the center of the roof.

DoRe climbed down slowly. Like most horsemen, sooner or later one limps. He walked into the stable, his lopsided gait giving off an irregular beat.

Looking around, he said admiringly, "Best stable in Virginia. Miss Catherine thought of everything."

"That she did," Jeddie agreed. "The hardest part of building this stable was getting her father to agree. We still use the old stable." He indicated it with his eyes as he led Serenissima into her stall. That was in an older, smaller stable twenty-five yards behind this one, a covered hallway connecting them.

DoRe shook his head. "Francisco wouldn't spend a penny on a walkway, but he'll order furniture from France."

Moses, glum, said nothing.

As she'd seen the mare arrive, Catherine walked from the house to the stable. She handed an envelope with tips to DoRe and one to Moses.

"She's a beauty. DoRe, did you talk Francisco into this? He can be hardheaded, you know?"

DoRe grinned. "No, Miss Catherine, you did."

Moses knelt down on one knee. "Miss Catherine, I beg you to help me."

Shocked and fearful, DoRe put his hand under his son's armpit, hauling him up. "Pay him no more mind than if he was a goat barking."

Eyes filling with tears, the young man disobeyed his father. "He violates my Ailee. He forces her, Miss Catherine. She has finger marks on her throat and sometimes a black eye and Missus Selisse beats her, declares she entices him." Trembling, Moses sobbed, big racking sobs.

Catherine, distressed, touched Moses on the shoulder as she looked from his father back to him. "Sit over here, Moses. You, too, DoRe. Jeddie, please fetch these men something cooling."

Led by Catherine, the two men dropped onto stacked hay bales. She pulled one into the aisle while DoRe swiftly put another bale onto that.

"Miss Catherine, this isn't a fitting chair for you."

Catherine smiled her dazzling smile at DoRe. "It's not only fitting, it's welcome. I've been standing and talking to my father for over an hour. You know how Father can go on."

Nodding, smiling, DoRe sat down. "Do, Miss Catherine, do. But he knows what he's talking about."

Moses was crying still. Looking over at Catherine, he said, "You have your mother's heart. Oh, please, help Ailee, Miss Catherine."

Jeddie returned with lemonade; Bettina had fixed a pitcher and a tray with four glasses. Before Jeddie reached the stable, Bettina hustled up behind him.

"Gimme that tray, Jeddie. You have no more couth than is on a yellow stick."

Meekly, the wiry young man allowed Bettina, who

had tied on a brighter headscarf than she wore in the kitchen, to take the tray. Jeddie followed.

Catherine looked up. "Oh, Bettina, thank you."

"Jeddie, pull over another hay bale," Bettina ordered. "Now you all refresh yourselves. I know you two men are hungry, but I wanted to find out would you like something cold on this September day or something warm?"

While the soul of hospitality, Bettina also wanted to visit a bit with DoRe, who had lost his wife two years back. She knew a good-looking man when she saw one, and a hard-working one, too.

DoRe stood up, as did Moses. "Oh, Lord, an angel can't cook as good as you."

Waving him off, Bettina repeated, "Cold or hot? I have stuffed eggs, sliced chicken with crisp skin and my special tiny potatoes, in a bit of crème with parsley. That's to set you up for peach pie. Oh, I forgot the biscuits, butter, and you know my raspberry jam. You two men need to fortify yourself for that drive home."

DoRe held up his hand. "Bettina, stuffed eggs, cold chicken, you are temptation itself. Our missus would kill to get your cold-chicken recipe."

Bettina, with an edge to her voice but smiling, said, "She'd have to."

"Can we help you carry anything?" DoRe offered.

"No, the girls can help." She shot a look at Jeddie. "You get on in the tack room and fix up some kind of table, you hear?"

"Yes, ma'am." Jeddie nodded.

As Bettina left, Catherine watched her walk, head high, singing to herself. Jeddie sped into the tack room.

Catherine returned to Moses. "Shall I assume everyone knows?"

"Can't hide the bruises." Moses wiped his eyes.

"I say leave it," DoRe added. "It's the way things are, and Master will flay Moses alive if he gets in the way."

"Yes, he will. Francisco's evil temper is no secret," Catherine agreed.

"You have your mother's heart and your father's brain. That's what folks say about you. I will do anything you say to help my Ailee," Moses pleaded.

"Yvonne is the head woman over there. Can she help?"

"She tries to keep Ailee busy, away from him," Moses answered, "but he comes looking for her when he wants her."

"Is there anyone who has it in for Ailee? Another pretty girl? A field hand who wants her?"

"All the men want her, but she's mine." Moses uttered this with pride. "She's a good girl. She pays them no mind. She's polite. I don't think any of the girls want to hurt her."

DoRe interjected. "They're glad he's after her and not them."

"Yes, of course." Catherine understood. "Can you think of anyone who would feed the missus anger or foolishness?"

"She don't need no help," Moses bitterly replied. "Sheba fans the flames."

"Yes, I'm afraid she doesn't," Catherine agreed. "And you're right about Sheba."

Bettina arrived with two girls pulling a little wagon. Didn't take five minutes for them to fix up the table in the tack room. Jeddie stepped back. Never interfere with Bettina at the helm.

The middle-aged, well-padded good woman did thank him. "And you can eat some of this, too."

Catherine walked into the tack room. "Bettina, you outdid yourself. Of course, you must sit down and join us. And the girls, too."

"Those worthless girls have work to do at the big house." Bettina smiled at Catherine, then turned to glare at the girls, who curtsied and left.

Catherine smiled. Bettina's desire to shine was quite obvious, and she did shine. As they all sat at the make-shift table, Catherine couldn't have given a fig that this truly wasn't protocol for the lady of a great estate. Catherine did what she wanted, one of the reasons she occasionally frightened her father and delighted her husband.

As they ate, Catherine, after asking permission from Moses, drew Bettina into the problem. There were two reasons for this. DoRe loved his son, and if Bettina could help, well, that might help Bettina, clearly taken with the man. The other reason was Bettina had a good head on her shoulders. She knew a whole lot about a whole lot of people.

Bettina listened gravely, looked at her mistress, then at DoRe. "You need to keep Moses far away from the master. I know you can't always do that. Keep your boy level."

Moses cried out, "How can I be level when he's hurting my woman? He beats her, Bettina. If she doesn't do his bidding, he knocks her around."

Bettina reached over, put her hand on his forearm. "Moses, trust in the Lord. You've trusted Miss Catherine and now you've trusted me. If this can be solved, it's women who will do it." She took a deep breath. "Masters sleeping with pretty slaves is as old as your name, Moses."

"Beating them isn't," Jeddie couldn't help saying.

Catherine loved Jeddie, not only because they'd played together and worked with horses since they were children, but because of moments like these. He was like a brother. She truly loved him, and it never occurred to her that he would want to be free.

As for Jeddie, he could imagine freedom, but not life without Catherine.

"True, so true, but the Lord has set this burden upon these fine people." Bettina looked at DoRe with sensitivity. "Even Mr. Jefferson takes up with his beautiful Sally." She inhaled again deeply. "Whether a woman wants the master or not, there are gains to be had. Gains, indeed. With those gains like a serpent's tongue flickering comes the jealousy of other women, our women, their women and a few men."

Catherine quietly affirmed Bettina's thoughts. "Maureen Selisse more than fulfills your prophecy."

"She would," Bettina said with disgust. "Moses, hear me. You have been given a terrible trial, and so has Ailee. You must bear it as long as you can. I will set my lights to this—"

"And I," Catherine pledged.

"But it will take time," said Bettina.

As the two men prepared to leave, Catherine took Jeddie by the arm, walking out the other side of the barn so Bettina might have a few moments with DoRe.

"I hope the mare catches." Catherine used the term for a mare becoming pregnant.

"I hope Ailee doesn't," Jeddie answered.

She squeezed his arm, then released him. "Jeddie, pray that she doesn't, because Maureen will kill her. Remember, Mrs. Selisse is barren."

Bettina now walked back to the house. Catherine hurried to walk with her while Jeddie returned to the stable.

"The sorrows of this life," Bettina murmured, voice low.

"Come with me, Bettina. Let us speak with Father."

Entering the house, they found Ewing Garth in his study, shirtsleeves rolled up. A sheaf of papers commanded his attention. He was a neat man; tidy piles rested on his desk. A graceful bureau, of bird's-eye maple and crafted to his specifications, held his current papers, maps, and blueprints. He had it specially built five years back by a master cabinetmaker, Howard Holloway.

He removed his spectacles, turning to them, smiling. "Aha, I am about to be dragooned into something."

"Yes, you are." Catherine stood before him, as did Bettina.

She then concisely outlined the problem.

Face darkening, Ewing clasped his hands together. "What can one do?"

"You can buy Ailee," Catherine firmly said.

Ewing leaned back in his chair. "My dear. I can't buy every woman so used by her master."

"Using is one thing, Father. Violating and beating is another, and don't forget Maureen."

"Feral, aren't they?" Ewing blurted out.

"Mr. Ewing, whatever you did for one of the least of these brothers and sisters of mine, you did for me," Bettina intoned, her voice melodious.

Ewing's hand flew to his eyes, tears rolled down. "Ah, my beloved angel."

His late wife would quote this from Matthew 25:40.

Catherine leaned down to kiss her father. "She's always with us, Father."

"Yes. I lose my way. She brings me back. I will send Jeddie over tomorrow with an offer."

• • •

Later, twilight filling their senses, a few bats zigzagging overhead, Catherine and John walked together across the lawn. She'd told him what had transpired.

In the distance they saw Ewing standing in the family graveyard before his wife's handsome statue, lamb recumbent, holding a cross.

John Schuyler put his arms around Catherine. "Promise you won't die first. I couldn't go on."

Surprised by this outburst, she said, "We do not get to pick our hour, but if God is kind, He'll take us both at the same time."

"No, me first. What about the children?"

She laughed. "Ever my practical John. Well, we'd better apply ourselves to the task."

9

Monday, July 18, 2016

"You could have told me," Harry complained to Cooper. They were in Harry's kitchen, and had just split a piece of delicious carrot cake.

"Busy weekend and I worked all weekend. Little stuff, but endless. One fellow forgot his emergency brake and his truck rolled backward into the pond. Unfortunately, he was in it. Stuff like that."

"Get him out?"

Cooper nodded. "Oh, yeah. Took the fire department, me, and his golden retriever. One of those weekends."

"Well, so then how did Barbara Leader die?"

"Thallium chloride. The family had requested an autopsy so the body had been sent to Richmond to the state medical examiner's. They found it in her system."

"What's thallium chloride?"

"Kind of like potassium chloride. Mimics a heart attack. Just stops the heart. Usually it's injected, but she had no injection marks. You die pretty quickly if it's injected, like a suffering dog the vet puts down. It's quick. We're hoping the final report from the examiner's office can determine how this lethal drug got into her system."

"Coop, could it be a mistake? An accident?"

Cooper shook her head, then added, "We've checked the usual. Financial problems. Marriage difficulties. Depression. Alcohol. Theft. Remember, anyone in the medical profession with a bit of brains can figure out how to steal drugs and then sell them. But Barbara's life was in good shape, so that also rules out suicide. At least I think it does."

"Do people use thallium chloride to kill themselves?"

"There are other ways to do that with substances more easily acquired, but I'm sure it's been done somewhere by someone." Cooper shrugged.

"I liked her. We all liked her. We weren't close, but when we were kids it was a small community." Harry crossed her arms over her chest for a moment.

"Turn on the TV, will you?" Cooper said.

"Sure." Harry picked up the remote from the kitchen counter, turning on the large-screen TV affixed to a wall.

The cats and dog, asleep in their fleece-lined beds, paid it no mind. They were accustomed to Harry checking The Weather Channel frequently.

Harry flipped through until she came to the local news, which is what Cooper wanted to see. A remarkably clear picture of Edward Cunningham with local reporter Bill Coates appeared. Former governor Sam Holloway's grandson was being interviewed regarding his Senate campaign.

"You don't think there's a war on women?" the reporter asked.

"That's a Republican problem, not mine," said Eddie.

"Mr. Cunningham, you are perceived as an old-time Democrat by many, which is really a new-time Republican. Two bills are before the state Senate, one on removing special requirements from clinics that perform abortions, costly requirements put in place by our previous Republican-controlled legislature, and another bill purported to close the pay gap between men and women for equal work. What is your position on both?"

"Well, Bill, I learned from my grandfather. He was criticized by the head of the Democratic Party in Virginia in the late sixties before being elected governor. My grandmother, a nurse, continued working throughout Granddad's career. The party fellow said, 'Sam, can't you keep that woman in line?' And Granddad quipped, 'No. That's why I married her.' That ought to tell you how I feel about women."

"Slick." Harry's eyebrows rose.

"Didn't answer the question," Cooper replied.

"Do they ever?"

The two watched the rest of the news. No mention of Barbara Leader.

"You don't have to report that the accident is now regarded as a suspected murder?" Harry questioned the deputy.

"Do. But Rick and I will wait until we have the final medical examiner's report. Gives us a little more time."

Clicking off the TV, Harry sat at the kitchen table. "Are you sick of this women stuff? I don't want to hear Eddie Cunningham's opinion on women."

"Bored and insulted." Cooper sat across from Harry. "If anything is brought up as a woman's issue, it means whoever is bringing it up sees women as second-class citizens. Plus, they're assuming we all think alike. That's the ultimate insult."

"Well, we're unequal on the money front, but I take your point. The media and politicians think we care only about so-called 'women's issues,' and in Eddie's case, vote for or against."

"What it really means, Harry, is there's money and political gain to be had focusing on women as separate from men. There's Eddie, pulling an old-boy routine, using his grandfather and grandmother, and I pretty well think he has no concern about equal pay for equal work or any of it."

"Mmm, seems to be the case. I mean, other than trotting out Chris and the two kids, he steers clear of anything that could be construed as human rights. Ranting against welfare, immigration, on and on. Makes me suspicious, but I'd be even more suspicious if he wasn't working to promote business, create jobs. At least that's in his campaign. Anyway, it is boring, but Barbara Leader's mysterious death is not."

"No."

"So back to that. If someone killed her, they would have had to have some medical knowledge. Had to know where to get the stuff."

"We've been checking hospital records, doctors with whom she had a working relationship. I've been on it. So far nothing."

"It's like finding a needle in a haystack, isn't it?" Harry commiserated.

"It is, and I always hope I don't sit on the needle," Cooper said.

10

Monday, September 13, 1784

Peter Studebaker, a wagonmaker from Huntington Township, York County, Pennsylvania, sat in an empty classroom with Captain Bartholomew Graves, lately of the Royal Irish Artillery. He had come to deliver a letter given to him from Charles West, as well as to talk a little business.

Schoolteacher Bartholomew smiled at Peter, a man of middling years like himself. "Your business flourishes," he complimented his visitor.

"Which is why I've come to you. As an artillery officer, you must be good at math." He chuckled. "Your students I'm sure profit from this."

"Ah, Mr. Studebaker, if only I could get them to sit still."

Both men laughed at this, and Peter glanced at the floor, then up at the rugged veteran of the British Army. "You had to carry cannon over rough ground and at times at high speed. What I am interested in, sir, is the manner of axle. My son and I mean to make the strongest wagons in Pennsylvania. Axles."

"Always the weak spot and the rougher the ground, the more damage," said Bartholomew. "A wheel can fly off. That can be replaced or mended, but when an axle breaks, without proper tools and a forge, that's the end of it."

"I have heard of your success on the battlefield."

"You flatter me. If I'd been successful, I'd not have been captured at Saratoga."

Peter slapped his thigh. "Ha. Ah, but then war must be such confusion, smoke, noise, if a man can't hear the trumpeter or see. To simply live is a victory. But I know you were not here at Camp Security."

"No. I was down at The Barracks outside of Charlottesville. Hearing piecemeal reports of the southern campaign, I felt the Crown would lose this war, and I tell you, sir, even if it sounds treasonous, I began to see that you should win."

"Indeed." Peter nodded.

Bartholomew held out his hands expansively. "I determined to live in a new land, a free land and one where my lowly birth would not impede my progress."

"But you, sir, attained the rank of captain." Peter knew some of Bartholomew's past. The Irishman was well liked; his friends often told some of his tales.

Bartholomew leaned forward, his chair creaking a bit. "I had outlived my senior officers, all of them having purchased their commissions. Not a brain in their heads. And then I secured some promotions through combat. Ah, Peter, war is a terrible thing, but we always make advances. And so the next war will be even more terrible than the one that preceded it."

Wryly, Peter replied, "I hope, sir, some of those advances involved axles."

Now it was Bartholomew's turn to slap his thigh and laugh. "What would you have me do?"

"Come to my shop. Look at the axles and the wheels of each of my wagons. I will pay you."

"We can talk about money later, Peter. I will ride over this Saturday."

Peter changed the subject. "Do you like teaching? I wonder, it must seem dull?"

"Ah." Bartholomew grinned. "The boys at York County Academy are not dull—wild, perhaps, not quite what the Episcopal Church had in mind—but I have an affection for them. Perhaps I recall my own misdeeds when I encounter theirs."

Peter nodded. "Yes. It goes so fast, does it not? Time?"

The former captain shook his head. "Sometimes in my sleep I can hear my mother's voice." He waved his hand. "So long ago, but Peter, we are here and we must make the most of it."

Smiling as he rose to shake hands, Peter agreed. "Indeed, good sir, indeed. Please send my greetings to your excellent wife."

"Mary will be pleased."

After Peter left, Bartholomew put the envelope from West in his pocket. His mind went back to the Revolutionary War for a moment.

Separated from his unit, thanks to a ferocious barrage at Saratoga and a thrashing infantry charge, Bartholomew Graves wound up being captured by a large, handsome, decent man, John Schuyler. He also marched all the way to Virginia with another prisoner of war, the young Captain Charles West. It was Bartholomew, held at the camp in Charlottesville, who counseled Charles near war's end to escape and paid him to forge discharge papers. The future was here in America.

By war's end, Bartholomew was working his way up the Wilderness Trail, finally reaching the Mason-Dixon Line.

He remained in Hagerstown, Maryland, until war's end, where he worked for a lawyer who needed a man who was good with numbers. All artillery officers are good with numbers. But once the war was over, Bartholomew headed for York, not all that far. He'd heard this town just west of the Susquehanna River boasted good land, plenty of work, and a great deal of construction. Also, while predominantly Lutheran, they were not inhospitable to Catholics. He was not terribly religious, but he was Catholic.

Doing odd jobs to get by, he heard a vacancy had opened at the Academy affiliated with St. John's Episcopal School. Having been buffeted by the anti-Catholic laws in England and the king's service, he hesitated to apply. Allowing people to worship as they pleased was not the same as hiring them. But Mary, the young woman whom he was courting, told him, "Barth, just go. No one is asking you to renounce your faith." Mary giggled. "What little there is of it."

Baited, he did go, and the Rev. John Andrews hired him on the spot. So Bartholomew Graves became a mathematics teacher, and shortly thereafter, a husband to Mary.

It was a perfect early September day in York County, absolutely delightful. Walking through the streets, he passed gardens filled with chrysanthemums. There was color everywhere. His step quickened. He swung his gentleman's walking stick with vigor to match his step.

Opening a low wooden gate, he stopped to admire the small brick dwelling. There were flowers in front, a vegetable garden in the back. The door, painted blue, sported a brass pineapple knocker, a gift to his wife.

Chickens cackled out back. Opening the door, Bartholomew was greeted by a beagle. He knelt down to pet the dog.

"Barth?"

"Yes, my dear." He went into the kitchen, herbs hanging by the window, cabinets wiped clean, the floor clean, strewn with fresh rushes. Mary would brush them out, put them in the garden. She swore the bit of blood from her lamb chops or beef brisket that fell on the straw was the reason her garden flourished.

Wiping her hands on her apron, she walked over to him, put her hands on his cheeks, and gave him a welcoming kiss. "And did you thrash the little hellions?"

"Not today, my love, but I had a most interesting visit from Peter Studebaker."

"The wagonmaker?"

"Yes. He would like me to help him. He feels I can, as I had to move heavy cannon over bad roads, onto fields. Said I would."

"Now, don't you go giving away the store, Bartholomew." Mary used his full Christian name. "You are too generous. Too generous by far."

He waved his hand. "He will pay, dear."

"What you are worth, I hope. I can't run a house on a pittance. We could use some help, and, my dear, you need a horse. Such would help on the burden of this house."

Smiling, for he heard this refrain often, he said, "A house. You deserve a castle. You deserve servants in livery and a coach-in-four with matched horses and jewels." He ran his fingers down her cleavage, as she wore a lower-cut dress, given the weather. "Jewels that will rest on your natural jewels."

Mary took his finger and lightly bit it. "You are no good, Bartholomew. I knew it the minute I looked at you. I said to myself, 'There is a no-good man, but, oh, there's something about him.' And here I am. Married to the same." She laughed, then turned to tend her oven.

All the windows and doors were open to let the heat escape. Unlike Virginia, these Pennsylvania homes did not have summer kitchens. While the heat came up in the summer, it didn't last as it did in Virginia, and fall skidded in earlier, a perfect fall with robin's-egg-blue skies, Canada geese flying overhead, fields waiting to be harvested. York County was rich in soil and water, and was stirring with industrious people. Walking through town, one could hear the hammer of blacksmiths, the rumbling of wagons, the shops making all manner of goods.

"What's for supper, love?"

"Shepherd's pie. Oh, I know it's a bit early for shepherd's pie, but I just felt like it. Won't be long." She brushed back a stray hazel tendril.

He took the letter from his pocket. "From Captain West. Peter Studebaker was given it by a drover when Peter was in Littlestown."

The two men kept up a leisurely correspondence, both being former officers in the Crown's army and choosing to live in the former colonies. The colonials rarely used the post except for business. First, it was slow. Second, it was expensive. Two sheets of paper might cost twenty-five cents, and the recipient had to pay. So letters were often passed along hand to hand. But West and Graves, Europeans, used letters to catch up with each other. Each man observed these "new" people with interest. Unlike the "new" people, they did not consider personal mail a luxury. They considered it civilized.

Bartholomew sat down to read. He didn't need spectacles, quite unusual. "Mary, he says all is well. Ewing Garth bought more land west of his current estate. The orchard is thriving. The hard winter seems to have helped this. He doesn't know why. He has accepted a commission to design a Lutheran church, to be called St. Luke's—"

Mary interrupted. "Are there many Germans there?"

He nodded. "Not as many as here. A few Swedes and Italians. Like here, my dear, so many Italians who fought for King George escaped from the prisoner-of-war camp."

"Truthfully, the guards at Camp Security here looked the other way," Mary said. "My father said we needed men to work since so many were in the army. I hope never to see such times again."

"God willing, you won't, my dear." Bartholomew looked up from his letter and smiled. "He also writes that John and Catherine are well. His Rachel is radiant. No children yet, and Ewing is becoming fretful." Bartholomew laughed loudly. "Such things take time and skill."

"I'm going to pray for you," Mary teased.

"No, dear, pray for them." He laughed uproariously again, then returned to the letter. "Charles writes that there has been some exceptional brutality on a nearby estate regarding slaves. He says the longer he sees this institution the more he feels it is wrong, even though the Bible condones it." Bartholomew looked up at Mary. "I don't know what's worse, being a slave or being an indentured servant." He sighed. "I rather think this will resolve itself. Hellam Township has seven slaves and more indentured servants. I have no idea how many such people work in York County, but, Mary, the day will come when we visit Virginia. It's different."

"Because of slavery?"

"Different in many ways. A few very rich planters control the state."

"Well, let us not forget those very rich merchants in Philadelphia."

He smiled at her. "Quite. I think it will always be a few at the top, some in the middle, and the rest below, but I see this home you have brought to life. I see glass in the windows, a hearth with a good draw, fancy, a feather bed. I think we live quite well."

Mary came over and kissed her husband's cheek. "You see to that, Barth. I knew when I looked at you that you were a man who would succeed."

"I thought you said I was trouble," Bartholomew teased. "And do you know what I thought when I first saw you? There's a colleen worth fighting for! And there's a girl of strong opinion!"

"You like the strong opinion?"

He shrugged. "I had no choice."

She swatted at him with a clean wooden spoon. "I ought to crack you wicked hard."

"I am never bored. And I am well aware that you with your rosy cheeks, your heavenly bosom, your full figure, you could have won any heart you wished. But you accepted me, a captured fellow, a man fifteen years your senior, gray amidst the black hair, in my mustache, even, you picked me."

Mary pursed her lips, as if she'd just made a practical decision. "You actually listened to what I had to say. Father and Mother were worried, of course." She walked back to the stove. "All that's behind us now."

"Are you happy, love?"

She turned to look at him. "I am the happiest woman in York County."

"Then I am content."

11

Tuesday, July 19, 2016

At eleven o'clock in the morning, the mercury read eighty-one degrees. With seventy-five percent humidity, cloud cover blocked the sun. Accustomed to working outside in all weather, Harry paid no heed to the drizzle turning into a light rain. Chores finished, she ducked into the house, changed her shirt, did not change her jeans.

"*Where are you going?*" Tucker followed her. "*You've that got 'I'm going somewhere' air.*"

She swapped her wet baseball cap for a dry one, tucking her hair into it as best she could. Harry, like most women, moved through hairstyles. In high school she wore her hair shoulder length, tied into a ponytail at the nape of her neck when playing volleyball, softball, basketball, whatever was in season, plus riding at home. In college, she went through the buzzed-hair phase and thankfully got through it. Over the years, she moaned and groaned along with Susan and her girlfriends about what to do with their hair. Do you spend a fortune at the beauty parlor? Do you go for flash or convenience? These days, it seemed even the area's two dedicated bombshells, BoomBoom Craycroft and Alicia Palmer, elected convenience. However, one must realize convenience does not preclude coloring because Susan pitched a fit about the ever-increasing gray hair. Harry, with a touch of gray, refused to color her hair. Her rationale was she could buy bags of good alfalfa for the price of one color job. So Harry kept her hair in what used to be called a short pageboy. It was straight as a stick, so the cut worked. While it pained her, she spent money on a good haircut.

Tucker watched as her beloved human fussed for all of ten minutes, smacked on a touch of light lipstick, walked through the house.

"*Hey, where are you going?*" Pewter asked.

"*I don't know, but we're going.*" Tucker quickly thought to zoom to the car, sit by the door.

"*If you're going, I'm going.*" The fat cat stretched, then followed Tucker, not that she would admit affection for the dog.

Asleep on the counter, the tiger cat roused herself and leapt down. Now three furry creatures trailed Harry until Tucker charged ahead.

"*Oh, she pulls that every time.*" Pewter sniffed. "*You know, the panting, eager, I-can't-live-without-you look. Please, have some self-respect. I prefer proper deportment.*"

"Of course you do." Mrs. Murphy's voice carried a hint of humor.

Mrs. Murphy knew that oh-so-proper deportment could fly out the window in a skinny minute. Harsh words would be uttered, claws unleashed, and more than occasionally, a bloody nose followed. No matter what, fur flew.

The light rain didn't provoke a run, but Harry walked briskly. Looking down at the three musketeers, she opened the cargo door of her Volvo station wagon and they jumped in.

Once behind the wheel, she turned on the motor, checked the dash should any vital signs be amiss, then read her mileage: "198,762. You know, gang, soon time for a new car. This isn't even that old, but boy, do we rack up the miles."

"Your truck is from 1978," Tucker reminded her, which was decades and decades before his birth.

Harry's father had bought it when she was just four years old. She babied that truck; she used it hard, but she still babied it. She replaced hoses long before they wore out. Years ago, she had the entire engine dismantled and cleaned. She was beside herself with joy. Early this spring, she had the silver-and-blue truck painted. People, almost always men, constantly tried to buy that truck from her. Why would Harry part with a truck that wasn't controlled by computer chips, that used manual transmission, and, best of all, that when she cut on the motor the satisfying burble of a powerful V-8 engine sang to her?

The Volvo did not sing to her when she turned it on, but being a station wagon and well built, she learned to appreciate its good qualities and she learned to drive by computer chip. Not that she liked it.

The animals enjoyed the Volvo because they had beds in the back and they could see well out of the cargo window. And with a half leap, all three could move up into the second row of seats or even the first. Mrs. Murphy, in particular, wished to help Harry drive. Human eyes left a lot to be desired, but then they couldn't help it. The tiger cat believed she helped ensure safety.

Harry remembered what her father had told her about rain: The roads are more dangerous when the rain begins. She drove accordingly, reaching the Ivy post office in twenty minutes.

Cracking the windows a bit, she hopped out, pushed the door open to the narrow post office service counter at the end. The post office boxes were on her right as she walked down. The metal boxes filled the wall, which was maybe eight feet high and twelve to fourteen feet long. It was a small post office, so not too many post boxes.

It reminded her of her old post office in Crozet. She became the Crozet postmistress right out of Smith College after the postmaster, George Hogendobber, died and people were desperate for someone to run the old country office. Harry took the job, no other prospects at the time, figuring it would be temporary. George's widow, wise and kind Miranda, helped her enormously. Ten years later, Harry still sorted mail, pushed the carts with the cats in them, spoke with everyone who came into the post office, which was to say all of Crozet.

But times change. New people moved in, their houses with granite countertops and controlled lighting. People of some means, mostly quite nice but demanding. A little country post office would never do. Plus, Harry ran out of post boxes, had a waiting list that stretched into next week.

The federal government built a new, large, gleaming post office. The job of running it was offered to Harry but with an appalling list of restrictions, including not being able to bring Mrs. Murphy, Pewter, and Tucker to work. She declined, but she did miss the daily contact. She also missed hearing the old uneven wooden floors creak, the sound of a metal box opening from the outside, requests for the prettiest stamps, especially ones featuring flowers, birds, or historical sites. Stamps had become little works of art during her tenure. She still loved looking at them.

All gone. Well, not the stamps, but the wonderful feeling of being crowded into an old building hard by the railroad, where before her time the mail sack hung on a large hook, the arriving mail tossed onto the siding.

The Ivy post office was not nearly as charming or old as her old post office, but it had a nice young fellow as postmaster. Harry liked to stop in and catch up on the news among her old colleagues throughout the area.

"James!" she called, as he wasn't up front.

"Be right there."

And he was. "Harry, what's new?"

"Good hay crop, sunflowers look good."

"So far, a good year."

"How are you doing?"

"Okay. I was so sorry to hear about Barbara Leader dying in that car accident. All of Ivy"—he mentioned the little crossroads—"everyone's in shock."

The Leaders owned a pretty house on the south side of Route 250 not far from the post office. They were regulars at the post office; at Duner's, the restaurant; and at Ivy Family Chiropractic, where both Barbara and her husband got the kinks out.

"Me, too. She was a year behind me in high school. Isn't it funny how you know more kids older than you or in your class than younger?"

"Because they boss you around. I was so glad when I became a senior. I thought I'd boss around people, but I was too busy." He laughed at himself, then pulled out a sheet of drawings. "Look what stamps are planned for next year. I know how you like stamps."

Harry examined the ones drawn from nature. "I liked the songbirds issued in 2014. The color was extraordinary and maybe people learned something about goldfinches, painted buntings. I like color."

"Me, too. Did you ever pick a favorite?"

"Yes. Martin Johnson Heade's painting from the American Treasures series."

"Remind me."

"Giant Magnolias on a Blue Velvet Cloth, circa 1890. My all-time favorite. Oops, here comes a customer. Good to see you. When you have a minute, look up the stamp on your computer."

"Will do. Good to see you, too." He greeted a lady wearing Bermuda shorts. "What can I do for you?"

As she pushed a small package onto the counter, Harry returned to the parking lot, turned on the motor, air-conditioning filling the interior immediately. She sat there for a minute, but before she backed out, Cooper, in a patrol car, pulled into a spot in front of the store next to the post office. This little place carried such healthy hanging baskets, small shrubs in pots, a wide variety for such a small place.

Harry left her Volvo running, no worries about theft, and sprinted through the rain over to Cooper.

"Coop."

"Get out of the rain."

"I can sit with you or you can sit with me. I have the kids."

"I'll sit with you for a minute, but I need a drink. Want one?"

"No, I've got my little cooler in the car as always. I can give you one of those carbonated grapefruit drinks."

"I'll take it." Cooper got out of the squad car, locked it, followed Harry back to the station wagon.

"Coop!" All three animals greeted her.

She turned and smiled. She wanted a dog, but her hours were just terrible. Wouldn't be fair to the dog. Harry handed her the grapefruit drink, Pompelmo, made by Sanpellegrino.

"What are you doing out here?"

"Oh, a complaint. Some new people who bought near Verulam woke up to see cattle in one of their fields. The wife wanted me to get them out of there before they destroyed her hydrangeas. I said, 'Ma'am, your hydrangeas are up here at the house.'

"She then complained that I wasn't taking her problem seriously." Coop was still feeling the anger. "I handed her my card, pointed out the HQ number, and suggested she call if she was unsatisfied. She blinked, surprised, I think, then said was I going to get the cattle out of her pasture? I replied with the greatest pleasure that no, I was not. She needed to call Animal Control."

"Good for you, Coop. You're not a hired farm worker." She paused, then shifted gears. "Been thinking about Barbara Leader. I know you've been checking out hospital records and doctors' records concerning thallium chloride. I'm assuming since you haven't told me anything you haven't found anything unusual."

"Not yet."

"I keep coming back to what did she know?" Harry seemed to be deep in thought. "Something about a doctor, another nurse, a hospital administrator. Any of those people could steal drugs and use or sell them, and obviously they wouldn't be using thallium chloride. It would be one of the opiates."

Cooper looked at Harry. "Right."

"Maybe Barbara knew something about another patient, like Governor Holloway, for instance."

Cooper said, "We thought of that. So far nothing. Politicians of Governor Holloway's time, their secrets almost always involved extramarital affairs or booze or both. We've investigated his past and that of a few of Barbara's other patients who were high-profile doctors or businessmen. They all drank. It was a big part of the culture, but no one was a raging alcoholic. As for affairs, they indulged, but Governor Holloway did not, or if he did, not a hint of it."

"It appears that once he married Penny he had no interest in other women," said Harry. "Millicent would have sniffed that out. Susan's mother can't keep a secret."

"It's not usually a daughter who ferrets that secret out." Cooper smiled. "The worst blunder that Governor Holloway appears to have made was his anti-integration stand. Aroused a lot of passion for and against at the time, and I bet there are still people who can get worked up about it. Maybe we're too young, but I think it's all water over the dam."

"For which we can be grateful. I'm glad I didn't live through it. I mean, we aren't out of the woods. There's lots to be done, but not like then. It's hard to believe people believed that stuff."

"Believed and screamed about it." Cooper at that moment wanted a cigarette, which she had given up for the second time this year.

"Anyway, why would a nurse be killed over an old segregation issue?" Harry pondered, then brightened. "Maybe this is something we've never dreamed of."

"I don't know, Harry. How many ways can you frighten or outrage people so they will kill you?"

"Maybe more than I'd like to consider," Harry somberly replied as the rain splattered the windshield.

12

Wednesday, July 20, 2016

Harry, animals in tow, turned left into a big development, Old Trail. The first row of commercial buildings matched the homes not in size but in style. Nice balconies jutted out on top of the two-story buildings. She parked in front of a mint-green clapboard-frame building. The rain intensified.

They sat.

"I can't leave you until the rain slows a little," Harry announced to her friends, not that they cared. They were happy to be on a ride with her.

Pewter settled down in the leather seat. "*She could leave us. Just keep the air-conditioning on.*"

"*If she keeps the engine running, someone can steal the Volvo,*" Tucker said.

"*Who would steal a car or wagon? When is the last time a car was stolen in our county?*" Pewter huffed for a moment.

"True, but if someone did steal this, we'd be in the wagon," Mrs. Murphy explained.

"There is that," the gray cat agreed. *"But tell me this, all these new cars have every screen, knob, push-button whatever. So why can't they build a car that you can turn off the motor, leave, but keep the air-conditioning running?"*

"Too expensive to figure out," Mrs. Murphy replied.

"It seems like everyone everywhere is mired in debt. Aren't you glad we don't have to worry about money?" Tucker breathed relief.

"We don't have bank accounts." Mrs. Murphy said the obvious.

"I would never go into debt." Pewter puffed out her gray chest.

Neither Mrs. Murphy nor Tucker would touch that one. A long silence followed.

"You all were chatty," Harry remarked. "Now cat got your tongue?"

"Ha." Pewter stuck out her tongue.

For a split second, it occurred to Harry that her cat had understood her. Then she discounted it.

The rain continued, softly now. Harry cracked the windows a bit.

"Not one drop." Pewter gave her the evil eye. *"Not one drop on my fur."*

"I won't be long, but if it starts to rain harder, I'll come out and we'll go home. I can always come back here later."

Pewter disbelieved the promise, knowing how Harry

could become embroiled in conversation. "*That's what she says now.*"

Pushing open the clapboard-frame building's white-painted wooden door, Harry stepped into a pleasant waiting room, framed posters on the wall: Toulouse-Lautrec, World War I recruiting posters, shipping posters, airline posters from the forties, color stills of the company's video work, all dramatic, colorful.

An attractive woman, early forties at the most, came out of her office.

"Hello, I'm Mary Minor Haristeen, Harry. I called earlier about revamping my farm website."

"Yes, of course. Rae Tait. Sit down here. I'll show you some of our work on the big screen." She wasted no time pointing to a chair, upholstered in dark beige.

"When I called, I didn't think you'd work this fast."

"Well, Mrs. Haristeen, your project intrigued me. Sunflowers. Hay. Organic farming is becoming good business. You need to look at a few sites first. I hope we're the firm for you, but, well, see for yourself."

Rae sat down by a long keyboard, much like a director's board in television, pushed switches, popped in a DVD. "This was for women's crew at UVA. You see a bit of a practice, the boathouse, then you see everyone traveling to the nationals. *Action*. Action is always preferable to talking heads."

"It is, and please call me Harry."

"If you call me Rae. Okay, this one is for Harkaway Stud. I needed help because I don't know much about horses. I looked at the websites for the big studs in Lexington, gorgeous work, but they have big bucks to spend. Harkaway, just getting off the ground, did not."

The DVD played out, horses seen on the tracks are then viewed walking in the paddock once at stud and finally standing still so the viewer can closely examine conformation.

"That's Justin doing the narration. Good voice," Harry remarked.

"All you horse people know one another." Rae smiled. "I learned that. And I learned a person needs to know a great deal to be successful in the equine industry. Huge in our state."

"And even then, Rae, something like a rise in gasoline prices can really hurt you. Remember, the mares have to be vanned to the stallion, which usually stands in Kentucky, New York, Maryland, West Virginia, even Florida."

"Never thought of that. Okay, here's one that called for a lot of thought."

The DVD opened with Edward Holloway Cunningham talking to an African American couple in front of their tidy brick house. The voice-over filled viewers in on rising taxes yet lowered services. There was a shot of Cunningham walking on UVA's lawn, the Rotunda in the background. Other images showed a dynamic young man shaking hands, talking to all kinds of people, mothers pushing strollers, a garage mechanic, a farmer. Cut to his grandfather sitting at his library at a large desk, poring over law books. The voice tells how he often asks the old man for advice. Finally, there's a picture of all the Holloways: the ex-governor; his wife, Penny; his two daughters: Eddie's mother standing to his right, Millicent Grimstead, Sam's other daughter; Eddie's wife, Chris, is next to him. In front of the candidate stand two children, a boy of about six and a little girl, maybe four. Adorable, of course. The images, the flow, were good. The script was what one would expect. Eddie wanted an easy-to-access website, the old one now outdated. He attacked his rival as a spendthrift while concentrating on his tightfisted monetary policies. He vowed to shrink government, fight for workforce, not welfare, and to combat the delusional left, as he called them, every step of the way. The website would be constantly updated, too. This was a plum assignment for Crozet Media.

"He certainly has the advantage of name recognition," said Harry.

"Yes, he does, but with his grandfather's illness, Edward felt it was imperative to get good footage of the two of them together." Rae put in another DVD. "Some of these images will fold into Edward's website. We're still sifting through them. We don't want to overdo the family connection."

A terrific shot of Governor Holloway in his World War II Navy uniform, followed by a photo of him taking the oath of office to be governor, followed by a final picture of the old man walking upright, hair gleaming silver, looking up over the horizon.

"Very dignified." Harry admired it.

"Good. I'm glad you like it. Crozet Media, us, had access to the old photos when we shot Edward's footage. I'm being blunt, but Edward—indeed, most men running for office these days—have no military service record. He's leaning on his grandfather's heroics pretty hard." She then changed subject. "As you have seen, we've created websites for a variety of clients."

Harry smiled. "I liked what I saw. Each website is individual, tailored to the task or the company. I guess for me you want shots of the crops. The sunflowers are dramatic."

"Raindrops on plump grapes," Rae continued. "I assume you have horses, a shot of them in the field."

"But I'm not selling them."

"Harry, this is Virginia. Anything with a horse in it gets attention. We'll do a storyboard. Easier to make changes. We are very efficient. How does that sound?"

"And when this website is done, you can cross-reference to other sites where there might be an interest? I'm not conversant with all the new technologies."

"I can. Each of those videos you watched has a presence or an ad on other Web formats. You reach an amazing amount of customers. It's an inexpensive form of advertising, compared to traditional advertising, which is through the roof."

"Can I stop anywhere in the process?"

"Yes, of course."

"Who writes the copy?"

"Usually I do, but you can do it or help me. You know your farm better than anyone. There's a lot of information and territory to cover."

"How much will this cost?"

"Tell you what, I'll ballpark it at two thousand dollars, but I can be much more accurate once we shoot. I'll break it down by hour. If we go over the time limit, we'll stop or keep going. Up to you."

"Want to come by next Wednesday?"

Rae walked into her office, brought out her diary as well as her cellphone containing her schedule on it. "Wednesday I'm shooting at Keswick Club. What about Thursday?"

"That day doesn't work for me. What about Friday?"

Rae nodded. "Perfect." She looked up into Harry's eyes. "Don't you wonder when you schedule what happens to your time?"

Harry laughed. "We're all overcommitted."

"I don't know how people with children do it." As Harry stood up, Rae extended her hand. "I look forward to this."

"I do, too. Before I go, where did you go to college?"

"Savannah School of Art and Design."

"Ah." Harry grinned, opened the door to heavier rain. "The best."

She slid in the driver's seat, wet on the left side, but it wasn't terrible.

"I could have drowned." Pewter wailed, quite dry sprawled out in the back.

"A raindrop fell on the tip of her tail. It's too terrible for words," Tucker solemnly intoned.

Whap!

"Ouch."

"Pewter, let's go back up front." Mrs. Murphy hustled the fatty forward before a real fight broke out.

Once in the passenger seat, the tiger next to her, Pewter squinted at Harry, who started the motor, shut the windows. *"Nobody has any idea how much I suffer."*

13

Tuesday, September 14, 1784

Bent over his drafting table, Charles West squinted, moving the T square farther up the page. Karl Ix had built him a table to his exact specifications. It raised and lowered, plus the flat surface would tilt.

Piglet snored under the table.

A rumble of not-too-distant thunder awakened the dog. Charles walked over to the handblown glass window, four rows of panes horizontally, six vertically. He needed lots of light. Having seen Mr. Jefferson's windows, which doubled as doors when slid upward, he had copied the design, somehow managing to pay for the considerable expense.

"Those are boiling black clouds," Charles said out loud.

Thunder cracked again, closer.

"Staying inside is a good idea," the corgi advised.

Although the sun had not yet set, a pitch-black sky had blotted out the late-afternoon light.

Peering out the window of his and Rachel's tidy house, he looked south toward the main house built on a soft rise and saw candles moving from room to room in Ewing's house.

"Piglet, storms do pass over England, but here in the summer it's almost every day, or so it seems to me. This one"—he paused, whistled low, which made Piglet bark—"is flying, just flying, toward us." No sooner had he said that than the west wind picked up, trees bent toward the east, their leaves fluttering like supplicants.

Although she had been working with her father, Charles worried about Rachel. He lit a candle, carrying it in a curving brass candleholder to each downstairs room facing west.

"Dammit." The house was a simple four-over-four with a wide center hall. He put the candle on the hall table, placing a hurricane glass over it. He opened the front door and rushed outside from window to window, flicking the shutter holders, wrought-iron *S*'s resting on their sides, to an upright position. Closing the shutters, he dropped each small wrought-iron *S*.

"Come on, Piglet." He hurried back in the house, bounding up the stairs two at a time. This proved more difficult as the wind now smacked the house. He lifted up a window, leaned out to pull a shutter closed. Fortunately, the wind pressed the shutter against the house so he could pull the other one shut, fastening them together from the inside with a wrought-iron bar that was longer than the *S*'s downstairs and inside the shutters.

There were only two rooms upstairs on the west side, but by the time he reached the second one and opened the window, the wind had blown the coverlet off the bed. Reaching out as far as he dared, he flipped one dark green shutter shut. The other one began banging against the house. He leaned out farther while Piglet grabbed his breeches, bracing himself.

The shutter flapped back with a bang. Got it.

Soaked in the front, Charles reached down to pat his friend. "What would I do without you?"

"*True*," replied the sturdy but small dog.

Their bedroom, on the east side, seemed safe. The west side of the house felt as though a giant was slapping it with his open hand.

Charles peeled off his sopping shirt, hung it over the banister. Both man and dog thumped down the stairs.

Once in the kitchen, which ran the length of half the house, he opened drawers and found a dish towel. Wiping his chest made the soft red-gold hair stand up.

Back to the hallway, he picked up the candle, retreating to the main room where they would entertain visitors. Slumping in a chair, he listened to the wind.

"Come on." He patted his thigh and Piglet without too much effort leapt up as Charles grabbed the fellow under the armpits.

The house shook.

• • •

While those two huddled together, Catherine, Jeddie, and John stayed in the main barn. Jeddie and the young boys he was training brought all the horses in when they perceived the temperature dropping, the black clouds rolling up behind the mountains. All the broodmares were safe and sound, in their special barn, nickered. They didn't like the storm, but they were safe.

Catherine visited each horse in the main barn, offering a handful of oats. Some took them, some didn't, but not one thrashed around in his stall or made a fuss.

A gust of wind shot down the center aisle. Cleaning rags blew around. In their hurry to bring in the horses, the boys threw rags over the stall doors, all of which had Dutch doors inside and out. The outside doors were shut.

John slid down the ladder from the hayloft, his hands and feet on the outside. He'd closed the hayloft doors, open to ventilate the hay and the barn.

"Black as the Devil's eyebrows," he remarked to his wife and Jeddie, standing with Reynaldo.

"I didn't know anything was coming until I heard that horrible thunder." Catherine felt another mighty gust of wind. She headed for the doors facing northwest. John sprinted ahead of her, as did Jeddie. The men pulled the massive doors shut, leaving the ones on the other end open.

"No point standing here in the aisle," she said. "We can sit in the tack room." A moan of wind overhead caused her to look upward.

Jeddie shook his head. "An evil spirit."

Catherine walked into the room and little Tulli, one of the small stable boys who was learning to identify the different kind of bits, was shaking.

"I don't want to see no dead people," he stuttered.

Jeddie tried to reassure him. "Oh, I was just talking 'bout spirits."

Catherine sat next to little Tulli, kicking her legs straight out to stabilize the old stool. She put an arm around him, rocked him.

John Schuyler smiled at his wife, realizing what a good mother she would be, how she loved children and animals.

"Tulli, don't worry yourself about spirits. You are surrounded by good spirits. You can't see them, but they'll protect you."

Jeddie picked up a bridle, a simple snaffle bit. "I always like what you say, Miss Catherine, about how any bit is cruel in the wrong hands. I'm trying to teach Tulli soft hands. He rides Sweet Potato."

"I've seen him."

Sweet Potato was a pony, and like most ponies, highly opinionated and smart.

Another blast of wind, branches creaking, quieted them.

Tulli started shaking again. Catherine pulled him closer.

"Do you remember your poppa?" she asked.

"A little. I remember he could juggle horseshoes," the child said.

His father had died when Tulli was five. The man was cutting firewood for his family. When he didn't come in the cabin, Georgia, his wife, walked out to see why he was taking so long. He laid on the ground, on his side. No one knew what took him away, but Georgia comforted herself and her two boys by telling them he didn't suffer and God needed a strong man to fix things in heaven.

Tulli thought there was plenty to fix at the cabin, but even then he had sense enough to keep his mouth shut.

At the big house, Ewing and Rachel put away his papers when the storm started. It was too dark to read, anyway. Rachel liked helping her father. She listened closely to him when he spoke of buying land. Catherine did, too, but she was more interested in her father's multiplying business holdings: tobacco, hemp, corn, buildings by a landing on the James River in Scottsville, properties on the Atlantic down in North Carolina. Rachel liked the land itself. Watching her husband, Charles, create plans for building interested her. She couldn't pass by places now without imagining a house or barn on a special site with good drainage.

Ewing enjoyed his daughters' company. He liked teaching them. Both were prudent and never bleated about what they knew. Both sisters learned very early to listen. That way, you learn a lot more than you do if you talk.

Father and youngest daughter retreated to the kitchen.

"Knew it would be bad," Bettina announced. "Knew it would be bad when the chickens ran under the henhouse. Chickens always know. Uh-huh. Always."

"I don't know if I've ever seen the sky so black." Rachel observed the fury outside the kitchen door, opened it, as it was on the north side of the house. Wind blew small limbs, odds and ends not tied down in front of them, but didn't blow into the kitchen, as the wind came from due west.

Ewing sat down at the kitchen table. "I remember a storm like this when Isabelle and I were first married. Just about blew us to bits. The river rose suddenly. No one understood why, 'cause there wasn't that much rain. Must have been 1759, 1760." He shook his head. "Where does the time go? Seems like yesterday."

"Does," Bettina forcefully agreed. "Seems like yesterday I could touch my toes."

"You can still touch your toes. Put your foot on the chair," Rachel teased her.

"You just wait, Miss." Bettina laughed and so did Ewing.

The storm blew over; clouds hung, though. The sun set, but the only sign was a glimmer of lighter clouds over the mountains.

Everyone checked outside. Branches down, a farm wagon tipped over on its side. Not too bad, considering.

Catherine and her beloved John walked home.

Charles met Rachel as she reached the low gate. "I was worried about you," he said to his wife.

"I stayed with father." She looked around. "Let's open up these shutters. Just in case the heat comes up. Hope it doesn't. Be lovely to sleep in a cool night."

They opened the first-floor shutters. Charles opened the ones upstairs.

Later, Piglet was curled at the end of the bed as Charles built small stairs so he could get up and down. He and his humans slept soundly.

Rachel never imagined she would allow a dog on the bed, but Piglet didn't seem like a dog; plus, it made Charles so happy. She reminded herself that Piglet went through the war with her husband, so nothing was too good for the corgi, and of course nothing was too good for Charles.

In the middle of the night, the farm dogs set up a howl. Piglet awoke and howled, too.

Charles ordered him, "Pipe down."

"*There's someone here,*" the corgi answered.

The other farm dog called out, "*Intruders!*"

No one paid any mind. The humans went back to sleep.

"*There's someone here!*" Piglet insisted.

14

Wednesday, September 15, 1784

Piglet, nose down, followed a trail of fresh blood. Yesterday's thrashing rains and the early morning's cool temperature helped the scent stick. Above, the low clouds showed no promise of dispersing, nor did they show promise of more rain. The stagnant cloud cover also helped the corgi.

His nose filled with information. A grouse had scuttled at wood's edge near an hour ago. An entire flock of wild turkeys left their distinctive signature scent as well as a few feathers. Once he got into the woods, a vixen was close. Then Piglet picked up traces of fading human scent. Someone had brushed by thick bushes.

Intrepid, Piglet continued. In the few places where blood splashed, the odor was overpowering. Otherwise, he followed drops magnified by the dew.

A rocky overhang stopped him. Good place for a bear, but this small cave under the overhang was disguised by

saplings and bushes. Strong now, the smell of blood made the corgi cautious. He ducked behind joe-pye weed, high and blooming. He could hear humans talking, crying.

A deep voice ordered, "You go on. They'll miss you before they miss me."

Bettina stepped out; worry creased her face. "I can't come back until dark."

The deep voice that Piglet now recognized as the slave Father Gabe called softly, "No worry. I've got rags and good water here. I'll stop by the kitchen. So you'll know."

Not a small woman, Bettina stomped away.

Piglet crept forward, belly low to the ground, until he could peer into the disguised place. A young man lay with his back against the rock, a deep diagonal wound across his broad chest. Next to him sat a beautiful woman, or she had once been beautiful. Her eye socket had been damaged. The cheekbone underneath had been smashed. Her right hand, wrapped in a clean cloth, bled through. Tending to them was Father Gabe, an old man with medical knowledge and some folks said more than that. He gently placed a compress on the woman's cheek. She didn't wince. The young man would awaken, then fall back to sleep. Piglet knew he'd lost a lot of blood because he'd followed it all the way here.

Turning for home, the little fellow wanted to tell Charles, but how?

• • •

Ewing Garth was up at dawn. He walked into the kitchen for his full breakfast at seven in the morning. He'd brushed his teeth, nestled in his chair to be shaved, then dressed. This was a leisurely morning, which he preferred. The big breakfast prepared him for the day. While he was never averse to eating, a big breakfast could hold him until one or two o'clock, when a light meal sufficed until supper. But in the summers and early fall even supper was light, unless he was entertaining.

Serena, a young woman helping Bettina, had her back to him and was just putting the finishing touches on Ewing's poached eggs. He was most particular about his eggs.

"Good morning." He beamed.

"Morning back at you." Bettina turned, eggs now on the dish, placing it before him. "Serena, where's Master's coffee?" Returning to Ewing. "Chicory coffee this morning. That bit of tang to the air just whispered to me, 'Chicory for the master.' "

"Bettina, you're a mind reader." He savored those eggs and that cup of coffee.

Now placed before him were biscuits light as air, an array of jams and honey. They came from the summer kitchen, still in use due to the fact that the day would heat up, no point using the kitchen even in the cool of the morning. The last thing anyone wanted was for heat to be hanging around as the mercury climbed upward.

Serena placed a plate of sausages in front of him, along with condiments.

"Serena, did you make this sausage?"

"Yes, sir."

He tasted one, then nodded his approval. "Bettina, your pupil is learning her lessons."

"If she don't, I'll beat her butt with a wooden spoon."

"Perhaps you don't have to go that far."

He'd finished his breakfast, walked down the hall to see Roger, his all-powerful butler, speaking closely to his son, Weymouth. Weymouth shaved Ewing. The young man, so dexterous, was a fine barber.

On seeing Ewing, both men straightened up, nodding to him as he turned into his office. Just as he retrieved the papers that he and Rachel secured yesterday, he heard voices. Roger had opened the door.

"Drat," he uttered, placing a paperweight on the papers.

What now and whom? Why was it so hard to get anything done in peace?

At his opened door, a serious Roger, voice low, said, "Master, there's two men here from the constable's office who say it is of the utmost importance to talk to you."

Ewing, never fond of officials, wondered what they wanted. "Show them in."

It was always something.

He stood up to greet the men. Hiram Meisner, the head constable, hat in hand, bowed slightly as did Dennis McComb, his deputy. Hiram was a man of middling status with a decent frock coat, tidy tricorn, and thick leggings. He smiled tightly.

Dennis said nothing, which was just as well. Dennis had no reputation for either sense or etiquette.

"Begging your pardon, Mr. Ewing," Hiram said. "We are here on a most serious matter."

"Please, gentlemen, sit down. Is it so serious you can't enjoy a cup of coffee?" Ewing pleasantly offered, knowing neither man would detect the sarcasm.

"Thank you, no. I will come directly to the point. Francisco Selisse has been murdered by one of his slaves, who escaped. This wretch took with him another slave, a woman of great beauty. We will capture them and we ask for everyone to be alert. The woman is possibly a captive or a shield. We do not know, but we feel the man will not hesitate to kill again."

Ewing narrowed his eyes. "I see. And what of Mrs. Selisse? Is she safe?"

"Yes. Not in her right mind, which is more than understandable. She witnessed the murder. Her lady's maid Sheba says her mistress caught the slave Moses assaulting her husband. Sheba says Mrs. Selisse picked up a small split log—they were in the main room, in front of the fireplace—and swung at the man. He pulled a long knife from his waistband, drove it through Mr. Selisse's heart, grabbing the other slave by the wrist. That's all we know."

Bettina also listened, ear to the door in the next room.

"How very terrible." Ewing lied because Francisco was not a man he would mourn. "In the interests of safety for my own family, might you tell me if you saw the body and the wounds?"

"Blood over his waistcoat. Sheba said Moses pulled out the knife, keeping it."

"Head smashed like an old pumpkin," Dennis blurted out.

"Mr. McComb, that's quite enough," Hiram angrily scolded the man he loathed working alongside.

"Terrible," Ewing again said.

"The killer, Moses Durkin, possesses great strength, so should you see him, you must be wary. I would carry a pistol until he is found," Hiram suggested.

"Quite right, Constable." Ewing rose. "Are you sure you won't fortify yourself with some coffee? This will be a long and trying day for you."

Hiram rose, tapped Dennis on the shoulder so he, too, stood up. "Mr. Garth, thank you. Again, I am sorry to disturb you with such news."

"I'm glad you did. We need more men like you, Hiram." He shook the constable's hand.

As the two men left, Roger silently glided to the front door, which he opened. Bettina tiptoed back into the kitchen.

Once in the kitchen, Bettina sagged into a chair. She'd been up most of the night helping Father Gabe clean Moses's wound. No one could set Ailee's bones or tend to her eye. All they could do was put compresses on the wreckage.

Serena came and stood next to Bettina. "What do we do?"

Bettina reached up, patted Serena's hand resting on her shoulder. "We say nothing."

"I can slip down and take some food."

"I know you can, honey, but we can't go down in the day. Anyway, right now they hurt too much to eat. We'll take food down after sundown, and perhaps some liquor to kill the pain."

"Bad?"

Bettina nodded. "She'll not see out of that left eye. He'll heal, but, oh, it's a long and ugly wound."

Serena kissed Bettina on the cheek. These two had played their parts. Bettina would fuss at the younger woman; Serena would do as she was told, occasionally tossing her head or glaring back. The white folks loved it, and truth be told, so did Bettina and Serena. This bit of theater gave them a conduit for emotion. Then again, playing to an eager audience somehow lifts one up.

Roger came back to the kitchen. After checking, he closed the door to the hall.

"And?"

She held up her hand. "I hope we can save them, Roger. We can keep them from being found, although I don't know how long. I don't know how we can get them out."

Roger dropped his eyes. "They'll hang Moses."

"And they'll return Ailee to that bitch!" Bettina spat, surprising both of them by swearing.

"Which one, the Missus or Sheba?" Having been at the Selisses, Roger hated both women.

"I don't know what to do." Bettina sighed deeply, fighting back tears.

Roger came and held her other hand. "The Good Lord will show us the way."

Hearing Ewing's footfalls, Serena ducked out back to the summer kitchen and Bettina began clearing the table. Roger walked into the hall.

Ewing said to him, "The Bible tells us it is wrong to kill, but I'm not so certain that Francisco didn't deserve it. I wonder sometimes, Roger, I do wonder if lives would be changed, or even history, by killing the wrong man at the right time."

"I don't know."

"Well, neither do I."

Catherine watched as Hiram and Dennis rode out on their errand. Rachel, standing next to her, did also. Already at his drafting table, Charles knew nothing of it. With the sisters, John also watched.

"You know they want something from Father," Rachel noted.

"Ever notice hardly anyone comes to him to delight him or bring him a book? Everyone wants something, as you said." Catherine saw Piglet amble toward them from across the field.

"Piglet, tired of drawing?"

"Follow me. I can't get Charles to follow me."

"Well, back to my husband." Rachel smiled.

Catherine looked up at hers. "I know, you and Karl are going down to check the bridges."

John nodded. "I don't think there has been that much rain in as short a time since we built them during the War, but then perhaps there was while I was fighting."

"No. I think last night was the worst."

"We'll find out how good an engineer Karl is. If those supports didn't hold or cracked, we've got a big job in front of us."

She kissed him. "You're equal to it. Why, John, you could just stand in the water and hold the bridge overhead."

He laughed. "I'm not Hercules."

"You're my Hercules."

"Will someone pay attention to me?" Piglet sharply barked.

"You're making me dizzy, turning in those circles." Catherine leaned over to pet the dog, who looked up at her with big brown eyes.

He took a few steps, turned to look at her. *"I know something."*

Walking away, Catherine found her path blocked. Piglet circled behind her and nudged her leg with his nose.

"Follow me."

Knowing a fair amount of animal behavior for a

human, she turned and followed Piglet. The beige fellow would hurry ahead, nose to the ground, stop and wait for her. It occurred to her after five minutes of this to look down as she approached the edge of the woods.

She saw blood.

The thick woods rested on level ground that dipped down, eventually to a feeder creek. Much rock lay near the bottom. In some cases sheer rock faces loomed over narrow deer trails, unusual for this land, but common as one got into the Blue Ridge Mountains. Other places had flat rock beaches, or rocky sides and a few large boulders, like this area. A narrow trail followed the creek. One could travel it without detection. This portion eventually flowing into Ivy Creek was one of them.

Her senses alert, she followed the dog and followed the drops of blood. Piglet stopped near the hidden cave. Motionless, he pricked his ears. Catherine took his advice and stayed still, too.

She heard a moan, then Father Gabe's voice. Catherine listened for what seemed a long time, then silently turned, headed back.

Back on higher land, she ran to the big house.

"Bettina!"

Having fallen asleep in the kitchen, Bettina startled, sat up straight.

"Bettina." Catherine stepped into the room. "Something's wrong."

Just then, Ewing opened the kitchen door from the hall side. "Darling, Francisco's been killed. Come into the office and I will tell you what I know. Weymouth!" He called out.

Weymouth appeared. "Yes, sir."

"Go fetch Rachel, Charles, and John. Now."

"Yes, sir."

Ewing looked at his daughter. "I only want to tell this story once, but seeing you, I know I will tell it twice." And so he did.

When the others finally gathered in the library, the tale now told, Rachel looked to her father and then to Catherine. They all knew one another inside and out.

"Father, do you want us to search?" Rachel asked.

"No, my dear. We leave this to the constable. If I were a runaway slave, I'd make for the river."

No one said anything, but then John nudged forward another opinion. "Yes, sir, that would be the fastest way out of here, but it might be the first place people would look and I expect there are militia men or others on the river now."

Ewing wrinkled his brow. "I suppose so. They'll kill Moses. There will be a show of legality if they can even get him to the courthouse, but he will die."

Not being an American and never facing such a situation, Charles asked, "What would happen to anyone who assists him or Ailee?"

Ewing exhaled loudly. "Up to the discretion of the judge, but even if a man was not accused of stealing another man's property or helping a murderer, he would be ruined for life. Certainly he would have to leave Virginia."

"Yes, yes, of course," Charles replied in a low voice. "And where could such a person go? Every state has slaves."

"There are some states which are talking about changing that," said Catherine. "Vermont most especially, but I have heard Pennsylvania might be leaning that way."

"It will ruin businessmen," Ewing said.

"Not if it is done in stages, Father, which some people have suggested. It's not a popular idea, but it is interesting, is it not, that a few people in a few places are thinking of such things?" Catherine added this as though of little consequence.

"I suppose." Ewing folded his hands together across his middle. "The world is changing too fast for me. So many improvements, and then again, a falling away from the old ways. Such ideas will create turmoil."

"Yes, they will," John agreed.

Unbidden, Piglet came into the room. He stared right up at Catherine. They shared an enormous secret, a crushing burden.

15

Friday, July 29, 2016

"Me, Me, Me!" Pewter rolled around in the dirt by the barn, stopping to reveal way, way too much white tummy.

"I wouldn't display that much fat if I were you," Tucker yipped.

"I'm not you, *Wormdog*," she hissed.

Holding a small boom with a sensitive mike, Deon Watts, the soundman, pleaded, "Is there any way to put up the animals?"

Harry, in a dark blue shirt in high contrast to her tall sunflowers, replied, "I can try, but they know the way in and out of everything. Let me see if persuasion will work."

Rae Tait and Bethel Carson, the videographer, took a short break.

"Pewter, Tucker, shut up. If you don't, this will be ugly and I'll carry you back to the house and put you in the basement."

Feeling Tucker was wrongfully chastised, Mrs. Murphy walked over to sit next to the dog.

"Brownie!" Pewter spat.

"Come on, Pewts, I don't want to sit in the basement and neither do you." Mrs. Murphy loathed the boring basement. Given their great hunting abilities, there weren't any vermin in the basement to help pass the time.

Harry then tried her hand at direction. "If you shoot them there, together, then pan to the sunflowers, overlarge egos may be appeased. And then, of course, when we walk back to the barn, they'll run ahead and that will make a good shot. Mrs. Murphy might even climb on a paddock fence and call to the horses. Never hurts to entertain a bit, does it?"

The three looked down at the animals, then to one another.

Rae shrugged. "Why not? If you can just keep them quiet. Let's try this again. Take four."

Ignoring the rising heat, Harry smiled at the camera. She turned away slightly, sweeping her hand toward the beautiful field of sunflowers. "This riot of color will be harvested in a few weeks, depending on rainfall and sunshine. The sunflowers will grow higher, the heads larger. No pesticides are used. The seeds are removed, placed in large sieves. We shake them out and divide by size once they are completely dried out. I'm surprised musicians don't use the sound, softer than castanets but swishy." She half giggled.

"Did she write this?" Pewter whispered.

"*Shh.*" Mrs. Murphy bumped Pewter, who sat on her haunches with Mrs. Murphy and Tucker.

Harry rattled on. The footage and soundtrack could all be edited down. From the sunflowers they shot footage of the Ambrosia corn and the Silver Queen, Harry explaining the difference in taste, the Ambrosia being sweeter. She discussed the types of pests, especially corn worms and blight. Corn spiders performed useful service against some of the pests, and she declared she lost about ten to fifteen percent of her annual harvest to damage because she refused to use pesticides. A few old pear trees were next, and Harry explained that she had no orchard but she wanted to keep some of the old varieties growing and healthy. She put her hand under a pear, large already.

"This is a Sewickly pear. Used to be acres of them in the forties and fifties, my dad said. Harder to grow, more susceptible to fungi and other things. They've been overtaken by Fuji pears and a few other types, all good, but we lose diversity." She then walked to some appealing peaches, almost like a drawing, and continued, "These are Alverta peaches. The same story as the pears and"—she continued walking—"here are Black Twig apples." She paused. "I don't sell the fruit. I don't have enough, but my friends and I use them, bake with them, and also can some. Each of these varieties has a distinctive taste, quite different from what you are accustomed to in supermarkets. I just don't have the

money or manpower to install a profitable orchard using the types from past centuries."

"Cut." Rae beamed. "This is fascinating. People will be interested. Can you tell me why this is important to all of us? Even though they are more difficult to grow, so to speak, what's the payoff for the consumer?"

Harry nodded. The cats took the opportunity to climb up into the Black Twig apple trees closest to Harry. Pewter stretched herself along a branch, thinking a languid pose might look better than some old apples. More sensibly, Mrs. Murphy sat in the crook between the trunk and the first low, heavy branch.

"Rae, should we move the cats?" Bethel inquired.

Rae studied the new composition. "No. We can always cut it if we need to. I think this adds some fun to the enterprise. Okay, roll 'em."

Harry leaned against the trunk. "The reason we don't want to lose the old fruit trees is pretty simple. Yes, they may be more prone to certain types of pests, and yes, the fruit is usually not those huge red or green apples you see filling display boxes at the market. Often these varieties have a stronger taste, some sweeter, some tart, but the critical issue is diversity. What if a virus or fungus wipes out, say, Golden Delicious? It takes years to develop an orchard; the trees mature at their own rate and early harvests aren't as good as later ones when the tree is in its prime. I see this as one of the most important issues in agriculture, the diminishment of diversity."

"Cut," Rae called out. "Harry, that was very clear. Something I never considered."

Harry smiled. "People don't live close to the land anymore. They take food products for granted. You know, it's not like the American public is purposefully limiting their choices. They don't know any better, and really, the big supermarket chains are determining the varieties. That's how I see it. So naturally, a shopper will pick the biggest, shiniest red apple they can find or the roundest peach."

Deon piped up. "I do."

"Me, too," Bethel added.

"Okay, how about a shot of your vineyard?"

"Great." Harry headed toward her small vineyard and heard a cry and a plop.

"I told you not to stretch yourself on the branch," Mrs. Murphy chastised Pewter, who had fallen out of the tree.

Despite her bulk, the gray cat had twisted so she didn't land hard, but she didn't land on all four paws, either. Her front paws hit the ground while her hind end sort of flopped down.

Hard at Harry's heels, Tucker glanced back, deciding to keep a tight lip.

Arriving at the vineyard, Harry pointed to a low hill. "If you do a shot of me, whatever, you'll be able to see the whole vineyard from that spot. This is only one-quarter of an acre, and when I planted the grapes, four years ago, it cost me fourteen thousand dollars. More expensive today. Your first year's grapes you must leave on the vine. After that you can harvest, but the grapes aren't at their best for a few years more, depends on the variety. Growing grapes is expensive, fraught with sorrows."

Rae spoke. "Bethel, shoot this. And Deon, what we can do to add interest is do this section as a voice-over. Okay, shoot the close-up of the vines and then a tight close-up of the grapes. Let's all go to the rise, where, Harry, talk to us again as you just did, but condense it if possible."

Once on the hill, Harry did trim her comments.

Rae then nudged her. "What sorrows?"

"Right." Harry spoke, her voice pleasant to hear, a soft alto. "Regardless of how vigilant you are, even if a viticulturist keeps dogs in the vineyard to chase away the deer, the birds will take some of your grapes and occasionally, especially if you don't have dogs, the foxes will strip off the lower vines. Foxes love grapes. Aesop was right."

Rae motioned for Bethel to shoot Tucker, who was on all fours, the picture of alertness and service. She then pointed to the dog, and Harry, a quick mind, understood.

"While I don't keep a Great Pyrenees, I do have this loyal and tough corgi, and Tucker chases off the deer. Actually, she'd be happy to herd them."

Tucker puffed out her chest. *"I'm an all-purpose dog."*

"I chase rabbits. Oh, I am death to rabbits," Pewter competitively boasted.

"Save me," Mrs. Murphy uttered under her breath.

On the hill, Harry repeated herself more succinctly, mentioned foxes and Tucker's good deeds.

"Cut. All right. How about we go back, shoot some exteriors, and we should have it?"

"Rae, how long will it take to edit?" Harry asked.

"We'll have a rough cut by next week. You can see it and then we can tweak it. If we need more footage or you think of something else to add, we can come back. We should have this ready for you no later than mid-August, on budget."

Walking back to the barn, grasshoppers flying and making that *tic-tic* sound as they hit things, Pewter ran ahead. Mrs. Murphy and Tucker moved at a more dignified pace as they walked ahead.

Upon reaching the pastures, both cats climbed to the top of the fence, each sitting on a post. Bethel captured this. The cats meowed.

In the paddock with Tomahawk, Shortro lifted his head; the grass tasted so sweet.

"Let's go see what she wants."

Tomahawk, older, grass blades sticking out of his mouth, replied, *"Pewter is showing off."*

"Hey, we can, too." Shortro snorted, bucked, twisted, then thundered up to Pewter, skidding to a stop.

Tomahawk followed suit, kicking his hind legs higher than his head, which nearly touched the grass. *"I may be old, but I can still keep up with you."*

"Good footage," Rae remarked as Bethel kept the camera rolling.

"We don't lack for drama here." Harry laughed. "It's just different than all the cop shows."

"The horses come when I call." Pewter sang out, then touched noses with Shortro, who was sorely tempted to push the cat off the fencepost.

Bethel swung the camera upward for a long shot of the sparkling white stable, a glittering copper weather vane, a galloping horse on top. Peering out from the cupola, which the humans couldn't see, was the large owl, Flatface, nesting up there as she had for years. Damn noisy humans and animals. She ruffled her feathers, moved from side to side, then closed her eyes.

"You must have shined your weather vane," Rae remarked as they walked closer to the barn.

"Lost it in the storm. That's a new one and I about died when I paid for it. Found it on the Internet. Exactly what I wanted. One thousand dollars. I balked, but my husband said the stable wouldn't look right without it. Does look pretty good, doesn't it? It will be verdigris by next year."

"That's a good look, too." Rae nodded, then glanced around. "How about one last shot? You driving the John Deere down the farm road. We'll probably start the video with that. Maybe." She looked at Bethel. No response. "Okay, we'll have to see the footage."

Harry led them to the equipment shed. "Deon, how about I take out the old 1953 John Deere, the one we call

Johnny-Pop? The cap on the exhaust stays open when you're going, but it claps up and down when you start or slow down. It's a distinctive sound known to most old farmers or farmers who don't have the money for a big John Deere with all the add-ons. About two hundred thousand dollars if you buy, say, a new 90HP, a hay baler, a drill seeder, a bushog, and that's for starters. Oh, they've got computers in them, closed air-conditioned cabs, radios. Unbelievable. I go out on Johnny-Pop, wear my straw hat, and hope I don't hit digger bees."

Deon liked that she was thinking about the soundtrack. "What about the big tractor?"

"That's an 80HP John Deere, 1987. Real steel. Today, lots of plastic. A great workhorse, but it doesn't make the same sound as Johnny. Course, it's a lot more horsepower than the old boy."

Harry climbed up into the driver's seat. She'd painted a turtle on the side of the tractor. If it's possible to love a machine, she did. She could always picture her mother on Johnny-Pop.

Tucker whined. Harry stepped down, a big step, picked up the dog, lifted her up into her special seat attached to Harry's seat. The cats observed this with disdain.

"I wouldn't go up there. Think of the pollution from the exhaust." Pewter sniffed.

"Bullroar," Tucker, big smile, called down.

"Come on." Mrs. Murphy gleefully grabbed a heavy beam. She climbed up with grace and speed and then

walked over everyone on the crossbeam. Pewter followed suit. Bethel shot it.

"A dog can't do that," Pewter crowed.

Harry backed out. Super-alert, Tucker headed down toward the fields. And Johnny did pop. A backfire added to the excitement.

The crew left by one in the afternoon. Harry fed everyone lunch before they left, which they happily accepted. Sitting around the kitchen table, she heard their stories, how each wound up in this field. After eating their food, Mrs. Murphy and Pewter listened, as did Tucker. Harry gave them some chicken slices, which made everyone quite happy.

The remainder of the day, Harry weeded her small food garden behind the house. Took longer than she wanted it to; the heat slowed her down. Stopping for water breaks, she'd peer down an aisle of tomato plants or squash rows. She just knew the weeds popped up as she looked down the rows. The cats slept in the house, and even Tucker, her shadow, fell asleep under the tree where Matilda, the blacksnake, hung out, literally.

By five o'clock, Harry had had it. Took a shower, made a huge salad with fresh lettuce, cranberries, sunflower seeds, other nuts, shredded cheese. She peeled and sliced hard-boiled eggs.

Wiping off the counters, Tucker awakened, ran to the back door. *"Cooper!"*

The dog and two cats could recognize cars and trucks by the sound of the tire treads. Each vehicle, thanks to model, age and use, wore out their tires in a distinctive fashion. If Tucker hadn't recognized the sound, she would have signaled that an intruder was coming.

Looking out the window over the sink, Harry wiped her hands on the dish towel, hurried out to the screened-in porch, opened the door as Cooper emerged from her car. "Perfect timing. Come test my cranberry salad."

Cooper walked over as Harry held the door open. "Harry, give me a minute. Thanks for the offer, but I'm still on duty. Friday is my late-night day."

"Sure." Harry closed the door behind her. "You can sip some iced tea, can't you?"

Sitting in a kitchen chair, as a friend and neighbor, Cooper need not have been invited to do so, but now she nodded. "Sweet tea. I need the sugar."

A new person or acquaintance would have been invited by Harry to pull out a chair. Cooper was considered family, just as she could walk in the back door unannounced. By such subtleties, southerners know one another and know their place.

"A sprig of fresh mint?"

"Uh-huh."

Setting the tea in front of her and grabbing one for herself, Harry said, "What's wrong?"

"Crozet Media came out here today, right?"

"Yeah. I told you I was hoping to create a professional website to help promote my produce."

Taking a refreshing sip, Cooper nodded. "You did, but I have to check. Everything went fine?"

"Great. A lot of fun. Mrs. Murphy, Pewter, and Tucker got into the act. I'm sure they'll be stars."

"So when did the crew leave?"

"Oneish. Why?"

"Their office has been trashed."

16

Thursday, September 16, 1784

So very becoming in a pale rose light silk gown, Sheba almost outshone her mistress. Maureen Selisse wore shimmering blue, her blonde hair with streaks of gray coiffed in the latest fashion. This being her husband's funeral, Maureen took advantage of the situation to mourn with the smallest of lace kerchiefs covering the top of her head. The proprieties must be observed, and a lady is always covered in the house of God or for a sacrament. This particular house, Episcopal, was unadorned. It wasn't that the Episcopalians of central Virginia ignored their churches, but all that red, gold, blue, gold, more gold, candles, lavish painting, and hangings smacked of Rome. Then again, red smacked of the recently defeated enemy. Perhaps the time would come when the Protestants of the state might add a bit of color and comfort—those pews were unmercifully hard—but who could predict?

Francisco's casket was closed, with a spray of late-summer daylilies. Situated at the front of the church, the altar and priest were three steps upward on the raised floor behind the casket.

Often funerals were conducted at the home of the deceased, but Maureen wanted everyone to attend a church funeral and, of course, for all to see the honor she paid her murdered spouse. And she did pay him honor.

The service from *The Book of Common Prayer* was a dignified one, filled with the simple, beautiful phrases from the seventeenth century. It pleased everyone. Some of the pleasure derived from the fact that it didn't last too long.

The church service was followed by a subdued procession, ladies under their parasols, to the expanding graveyard. Francisco was set aside an open grave but not put into it, and Maureen sagged onto Sheba, who held her up with the help of Yancy Grant, planter and horseman. Maureen was carefully walked back to a repast under large trees, the church meeting room deemed too small. Once Maureen was seated at the head of the table, many of her slaves in evidence, Francisco's last meal began.

In livery, DoRe stood at a distance at the open carriage, the very latest painted Charleston green with gold pinstripes.

Catherine stood on one side of her father, Rachel on the other. Their husbands were next to them, and the group slowly walked to the occasion.

In a low voice, Ewing said, "I see Yancy Grant hasn't lost a minute."

No, he had not. He danced attendance and feigned sorrow upon Maureen, herself not averse to the attention but only slightly encouraging it. She sat in the catbird seat. Yes, a bit plump now but not overly so, she retained much of her good looks, which were tremendously enhanced by the fact that Maureen Selisse was now one of the richest widows in Virginia.

Catherine smiled, said to the family, "They aren't punishing DoRe."

Ewing wisely nodded. "People know he tried to restrain Moses in his wild passion for that girl."

"She was very, very beautiful," Charles West noted, then hastily added, "And Francisco was not renowned for his restraint when it came to a beautiful woman. How many times have I caught him staring intensely at my Rachel? I think I would have killed him myself."

"Now, Charles." Rachel's admonition carried affection.

"Was any woman safe?" John Schuyler half snorted. "I would never have left Catherine, Rachel, anyone, alone with that man."

"It was almost an affliction," Ewing mused.

"In the end, it was a fatal one." John put his hand over his wife's hand, which rested on his arm, again quite the proper way for a lady to walk slowly with her husband.

"No sign of either Moses nor Ailee?" Ewing remarked.

Catherine felt herself stiffen, then relax. "Not yet, but I would think they'd be downriver by now or, perhaps more prudently, up in the mountains."

"Mmm," Ewing murmured as they reached the long table, parishioners, business associates, friends, neighbors enjoying the food, one another. "My darlings, allow me to stand in line and pay our respects first and then you all may follow when the hordes clear."

"Yes, Father," both daughters agreed.

Ewing patiently took his place, but due to his reputation and wealth most men moved him forward. He was quick to thank them, as well as remember who knew their place.

Upon reaching a seated Maureen Selisse, Ewing bowed low. He took her hand, brushing his lips over it. "My dear, my poor dear. You are so brave."

Exactly what she wanted to hear.

Lowering her eyes then raising them, she fluttered her eyelashes. "Oh, Ewing Garth, I can't think of anyone the sight of whom could lift my spirits but you. You know, my dear Francisco always said you were the smartest man in this county and beyond. I do not know how I will recover from this dreadful event, but I will. He would expect it of me, you know."

"I do and you will. Now I must reluctantly leave you as the line behind me grows, a testimony to your late husband and a great show of respect for you, madam."

He moved away while her bosom heaved a few practiced heaves. Sheba patted her mistress's cheek and forehead with a Belgian lace handkerchief.

"Now you take a sip of this, Missus. You mustn't overextend yourself." Sheba forced a few sips of iced tea or what looked like iced tea on her owner.

Bettina attended because Catherine insisted she and Rachel needed her. Also as head woman at the estate, Bettina should be seen, especially among the other slaves.

Bettina, next to Jeddie, who was dressed as a postilion, put her hand over her mouth to hide the sneer. "Sheba is so full of the milk of human kindness, she moos."

Jeddie stifled a laugh. "Do you think she gets all of Mistress's clothes? Sheba's clothes are better than most of the white folks' here."

Bettina looked him up and down. "And who is in a most expensive uniform?"

"Uh."

"Uh-huh. Sheba is how Maureen tries to put us under her thumb. She wears the jewelry, her dress is better than Sheba's, but Sheba is just a rung down on that ladder, and having her lady-in-waiting so bedazzling shouts her wealth and her power. And you be careful. She does have power and she can be cruel."

"Yes, Bettina."

The other reason Catherine insisted Bettina accompany the family to the funeral was it might give Bettina a chance to speak with DoRe. Looking about, she saw

DoRe standing by the exquisite carriage under large oak trees. Bettina walked toward him, her head high.

He smiled wanly when he saw her. "Bettina, I don't believe I have ever seen you without your apron until now."

She placed her hand on his, then withdrew it. "DoRe," she whispered in his ear, "your boy is alive. I can say no more." She kissed him on the check. "Our only hope is silence."

Sensible to what she was really telling him, his eyes misted. He took both her hands in his, then looked over to the open grave. "The silence of the grave."

He kissed her back and wiped his tears, and she returned to Jeddie. You never knew who had the searching eye, and she didn't want Sheba to see her lingering with DoRe. Looking at Sheba, she realized she was in no danger. Sheba was too busy fulfilling her role as the ministering angel.

Hiram Meisner stood at the back of the crowd. As a county servant, he was not of this group, but he was allowed there, as was everyone who wished to pay their respects to the grieving widow. Hiram watched everyone.

Catherine, John, Rachel, and Charles paid their respects, followed by Yancy Grant swooping in for a second pass.

"Might I fetch you some refreshments?" asked Yancy.

She smiled up at him. "Thank you, Mr. Grant. Sheba will see to that."

Jeffrey Holloway made his way to Maureen. Of medium build, strong-jawed, blond, and tremendously handsome, Jeffrey, of the middling orders, harbored ambitions. Hardworking, careful of drink, he had a decent reputation for a young man. His lack of education, and the fact that he worked with his hands as a cabinetmaker, proved a hindrance to the advancement of his station. Jeffrey bowed to Maureen even lower than Yancy, as he should, being lower down on the social scale.

"Mrs. Selisse, allow me to express my sympathy." The handsome Jeffrey Holloway tilted his head upward to look deeply into her eyes.

Maureen didn't know Jeffrey. The handsome fellow's dealings had been only with Francisco.

Yancy, discounting him, half turned his body to Maureen, interrupted whatever Jeffrey was going to say.

"Madam, you inherit complicated business and legal matters. Consider me at your service."

She smiled up at him, then focused her attention back on Jeffrey.

"Madam, you helped your husband in numerous ways," said Jeffrey. "Your acumen is well known. I think what Mr. Grant means to say"—he stared right at Yancy Grant, whose face registered surprise at this upstart—"is that we all want to protect a beautiful woman alone in these turbulent times. As you can see, Mrs. Selisse, I am not a man of Mr. Grant's standing, but I wish to see to your comfort and safety. If you need anything, pins, flour, a book from Europe, call upon me. I will do your bidding."

With that, Jeffrey bowed again, not as low, took her hand and kissed it, again looking directly into her eyes with his remarkable green ones.

Yes, Maureen had loved Francisco once, and yes, she was mourning. That mourning abruptly ended. Her bosom lifted upward, she let her hand linger in his, then whispered, "I shall call upon you, sir."

Inclining his head slightly, with a hint of a smile, Jeffrey then looked directly at Sheba.

Sheba got the message.

So did Catherine and Rachel, observing the brief transaction. Missing it were John and Charles, engaged in a conversation with the aging former commandant of The Barracks. Then again, they would have missed it even if they had seen it.

Rachel quickly slipped her arm through her sister's, propelling her away from the table and away from clouds of chat.

"Jeffrey Holloway!" Rachel breathed.

"All the wolves circling Mrs. Selisse. She's the one with the longest fangs. You'd think some of these men would have the sense to, well, I don't know. If nothing else, they might try to determine what truly happened."

"She'll never tell," Catherine flatly stated.

"Why?"

"Maureen Selisse is the unstained widow, the hapless survivor of a slave attack on her blameless husband."

"You don't think she killed him, do you? Women do lose their minds over such things."

Catherine shrugged. "There's more to this than anyone knows. Sheba knows. I'm sure of that."

"She'll hold it over her mistress's head for the rest of their lives." Rachel, quieter than Catherine, missed little.

"Wouldn't you?" asked Catherine.

A long silence followed this as they paused under a majestic tree.

"Yes, I suppose I would," Rachel said at last. "One has to use what one can to live. I hate to think about it, though."

"I'll make you a bet."

"What are we betting, before I agree?"

"Your hand is better than mine. I want embroidered pillowcases, rich blue against the white."

"How many pillowcases?"

Catherine smiled. "Rachel, don't be peevish. I know you. Four."

"All right. What I want if I win this bet, whatever it is, is a trip to the milliner in Scottsville for a fall hat."

"You think big."

"I need a new hat, something with feathers for the season. I'm tired of gauze and ribbons."

"I am, too. Here's the bet. Maureen marries Jeffrey before one year of proper mourning."

Rachel considered this. "That's quite a bet. A flirtation is one thing. Should she engage in more than that, she is a widow. That's some protection, but to marry a man without money, a cabinetmaker working with his father, oh, I don't know. That is a big step. What does she gain?"

"A Greek god and the fountain of youth."

Rachel stared at Catherine, then back at Maureen and then to Jeffrey. He was now politely speaking to the priest who officiated the ceremony. "I see what you mean. Sister, do you think age will affect us so?"

"No. It didn't bother Mother."

Rachel smiled, then led Catherine back to the funeral feast.

Carriages filled the road heading west toward the mountains. Most turned off on Three-Chopt Road, a few turned right to clop along the road to The Barracks. More farms were springing up in the area as more people flocked to Central Virginia, especially now that the native Indians had been driven across the Blue Ridge Mountains into the Shenandoah Valley.

By the time Ewing Garth, the Schuylers, and the Wests reached home, the sun was setting.

"Like a torch behind the mountains," Ewing said.

"I never tire of it," Catherine replied.

With help from Tulli, Jeddie took the carriage. Bettina asked if Ewing needed anything and he said he did not. She walked briskly back to her cabin.

Catherine looked down the distant row. The children played in front of their cabins, the boys ran after a hoop, the girls ran after the boys just to bedevil them. No sign of Father Gabe.

Late that night, Catherine slipped out of bed, changed into a shift, put on working shoes. She let herself out of the back door, thinking John remained asleep. He did not. He rose, looked out the window to see his wife heading for the woods. He also saw Piglet emerge from Rachel and Charles's house. Catherine carried what looked like a blanket. He pulled on his socks, pants, and boots to follow.

This time, Catherine stopped before the cave, then called softly, "Father Gabe, I mean no harm."

Bettina surprised her by stepping outside. "Missus—"

Catherine held up her hand; with the other she offered the thin blanket. The September nights could become cool, and this was one of them. "How are they?"

Bettina motioned for her to come inside. Piglet followed. Moses, feverish, moaned. Father Gabe soaked strips of cloth into a bucket of water, then wrung them out, carefully placing them over the inflamed wound.

Ailee sat on one side of Moses, holding his hand.

Someone had built two rough beds. Catherine now knew that other slaves knew. She also knew no one would tell. This would risk all of them.

Moses moaned louder. Catherine knelt down, inspecting his wound more closely.

"If he screams—" She didn't finish.

Father Gabe reached down for rawhide strips an inch thick, long enough to tie around Moses's head. This gag allowed him to breathe.

Tears rolled down Ailee's cheeks; her smashed cheekbone and cloudy blind eye glistened. Catherine wished she had something, anything, for Ailee's pain, as well as Moses's pain.

Bettina whispered, "He's burning up."

Catherine placed the back of her hand on his cheek. "Dear God."

Piglet barked. *"Someone's coming."*

Catherine reached down to hold the dog's jaws shut when John shocked all of them by walking into the hiding place.

"John, oh, John, I wish you hadn't found me," Catherine blurted.

"I . . . you woke me up and I watched." He took in the situation. "He's in a bad way."

"We're hoping to break the fever," Bettina informed him. "Father Gabe has been putting compresses on his wound and on his head. The fever's climbing."

Having seen men fall in battle, John knew what happened next. "The stream isn't far from here, is it?"

"No, it's right behind and below," Catherine answered.

"All right, then. Father Gabe, help me lift him up."

Father Gabe took a big step back, afraid of the big man.

Bettina spoke for the old healer. "Tell him what you want to do."

"Yes, forgive me. Father Gabe, the waters are cool and swift. If I hold him in them, perhaps the fever will come down. I've seen this done."

The old man nodded, lifted up his rattle gourd with the colored ribbons hanging from the neck, reached toward heaven with it and then the four corners of the compass. He put the gourd down and went to the other side of Moses. He lifted up Moses's side as best he could.

Bettina joined him, as did Catherine. Together they helped roll Moses, moaning louder, into John's arms. Now John could stand up, his burden secure.

Catherine followed her husband down to the creek, as did Bettina. Father Gabe held Ailee back. The dark night made walking difficult, but all feared lighting a candle. The light could be hidden in the cave but not outside. Piglet led the way.

At the creek, about four feet deep at this spot, John laid down Moses, pulling off his boots and socks.

"We need to strip him," John ordered.

Catherine knelt down to remove Moses's pants when Bettina knelt beside her. "Let me do it, Missus. You keep watch. You and Piglet."

John picked up the naked man, gingerly finding the best way into the water without dropping Moses, who weighed about one hundred eighty pounds. Once secure in the stream, he held one arm under the man's back, the other under his buttocks. Moses dropped his head back. Catherine knew John possessed the strength of a bull. Now she learned how patient he was. He stayed in that stream, teeth chattering for a half hour.

"Honey, come out," Catherine said.

"Perhaps a bit longer?" John asked.

"Long enough. Let's get him back up and see if this has helped. If you can put him down, you can get your socks and boots on. You can't carry him barefoot over these rocks and stones."

John came to the edge, lifted Moses up and over. When he stepped out, Catherine used the hem of her dress to dry his feet. Bettina dropped her head rag over Moses's genitals.

Piglet again led the way. The three could hear animals moving about. One owl called overhead, then stopped. They heard the needles on the pine branch swish.

Back at the small cave, John placed Moses on the makeshift bed. Ailee reached for him, felt his forehead. She uttered a low noise. Father Gabe put his head to his chest, listening to his heart. Then he, too, felt his fore-head.

"Better," Father Gabe said.

"Father Gabe, can you pack the wound? Anything like beeswax with all those herbs you have?"

"Yes," Father Gabe replied.

Teeth chattering still, John sat down on the dirt. "Do you need more clothes?"

Bettina answered, "No, but if we do, they're easy to come by."

Catherine gently touched Ailee's good cheek. Tears flowed again. "Ailee, we can't save your eye, but when the swelling goes down, Father Gabe may be able to shift your broken bones back into place."

Ailee nodded.

With his hand on Piglet's head, John told them, "We can't come here again. We can't take the chance of leading someone down here like I followed Catherine. If you need something, tell me. I will place it on the high shelf in the hay barn."

"The tack room is better," said Catherine. "We can put whatever you need on the highest shelf there. We will never tell. When this is all over, we will never tell about this hiding place."

John nodded in agreement.

"Bettina, come back with us. You've got to get some sleep. Father will notice if you're not yourself tomorrow. He depends on you so."

Bettina sighed. "Father Gabe, can you manage?"

He asked for the child. "Send me Tulli."

"I will." Bettina rose, touched Moses's cheek, then Ailee's. "May the Lord bless thee and keep thee."

No one spoke until reaching the high meadow beyond the woods. Candlelight in the houses, cabins could be seen in the distance.

Bettina said, "Thank you."

"Is Ailee all right—in her mind, I mean?" Catherine inquired.

Bettina nodded. "I think so, but she has lost the power of speech. She opens her mouth. Silence."

Thinking ahead, John offered an idea. "If and when Moses recovers, we must get him out. How, I don't know. There must be a way to disguise him."

"Let's cross that bridge when we come to it," Catherine remarked, tired and troubled. "There's no way we can smuggle out Ailee. The smashed cheek, blind eye will give her away. Hiram and Dennis know about that. Sheba's told her version of the murder to all and sundry. Rachel and I heard it at the funeral, but we heard pieces of it from others."

"Ailee will not stand for murder," John stoutly said. "No one has accused her of that."

"She'll be returned to Mrs. Selisse and Sheba," Bettina bitterly replied. "They'll kill her. They'll take their sweet time about it, but they will torture and kill her."

Catherine whispered, "I fear you're right. When Moses is able, he can tell us what really happened."

John looked up at the stars. "We have to separate them when the time comes. Catherine, Bettina, you do nothing. You can lose everything."

"It's too late for that now," Bettina replied.

"She's right, John. We're all in this together."

"No, you're not. Bettina can pretend to be ignorant. You can, too. I can always go back to Massachusetts, even if I'm found guilty. We'll find a way."

"If you go to Massachusetts, I go with you." Catherine's voice brooked no argument. "It's father and

Rachel I worry about. We have to save Moses and Ailee and protect them, too."

John rubbed his forehead with his right hand. "God help us."

"He'll have to," Catherine said.

17

Saturday, July 30, 2016

Although the mercury climbed up to ninety degrees by one in the afternoon, the humidity hung at thirty-seven percent, quite unusual for Virginia in the summer.

On scaffolding, Harry and Fair started painting the outside of the equipment shed at seven A.M. Using rollers on long poles, they made quick work of it, each painting on a different side, then both painting across the broad back of the shed. The low humidity helped considerably.

Back on the ground, they stepped away to study their handiwork.

"Looks brand-new," Fair bragged.

"I wouldn't go that far, but it does look good. We've still got to trim, remember, bright white."

"Well, that can wait until tomorrow. I need to shovel an avalanche of paperwork." He draped his arm around her shoulder. "Tell you what. If you put the paint away, clean the rollers, I'll make lunch. I might surprise you."

"You just did." She smiled. "I'm assuming you want to leave the scaffolding stand?"

"Yeah, we can knock out the trim tomorrow. I don't see the point of painting the interior support beams, do you?"

"No, the barn swallows will just poop all over them. I don't think there's a building on this farm except for the house that doesn't have barn swallows. I love to watch them dart about."

Sitting nearby in their nests for an afternoon, two couples heard Harry.

The oldest male, Luciano, puffed out his chest. *"But of course."*

The younger male, shoulder to shoulder with his mate, remained silent. No point in adding to Luciano's statement. That the bird's name was Luciano already broadcast how he felt about his singing abilities.

Closing the five-gallon paint cans, Harry carefully tapped all the way around them with a light hammer. She'd paid good money for this exterior paint and she wasn't going to waste any of it. That task gave way to setting the rollers in sharp-smelling cleaning fluid. Harry used only oil-based paint for exteriors. Cleaning rollers and brushes was indeed a time-consuming chore, but she never repented of her commitment to oil-based paint. She didn't care what the paint companies said about latex, she thought oil-based better, especially for exteriors.

Swishing around the rollers, she then lifted them out, swished some more, then dried them, hanging them upside down in the shed. Harry poured the fluid into a can used for that purpose and closed that lid. Vigilant about anything she thought could damage soil, creatures, or plants, she never tossed out oil, diesel fuel, gasoline, paint thinner. She found uses for them or let them dry up in their containers.

Every outbuilding had a frost-free pump, either inside the wall or outside. At the equipment shed she stood outside and washed her hands, the flow of water gushingly strong.

A female barn swallow swept past Harry, climbed high, then dived straight at her, turning at a right angle at the last minute.

"*Whee!*"

Harry ducked her head back which encouraged the beautiful bird to show off even more. By now the female barn swallow was joined by Luciano. The two of them put on quite a show, adding a bright chirp now and then. Harry laughed. She loved all the creatures on her land. Well, maybe not chiggers and ticks, but she even liked the snakes. She learned from other animals.

Finished cleaning up, she entered the kitchen.

"You did make lunch." She sat down. Before her was a huge Cobb salad, as well as a large glass of untea, unsweetened iced tea.

Proud of himself, Fair sat opposite her.

Before they got the forks to their mouths, Tucker rushed to the door, signaling a visitor. She didn't bother to bark, which meant a friend was here.

Harry half stood up. "Coop. If there's not enough, I can split my salad. It's so large."

He rose. "Sit. I've got enough."

"She'll say she's not hungry."

Fair laughed. "We've heard that before. You can wear her down."

"I could use some of that bacon." Pewter lifted her nose.

"Me, too," Mrs. Murphy and Tucker agreed.

Coop knocked on the screen door, opened it, then walked through the kitchen door. "Sorry to barge in."

"You're not barging in. Sit down. There's enough for all."

"No, no, I couldn't do that," Cooper demurred.

Fair placed a large bowl on the table, towered over her and she was relatively tall. "Sit down."

He then brought over a napkin and utensils. "Sweet or unsweet?"

"Uh, sweet."

She speared an egg slice in the salad, each person enjoying the cold food. Tucker sat by Fair, Mrs. Murphy took Harry, and Pewter felt she could work over Cooper.

"The shed looks great," Cooper remarked. "One of these days I'll paint mine."

"We'll do the trim tomorrow," Harry informed her. "The best part is the day was bearable. If you stand out in the sun it will get you, but we painted the unshaded side first, early. Wasn't bad."

"It's a good day."

"And this is a good salad by my talented husband." Harry smiled.

Cooper stared at Fair. "You know, you make me believe having a husband is a step forward."

"Depends on the husband." He laughed. "And I can still pluck her last nerve."

Pewter reached up to pat Cooper's leg. *"What about my nerves? Smelling that delicious ham, bacon, and even the cheese rattles me. I need some food, your food."*

Of course, Cooper dropped a thick piece of cubed ham.

"Don't spoil her," Harry admonished her neighbor.

"And you don't?"

"Well, she can be a pest," Harry rejoined.

"Here, Tucker, you're behaving like a good dog." Fair dropped an egg slice.

"I am a good dog."

Harry gave Mrs. Murphy a ham cube, which Pewter eyed, deciding not to start a fight.

"Are you wondering why I'm here?" Cooper asked.

"No," Harry replied.

Cooper sipped the delicious tea. "Not even a little bit?"

"You're our neighbor," Harry said. "What's to wonder?"

"Can you tell me if you noticed anything odd while working with Rae and her crew? An offhand remark, perhaps she mentioned that things have gone missing before. You notice things, undercurrents."

"They were all very professional. What I did notice when I first went to the office to discuss what I needed were the posters on the wall and small framed photos of some of the work. I assume it was some of their work. Rae also showed me other websites, mostly farms, business ones, and some campaign websites from last year."

"Did you notice equipment on a table or shelf?" Cooper asked.

"I did. All the sound equipment was stacked on a table and the big keyboard was on the desk in the middle of the room. Why?"

"None of the expensive equipment was touched. The robber or robbers were interrupted by Deon returning. He came in the front door and whoever went out the back."

Harry whistled. "There's a fortune in equipment there."

"Which is why I doubt the motive was robbery."

"Had to be something recorded by Rae's crew," Harry mused. "I have a suggestion. I'll be willing to help, let's sit down with Rae, Deon, and Bethel and review footage."

"Why can't we just look at it on our computers?" Cooper wondered.

"We can, but that's the final edited website version. Perhaps there's something compromising, something not on a final version."

"Well—" Cooper was thinking.

"It could be something tiny, maybe a line of cocaine on a far table, the outline of a still in the distance near water, a poached deer, you know, out of season. It could be anything, but whatever it is, if there is something, it might offer a clue."

"Normally, I'd say that's far-fetched. This is an attempted theft." Cooper inhaled deeply again. "Rae's company specializes in websites for farm products, Thoroughbreds, local and state political campaigns. I suppose it can't hurt to take the time."

"Maybe whatever it is could cost someone a job, money, maybe an election," Harry wondered, as did Fair, leaning forward in his chair.

"Rae is a Democrat, not wildly liberal, but more liberal than her customers," said Coop. "And I didn't know this, but these Web people as well as advertising agencies are divided up by party. Charlottesville is a liberal Democratic town; all those videographers were already on the party payroll. Well, not the party, but anyone running for office from the area used certain people. Being a fairly new business, Rae took what she could get. She was so good she wound up shooting websites for those nonliberal candidates."

"Did Ned tell you that?" Harry inquired about Susan's

husband, Albemarle County's representative to the state legislature.

"No. Rae did. But talking to Ned is a good idea." Maybe he'd have an idea of what might be hidden on the missing tapes.

18

Monday, August 1, 2016

Harry and Cooper sat in the small Crozet Media screening room, piles of DVDs before them. Those DVDs represented the finished product. A smaller pile of outtakes sat next to that.

Cooper stuck her long legs in front of her once in her seat. "Harry, two hours, that's it."

"I know, but look at it this way." Harry turned around for a moment to make eye contact with Rae. "You have nothing to go on regarding Barbara Leader's death. That was followed by this break-in."

"I don't see how they can be connected," Cooper grumbled.

"Well, I don't, either. But if we look at website outtakes and some websites of those who knew or worked with Barbara, maybe something will pop up. You're only losing time."

Rae stepped in. "When I sifted through my list of clients with Harry she knew some of the people who knew Barbara. Of course, we have no way of knowing a casual acquaintance. As it turned out, not many of my clients did know Barbara. Let me start with The Barracks."

Harry filled Cooper in. "Barbara kept a horse there for years. Occasionally I'd see her in the ring."

"We shot this last fall." Rae punched some keys on the large keypad, and an image of The Barracks's sign out on Garth Road appeared. Next a moving shot through the gates revealed the land beyond, fenced, the mountains in the far background, and to the viewer's right the large main building of The Barracks. From there Bethel had walked through the aisle, shots of tidy stalls, contented horses, and thence into the large covered riding arena, the big draw of this place. Over this, Claiborne Bishop's voice explained the dimensions of the ring, the footing, while two riders in the background were taking a lesson over fences.

Once outside, Claiborne introduced horses in the near paddocks, the house she shared with her husband, Tom, in the background. The brilliant fall day added to the allure. This was the slick final product Rae produced.

Now she slipped in a DVD. Claiborne stood by the fence, and a flaming chestnut horse thundered up, looking stunning, and then pooped as if on cue.

Harry chuckled.

"Wait until you see the next one." Rae gave them a little anticipation.

Back in the main stables, two teenage girls washing

one of the horses obviously didn't know footage was being shot. A few harsh words were spoken. The blonde reached around the horse with a wet chamois, flicking it at the dark-haired girl, a few pounds overweight. That fast, the larger girl turned her hose on the blonde. The wet-T-shirt moment would have been appreciated by most of the male audience, but it might not have done The Barracks much good. Amazingly, the horse stood quietly through it all, not even folding back her ears.

That was it for The Barracks outtakes.

One hour later, the group had seen most everyone who went to school, worked with, or knew Barbara, if they had websites.

"Okay, last one," Bethel said. "Edward Cunningham at Big Rawly. We had so many delays, interruptions. We're still piecing footage together for his new campaign website. Won't be long until it's up."

Edward, sleeves rolled up, no necktie, wearing beige pants and loafers, was walking through the living room, opened massive double doors to the outside slate patio, stepped down, and stepped on a rubber ball.

"Goddammit!" He bent down to pick up the ball, chucked it out on the lawn in disgust.

A golden retriever appeared, entering the frame from the left, joyfully chasing the ball, bringing it back to Eddie. He dropped the ball at Eddie's feet. Picked it up. Dropped it again.

"Piper, leave it."

Piper experienced a moment of canine deafness.

Frustrated that the ball was slimy, Eddie yelled, "Chris, will you get out here!"

Entering from the right, pretty Chris appeared, wearing the fisherman's top favored by Picasso, white clam diggers, and navy blue espadrilles. Ball in hand, she coaxed the golden to follow her.

Chris Holloway Cunningham, the perfect country club wife, should have stayed in the video. Poor Eddie, flummoxed by the dog, spoke his lines too quickly.

Off camera, Rae's words could be heard. "Cut. Mr. Cunningham, take a deep breath, slow down. Actually, the dog looked great, but we'll leave using her up to you."

Another outtake showed Eddie in the impressive library, his grandfather there also. His grandfather, the former governor, sat behind the desk. Eddie's father, Taylor Cunningham, dropped a book as he entered the library. He laughed, picked it up, and said to the camera, "Marcus Aurelius, one of the governor's favorites."

In the last outtake, Eddie was promising he would fight the creep of federal government as a senator. He called upon the memory of Sam Holloway defying Washington while standing at the entrance to the state house when he was loudly interrupted by the governor complaining from his desk in the background.

A middle-aged woman slipped in, handed him a glass filled with ice and a splash of amber liquid. She pressed a pill in his hand.

Harry recognized the woman as Barbara Leader.

Barbara leaned down, whispering in the governor's ear.

He grinned, popped the pill, drained his glass. His energy returned and his face became more animated. *He became more animated.*

He looked directly at the camera, his voice booming. "I want to explain why I fought the federal government forty-five years ago. I apologized, but I've never really set the record straight."

Standing in front of his grandfather's desk, Eddie froze.

Women's voices filled the background. Entering the frame from the right came Barbara Leader, again followed by Penny and Millicent Grimstead.

Eddie hurried to stand beside the governor's chair. "G-Pop, the federal government is like a giant kudzu plant. They want to cover us all and control us all."

Standing, the old man, still handsome despite his illness, boomed, "It is the obligation of every generation to keep the central government in check. I *was* right about that, but I chose the wrong issue and I regret it. I will die regretting it."

"G-Pop, you fought the good fight." Eddie glanced up at his grandmother and aunt.

"Edward, you sorry ass, I hate an overly centralized government. I hate an imperial presidency, but sometimes only a strong president and Congress can right a terrible wrong. Segregation was such a wrong. I cannot, I will not, abide you using me to cloak your intentions."

"Daddy, Daddy, come on now," Millicent cajoled.

"I'm not going to be used like this!" he shouted.

"Honey, Millie and I will work with Eddie. You come on. You're going to overtire yourself. You need all your strength to fight the leukemia."

Shaking with anger and effort, he refused to allow his wife and daughter to lead him away, but he did go.

Penny's voice could be heard off-camera. "Come on, honey. They can do a video just of you."

"I'm ready to talk," he hollered.

"Please, Daddy, this is for Eddie's website."

"Maybe people interested in him should hear me out! I have something to say."

"Of course, you do, dear." Penny's voice was clear. "You were the most eloquent governor of Virginia since Thomas Jefferson."

Then Barbara's voice could again be heard. "Come on, Governor, we'll have our own party."

On camera, Eddie sank into the chair just vacated by his grandfather. "Give me a minute." He looked into the camera. "He suffers these outbursts. A lot of anger. I blame the medication. They're filling him full of too much stuff." That was the end of the footage.

Cooper pulled her outstretched legs back. "Poor fellow. Do you all remember anything else?"

"No," Deon answered. "As you've seen, most of the outtakes are flubs. Maybe a wind came up, messed up the sound for an outside shot. Pretty much what you'd expect. Well, maybe not the governor, but I guess that's what happens when people get that old."

"Or that medicated," Harry added.

"Scares me," Rae admitted. "Doctors pumping you with God knows what."

"You don't have to be old for that." Harry feared overmedication, too.

"Right," Deon agreed.

Rae said to Cooper, "I didn't question Edward Cunningham why he wanted us to shoot this footage."

Cooper stood up. "We all saw the governor's condition. I would guess Edward needed a video of him. The old man is frail, but he's still presentable and still powerful."

Fed up with politics, Harry said, "Elections are now never-ending. Edward Holloway Cunningham has his website. The amount of money spent these days on running for office is astronomical."

"A big waste of money," Deon said. "All that money could be put toward fixing some of our problems."

"True, it is, but that money is coming to us," Rae reminded him. "For which I'm grateful. It's all ego, don't you think?"

Bethel grimaced. "I know when I'm old enough to retire there won't be any money in Social Security. All that money taken out of my paycheck and Deon's paycheck will be squandered."

"Yeah," Deon simply agreed.

"Well, you could run for public office," Harry suggested.

"And be like them?" Deon's eyes widened.

Rae quietly added, "I really think when most people take that path they want to do good. Then the process corrupts them."

"As a public servant I can't partake in this discussion," said Cooper. "But I can also tell you Albemarle County has a good sheriff. We are chronically underfunded and people want more and more services. Harry's right. You all should run, or find someone young who you like, and encourage them."

Harry added, "Someone young who isn't corrupted."

Deon felt cynical. "Yeah, but won't they become corrupted, like Rae says?"

"You can always hope that a few won't," said Harry. "I don't think anyone can corrupt Ned Tucker or could corrupt the late Emily Couric or Mitch Van Yahres, before your time. They were liberal, but I trusted them. We all did. But such people are few and far between now." She stood up. "Maybe it was always this way and we think times were better in the past."

"Do you think Governor Holloway was corrupt?" Deon asked.

"When he was governor, it was the Old Boys' Club, you scratch my back and I'll scratch yours. They didn't think of that as corrupt. I doubt that Governor Holloway or generations of Virginia governors questioned how business was done." Harry vividly remembered her parents discussing politics.

"It's still the Old Boys' Network." Deon, a young man of color, distrusted most all elected officials who were white.

Harry thoughtfully answered him. "Maybe it's a shadow we'll never shake. Little by little, the process opens up. I guess my question is, will it open up enough in time?"

"Hmm." Deon listened.

"I'm going to be forty-two on Sunday." Harry looked at Rae, Bethel, and Deon. "Sounds old to you, I'm sure, but it's not that old and yet, I think about things a little harder, I feel things a little deeper, and I know I can't turn my back on our problems. By the time you're forty you know you have to step up to the plate. Otherwise you've left politics to all the creeps."

"That means you'll be working on Ned's campaign next year." Cooper smiled, then turned to Rae, Bethel, and Deon. "Thank you for your time. I may be back to ask questions as they occur to me. We'll try to get to the bottom of this peculiar break-in. The good news is no one stole your equipment."

Back outside, Harry climbed into Cooper's squad car. "What an outburst."

Cooper nodded. "It's got to be painful being used by your grandson, used in a way that dredges up old hatreds."

"Maybe they aren't so old." Harry fastened her seat-belt.

"I don't know. I sure hope not."

"I do, too, but Eddie wants to make political capital out of them."

19

Saturday, September 18, 1784

Not wishing to offend, Jeddie bowed slightly to Jeffrey Holloway. "If you wait here, sir, I will fetch Miss Catherine."

Handsome Jeffrey inhaled the fragrance of cleaned oiled tack. The bridles hanging on the tack room wall, bits gleaming, saddles on racks, also perfect, announced a well-run establishment.

Outside, divided into separate pastures, the horses grazed, mares separated from geldings, driving horses from saddle horses.

In the distance, Catherine approached with Jeddie. Struck by her grace, Jeffrey smiled.

"Mr. Holloway," she greeted him, "to what do I owe the pleasure?"

Inclining his head, executing a half bow, he bounced back up, "Mrs. Schuyler, I've come to inquire if Serenissima has been bred?"

"Ah, Mrs. Selisse is taking an interest in affairs. That's a good sign," Catherine remarked. "Yes, she has been bred, but I would like to keep her for one more week. Of course, if Mrs. Selisse wishes her returned immediately, we will do so. There's never a guarantee about these things. I hope she has caught, as it promises to be a fine breeding. Francisco relished an outstanding horse."

"That he did." Jeffrey cleared his throat. "You may be wondering why she sent me here."

Graciousness itself, Catherine intoned, "I'm delighted that she did. You saw the crowd around her at the funeral. None of them horsemen, except Mr. Grant, of course, and I think of him as a gambler first." She smiled conspiratorially.

Jeffrey's face flushed. "Madam, I'm not much of a horseman myself. Yancy Grant fancies himself the best in the county, although we all know pride of place belongs to you."

"You flatter me, sir."

Taking all this in, Jeddie glanced out the barn doors. Covered in mud, John Schuyler walked toward the barn.

"It's not flattery if it's the truth." Jeffrey smiled and Catherine knew Maureen had to be under his spell. "Mrs. Selisse sent me, as she is not yet ready to pay calls. Also, she fears that Yancy Grant will try to buy Serenissima from her. She is unsure of the mare's true value, but she knows you will tell her the truth. She asked me might I inquire of you if you think she should sell the mare? Grant has offered her four thousand dollars."

"A fine sum, Mr. Holloway, but Serenissima, especially if she's caught, is worth far more."

Jeffrey's brow furrowed. "I knew he'd try to take advantage of her. Beg your pardon, I shouldn't have—"

Catherine shook her head. "We all know what Yancy Grant is about. He wants to win, he wants the best horses, and I suspect he wants Mrs. Selisse."

John strode into the barn at that exact moment. "Hello, Mr. Holloway."

"John, you've arrived in the nick of time," said Catherine. "I was being indiscreet and spoke much too directly about Yancy Grant."

Her husband came alongside her. "Ah, well, no harm done. Mr. Holloway will keep a confidence."

"Of course, I will," Jeffrey responded, pleased to be taken seriously by his betters. Plus, he liked them. They were close in age.

"Husband, might I ask what you've been doing?"

"Charles and Karl wanted to reinforce the bridges over the narrow deep ravines. They held. We knew that, but you know how those two fret, so I've been waist-deep in water, as have they, as well as all the men we could pull off their chores. Done."

"Mr. Garth has the gift of seeing into the future." Jeffrey admired the older man. "The work he did on the main bridge during the war has opened up commerce. Mr. Garth just sees what we do not."

"That he does," John agreed.

Catherine invited Jeffrey to come up to the big house, enjoy a sip of tea or something stronger.

Studying her husband, she shook her head and laughed. "As for you, don't set foot in that house until you're cleaned up. Father will fret. He won't say anything, but he'll fret."

"I know it." John grinned. "Mr. Holloway, a pleasure to see you."

As Catherine and Jeffrey walked up to the elegant brick Georgian structure, Jeddie returned to Serenissima, who was munching away in her large paddock. "Beauty, I won't let Yancy Grant buy you. I don't want you to go back to Mrs. Selisse, either."

He climbed on the stout fence, legs dangling, and wished, just for one day, to have the money that Ewing had. Jeddie would buy Serenissima because she was fine, but mostly because he loved her.

The mare felt the same way. Sometimes two creatures strike a chord in each other, and this was the case.

Once in the house, Catherine called out, "Father, we have a visitor."

Ewing replied from his office, "Yes, dear."

"I don't wish to disturb him," Jeffrey said.

"Mr. Holloway, my father will be glad to see you."

With spectacles pushed up on his head, Ewing popped out of his office. "Ah, please have a refreshment. Warmed up a bit today. Catherine?"

"I already asked him. I'll dash back to Bettina and Serena. Where would you like to entertain, Father?"

"Let us sit in my office. It's pleasant today." He looked at Jeffrey. "If you can bear being surrounded by piles of papers."

"I look forward to your company." Jeffrey had always been well treated, even though of the middling classes but this was a bit warmer.

As the two men chatted, Bettina and Serena came in with drinks, a tray of cookies. Catherine followed.

"Sit down, my dear."

Jeffrey informed Ewing, "Mrs. Selisse sent me a message if I might inquire about Serenissima. She's trying to attend to her husband's business."

"Perhaps there are too many horses," Catherine casually remarked. "Without Francisco she needs only four carriage horses and two saddle horses. Then again, she may wish to keep all, as a reminder of her husband."

"She may be ready to part with a few," Jeffrey allowed. "There's much to do for her. She must manage the crops, the slaves, and deal with her husband's many interests beside that. Some of those men are"—he paused—"perhaps not operating in Mrs. Selisse's best interest. I cannot say as much to her. At this time, casting doubt on others would only add to her sufferings."

Smiling broadly, Ewing answered, "No doubt, sir, no doubt, but they underrate the lady. She is fortunate to have you quietly protecting her. Of course, she needs time—the shock, you know, the terrible shock—but I trust she will refrain from major business decisions until she has put this dreadful event behind her."

"Yes." Jeffrey sipped his tea, refusing spirits. "There has been no sign of Moses or the woman. It's as though they've vanished."

Voice modulated, Catherine remarked, "It may be better if they have. Mrs. Selisse has been through enough."

"Oh, I quite agree, but her lady's maid seems intent on revenge. Says her mistress should have satisfaction."

Ah, yes, Sheba at work.

"Perhaps." Ewing changed the subject. "How is your father?"

"Well, thank you."

Ewing pointed to his special bird's-eye maple bureau holding his papers. "You were small when your father crafted that for me. No one better, not even in Philadelphia. And the drawers slide as evenly and well as the day he delivered the bureau."

Jeffrey smiled. "I'll be sure to tell him."

"And you, too, have taken up the profession?" Catherine made polite conversation, although it wasn't really polite, she was reading between the lines.

"I work with Father, but my heart's not in it. I prefer being outside, but we do not always get to choose how we will make our way in the world."

Seizing the moment, Catherine smiled at him. "Yes, I have often thought of that. One never knows what lies ahead. I suppose you have to keep your eyes open, as my father always counsels me. And if you would, please tell Mrs. Selisse if she needs anything at all, we will do our best to assist. She has been fortunate to have your concern." This was uttered with warmth.

Jeffrey dropped his eyes for a moment, then returned her gaze. "I can't stand to think of Mr. Selisse's business associates trying to take advantage of her at such a time. Your interest in her well-being will help her, I'm sure. I do believe women know better about such things than men."

After he left, Catherine waving him off at the front door, she returned to her father. "I made a bet with Rachel."

"And?" His eyebrows raised.

"I bet that Jeffrey Holloway would marry Maureen Selisse before a year's time. If I win, she owes me four embroidered pillowcases. She has Mother's hand, you know."

"She does. Very artistic, Rachel. Well, what does she win?"

"A new hat from the milliner."

He tapped the arm of the chair, laughing. "It is a fascinating bet."

"He hasn't let the grass grow under his feet." Catherine used the old saying. "He's obviously attentive and handsome."

"And young." Ewing broke into a broad grin. "Ah, well, this is a bet I shall avidly follow."

• • •

Once in the kitchen, Catherine relayed the visit to Bettina.

"Sheba will demand her pound of flesh." Bettina used the line from Shakespeare even as she didn't know its provenance.

The woman soaked up everything, even though she couldn't read. Her mind was broad and retentive.

"No doubt." Catherine leaned against a thick counter. "How are they?"

"Better. His fever's down. He can think more clearly. We must find a way soon." Bettina didn't wish to speak directly, nor did Catherine.

"I will speak to John."

As Catherine left the big house, sun noon high, she saw Father Gabe standing before her mother's grave. He stared directly at the tombstone. Fetching a small, sharp stone out of his pocket, he scratched something at the rear of the stone.

Seeing this, Catherine stood still, hidden behind a large black gum tree. He spoke as he marked the base of the fine monument, but she couldn't hear what he was saying.

Once Father Gabe left, Catherine carefully made her way to her mother's grave. She walked to the back of the beautiful sculpture, the recumbent lamb with a cross between its front legs. This was on a sizable marble rectangle, the right side of which had Isabelle Garth's name, birth date, and death date. The left side showed Ewing's name and birth date. His intent was to be beside his beloved wife for eternity.

A small cross had been scratched on the back of the base. Catherine knew Father Gabe would never disfigure her mother's tomb. This small cross had to carry some deep meaning, but what?

20

Tuesday, August 2, 2016

"He has good days and bad days," Penny Holloway said as Harry shoveled mulch for Susan from the back of her F-150. "Sometimes the medication agitates him, just sets him off, but he tries to stay upbeat. It's better if his mind is occupied."

Waiting for her mulch pile to grow bigger, Susan stood next to Penny.

Her grandmother had dropped by for a visit, needing a break from tending to the governor.

Penny smiled, looking up at Harry on the truck bed. "Harry, you will never gain an ounce."

"No, but I will." Susan laughed. "If I so much as look at a chocolate-chip cookie, a pound."

"Oh, your mother always says the same thing. She kept her figure and so have you."

Susan exaggerated her pain. "G-Mom, it's so hard."

"A woman must suffer for beauty," Penny responded.

"The French said that first, of course. You know, when Sam was governor, we met so many people when we traveled on government trips. Every time I was in Paris, the women had perfect clothes, perfect hair, perfect makeup, and, of course, perfect deportment!"

"That is irritating," replied Susan, who knew Paris well.

Harry told on herself. "I'm safe. No one will ever accuse me of being fashionable."

Susan compressed her lips, thought for a moment, then actually said, "Well, Harry, that may be the case, but you will always be the one with the best body."

"Don't forget BoomBoom." Harry mentioned a classmate who was quite beautiful and with a tremendous bosom, hence her nickname.

Her given first name was Ursula.

Penny laughed, then lowered her voice. "Too much to carry." She paused, then turned to Susan. "When I look at you, I see your mother at the same age. How the time goes and what fun we had. She'd canvass door to door when Sam would run for office and she swore she would never marry a politician. She didn't." She paused again.

"Daddy liked banking and Mom did, too," said Susan. "I thought I was safe when I married a lawyer," she forthrightly admitted. "Ned kind of slid into politics."

"You get used to it." Penny sighed. "I wish Sam and I could do it all over again, I wish we could correct our mistakes, accomplish more of what we hoped to do, but as you know"—she looked directly at Susan—"so much of that depends on who sits in our legislature."

"Ned's eloquent on that." Susan smiled. "My ever-so-levelheaded husband can actually swear like a sailor—just to me, of course."

"How do we know he's not swearing at you?" Harry jabbed her.

"He doesn't need to do that." Susan sweetly smiled. "You'll do it for him."

Penny laughed out loud. "You two. Never ends. I remember one time when your father built a sandbox. Do you remember your sandbox?"

"Do," Susan replied.

"We all called it the Taj Mahal. Never saw anything like it. Well, the two of you, such lovely little girls, were playing in there, building castles, and the next thing your mother and I heard was screaming. Out we ran, and you, Harry, had torn out a side of the sandbox. How a child of six could have done that I don't know. Susan, being the lady she is, hit you over the head with her sand bucket. It took two adult women to separate you."

Harry pointed her shovel at Susan. "Violent. I've always known you had a streak of violence."

Ignoring this, Susan motioned to the ever-growing pile. "Well, let's fill up our wheelbarrows."

Hopping down from the truck bed, Harry said to Mrs. Holloway, "If you need mulch for your gardens, I'm happy to bring some over."

"What do you charge?"

"Not a thing. I don't charge Susan anything, and right now I like you better than Susan."

They all three laughed.

"I will leave you girls to it," said Penny.

"A quick question before you go." Harry stuck her shovel into the large pile. "Is the governor really writing his autobiography?"

Penny threw up her hands. "Driving me crazy. 'Honey, do you remember what LBJ's oldest girl wore the first time we were invited to the White House?' 'Honey, whatever happened to that officious fellow who ran The Valentine Museum when I got elected to the state Senate for the first time?' Yes, oh, my, yes, he is writing his autobiography. Thankfully, Mignon's a treasure."

Susan smiled. "G-Pop likes to talk."

"These days, you can't have one fact wrong or the media pounces on you." Penny shook her head. "Sam and I were in politics when you could actually get something done. It's so vicious now."

"You all didn't have the easiest time," Susan said sympathetically.

"No public servant does. And sometimes one has to say and do things he doesn't believe because if you don't you won't get elected or reelected. I always thought the trick to politics was knowing not what you can do but what people are ready to accept. Your conscience can take a real beating."

"Neddie says one of the greatest moments of the last

half of the twentieth century, speaking of conscience, was when LBJ signed the Voting Rights Act."

Penny slipped her arm through Susan's. "When it happened, Sam simply said, 'There goes the Democratic Party in the South.' And he was right. But so was LBJ. Of course, I couldn't publicly say anything at the time, but I could to Sam. He didn't see it then. He learned. But we all learn." She pulled Susan to her, gave her a squeeze with her arm now around Susan's waist. "Now what are you talking about, putting on a pound?"

As she released her, Susan glowed. She had worked to lose extra weight a few years ago and she worked even harder to keep it off. Oh, how those pounds want to sneak back.

As Penny drove away in her Subaru Outback, which she adored, the two women watched her go.

"I hope G-Pop has time to finish his autobiography," Susan said. "Leukemia is a terrible disease. You know it's not going away ever."

"Right, but aren't the drugs better now? People can last longer."

Susan nodded. "What I notice about terminal diseases is how up and down people's health seems to bounce. Some of that is getting the medication right. Pill A can create problems with pill B. But he's ninety-six, frail, and he really can't have too long."

"Guess not. What I've noticed about terminal diseases, since we're on this dismal subject, is, well, have you ever noticed that sometimes before a person dies they'll have a really good day? A day where they're up and about, happy, talking to everyone, or if they're in the hospital, they sit up and seem just fine."

"Odd."

"Know what else is odd? When Eddie first got elected he was conservative, of course, but more middle of the road. Now he can't run to the right fast enough."

"Plucks my last nerve," Susan growled.

Harry shrugged. "Maybe these days no one can be middle of the road."

Susan nodded. "Much as he irritates me, he has done some good things. He tried so hard to legalize marijuana for medical purposes. He squared off against the Committee for Courts of Justice."

"Yes, he did." Harry remembered. "And he hasn't backed down on it, either."

"I will hand it to him when it comes to medical issues, he's far-sighted. His oversight of the Virginia Board of Pharmacy and the Drug Control Act is pretty tough. So he's not completely knee-jerk on this right-wing stuff."

"Mmm. Do you think he cares about those issues or is he courting the older citizen vote or those people with medical conditions?"

"Harry, of course he is, but I actually think he cares, too. Cares about education, as well. What it comes down to is I'm not being one hundred percent fair. Eddie and I have never seen eye to eye."

"Maybe we're all a mixed bag."

"Or just mixed up." Susan laughed.

The two worked for forty-five minutes in Susan's garden spreading the mulch. The temperature in the mid-eighties, not bad for August, felt worse because the humidity hovered at sixty-five percent. The two felt this keenly since this unusual, glorious summer the humidity remained in the fortieth percentiles and for a few days even dipped down into the thirties.

"Whew. Done." Susan wiped her brow with a bandana. "Come on, let's go have a Co-Cola."

"Be in in a minute. Let me put up the shovels."

By the time Harry joined Susan, two tall glasses filled with ice and Co-Cola sat on the kitchen table. A plate of quartered tuna-fish sandwiches and egg-salad sandwiches sat in the middle of the table.

"I'm starved." Harry plopped down in a chair, but she waited for Susan to sit before reaching for all the delicious food.

"I can't wait to see all the photos when G-Pop's book is done," said Susan. "I love photos of people when they were children, then young adults."

Stuffing her face, Harry nodded, swallowed, then asked, "Did you see the news this morning?"

"No, why?"

"Oh, a brief interview with Eddie. He was attacking the current governor for not doing more to aid economic recovery."

"It is slow, but Ned says jobs are creeping back. He also says it will never be like it was before the crash. So many small businesses were put down, so to speak, and the coal industry, others, destroyed by a Congress offering no alternatives."

"Eddie mentioned that." Harry reached for another sandwich. "These are really good." She then returned to the subject at hand. "Eddie fired off facts and figures. He said that in 2007 there were sixty-four jobs for every one hundred Virginians over sixteen. But now it's fifty-nine jobs for every one hundred Virginians over sixteen. Gotta give it to him, he can argue effectively. When he was sent to Taft, he got such a good education. From Taft to Yale and then UVA School of Law. He did his homework. I just wish he weren't so right-wing about some issues like race, immigration, that stuff."

"Taft changed him," said Susan. "Be like you or I going to Madeira or Westover. It's so different from high school, public high school. Speaking of jobs, if I were young today, I'd try to work my way up in these research institutes. I'm willing to bet you that the figures Eddie Cunningham used came from the Commonwealth Institute for Fiscal Analysis. Everybody uses them, and the real brains there belong to Laura Goren."

"Never thought of that, of research. I admit that I do take notice if a senior officer or analyst or someone running for public office is a woman."

"Me, too. Doesn't mean I agree with them."

"Susan, you don't even agree with yourself."

The two laughed uproariously.

Then Harry asked, "Where's Owen?"

Owen was Susan's corgi, brother to Tucker.

"With Ned. He took Owen to town with him today. Said he misses the dog. Didn't say he missed me."

"Men." Harry smiled.

"What did our mothers say?" Susan reached over to poke Harry.

In unison the two chanted, "Men, you can't live with them, you can't live without them."

21

Saturday, September 18, 1784

The first hint of fall filled the crisp late afternoon air. Catherine and Rachel investigated the gardens around the house, thinking to make cuttings for their father and husbands. Ewing especially enjoyed cut flowers, as his late wife had filled the house with them.

"Do you ever wonder how Mother organized her gardens?" Catherine asked. "By color, by size, by season. I don't know how she did it nor where she procured the seeds."

"I don't know, either. She did teach us how to weed, when to turn the soil, she had a gift. I like that she put the tall flowers in the back, the lower ones in front."

"You have more of her gift than I do," Catherine truthfully stated.

Pleased by her sister's praise, Rachel's open face glowed. "I want to create an English garden at our house. Charles promises to help, but he says he doesn't really know that much about it. Oh, he knows about the geometry, the pathways and such, but he said he doesn't know what will grow here, as opposed to what grows in England."

"Boxwoods." Catherine laughed.

Spotted in the distance, a well-dressed rider captivated their attention.

Rachel, shielding her eyes, identified him. "Yancy Gates."

"Come with me." Catherine started for the main stables.

Both women reached the sparkling-clean stable shortly before Yancy arrived.

Putting up one of the saddle horses, Jeddie smiled as Catherine and Rachel walked in.

"Jeddie, Yancy Gates will be here any minute. Is everyone groomed?"

"Everyone but King David." He mentioned one of the driving horses. "I put him in light work this morning."

"Call Tulli over to wash him. I'll tend to Yancy. I suspect he wants to talk about Serenissima. Rachel and I will entertain him. If I need you, I'll send Tulli to fetch you."

"Miss Catherine, why don't I work in the broodmare barn? Close, especially if he wants someone pulled out."

"Of course." She placed her hand on his shoulder, then dropped it just as Yancy Grant reached the stable. A slender lad of fifteen, Ralston rushed up to hold his horse.

"Should I untack him, sir, and rub him down?"

"No, I won't be long. A drink of water, perhaps." Yancy treated the youngster kindly.

Many people ordered their servants and slaves about, but Yancy appreciated anyone who worked with horses and he knew anyone in Catherine's stables was good, even if very young.

Catherine and Rachel strode out to greet him. "Mr. Grant, how good to see you. Can we offer you a libation?" Catherine, the eldest, took over.

"Or biscuits. Bettina made a batch this morning," Rachel added.

Looking at these two sisters, so beautiful, he smiled. "Thank you. I happened to be over at Pestalozzi's Mill and thought to come by, as it is near. May I look at Reynaldo?"

"Of course." Catherine then called out, "Jeddie."

He appeared as if by magic the minute her voice lifted. "Miss Catherine."

"Mr. Grant would like to look at Reynaldo and"—she lifted her chin ever so slightly—"allow me to show you his younger half brother."

"I'd be delighted."

Jeddie motioned to Binks, a short twelve-year-old, to follow him. Within minutes, the two brought out Reynaldo and Crown Prince.

"Jeddie, trot Reynaldo for Mr. Grant. Straight up to us, then away, and then in two circles, opposite directions."

If Reynaldo favored one leg over the other, this imbalance would show in the circles, especially on an inside leg. Yancy Grant knew how to study a horse.

After Jeddie trotted the sleek animal, Catherine instructed, "Now pass him in front of us."

"Majestic creature," Yancy admiringly muttered.

"Binks, do the same with Crown Prince."

Completely at ease with the stallion, the younger boy did as he was told.

"All right, you can put them back in their pastures." She turned to Yancy. "Unless you'd like to see more?"

"Serenissima, after these two are turned out," he prudently requested.

Rachel briskly walked up to Jeddie and Binks, informing them as to Yancy's request. The three of them waited at the fence. When Catherine and Yancy reached them, Rachel opened the gate and Reynaldo walked in first, followed by Crown Prince. Then each horse was turned to face the people, their halters slipped off. Both stood for a moment, then joyfully ran into the pastures.

Yancy's eyes never left them.

"You can see that Crown Prince is lighter than his half brother. Built for speed, whereas Reynaldo is built to carry me up hills, down hills, through streams."

"Same dam?"

Rachel interjected, "Catherine's favorite mare, Queen Esther. She's in the next pasture."

The three horses, with the two young fellows behind them, walked to an adjoining pasture separated by about twelve feet, so no hanging of heads over fencelines.

"I remember Queen Esther." Yancy smiled upon seeing the mare. "Of course."

Not only did he remember Queen Esther, he knew her bloodlines and most of her get. Why he was being coy only he knew, because both sisters knew Yancy was a fervent student of bloodlines.

Catherine called the mare over for a nuzzle. "She's dear to me."

"Serenissima?" Yancy underlined his own, pretending not to remember Queen Esther by identifying Serenissima.

"Here to be bred, before Mr. Selisse's unfortunate end. I'm keeping her until I'm quite sure. You're the second person to check on her."

His eyebrows raised, his voice did, too. "And who might I ask was the first?"

"Just this morning Jeffrey Holloway came to check on her condition."

He snorted. "He's a cabinetmaker, not a horseman."

Rachel coolly observed while Catherine acted nonchalant. "True enough, but he mentioned that he wished to see to Mrs. Selisse's mare, she being under such duress."

Yancy's face reddened, but he composed himself. "Upstart."

Catherine shined her best smile upon him. "Well, he certainly doesn't know horses as you do, but then how many do?"

"You flatter me." A worried look flashed over the anger. "That poor lady is under great duress, as you stated. I can't see how Jeffrey Holloway can relieve any of it. He has no experience managing slaves, he has no business experience other than that of a tradesman. Ladies, I fear, his motives are"—he paused to effect—"for personal gain."

"Oh, Mr. Grant, I hope not. She has been through enough," intoned Rachel, now in on the game.

If Yancy could win over Maureen Selisse, his moderate fortune would be enlarged by a great one. Not that he would hint as such, but his feelings about Jeffrey Holloway betrayed his own motives—plus, Holloway was incredibly handsome and young. Yancy was not a bad-looking man, but was middle-aged with a paunch. He could not have been immune to the figure in his mirror.

He shook his head. "Women in distress can be easily swayed. I have seen it."

"You are kind to be so concerned." Catherine fed his vanity.

In Yancy's defense, he deserved some of that vanity. He'd supported the revolution, worked tirelessly for the cause, kept his estate afloat during the financial debacle that followed. Like Ewing, he had a broad vision.

Settling down, he walked back to the main stable with the ladies.

The slender fifteen-year-old Ralston stood outside the

stall into which he had put Yancy's horse. Catherine nodded to him, so he opened the stall door.

"Mr. Grant, please consider staying and enjoying a drink, some food?" Catherine repeated her offer.

"Thank you, but I'd best get back."

Rachel asked him, "Have you heard, sir, any news of the slave who killed Mr. Selisse or the woman?"

"No. No one has. They've vanished. For now. If they can be found, that will relieve Mrs. Selisse. I can imagine she fears their return, and she may fear for her own life. It was a vicious business." He swung himself up in the saddle without using the mounting block. That damned Jeffrey Holloway might be much younger, but Yancy could swing up like a young man and he knew he could outride Holloway. Still, he was worried.

"You honor me by wishing to look at my two boys; I call them my boys." Catherine looked up at him while thinking about how to tell Rachel not to discuss Moses without giving anything away, although Rachel didn't know the fugitives were on the farm.

Peering down into Catherine's gorgeous upturned face, he smiled. "I shall send over my best mare. We can discuss terms later, but I would like her put to Crown Prince."

She shamelessly flattered him. "Your best mare will make Crown Prince's future."

• • •

Yancy made one more stop before returning to his own estate. He called out at Dennis McComb's small cottage on the way home.

It was now late in the day and Dennis had done all he was going to do for the county. His young wife could be seen in her flourishing garden at the rear.

Hearing Yancy's voice, Dennis came out. "Mr. Grant. No trouble, I trust?"

Damned if Yancy was going to dismount and mount again. He reached into his waistcoat pocket.

"A down payment."

Dennis took the coins from Yancy's hand. "Yes, sir?"

"There will be fifty more when you bring in Moses. If you find the woman, sixty, but Moses, bring in Moses."

"We're doing all we can, Mr. Grant."

"Damn the constable's office, Dennis. You do what you must, you hear me, and don't tell Hiram. Hiram lives by rules. If you must bribe people, do so. I will make good any expenses, but find that killer. A lady's peace of mind depends on it."

Thrilled at the possibility for future gain, Dennis promised, "I will find them both."

22

Thursday, August 4, 2016

"I thought I heard someone out here," Mignon greeted Harry.

"Sorry, I tried to be quiet." She finished spreading the mulch on Penny Holloway's front plantings.

"You were, but the truck makes a rumble. I'm taking a brief break from making notes with the governor. Perhaps sometime I can interview you, since you know the family so well. And Susan is your best friend."

"Most days. Other days we fuss."

The petite woman laughed. "Family history is how I became interested in Virginia history and beyond. Like the Holloways, the Skipworths have been here a long time."

"Well, you're standing on a pile of history." Harry smiled. "Big Rawly goes back before the Revolution. French inspired, all these buildings. Gives it an exotic look."

Mignon replied, "You do know the history around here."

"I was raised here, but a year ago I found myself learning a lot more about The Barracks prisoner-of-war camp. Also, I'm a congregant at St. Luke's Church, which was the first Lutheran church this far west."

"Very beautiful. Designed by an Englishman. Working for the governor, I've been poking around western Albemarle County. Everyone focuses on Monticello and Ash Lawn and, of course, the University of Virginia, but a great deal happened out here. It was the Wild West for a while." Mignon clearly enjoyed research, her work.

"Funny, isn't it? Nothing is really lost. We just have to find it."

"Good way to put it," Mignon agreed.

"If I learn about the past it's usually through farming practices, seeds, livestock," said Harry, ever the farmer. "My paternal family has farmed here since shortly after the Revolution. The apple hasn't fallen far from the tree, and as you know, lots of apples in Virginia."

"Oh, yes," Mignon said and chuckled. "Just this morning when I was reviewing the governor's first year in office as governor, he recalled the primary crops, which were corn followed by apples. He keeps right up with things. He informed me that Virginia now ranks sixth in the nation for apple production, ten thousand four hundred acres devoted to apples, one hundred ninety-five million pounds of apples. He's amazing how he can remember details. Can rattle off figures from the past and the present. He told me that the owner of all the land on the other side of Garth Road first started big apple orchards."

"Ewing Garth," Harry added.

"Yes."

"Garth also grew peaches and pears, the old varieties. If I ever get rich, I am going to devote myself to growing the old varieties."

"I've never heard anyone say that. They usually say if they get rich they'll buy a new car, pay off debts, vacation in Hawaii."

Harry looked toward the Blue Ridge Mountains. "What could be more beautiful than that?"

"That's the truth," Mignon enthusiastically agreed.

Another attractive woman came out the front door. "Mignon, he's asking for you." She then looked up at Harry.

"Harry Haristeen," Harry introduced herself. "I promised Mrs. Holloway I'd deliver some mulch, and so I have."

Relief crossed her face. "Good. I'm Rebecca Colman. I'm here part-time since Barbara Leader's unfortunate accident. I'm learning what a good nurse she was," Rebecca said.

"Penny finally told the governor," said Mignon. "He was so upset. Rebecca, he'll warm to you. Just tell him he'll outlive us all." She smiled.

As Harry drove out, she passed Sheriff Shaw and Cooper arriving in Rick's squad car. She figured they had received the medical examiner's report on how Barbara Leader had died. These tests and reports often take weeks. This report was quickly done, no doubt because the deceased had been tending to an ex-governor.

Harry expected the news wouldn't be good.

23

Sunday, September 19, 1784

Twilight shrouded the mountains, the rolling hills in light blue darkening to a deeper blue. The last streaks of pink, gold, and flame faded to soft purple.

Catherine, John, Rachel, Charles, Ewing, and Piglet sat in the big house's back gardens. The graveyard was in the near distance and over to the right, in two neat rows, stood the slave cabins, logs chinked tight. Some, like Bettina's, boasted true brick fireplaces with chimneys. Others used charred logs for a fireplace, as had been used at The Barracks. Usually it worked. Sometimes, though, it caught fire. Karl Ix convinced Ewing to replace those charred log fireplaces with stone or brick. In the long run, it would save money. One by one, new fireplaces were being built. The hope was to have every cabin refurbished before hard winter.

Piglet snored at Charles's feet.

"I wonder, are the spirituals remembered songs from

Africa?" Charles mused as he listened to the distant singing.

"Perhaps, although the captured spoke different languages." John knew a little bit, as he had learned from an old fellow who kept three slaves back home in Massachusetts. Much wealth in Boston derived from the slave trade, from rum and molasses carried from the Caribbean. "So many Africans were already enslaved by other tribes. Maybe they brought their music with them."

Catherine knew that certain spirituals communicated information between estates. "Swing Low, Sweet Chariot" meant someone was dying. Could be the master or could be a slave all loved. "March on Down to Jordan" meant someone was moving through, hoping for freedom. She paid attention, because no one had sung that lately. This would have tipped off others, the news would have filtered to other places. This would endanger Moses and Ailee.

Catherine wasn't the only white person to understand the various meanings of spirituals. The constables probably knew more about slave life than the people who owned the slaves, since they were charged with finding runaway slaves. Few white people wanted the job. It was considered low, very low. The only thing lower was actually transporting slaves from Africa. Yet the need for labor was so great in the raw land that captains brought more and more men and women to the New World. Fortunes were made. Many of the men who made them chose to live and retire in seaport towns. Boston proved a most hospitable place, a thriving city, a good port with music, dancing, libraries, and Harvard. Its great appeal drew slavers, traders, and the ever-present and growing number of lawyers. But Providence, New York, and Portsmouth also had their allure.

Once their fortune was secure, other blackbirders sold their ships and moved inland. No one knew how they had made their fortunes as they slid into western Georgia or eastern Alabama. A few brave souls pushed into the Ohio territory. If their new neighbors eventually found out how they made the money, generous donations removed the scandalous odor. A few ex-slavers even founded great colleges. Most all gave generously to hospitals, churches, and places for the poor. Then, as always, any dubious trade was justified by saying business is business.

Catherine and Rachel did not question the system. Their mother had prepared them for their responsibilities to the servants, never called slaves. The mistress ran the estate, especially the house. To her fell the burdens of keeping the various often large personalities working together. If a romance among servants proved difficult or disruptive, the mistress exercised her responsibility to untangle this before violence occurred. Not that the lady of the house could always succeed in matters of the heart, but she tried. Health was a major concern. Nursing was a primary duty. The labors of a good mistress could be seen by all. This was one of the reasons Maureen Selisse had no true standing among other women. All she had was money. Her treatment of people, as it was thought by others, was disgraceful.

The story of how Moses killed Francisco was accepted by many. Others doubted it. People knew the Selisses had been brutal. Then, too, everyone who owned other human beings would have to confront, however briefly, the injustice of the system. The Selisses brought that injustice front and center. Some people whispered that Francisco deserved what he got.

A few people made the connection between this peculiar institution and the practice of kingship. If you lived under a good king or queen, the country thrived. A bad one created endless pain, suffering, and often death. Removed from politics as she was, Catherine was beginning to make these connections. The condition of Ailee's face made them for her. But then, too, working so closely with her father, Catherine began to look at the world the way men do. She understood profit. She also understood right from wrong.

"What did you think of the German's sermon today?" Ewing asked almost idly.

" 'By their work alone ye shall know them,' " John spoke up.

"It does make sense," Charles chimed in.

"It's awfully Lutheran," Ewing half grumbled.

"Father, he was Lutheran." Catherine laughed and the others laughed with her.

"Progress in designing a church?" Ewing asked of Charles.

"They are trying to raise the funds," said Charles. "I've made some rough sketches. I've designed two quads, each at a different level, and, well, sorry, I don't want to run on, but I do so hope they raise the money. Karl Ix is the engine behind this. He and Giselle"—he named Karl Ix's wife—"are devout Lutherans."

"No Episcopal church?" Ewing wondered.

"Father." Rachel reached over and touched his hand. "So many Hessians live here in the west of the country. They're Lutherans, and really, it's not so very different from the Church of England. I mean the Episcopal Church. Charles and I would be happy to attend."

"I hadn't thought of that." Ewing leaned back in his outdoor chair. "Ah, see how the last of the light outlines your mother's lamb with the cross? Glows. Yes, it glows."

"It does," Catherine enthusiastically agreed.

"I must retire," he said. "This week will be a busy one. Time to harvest the apples. Then time to put down some winter seed. I think I'll allow tough rye and winter wheat to root for a month before winter, perhaps even buckwheat. Comes up early in spring, giving the other grasses protection." He shook his head. "Paradise now, and yet it won't be even a month before the first frost."

"But Father, I love October. The color, the cool nights, the pleasant days." Rachel folded her hands together.

"You like the fall colors on you," Catherine teased her.

Charles winked at Rachel. "My bride looks ravishing in any color."

Ewing rose and the men rose with him. He bid his family good night, kissing his daughters. The young people sat there, chatting, dreaming, and then they, too, retired to their clapboard houses. Piglet lifted his head with a grunt to follow Charles.

Little by little, the singing stopped. Everyone went inside, for the night was turning cool.

Catherine and John waited before they ventured out. Piglet joined them. Catherine carried some food from the kitchen. John brought an old coat for Moses, too big for the man, but better than nothing.

Carefully, quietly, they made their way to the hideaway, the cool night air already causing a shiver.

Father Gabe looked up, as did Moses, Ailee, and Bettina.

Wordlessly, Catherine put down the food, as John did the coat.

John asked Moses, "Do you feel well enough to travel?"

"I won't leave Ailee," he stubbornly said.

John's deep voice reverberated against the cave walls. "Then you sentence yourself to death, and perhaps Ailee, too."

"I won't leave her."

Ailee looked at him with her good eye, but did not speak.

"Moses." Catherine's voice was soothing. "If captured, Ailee will be returned to Mrs. Selisse. She and Sheba will torture her. Ailee's life will be hell on earth."

Ailee took Moses's hand, kissing it.

Bettina affirmed this. "It's true, Moses."

Catherine sat on an upturned basket that Bettina had used to carry food. "You asked me to help you. Things happened so fast. I couldn't keep Francisco away from Ailee, but I can help you now." She paused. "The truth. Who killed Francisco?"

He took a ragged breath. "The Missus."

Bettina moved beside him, placing her hand on his shoulder. "How?"

Still weak, Moses's voice was low. "He trapped her in the summer kitchen. He held her throat, he lifted her skirt, but this time she screamed."

Ailee began to cry. Father Gabe petted her head, a soothing touch, as one would comfort an animal.

Moses continued. "The Missus ran out of the house. Sheba, too. I ran toward the summer kitchen behind them. The Missus, seeing what she did, picked up a big knife and stabbed him. Sheba grabbed a log from beside the fireplace and hit him over the head. Then she attacked Ailee. I pulled her off, grabbed her wrist so she'd drop the log. As I turned, the Missus slashed me with the knife. Sheba, she was crazy wild, and so was the

Missus. Ailee's face bled; I couldn't even see her eye. So much blood."

"What then?" Catherine asked.

"I don't know. We ran. The Missus and Sheba stayed in the kitchen."

John asked Father Gabe, "Is Moses strong enough to travel?"

"His wound is healing. He'll regain his strength."

"Do you think he can get his strength back soon?" Catherine asked. "Enough to work, perhaps indoor tasks? Or tending horses? He can't be disguised as a traveler. He will have to work."

Father Gabe thought, then opened Moses's shirt. Healing from the inside out, the wound was still open. "I would have to bind it. He could tear it."

Catherine felt a knot form in her stomach. "The blood will give him away."

"I won't leave Ailee."

"Moses, you must," Bettina simply, firmly said.

Ailee kissed his hand again, tears from her eyes falling on his hand. Seeing tears from her blind eye brought Catherine to tears.

John changed the subject. "Do you need anything?"

"Shoes, they need good shoes," Father Gabe announced.

"We can get warm clothing. Shoes are hard." Bettina affirmed Father Gabe's request.

John studied Moses's and Ailee's feet. "I'll see what I can do."

Piglet growled. Father Gabe pinched the candle, cutting the light. All held their breath. Snuffling was heard outside, followed by the pungent odor of bear. Piglet growled louder, then shot out of the hidden cave. The bear ambled on, not terribly frightened of the dog. Puffed up, Piglet returned.

"Bettina, best to walk back with us, just in case the bear returns," John sensibly suggested. "Father Gabe, what about you?"

"I'll stay. I sleep here now, then go up at dawn. Some of the children come down."

"Can you trust them?" John questioned. "Little ones talk."

"Yes. Little they are, but they understand. They look at Moses's wound, Ailee's eye, they understand."

With the corgi, the three threaded through the woods, occasionally stumbling, emerging onto the high meadow, the stars brilliant.

John softly said, "Even if people believed Moses innocent, he'll still hang. Hiram and Dennis will see to that. Notches in their belts. They captured a dangerous runaway."

Bettina murmured, "God will show us the way."

"Bettina," Catherine asked once they could speak, "what does a cross scratched on a tomb mean?"

Eyes widening, Bettina inquired, "Whose tombstone?"

"My mother's. There's a cross scratched on the back."

Walking, Bettina finally answered. "A square means

asking for a curse. Those are put on the tombs of the evil dead. A cross on a tomb is a prayer, a request."

"For?" Catherine pressed.

"Health. Success in love."

"So it's not a curse?" Catherine was nothing if not shrewd.

"Not on your mother's tomb. A curse is marked by a square, like I said. Depends on whose spirit is being conjured."

"Conjured?" John had never heard of such a thing.

"The old faiths, the faiths from Africa, they believe you can communicate with spirits." Catherine tried to frame this as neutrally as possible because she didn't want to insult Bettina.

"A doctor, a queen, they have great power," Bettina enlightened him.

"Father Gabe can conjure," Catherine mentioned, which made Bettina stare at her. "Bettina, I know he can. I keep my mouth shut, but I do not deny the spirits."

On hearing this, Bettina relaxed. Most white folks mocked the old ways. "They are all around us."

"May I ask why my mother? She was no conjurer."

"Your mother was an angel. Your mother had power, yes, she did. She could see into the future. She knew when others would die or live. She knew when she was going to die. She was not afraid, but she didn't want to leave you and Rachel. She made me promise to watch over you, to keep good spirits about you."

Catherine did not doubt this. Her mother, always sensitive, would speak to people in their own language, their own ways, if she could.

John was mystified. "I mean no offense, but why would someone put a cross on Isabelle Garth's tomb?"

"To ask for her protection," Bettina half whispered. "We need to protect Moses and Ailee, and the baby when it comes."

Catherine put her hands together. "Oh, no. Ailee is with child?"

Bettina nodded. "We need kind spirits. We need the Old Missus. She would find a way."

24

Friday, August 5, 2016

Piled against the inside wall of the equipment shed, the siding was held in place by vertical stakes so it wouldn't slip. Although the boards and the metal sides weren't heavy, they weren't that light, either.

Harry and Fair painted the woodwork on the shed July 31 as planned. However, taking down the siding took longer. Working outside in summer tired Harry more quickly than working outside in the other seasons, although a deep snow could wear her out.

"We did a good job." She admired it as she walked outside, followed by the barn swallows. "Hey, that's too close."

A female flew right to her face, then darted away. "*Zap.*"

Mrs. Murphy crouched down as the bird returned for another pass. The tiger cat launched herself straight up, hoping to catch the saucy bird between her paws. Thin air was her reward. She came down on all fours.

"Barn swallows aren't worth it." Pewter, as always, generously gave of her opinion.

Sitting on her haunches, licking her front paw as though this was of no concern, Mrs. Murphy responded, *"Maybe not, but they taunt me."*

On cue, Luciano flew over Pewter and turned upside down like a jet plane, joyfully screaming, *"Fatty."*

Huffed up, Pewter took a swat at the devilish bird.

Paying no attention to the catcalling, Harry trudged back to the house.

The two cats shot ahead of her, separated, ran in a beeline to each other, leapt straight up in the air, bumped chests, and fell back.

"That's a show!" Harry laughed, always delighted to see animals play.

Asleep, Tucker didn't lift her head when the three walked into the kitchen.

Harry sat down in the house office, turned on the big computer that Fair had specially made for his work. He didn't mind Harry using it. She actually liked looking at the big screen.

The two cats followed her in.

"Don't bat at the screen. You'll push her into a bad mood," Mrs. Murphy warned the gray cat.

Already next to the screen, Pewter called down. *"Just words. Nothing good."* She then settled down, dozing.

Harry read, then typed other things in. Read again.

"Hmm. Leukemia first appears in the English language in 1873 in an English pathology text describing an over-

production of white blood cells, which the author, a Dr. Green, thought often attacked the spleen."

Mrs. Murphy jumped up to sit on the other side of the computer screen. Harry kept reading, clicking on more stuff.

Pushing back in her chair, she rubbed her chin for a moment. "*Leukos* means white in Attic Greek. You know, Mrs. Murphy, we've known about many diseases for thousands of years. We can describe them. Physicians to the pharaohs described cancers, heart attacks accurately. But no one knew what to do. We still don't. Here I'm reading about all kinds of new drugs. You can prolong life, ease the worst of the pain, but the truth is the stuff is going to kill you."

"You have to die of something," the tiger cat sensibly said.

Harry reached over, rubbed the cat's cheeks. "Governor Holloway doesn't have but so much time."

Pewter opened an eye, closed it again. *"He's old."*

Mrs. Murphy laughed. *"Doesn't mean he wants to die."*

Impulsively, Harry picked up the office phone, dialing Cooper. "Hey."

"Hey back at you."

"Work?"

"Long day. I'm on my way home."

"I know you received the medical examiner's report on Barbara Leader or you wouldn't have been on your way to Big Rawly yesterday."

"She was murdered. The odd thing was she had ingested the thallium chloride. They aren't a hundred percent sure how, but the consensus is she took a gelatin tablet, like a gelatin Motrin or vitamin, and it was inside the tablet. Once the outside dissolved, the drug could take effect."

Harry considered this. "Someone knew her routine if it was in a vitamin tablet or even a Motrin tablet. Do you think someone at Big Rawly did this?"

"No idea, although she was traveling toward Big Rawly."

"Right." Harry then asked, "Maybe the governor was the intended victim?"

"Given all the pills he's taking, you'd think he'd be long gone by now if that was the intent," said Cooper. "As it is, not to sound heartless, he will soon be gone."

"Right," Harry simply replied. The thought of the beloved old man's death saddened her.

25

Tuesday, September 21, 1784

"There." Charles sprinkled sand on the parchment. He tilted the skin to the side, and the sand fell into a small glass container.

Upon hearing the sand, Piglet's ears pricked up.

Catherine took the proffered document. "Remarkable."

Smiling, Charles added, "Forging discharge papers helped my comrades, the other prisoners of war, live unmolested once they escaped. Truth is, I don't think the guards or even your Congress wanted to find them. Still."

John leaned down to study Charles's writing on the document, beautiful flourishes. A hand like that took years to develop. "When you wrote letters to my mother, she thought they were pretty as paintings."

Rachel looked out the window; Charles's workroom glowed with light from the setting sun. "The autumn equinox," she announced before turning to the others. "Can Moses read at all?"

"No," Catherine answered. "But he'll know a manumission paper when he sees one. He will have to keep this on him at all times until he's settled, and even then." She sighed. "Rachel, Charles, I am sorry to draw you into this. John, Bettina, and I pray day and night for guidance. How do we save Moses and Ailee without compromising Father? And without compromising ourselves? You all know what will happen if either of them are caught."

Sitting at his drafting table, Charles solemnly reached up to touch his sister-in-law's wrist. "There might be another way."

John pulled a chair over for his wife and then for Rachel. He sat on a small high bench after removing papers, books, twine.

"What do you do with this?" John held up the twine.

"I put a little lead sinker on the end and use it for a straight line. Like we did when we built the bridges only wee, tiny. Sometimes if I can see something off the page, see all the dimensions, I can think better."

Catherine returned to the problem. "A plan?"

"I have been given the commission to design St. Luke's, as you know. Well, St. Luke's is a Lutheran church in a new land. I know Winchester Cathedral"—he smiled—"wouldn't fit here. And a Lutheran church must not be confused with Catholic, right? Or these newer faiths, the evangelical faiths. The Quakers. Lutheran is distinctive. It's still high church, but less"—he twirled his right hand as he tried to convey his meaning—"bombastic."

Catherine smiled. "You think the Church of England is bombastic?"

"After Harry the Eighth, it had to rival Rome." Charles smiled back. "The Dissolution scars still disfigure my homeland, and I truly pray such a terrible thing never happens here."

"It can't," said John. "We have the separation of church and state, thanks to James Madison, who crafted that for Virginia." John hadn't fought in the war for nothing.

"And let us hope it holds forever, but back to St. Luke's," said Charles. "There are few models in Virginia, but I know there are many in Pennsylvania. Captain Bartholomew Graves, whom John will recall, now lives in York. He says the churches there are uncommonly beautiful, both Episcopal and Lutheran. The good captain swears every second person is a Lutheran, but he mentioned a particular church, Christ Lutheran on George Street."

"Do you think they will change the street names?" Rachel blurted this out.

"Why? We were a colony of the king. Better to remember than forget," John levelly declared.

"If it's any further help, there's also a King Street, a Queen Street, a Prince Street, a Duke Street. The residents of York will keep their king and queen, which brings me to this church. It was a log cabin in the 1600s.

They say it is the first church west of the Susquehanna River. Over the decades, with trade increasing and people moving there, the church has been built out of red brick, all surmounted by a most beautiful proportionate steeple. It can be seen for miles around."

Rachel bestowed upon her husband her sweetest smile. "Charles, dear, what has this to do with Moses and Ailee?"

"Oh, I digress. What would I do if I didn't have you to bring me back to the path?"

"You'd listen to me bark." Piglet guffawed, which made the others laugh, although they didn't know what the brave fellow had said.

"Yes, dear." Rachel smiled.

"Yes, well, I will tell all and sundry that I must go to York to study these Lutheran churches, most especially Christ Lutheran. This will be a short visit. Karl can help me build a steeple, an example." He held up his hands. "A steeple to be looked over by the Lutheran pastors and their architects. We will hide Moses in the steeple, which I will cart up there on a wagon. The steeple will have slits so he can breathe and a door so he can step out at night and sleep in the straw, which will fill the wagon to protect the steeple. A steeple is the only structure I can think of that will work. It can be big enough that he can sit in it. When out of sight, we can pass food and drink to him. At night we can pull into an Ordinary, put the wagon under a shed roof or something. He can climb out, burrow under in the straw, and sleep."

No one uttered a word. Even Piglet remained silent.

Finally Catherine stood up, stared at the setting sun, the thrilling beauty of an equinox sunset over the Blue Ridge Mountains. "Charles, you may have found the way. I pray to God you have." She mused. "The changing seasons. How it marks time." She turned to the others. "I have involved each of you in a dangerous enterprise. Please do forgive me, but when I saw Moses and Ailee, when they first sought refuge here, my heart near broke. I could not turn them in nor turn them away." She paused for a long time. "Rachel, remember when Mother and Father would read us Bible passages?"

"I do."

"Remember how upset we were when she read to us about Cain and Abel? And Cain says, 'Am I my brother's keeper?' " She stared at her lovely sister, recalling their mother's liquid voice. "I believe we are our brother's keepers. I don't know what it means except that I must save these two souls. I think Mother would."

Quietly, with conviction, Rachel replied, "I think so, too. We are all in danger, Catherine, but it isn't your doing. It started with Francisco Selisse."

Charles ruefully added, "It started thousands of years before that. Catherine, what you've done has awakened us. If we are careful, if Moses keeps his wits, he will be safe with Captain Graves as a freedman worker. We can give the captain and his wife money to help feed and clothe him. In time, if Moses wants to move on, he can, just so long as he doesn't return here."

"He can never return," Catherine spoke with determination. "He will never see Ailee again."

"You two have not seen her." John spoke to Charles and Rachel. "Her face has been broken. She is blind in her left eye."

"Maureen Selisse wrought her revenge on a poor creature who was innocent." John surprised them with his vehemence. "Wicked. At least Francisco deserved what he got."

"Wicked and very female," Rachel opined, but without rancor.

"We aren't going to solve these foolish things," Charles said. "Karl and I can have the steeple built in two days. I'd like to cover the top with copper, but that will slow us down. Shakes will do for now. Can you ready Moses for the day after tomorrow?"

John nodded. "Father Gabe and Bettina will have to do that."

"Will they?" Charles asked.

"Yes."

"The other slaves know. Are Moses and Ailee safe? And what about us? Slaves talk just as much as any other group of people." Charles felt a creep of apprehension on his skin.

"They will keep silent," Catherine said. "Charles, think of what they stand to lose."

"What of Ailee?" Charles inquired.

"She doesn't speak. She has lost the power. If anyone were to see her, they would know who she is. She is so light-skinned. Everyone knows that, too. The story of Francisco's murder has strong legs."

Rachel looked at her sister. "Where can she go, and is she strong enough to travel?"

Catherine shook her head. "She's not strong enough. Father Gabe moved some bones back into place, but she will never look as she did, and she is blind in that eye. And yet the other side of her face remains so beautiful, so very beautiful. We must keep her until we can find a way. Moses can grow a beard. He'll look like so many other young men. But Ailee will only ever look like Ailee."

"She can't stay in that cave forever," Charles exclaimed. "I haven't been there, nor should I, but caves are damp and cold, and the nights grow longer and colder."

Rachel spoke this time. "Let's get Moses out first. Then we can attend to Ailee."

"There is another complication." Catherine took a deep breath. "She is with child. Bettina believes this to be so."

Rachel again spoke: "As I said, we will attend to Ailee later."

Walking back to their house, arm in arm, Catherine and John admired the sunset, now in full flame.

"Change," Catherine simply said.

"I welcome it."

"I do, too, but now I feel as though the earth is moving under me. I thought things were clear, right and wrong. Simple. Am I changing or are the times?"

He bent down to kiss her cheek. "Both. When I fought I knew what I had to do even if I didn't know how to do it. And I found a way. The cannonade, the whistle of bullets. War is both difficult and easy. This is not easy. Maybe, Catherine, everyone faces such moments or difficulties as we now find ourselves facing. The problem we have is certainly dangerous, but we will do the best we can."

"And we will do it together." She stopped, reached up, put her hand behind his neck, pulled his face to hers, and kissed him. "I love you so."

26

Sunday, August 7, 2016

"She looks so young." Harry's eyes misted as the photograph of her mother appeared on Fair's large computer screen. She was feeling sentimental. Her dearest friends had gathered at her house to celebrate her birthday, and now looking at these old photos was making her emotional.

"She was," Susan said. "Her senior year at Smith. I guess all your maternal side of the family attended Smith."

Harry nodded, then smiled as a photo of her father appeared. Standing in a vaulted doorway at Cornell, his arms were thrown over the shoulders of two fraternity buddies.

Photo after photo of Harry's family, grandparents, aunts, uncles, then the marriage photo of her mother and father at Greenwood Episcopal Church back in 1972. Two radiant young people, the bride's veil now off her face, the groom in a morning suit, with a large crowd of friends surrounding them.

Ned pointed to the screen.

"Hey, isn't that Samuel Holloway?"

"I think so. They were all good friends. There's Miranda and George Hogendober." Harry cited her longtime work partner and her late husband.

She missed working with Miranda as she missed the old post office.

Now peering over her shoulder, Miranda lamented, "George had hair in the photograph."

They all laughed.

The photograph that drew the biggest laugh was the one of Harry and Susan in the new sandbox, followed by another photo of the ruined sandbox.

Watching the screen from the side, Pewter called down to Tucker, *"She wore a bow in her hair."*

"Little girls did that. Still do." The corgi thought bows silly.

Sitting in Fair's lap, Mrs. Murphy enjoyed the pictures. Included here were images of long-deceased dogs, mostly German shepherds, and other kitties.

After the show, Harry, Fair, Susan, Ned, Miranda, the Very Reverend Herbert Jones, BoomBoom Craycroft, Alicia Palmer, and Cooper repaired to the kitchen. Susan pulled a giant devil's food cake out of the refrigerator and lit the candles, which glowed against the vanilla icing.

"How did you fit that cake in our fridge?" Harry wondered.

"Moved the shelves," Fair informed her, quickly adding, "Don't worry, I'll put them back."

"Okay. Blow out the candles and make a wish," Susan ordered her friend.

Harry blew them out in one big, long breath. "I'm not telling my wish."

"Can't. Then it won't come true," BoomBoom affirmed.

In the living room, thankfully cool, as Harry had put air-conditioning in the old farmhouse years back, the happy group ate their cake, drank some champagne, and reminisced.

"I can't believe we wore our hair like that in college," Harry mused.

Harry was moved. "I can't believe you all gathered up these pictures and took them down to Rae Tait and she did this, given all that's happening at Crozet Media."

"Said she had a wonderful time scanning them in." Cooper smiled. "It beats us asking her more questions."

"Such an odd thing." BoomBoom put her plate on the coffee table. "Why would anyone go through Rae's files when all that expensive equipment was there? The keyboard, soundboard, everything? Video equipment, apart from the cameras, costs a pretty penny."

Ned put his arm around his wife's shoulders as she sat next to him. "Well, you know they weren't druggies, or they'd have cleaned out anything that could bring a dollar."

"Cooper and I went through all that was left, the outtakes," said Harry, then looked at Cooper. "Did I just say too much?"

Cooper shrugged. "No. It helped to have two sets of eyes looking at the discarded footage, or I should say unused footage."

"The outtakes we saw from Ed Cunningham's website had the governor in some of them," said Harry. "Seeing him at Mom and Dad's wedding, I'm reminded what a handsome man he was. Still is."

"Many politicians are." Susan poked her husband, who laughed.

"Hey, not me," Ned replied.

"You are to me." Susan blew him a kiss.

"Ned, you're good-looking and not fat. That's a victory." Harry teased him. "I mean, you're even older than I am, or your wife."

"That reminds me." Susan rose, left the room, returning with a wrapped tube, a big bow in the middle. "Happy Birthday."

Harry shook the tube. "What's this?"

"Open it. Then we'll all find out," Fair encouraged her.

"Leave the empty tube," Pewter begged.

"Why? You're too fat to fit into it," said Tucker. A hint of malice pricked her ears.

Pewter shot over to the dog, boxed her ears, then returned to sitting under the coffee table.

"What was that all about?" BoomBoom wondered.

"Around here you never know." Harry laughed as she

gently edged out a piece of heavy paper. "What in the world?" Then she laughed. "I don't believe you!"

Susan held up the paper, which was a birth certificate. But this birth certificate had been backdated three years, so that Harry would still be thirty-nine. "See, your mother lied on your birth certificate."

Everyone crowded around to look and the certificate looked proper. They all laughed.

Alicia, unbelievably beautiful, like Sophia Loren is unbelievably beautiful, and who had been a movie star in the fifties and early sixties, studied the document. "Susan, can you get me one of these?"

Everyone laughed again and Fair poured more champagne. "To my wife. In my eyes, she will always be the most beautiful, the most fascinating, sometimes the most irritating, but always my girl."

They cheered.

Mrs. Murphy somehow managed to wiggle into the tube. Pewter maliciously rolled it. Harsh words were spoken and the tiger cat backed out of the tube, intent on her revenge. Two cats flew out of the living room. A crash in the kitchen did not bode well.

Harry shook her head. "Oh, we'll find it later."

"Must be wonderful not to know how old you are." Miranda laughed at the cats.

Tucker supplied an answer. *"We don't know like you know, but we know. Not so much years as memories. We remember everything."*

The humans talked, ate some more, drank some

more, and loved every minute of being together, as old friends do.

Harry piped up. "Seeing the governor like I said earlier, young, handsome, makes you realize the power of time."

"And burdens. Governor Holloway carried heavy burdens." Miranda offered that insight. "His mistakes will stick to him, but I hope what he did for us will, too. He built so many state roads, he protected our battlefields from developments, he tried to keep the peace—unfortunately, in the wrong manner, but I think he brought prosperity to Virginia."

"Being governor of Virginia means you have an easy or uneasy relationship with the president." Ned spoke from his experience in the House of Delegates. "We are loaded with military bases and we all benefit from the huge shipyard in Norfolk. Federal money pours into this state, but the governor has to be wary of the president. If the president is not of the governor's party, might not be a smooth ride. Anything affecting the military affects Virginia. And Governor Holloway's record on that is outstanding."

"Best to remember the good things. He's not long for this world." Miranda said what they all felt.

"They'll bury him at Big Rawly, won't they?" Boom-Boom inquired.

Susan said, "Holloways are always buried there."

Harry involuntarily shivered for an instant. "That cemetery gives me the creeps. That huge monument with the avenging angel on top, the flaming sword. Ugh."

"The Selisse tomb, the ravens like to perch on it." Reverend Jones laughed.

"It's like the Bizarre Scandal, isn't it?" Miranda considered the story. "The scandal about the missing infant which brought down the Randolph family, oh, 1793. The Selisse story is much the same. We will never know the details, except that a slave killed the master. So many stories."

"All done now." Fair smiled, feeling the glow of champagne.

Harry laughed. "Oh, Fair, nothing is ever done in Virginia. Everything always comes back to haunt us."

A booming howl followed by a long hiss and a clatter turned their heads toward the kitchen.

Eddie's voice carried into the living room. "This is an outrage. The state of Virginia must assign state troopers to protect my grandfather."

"What the—" Harry hurried into the kitchen.

Mrs. Murphy and Pewter had knocked the TV remote off the counter. In running away, one of them had pushed the on button.

Eddie Cunningham angrily spoke to Bill Coates, the Channel 29 reporter. Given that Sunday's news was usually tepid except for sports, this clip would blanket the state. "I believe my grandfather's life is in danger. We now know that his nurse, Barbara Leader, was murdered. I demand that the state offer him protection."

By now, everyone but the cats crowded into the kitchen.

Bill Coates pushed, "Why would anyone want to harm your grandfather?"

"You tell me!" Eddie's face darkened. "I believe this goes back to his gubernatorial term when he refused desegregation. Racial tensions are again high and I fear this has provoked some unbalanced person to want to kill him."

Bill Coates then looked at the camera and said, "Thank you, State Senator Cunningham. And now to the weather."

"Is Eddie crazy?" Alicia wondered.

"No. Clever." Ned calmly expounded. "It's dramatic. Tensions are high and Ed means to capitalize on them. He's throwing red meat to those people who want to turn back the clock, but he's doing it in a way where he can't be held to account."

"Ned, he doesn't need to do that," said Fair.

"He's laying his groundwork and the murder is a terrific gift. So many people are disaffected. Call attention to a racist event, a much-publicized racist event from the 1970s, make this murder look like revenge, you know, they got the wrong person, once he spins this out over the next week identifying Barbara Leader as the wrong person. Everyone will remember. He'll dominate the news, he can vent anger, which even liberals can understand, since he's defending his grandfather, worried about his safety. But Ed is aiming for a large constituency, much larger than he has now. It's low, but it's effective. To attack him for this makes the attacker look as though he has no family feeling. So Ed gets to have his cake and eat it, too."

"Could Governor Holloway be part of this?" Miranda wondered.

"My grandfather would not countenance it," Susan stoutly replied.

"True enough." Ned agreed.

Cooper sighed. "Rick and I wanted to spare the governor stress due to his condition, plus his feelings over the loss of a nurse he liked very much. We're going to have to call on him, though. Ed's statement pushes us to it."

"Obviously, my cousin doesn't give a damn about G-Pop's condition." Susan could have strangled Ed right then.

"Politicians don't care about people's feelings. They want to manipulate them. They themselves don't feel a thing except ambition." Alicia felt cynical, and she'd seen a lot in her life to provoke that.

"Governor Holloway's desegregation stand was so long ago. He's changed." Harry threw up her hands.

"Harry, there is no event too distant or absurd that can't be used to stir people up," said Ned. "What if those of Italian descent, you know, some young politician on the make, declares Al Capone was framed because of anti-Italian feeling? He was the victim of a government vendetta."

"Didn't they nail him on income-tax evasion?" Susan asked.

"He was too smart to be caught for his crimes, so they sicced the IRS on him," Ned explained.

"The more things change, the more they stay the same." BoomBoom couldn't resist the nearly three-thousand-year-old quote.

27

Thursday, September 23, 1784

The night, cool in the low fifties, ensured neither John nor Charles would fall asleep as they waited for Moses to emerge from the woods. The unpainted steeple was nestled deep in straw, tied tightly to wagon sides so it wouldn't slide. Inside, a cushion would allow Moses to sit comfortably. A jar of water and some biscuits and jam had been wrapped in a kitchen towel by Bettina. An old woolen shirt, socks, sturdy shoes, and a worn but presentable pair of breeches also had been neatly piled on the floor, as well as a black tricorn hat with black grosgrain ribbon where the crown met the brim.

Catherine thought Moses would need a hat when they felt safe enough for him to ride up with John and Charles, if that moment occurred. He had also been encouraged to grow a beard, which he was doing. By the time they reached York, his beard would be full.

Finally, Father Gabe, on one side of Moses, Catherine

on the other, led the young man to his new hiding place. Not completely healed, his wound caused some pain. John stepped down and he and Father Gabe gave Moses a leg up.

Tears streaming down his cheeks, the slave opened the door as he was instructed, bent over, slipped inside, and closed the door, latching it from the inside. Charles, prudently, placed a small latch on the outside, too.

John kissed Catherine, then swung up onto the cart, picked up the reins, and clucked, and the draft horse pair, Castor and Pollux, walked away. Piglet sat next to Charles.

Catherine and Father Gabe watched. He returned to the cave, where Bettina sat with a distraught Ailee. Catherine returned to her home but couldn't sleep for thinking of the flow of tears from Ailee's blind eye when she and Moses had to bid each other goodbye.

Dawn greeted John, Charles, and Moses, although Moses couldn't see it. They were now eight miles north of Charlottesville. Piglet awakened when the wagon stopped.

Trotting in the opposite direction came Dennis McComb.

Charles put his hand on John's holding the reins.

"Good morning, Constable," Charles flattered Dennis, as he was not a full constable.

Dennis stopped. "A fine morning. A steeple. And what might you two be doing with a steeple?"

Charles smiled. "You may have heard that I am designing St. Luke's Lutheran Church, which will be west of Mr. Garth's properties at Wayland's Crossing."

"I had heard that." Dennis enjoying letting them know he heard much in his official capacity.

Charles smiled sheepishly. "Well, now, Mr. McComb, something tells me you're not a Lutheran."

John sat there wondering what Charles was doing, but he remained impassive, as he was not the quick thinker that Charles was. His social graces, improved by his former captive, served him well, but with Charles such flourishes were effortless.

Serious of mien, Dennis uttered, "Presbyterian."

"A worthy sect, to be sure. Well, not being acquainted with Lutheran churches in the New World, I thought I'd best take this steeple to a former comrade-in-arms who knows Lutheranism well. He and his associates can make any corrections they see fit, for, as you know"—Charles lowered his voice conspiratorially—"one can make a misstep in such a delicate matter as ecclesiastical architecture. Don't want to smack of Rome."

"No, sir," Dennis replied with vigor.

"And might I ask what you are doing north of town at such an hour? No trouble, I hope? After all, the good citizens should allow you your rest."

Dennis smiled. "No trouble. I have been searching high and low for the murderous slave. Someone thought they saw a slave running in the night. Nighttime would be when he would move."

"I would have thought he'd be long and far away by now," Charles evenly replied.

"Too much clamor, sir. He or they would have never made it, no matter what direction they traveled in. They have to be here. It's a matter of time, and then, of course, they will move, and I intend to catch them. Murder is no small affair."

Charles's eyebrows rose. "Yes, of course. I would never have thought of them sitting tight, Mr. McComb, but then you are a constable and I am not."

Pleased, Dennis promised, "I will find them."

"If anyone can, you can," Charles complimented him.

"I will be on my way. Good day to you, sirs."

"And good day to you, Constable." Charles patted Piglet, now awake. John, reins loose, clucked to the matched pair of Percherons.

Once out of earshot, John remarked, "He's smarter than I thought."

"He's ambitious. Hiram Meisner is slack and Dennis McComb burns to succeed him. He won't shy away from whatever needs to be done. I've often thought that those who represent the law are as brutal as those who break it."

Further along, Charles called back, "Moses, all is well."

"Yes, sir," came the reply.

"Tap if you need anything, as we discussed," Charles reminded him.

"I will."

They rode along, then John said, "You study people. McComb. I hadn't thought of his wanting to rise."

"I was in the British Army, remember?"

At this, they both laughed.

Later that day, work with their father finished, the sisters walked down to Bettina's cabin. The children looked up as the two dazzling beauties came among them. They were a bit afraid of such powerful people.

Tulli sat next to Bettina on her front porch, peppers, thyme, basil, and other herbs all hanging from the porch rafters.

Bettina placed her hand on the boy's head, for she loved him as if he were her own. "Tulli, go on, now."

"Before you go, Tulli. I saw where you cleaned Sweet Potato's tack. Might you ride out with Jeddie and me tomorrow? We want to check the two bridges at the back of the farm and you could hold our horses. You would be a big help."

"Yes, Miss Catherine. Yes." He was thrilled to ride with the two best riders on the Garth estate and beyond.

Catherine gathered her light skirt to sit next to Bettina on her long bench. "If you're tired, Serena can make a stew. She's learned so much from you. Go to bed early."

"I believe that girl will grieve herself to death," Bettina half whispered.

Rachel sat on the other side of Bettina. "People do die of broken hearts."

"Yes, honey baby." Bettina reached for Rachel's hand. "Yes, they do."

"Ailee's not going to die," Catherine declared. "She'll live for the baby."

"If she lives," said Rachel, of practical mind, "she has to remain hidden, have a healthy baby, and live, and then what? Her face will give her away even if we managed to get her to Massachusetts or down to South Carolina. She will always be in danger as long as Maureen Selisse lives."

"And Sheba," Bettina sourly added.

"Two harpies," Rachel agreed.

"Let us consider this without emotion as though this were happening to someone in, say, Austria or, better yet, Russia, since they have serfs," said Catherine. "Our first task is to keep Ailee hidden, to make certain she doesn't entertain a notion to follow Moses."

"She won't," said Bettina. "He made her promise. He swore the day would come when he would return for her. He said she's worth dying for."

"Let us hope that's not the case." Catherine sighed. "But again, no emotion. What comes next?"

They sat there, smelling the thyme.

"The cave is the best place we have," said Bettina. "Can't build a fire there. Can't cook there. We can keep her in blankets and furs, but that's all we can do. I believe the cold will make her face more painful. Father Gabe examines her face. Says the cheekbones are knitting together as best he could push them back. But the eye bones, he says they are so delicate. She won't freeze, but she'll be miserable. Nights are getting cold." Bettina placed her hands on her knees, having released Rachel's hand.

"What about the cabin with the loom?" Rachel thought out loud. "It's at the end of the work row. The men never go down there. Father would have no reason to go down there and guests won't go down there."

The other two considered this.

Catherine replied, "It's a big room, but open. She would have no place to hide if someone did come there."

Rachel was hopeful. "Why can't the men build a loft? Ailee can hide up there if she needs to. There's a good fireplace in the weaving room. All it needs is an iron bar to hang a pot on it. Water nearby. It might work."

"Until someone sees her face," Catherine logically said.

"It's only our people along that row," Bettina added. "But you're right, if anyone did see her, the cat would be out of the bag."

Rachel racked her brain. "She could wear a large sunbonnet."

"In the winter?" Catherine was incredulous.

"Maybe, maybe." Bettina turned this over in her mind. "If her sunbonnet was longer on one side, she could pull it to hide her face. Winter, a scarf, something like that to cover herself with, I don't know."

"Bettina, we've heard that Maureen Selisse is offering

a reward for their capture and Yancy Grant is adding to it, for the protection of our citizens."

They didn't know that Yancy had also offered Dennis McComb a goodly sum, off the record.

"Ha," Bettina nearly shouted.

"But would anyone tell, anyone here?" Catherine pressed.

Bettina shook her head. "No. Never. And if they did, they wouldn't live out the week. If one of us didn't kill them when they walked off the farm, they'd be dead. Soon caught, anyway. How do you think Moses and Ailee got here that night? Hands, hands helping them along the creek, and there are other caves. It's the most direct route. The only person we can't trust is Sheba. She thinks she should be the missus. Lord, if you could hear her going on about how she's the granddaughter of a queen. Hell, I could be a queen. Tulli could be a king in Africa, but we aren't in Africa. Pride goeth before a fall."

"That it does," Rachel agreed. "Shall I ask Karl to have a loft built? No need to bother Father with it, and if he finds out, sees lumber being hauled down the row, or hears the noise, I'll tell him it was my idea. Didn't want to leave the fabrics and wool lying low. They should be high up. Someone should be in the weaving room. Which means we'd better put someone else in there."

"I'll think on that," Bettina answered.

A breeze rustled the oaks. "Sounds like fall." Rachel looked up to see the leaves moving, color just hinting at what was to come.

The catcalls of the children filled the air. The women tended their gardens behind their cabins. The men walked back home after a hard day's work. Long, slanting rays of the sun coated everything in deep gold. Horses neighed; cattle walked toward their quarters led by the old head girl.

The three women watched this.

Rachel asked, "What do you think happens after we die?"

Bettina turned to look at her, but since she had known Rachel in her cradle she was not terribly surprised by the change in subject, only by the subject itself. "Bible says we will all be united upstairs." She pointed straight up.

"How do we know there isn't an upstairs and a downstairs?" Catherine smiled impishly.

"Betcha there is a downstairs." Bettina pointed to the ground and they laughed.

"What brought that on?" Catherine asked her sister.

"It's so beautiful right now," said Rachel. "I don't want it to end. I want us to be together forever. I want to see Mother. I want to always hold Charles, and I even want that silly dog to sleep on the bed. I just"—she paused for a long time—"want us to always be together."

Bettina patted her hand. "In our hearts, we will."

28

Friday, September 24, 1784

"Beware of Greeks bearing gifts," Constable Hiram Meisner grandly pronounced.

"Sir?" Dennis McComb stood up as his boss, Hiram, walked into the blacksmith's shop.

Potter Manx, the burly blacksmith, apron covering his thighs, glanced up. "From the Trojan War," he explained to Dennis. "The Greeks couldn't defeat the Trojans so they withdrew their ships. The Trojans thought they sailed away. They left at the gates a large wooden horse as an offering to the gods, to peace."

"Oh." Dennis had never heard anything about this.

The constable finished the tale. "The horse hid Greek soldiers inside. That night after the horse had been hauled inside, the Greeks dropped a ladder, climbed down, opened the gates for their comrades, who had sailed back. They poured in. Hence the expression 'Beware of Greeks bearing gifts.' "

"I should think," said Dennis, amazed at the story, and the other two laughed at him.

"Ah, well, Dennis, best you stick to business." Potter focused on the mare's left hoof. "She needs time off. Give her two days."

"Well, it's lucky, then, that Mrs. Selisse has offered us an extra horse or two as we are tiring ours in the search," said Hiram. "Won't be the blooded horses but nonetheless . . ." His voice trailed off.

"Is Mrs. Selisse Greek?" Dennis inquired.

Hiram shrugged. "Selisse? Damned if I know. I thought Greek names ended in *os* and stuff like that."

"That boy Moses plumb vanished." Potter gently put the hoof down. "Hand me that pot, will you?"

Dennis handed the blacksmith a pot, a thinish black liquid therein. He painted it on her hoof.

"All her shoes are off. Let me finish this here. It will toughen the frog a bit. She's in good shape and she has good hooves, but our roads do their work."

The local roads were notoriously bad. Potholes, rocks, packed dirt. A few roads were corduroy, but most weren't, and a steady rain turned everything into a quagmire. A gullywasher often took the road with it.

"Aye." Dennis shook his head. "We haven't far to go and she had a nice pasture. Two days?"

Potter nodded. "Press on her frog. If she flinches she'll need more time, but I think she'll be fine."

"All right." Dennis looked at his boss. "I'll walk her to

the pasture. My wife will see to her and then, if you wish, we can go to Mrs. Selisse."

"You don't have a horse."

"How fast do you want to go?" Dennis asked.

"A walk." Hiram smiled. "We'll get there soon enough, where I'm certain we will receive an earful."

After dropping off his mare, Dennis walked alongside Hiram.

"Tops of the maples are red," Hiram noted.

"Willows already turning," said Dennis. "They're always early."

"You're fortunate to have a helpful wife. Then again, you haven't been married that long." Hiram laughed.

"She's a good wife."

"Dennis, she'd have to be, to put up with you." Hiram teased him and Dennis knew it.

Within the hour, they reached the Selisse estate. The peaches had been picked mid-August. The fieldhands stood on ladders in the small but abundant apple orchard, picking the last of the apples, which would be fed to stock. The cornfields boasted tall stalks with succulent ears. Summer slid into fall, a rich, bountiful fall.

In front of the house, DoRe took Hiram's horse.

The two men knocked on the front door. Sheba was glimpsed in the hall, but she wouldn't open the door. That was the butler's job. Everyone knew their tasks, their boundaries, and defended them.

Oliver, the ancient butler, opened the door. "The Missus is expecting you."

He led them to the rear of the lovely house, where Maureen Selisse sat on the same porch where she had entertained the Garths. Jeffrey Holloway sat beside her. As the two visiting men bowed to her, she fanned herself languidly.

Jeffrey, rising, indicated they should sit down. Then he turned to Maureen. "Madam, I will take your leave. I do not wish to intrude on your business."

She snapped her fan shut, pointing it at him. "You will do no such thing, Jeffrey. I want you to hear the constable and his assistant. You may gather something I miss." This was followed by a radiant smile, and then a less radiant smile at Sheba, who disappeared briefly before reappearing. In her wake came two women bearing a tray of refreshments and drinks. Maureen intended to bestow her hospitality on these public servants.

Hiram decided to take the bull by the horns or the horn from the bull, who knows? "Mr. Holloway, it is a pleasure to see you here. Mr. McComb and I have fretted over Mrs. Selisse alone on this large estate. Having a gentleman drop in on her is a comfort to us all."

Jeffrey smiled at them, then smiled slightly at Maureen. "Mrs. Selisse possesses rare courage."

"Gentlemen, please," she said, indicating the spread of food and drinks. "One of the stable boys ran up to tell us that you, Mr. McComb, walked. You must need some nourishment and a cool libation. It's warm, not intolerable, but warm in the sun."

"Thank you, madam. My horse is lame. Nothing serious, but she needs rest." Dennis accepted the drink handed to him by one of the ladies.

"I regret to report that we have yet to find Moses. Both Mr. McComb and myself have called at every farm, dwelling, even the small houses in Scottsville, the river captains, nothing. We have looked into reported sightings of strangers but—" Hiram again shook his head.

"You, sir, do not have enough help," said Jeffrey. "There are many calls on your time." He knew that Hiram could make his life miserable in a way he could not to those of higher station. "If you deem it necessary, I know many of us would join you."

Hiram considered this. "Thank you, Mr. Holloway. It may come to that. My suspicion is that neither Moses nor the woman has left the area. Someone is sheltering them. Had there been any movement at all, given how quickly we reported the news, I would have heard, but you know"—he looked straight up at Sheba—"slaves have many ways to subvert the law."

"They aren't the only ones," McComb added.

Hiram took over. "Mrs. Selisse, if there is a poor white who has cause to protect these two or who is holding them, waiting for a large ransom, which is also very possible, we will find them."

"I do hope so."

"Fortunately"—Jeffrey again soothed the water—"I believe that even though Moses and the woman were fool enough to dispatch Mr. Selisse, they would not be fool enough to return to harm Mrs. Selisse. But we can all understand this good woman's discomfort. This lady saw her husband murdered before her very eyes. I trust in good time you will find them and, as I offered, I know many men will aid you if needed."

"Yes, Yancy Grant offered the same," Hiram replied.

At this, Jeffrey's lips pursed together while Maureen took it all as her due. One fascinating development about Francisco's death was how many protectors stepped forward to cast their wing over her. Of course, men should, but so many? Perhaps Francisco should have died earlier? She looked at Jeffrey with a tenderness that did not escape him, nor the others.

So many men, yes, but only one so young and dazzlingly handsome.

Hiram and Dennis left, Dennis on Mrs. Selisse's borrowed gelding, a stalwart fellow.

That night, after supper, Dennis McComb told his wife the story of the Trojan horse.

"What an awful tale." Her hand fluttered to her breast. Although she had heard it in school, she pretended otherwise for him.

"Lies and deceit," Dennis mused. "Sometimes I think that's what holds the world together, a tissue of lies and deceit."

"Oh, Dennis, no. You're overtired and Hiram doesn't realize what a good man he has in you. It's wearing."

He smiled. She always made him feel better. "Sooner or later he will step down," said Dennis.

"Sooner better than later." She grinned, then wrinkled her brow. "Dennis, could it be possible that Mr. Selisse's killers are hidden in a Trojan horse?"

"What, my sweet?"

"They're hiding in someplace, something no one would question. It could be on a boat, or just on a farm somewhere, but someplace ordinary, or just"—she searched—"in something one wouldn't question."

29

Monday, August 8, 2016

"Here." Harry handed Susan an iron.

"I am not using my seven iron." Susan handed it back. "Give me a wood."

"No."

"You were born to irritate me. Give me my five wood."

"Susan, if I give you the wood, you will knock a real boomer. This is a tricky hole. You'll lay up in a bunker or the rough. If you take the iron, you won't hit as long a shot, but you'll land in the middle of the fairway. Then your second shot will put you exactly where you want. You're a great second-shot player."

Susan snatched the seven iron from Harry, looked down at the ball, then up at the fairway. Her swing, always fluid, picked up the ball and sent it exactly into the middle of the fairway. Still mad at Harry, she refused to tell her best friend that she was right. She strode down the fairway, making Harry drive the cart on the path.

Remembering she needed her putter, she then trotted up to Harry on the path, exchanged clubs, walked onto the green, and sank a beauty, making par.

She plopped back in the cart. "I hate it when you tell me what to do."

"Mmm-hmm." Harry hit the gas pedal, lurching forward.

They'd started at eight, but the rest of the morning progressed silently. Harry handed Susan woods or irons without a word and Susan snatched them from her. She finished the eighteenth hole four under par, a very, very nice score.

As they trundled back to the golf cart area, the little motor wheezing, Susan finally said, "Dew sure slows the ball down. On the other hand, I don't want to be out here at two in the afternoon."

"Course is perfect right now. Farmington has good greens keepers."

"Hell of a job. You know, I was thinking of going down to The Country Club of Virginia over the weekend. That's another old course. I need to push myself a little. I am going to win the country club championship this year if it kills me. Anyway, I know this course like the back of my hand. Thought I'd go to another old course and test myself."

"It is a terrific course, but just remember, no matter how well you know Farmington, the holes will be placed each day on the green in a different spot. The more you play this course, the more you will have seen a lot of placements. I'm not saying don't go on down there to Richmond, I'm just saying . . ." Harry trailed off. "Wendell Holmes!"

The springer spaniel greeted her. *"Hello."*

"What's G-Mom doing here?" Susan asked.

"She can still hit the ball." Harry so admired Penny Holloway, such a good athlete.

Most of the Holloways loved sports. Susan came by her abilities honestly.

"There you are." Penny had been chatting around the corner with an old friend. Hearing a golf cart return, she walked around to see who it was. "I was hoping it would be you."

Wendell Holmes ran back to Penny.

"Is everything all right?" Susan asked with trepidation.

"Your grandfather is as well as can be expected. It's not that but no, everything is not all right."

"What gives?" Susan used slang, but it was slang that her grandmother understood.

"Sam finally saw the interview with Eddie. I thought if I kept him away from the TV, he'd miss it, but they must be playing the darned thing every fifteen minutes. Your grandfather watched Eddie on the news this morning and he hit the roof."

"Oh, dear." Susan tipped the boy in the golf cart garage.

"Come home with me and see if you can help calm him down. You, too, Harry. I did not take Eddie's part, by the way. He should never have done that. Sam is so mad he accused me of being soft on Eddie." Wryly, she looked at Susan. "He knows you won't be."

One reached the front hall of Big Rawly by passing through the back gate of the Farmington Country Club, getting on 21 Curves to emerge on Garth Road, which was at the base of a steep hill. Old Garth Road dropped down to the hill where Ewing Garth's wide, sturdy bridge once stood. The state highway department had since widened the road, building a succession of new bridges over the creek over centuries. Still, if Ewing had returned to the twenty-first century, he would have likely recognized the spot.

They turned left on Garth Road, passed a subdivision carved from an estate, turned left onto the Beau Pre road, Oakencroft, the winery, in front of that. Took no time at all to reach Big Rawly, passing the graveyard.

Mignon and Millicent Grimstead heard them arrive and entered the hallway from the cozy TV room. When he wasn't in his library, the governor spent his time there in a recliner. Some days just walking to his library took too much energy.

"Calmer?" Penny inquired of her husband.

"Some. I'm glad you're here. You, too, Susan and Harry. He needs to vent. Maybe if he yells enough, he'll wear himself out." Millicent threw up her hands.

The five women ventured into the governor's lair.

"Penny, where were you?" Sam Holloway barked. "Wendell Holmes, I've been calling for you."

"Mom needs a buddy," the dog replied.

"Ladies, forgive me if I don't properly rise, but do sit down." As they were sitting, Sam started in. "You saw that disgraceful statement by my grandson? Certainly you did. Everyone in Virginia must have seen it!"

"I saw it at Harry's house," Susan answered her grandfather. "Miranda Hogendobber saw it. So did Ned, Fair, Alicia Palmer, and BoomBoom Craycroft."

As Sam had always admired Alicia from her movie days, he leaned forward. "What did Alicia think?"

Susan gilded the lily. "Terrible. Doesn't know if she can ever look Eddie in the eye again, much less vote for him."

"Ha! I've called him. He won't return my call. Mignon texted him. No reply. *Coward.*" Sam nearly spat that word out.

"G-Pop, he's riding on your coattails," said Susan. "I'm not making excuses for him. Eddie and I have never seen eye to eye, as you know, but politics is uglier than ever, and you are someone everyone knows. Look at the way you leaned on the federal government to build all the interstate roads. I can understand Eddie wanting everyone to associate him with you. I deplore it, but I understand it."

"Worrying about my safety. Oh, what a cheap shot!"

"It was." Harry felt that agreeing with him might calm him more quickly.

As it was, she did agree with him.

"He has enjoyed the advantage of my network, a network it took me seventy-five years to build," said Sam. "No, it's not the old Byrd machine with which I was only too familiar, but it is a network. The people may change, die, but the structure remains. I can call them off as easily as I called them on to get him elected, and by God, I'm going to do it."

Penny soothingly reached over to touch his hand. "Sugar, you can and you must. I know you will be discreet, but we can't have Eddie being so public, using you in such a fashion and, worse, darling, implying that you can't take care of yourself."

Sam glared at his wife, then relaxed. "The truth is I can't."

Susan picked up the thread. "G-Pop, a phone call from you and we are all better off. We don't need to be running for political office to be protected by you."

The governor fell back into his role of patriarch. He waved off Susan as though this was nothing, no matter at all, but already he felt stronger, on familiar ground. His wife, daughter, granddaughter, friend, and ghostwriter, all women, looked up to him. Sam was vital and needed. He needed to feel needed. The damned leukemia undermined that. His body might be failing, but he was still a man.

Penny stood up. "Sam, let me get you a drink. It's early, but a spot of bourbon followed by a tall glass of lemonade will refresh. Any other takers?"

"No, thanks, G-Mom."

"No, thank you, Mrs. Holloway."

"*Eddie!*" Wendell Holmes barked.

As he'd heard the voices, Eddie tiptoed into the room. "Sorry I didn't call right back. Crazy morning."

Sam got right to it. "How could you humiliate me like that?"

"I didn't humiliate you. You are an ex-governor and you deserve state protection." Eddie sounded smarmy.

"I am in no danger. Barbara Leader could have been killed for any number of reasons, none of which I can imagine, but not because she tended to me."

"G-Pop, you are an ex-governor known by all and there's still hard feelings about desegregation. You are vulnerable."

Enraged, the old man got out of his chair much faster than anyone could have anticipated, yanking a gold-tipped cane out of the large jar in which it stood. He smashed it over Eddie's head. "You slackass. You weakling. Get out of my house and don't you ever use my name again."

The governor swung a broken piece of cane at Eddie again.

A trickle of blood ran down Eddie's face. Hearing the ruckus, Penny came in, tray in hand. She put the tray down and wisely did not tend to Eddie.

"Edward, you had better go. I will speak to your mother."

With his hand over the bleeding wound, Eddie turned heel and left.

Shocked, but not entirely unpleased to see her cousin caned, Susan said, "I knew you could protect us, G-Pop, but that might be going too far."

The old man collapsed in his chair, but with a huge grin on his face. "I'll damned well kill him."

30

Monday, September 27, 1784

"Early fall, I think." John Schuyler inhaled the air, the faint aroma of leaves beginning to turn apparent.

"Autumn," Charles West corrected him, with one arm around Piglet. "Fall is when you lose your footing."

John shook his head, smiled. Charles's upper-class English pronunciation was bad enough, but fall was fall and that was the end of it.

Hauling their steeple behind, they'd crossed over the Potomac at Point of the Rocks, where a good, busy ferry plied its trade. A bit high, the river kept the ferryman and his sons alert. The river was never placid, and it swept along faster when its waters rose. Fortunately, the horses stood quietly, as did the other three passengers. Crossing a major river at sunrise held everyone's attention as a red, then gold path enticed one. So bright was the sunlight on the river, you felt you could walk on it.

On the Maryland side, carts and riders waited to be

ferried over to Virginia. Two hours later, the road was all theirs. Occasionally they'd pass another wagon, rider, or coach, but mostly the men headed north alone.

With their heavy load, the best they could do was twenty miles a day. They didn't mind, being in no particular hurry. The September days shimmered, the nights were cool, and wayside inns and ordinaries pleased them. The food was good, harvests were coming in. The houses they passed in the small towns boasted zinnias, asters, black-eyed Susans, many kinds of cornflowers, such bright reds, pale to deep yellow, purples, and the last white daisies of the year. On the Virginia side, the Virginia creeper was beginning to turn blood red. On the Maryland side the yellow willows were not yet dropping their leaves, but they would soon enough.

The farther away they moved from the river, the crisper the air smelled. The river odor had covered other scents until about two miles away. Charles noted how different a river's smell was from the ocean's. From that long trip across the Atlantic, with its stopover in the Caribbean with troops, Charles West would never forget the salty odor.

Hidden away, Moses remained silent, deeply saddened. If it was clear, they'd pull off the road to eat an apple or bread. Moses would come out, and the three men would sit under a tree, but he rarely spoke. Both John and Charles felt badly for him but at least he was alive.

"Did you see the big Chesapeake Bay during the war?" Charles asked John when they hit the road again.

"We thought your fleet would drop anchor there, disembark. From time to time a frigate, a smaller ship, would sail up, steal provisions or fire cannon. They say the Chesapeake is long and wide, enormous. What I saw, more inland, was big enough. I am surprised your navy didn't drop anchor there, unload troops."

"Ah, John, had we dropped anchor there and your boys knew it, they could have bottled up our entire fleet. Big fighting ships such as we have need room and wind."

John absorbed what his former enemy said. "I know little about naval matters, but I do wonder that your father didn't buy you a commission in the Navy. Is it not the premier—"

Charles interrupted, something he rarely did. "It is, but my father wanted me in the Army. When he attended Eton many of our admirals were boys there, too, and Father said he never liked a one. A few of my Eton fellows are in the Navy. A few are already commanders. No admirals yet. Not that any of us knew what would happen to us then, although we certainly knew what was expected of us."

"Which was?" John was curious.

"I would serve, marry well, which is to say marry an heiress. When my brother would succeed to the title, if he wished he could grant me my own land and the proceeds from such. If not, with my imagined wife's imagined money, we could buy something suitable to our station or live in London. It would have been a morass of intrigue, parties, races, fashion, and then of course we would send our sons to Eton, Harrow, or Winchester, and the cycle would start anew." Charles waved as they passed a carter hauling casks. "Spirits, I wonder?"

John smiled. "Could be molasses."

Charles returned to the subject of expectations. "I would have been as interested in architecture as I am now, but to pursue it in England I would have to pretend it was a hobby. Gentlemen don't become architects."

"What do they become?"

Charles smiled. "Lackeys to the king, which yields a veritable cornucopia of benefits as well as frustration. I could have won a seat in Parliament. Tory. It is not uncommon for a younger son to enter the church. The higher positions can be quite pleasant and then there is the Army and Navy. Hard on the wives."

"But you could pick your wife?" John was curious, for Charles rarely spoke of his past.

"Yes, but, John, the herd was thin. She had to be of my background. And she had to have money, hopefully pots of it. It was hoped she would come from a family that produced children without deformity or madness. You'd be surprised at how some families in England have madness, generation after generation. Even if a woman seems quite sane, it might show up later."

"Pretty?"

"To be sure, that would be an extra benefit."

"Charles, how could a man stand it?"

"The primary virtue of a woman is her money. You honor your wife, pay her every courtesy, especially in public, and then you keep a mistress or two, and they were pretty."

"Did your father do that?"

"He did. But I actually think my father kept a mistress because it was expected of him. He was not given to passion."

"Could the women also take up with a gentleman if she was quiet about it?"

"Some did, but within our class. Never heard of a woman taking a lover from a lower order. I expect it happens, but the thought was that women didn't take lovers until after two children. Supposedly they live for their children. The illusion is carefully polished."

John thought it suffocating. "I couldn't live that way."

"I couldn't, either. I stayed here." Charles smiled broadly. "And look what I found. My Rachel, my beautiful Rachel, who runs to my table to see what I have drawn today. Who makes me laugh. Who listens to my prattle. When Rachel looks at me . . ." Charles couldn't find the words.

"Yes," John simply replied. "When Catherine looks at me she sees a better man than I am, and then I try to become that man."

"Well put." Charles then whispered, "It makes Moses's situation painful to observe, painful to contemplate. If I were separated from Rachel, I would miss her so I would feel like dying. I never knew I could feel this way. John, I didn't know I had it in me."

John nodded, then turned to look behind him as they'd heard hoofbeats, coming at a trot. "My God."

Charles turned to see a grimacing Dennis McComb riding down the road toward them. "John, give me the reins. You're stronger than I. If he climbs in the cart, climb in with him."

John reached for the exquisite flintlock pistol wrapped in leather on the seat. Charles's father had given him the firearm when he entered the service, but when John captured Charles, he took it as the spoils of war. He never gave it back but occasionally would share.

Charles quickly put his hand around John's wrist. "No. Don't let him see it."

Dennis caught up with them, and with no preliminary banter ordered, "Stop the cart. I've been tracking you for three days."

Charles did as he was told. "*Whoa*, Castor. *Whoa*, Pollux."

John climbed down. "Mr. McComb, what's wrong?"

"You will let me examine that steeple with no interference." He pulled out his pistol.

"Of course." John swung himself up on the wagon. He reached out a hand for Dennis, who tied his horse—well, Maureen's horse—to the back of the cart. Taking John's hand, he was pulled up.

Dennis waded through the straw. "Lift up the steeple."

"No need for that. I can open the door. Let me just flip up the latch." John put his forefinger under the latch, pulled on the door. Pulled again.

"Dammit!" Dennis yanked on the door with his left hand, pistol in his right.

As he did, Moses unlatched it from the inside, Dennis fell backward as Moses charged out of the steeple to land on him, hands around his throat. Dennis fired wide, then fought him off using his pistol as a billy club. Moses had not yet regained his strength. This exertion reopened his wound.

John Schuyler put his hands around Dennis's throat. So powerful was the man that Dennis was dead in less than a minute. Choked to death with a broken larynx. John threw him on the straw. "Moses, get back in the steeple." Noticing the bleeding, John said, "We will examine that later. We need to move along before someone else comes along."

Charles called back, "Push him under the straw. When we find a likely place, we can throw him off."

Sweating a bit, John jumped down. Slightly loosening the horse's girth, he climbed up next to Charles, who had the flintlock in his right hand.

"You can put that away now," John said.

Charles wrapped the flintlock back in the leather.

"I'm glad I didn't have to fire it. Too much noise. No telling who it would bring."

"I could dig a big hole," Piglet offered.

John breathed deeply as Charles clucked to Castor and Pollux. "How did he figure it out?"

"I don't know, but if Hiram sent him, we will make it to York before anyone else reaches us. If we don't encounter bad weather or a band of thieves, we will make it."

"We will, but if Hiram sent him, he will go to Ewing. He will search the farm." John felt his stomach drop.

"We must rely on the judgment and intelligence of our wives if Hiram did send him." Charles was as worried as John, but why show it? "My judgment is we can't let an innocent man die. We've brought Moses this far."

"Yes," John opined.

They drove another two hours, the sun setting. A grove of thick trees lay up ahead on their right. They'd passed people walking, a few riding but the road had been quiet. Charles turned off toward a grove. He stopped the two gentle Percherons by the side of the road, climbing down.

John got down on his side. Happy to have a pause, the horses closed their eyes.

Back up on the wagon, John pulled out Dennis's body as if he were a sack of wheat. He threw his body over the side, jumped down. Taking Dennis's arm while Charles took his legs, they carried the corpse to the grove, swinging him twice to pitch him in.

Walking back to the cart, John wondered, "Maybe we should have gone through his pockets?"

"No. If someone finds him before the buzzards, they'll clean him out. If Dennis carried anything which might signify that it belonged to him, the thief will be thought the murderer."

"And his horse?"

"We give it to Bartholomew as payment. No one will travel to York, Pennsylvania, see that horse, and recognize it. I've never seen him on that horse. Must be new."

An hour later, deep twilight, they pulled off at a farmhouse and asked if they could sleep in the barn, feed and water their horses. Charles produced two silver dollars, more than adequate. The farmer took it.

Once in the barn, John unhitched Castor and Pollux, placing them in the small paddock. He filled up wooden water buckets and threw out fragrant hay. He then untacked Dennis's horse, put the gelding in an adjoining paddock, threw hay, and gave him fresh water.

With the door to the steeple open, Charles said, "Clear."

Stiffly, Moses stood up, stepped out.

Charles opened his shirt. "Stopped bleeding," he reported.

He jumped down, took a piece of cloth from the trunk tied to the inside of the wagon, dripped it in water he pumped up, and handed it to Moses, who put it on the wound.

John and Charles wiped down all three horses, patted them on their necks. The men then cleaned the horse collars, as well as the bridle and saddle from Dennis's horse.

"Ssst." Charles whistled low, for he spied a swinging lantern coming their way. Moses hurried back into the steeple.

A woman, perhaps in her fifties, the farm wife, carried a basket. "I thought you might be hungry." She smiled. "Three apples for your horses."

Charles reached into his pocket, pulling out another coin.

She put out her hand. "No, no, sir. You've paid us enough."

"You are very kind." Charles smiled.

"We start work at sunup."

"We will be on our way by then." Charles smiled again. "You've built a sturdy barn."

She smiled. "My father and his brothers. I believe this barn will be standing when I am long gone."

"No time soon, I trust."

"I take your leave."

Charles bowed slightly. "Good night, madam."

John called as he walked in from the paddock, saddle over his arm. "Good night."

Once they no longer saw the flickering lantern, the two climbed into the wagon and sat down with the basket between them.

"Moses."

Moses stepped out.

"Sit down. We've been visited by an angel." Charles

lifted the cover to the basket, and if she wasn't an angel, she certainly was a good cook. The aroma of sliced ham, corn on the cob, a heavenly apple cobbler, and a tankard of cold tea was shared.

Once they'd eaten, John and Moses scrubbed the plate, the big bowl, the wooden spoons, and the two knives, as well as the tankard, while Charles, retrieving his sketchbook, pulled out a well-wrapped bottle of ink he'd ground himself and a quill, then drew a certificate of thanks. He wanted to put the name of the owners of the farm in the center.

"Fletcher. Wasn't that the name?" Charles asked.

"Is," John, now exhausted, replied. "The owner introduced himself as Kevin Fletcher."

The name, in Charles's cursive hand, filled the center of the paper, and underneath he added the flourish: *Twilight Farm.*

That morning as the sun rose, the Virginians were already on their way. The carefully washed plate, bowl, tankard had been placed in the basket with the thank-you rolled up.

Kevin Fletcher picked it up, was going to wait until he'd done his barn chores, then thought he'd take it up to his wife.

She opened the basket, pulled out the paper, exclaiming when she saw it. "Kevin, what does it say?"

"'To Mr. and Mrs. Fletcher, thank you for your kindness.'" Then he traced the name underneath. "'Of Twilight Farm.'"

"How beautiful." She clasped her hands under her chin.

Her husband smiled. "Not bad."

Two hours down the road, John and Charles took a right fork heading northeast. With luck, they'd be in York inside three days, maybe two.

The gelding walked behind the wagon. John fashioned a rope halter for him so he wouldn't need to wear a bit.

Charles twisted to check on him. "Seems a fine fellow."

"We can't keep calling him Dennis's horse."

"We're heading for York. We could call him Martin Luther." Charles smiled.

John smiled, too. "Martin will do."

31

Thursday, September 30, 1784

"I know perfectly well if I had laid Francisco to rest at the church cemetery, sooner or later someone would build a tomb higher than his." Maureen Selisse lowered her voice to Catherine and Rachel. "You know how some people are. So the grave there was simply to place his casket in, and once the reception was over, we moved him back here."

Catherine admired the large rectangular marble. "The base is most impressive."

"His dates are already carved and so beautifully," Rachel added to her sister's praise.

With a flourish of her hand, Maureen remarked, "Italians. No one can work with marble like they can. One can be happy about King George losing the war for many reasons. Leaving behind Italians in the prisoner-of-war camps is one of them."

Shadowed by Sheba and Bettina, the three women

turned toward the house. Sheba couldn't stand Bettina. It was mutual, but both women put a good face on it.

"I can't believe my husband has been gone over two weeks. It already seems a lifetime," Maureen intoned, the grief perfunctory as her voice didn't register a note of it although she had loved him as a young woman. Time had taken care of that. "Tomorrow is already October, and such a lovely day. How was your apple crop, by the way?"

"Father is so happy he's planning to expand the orchard," Catherine answered.

"Perhaps I should as well. Your father has always said the soils and altitude beg for apple trees. Only Ewing would say 'beg.' Such a brilliant conversationalist."

"You bring it out in men." Rachel said this with a straight face.

"Tsh." Maureen again waved her hand. "You two ladies will have a light repast with me."

"We couldn't put you to such trouble." Catherine smiled. "I'm here on business."

"It is no trouble, and I long for conversation with ladies of quality. This place has been overrun with men since Francisco's terrible end. *Can they get me this? Am I planning to sell the southernmost acres, and if I am would I consider them first?* Dreary. When Francisco was alive he, as was natural, tended to such things. I had no idea men were so boring." She laughed.

The sisters joined in, then Catherine smiled slyly. "A

few are not. I find, Mrs. Selisse, if they are handsome, their conversation shines a bit brighter."

"Catherine, you shock me," Maureen said in jest.

Once seated, the food set before them by two young slaves doing their best not to catch the Missus's eye, the three enjoyed the cold soup, beginning the "light repast," which could have filled an elephant.

"Sheba!" yelled Maureen.

Hurrying into the dining room, Sheba looked at her mistress as though whatever was about to issue from her mouth would be the most important statement of all time.

"Do see that Bettina enjoys some lunch, and, Sheba"—Maureen looked coyly at Catherine—"see if you can wrest her biscuit recipe from her."

A half bob and Sheba left.

"Your Bettina is a woman of strong opinion." Maureen laughed lightly. "As well as one of the best cooks high or low."

"She does evidence strong opinion, and you know, Mrs. Selisse, she is often right," Catherine replied.

"Well, Sheba is not often right. She dithers. She picks out one necklace for me to wear, then tries another, and I can't get her to move faster. However, she is loyal and stood right next to me during that horrid assault. She could have run and she did not."

Rachel praised her again. "You could have run, too, Mrs. Selisse. Your courage has not gone unnoticed."

"I tell you the truth, I was so shocked I couldn't move.

Then a rage washed over me such as I never felt before in my life." Maureen frowned. "Well, let us talk of happier things."

"We could start with you telling us where you found that exquisite taffeta." Catherine spoke of the loose, sky-blue taffeta dress Maureen wore, bound with a beaded sash.

"France. Francisco always said France is the richest country in Europe, and when one sees the fabrics, the jewels, the furniture, just the furniture alone, he must be right. No one of even handsome means can afford it. One needs great sums, and I hear the king is not interested in such luxuries but that he would rather fix clocks. I can't imagine it. Must be some wild story."

"It does sound odd," said Rachel. "But then perhaps the clocks are gilded, encrusted with jewels," she added.

Catherine changed the subject. "Mrs. Selisse, you have created such beauty here, the house, your furnishings, your gardens. Your gardens alone are worth a trip from darkest Massachusetts." They laughed as Catherine continued. "I know that Yancy Grant offered you four thousand dollars for Serenissima. That is not enough."

Maureen's eyebrows raised. "Oh."

"It is a good price, but the mare has excellent conformation, an easy temperament, and she is with foal. She is worth more than that, even if you do not use her for a saddle horse. Yancy will run her, of course, then make a profit breeding her and selling the foals. Four thousand is too low."

"I see." She put her fork down.

"If you wish to breed the mare, I will help in any way. I do not want to see someone take advantage of you. But if you want to sell Serenissima, I don't know your plans, I will pay you seven thousand dollars."

Rachel burst out, "Seven thousand!"

This outburst was planned.

Maureen countered with, "Ewing Garth would pay that for a mare in foal for the first time?" The woman wasn't as dumb as some thought about horses.

"No, this is my money," said Catherine. "It is part of what Mother left to me. I don't want to see such a fine animal run to the ground. She is beyond compare, Mrs. Selisse. She reflects in the flesh what you have accomplished here." Catherine swept her arm away from her to indicate the whole farm.

As though an afterthought, Rachel said, "Have you been swayed by Jeffrey Holloway?"

Maureen, utterly focused now, looked at Rachel then Catherine. "Mr. Holloway?"

As though with reluctance, Catherine looked directly into Maureen's eyes. "When he came to inspect Serenissima, according to your request, he mentioned that Yancy Grant was trying to buy her and he, well, how shall I put this, he was not sure that Mr. Grant harbored your best interests but he, as a cabinetmaker, could not say much against Mr. Grant."

"Did he, now?" Maureen oozed fascination.

"Oh, Catherine, you know he's smitten with Mrs. Selisse," Rachel said.

As though appalled, Catherine said, "What is wrong with you, Rachel? After all Mrs. Selisse has endured, she doesn't need to worry about a young man's tender feelings."

"Now, now, Catherine, don't be too hard on Rachel," cooed Maureen. "Jeffrey Holloway has been helpful and he lightens a room. Of course, I had no idea."

What a fib.

"Well, you certainly can't miss the clumsy attempts of some of the other men," Rachel said. "At least Mr. Holloway is sensitive to your feelings. He would never push himself. He may be a cabinetmaker, but he is a fine man." Rachel glared at Catherine, who glared back.

"Rachel, will you please desist and—"

"Rachel, I am not offended," said Maureen. "I am pleased to know that you two are solicitous of my well-being. Yes, I know why many of these men are continually calling with this and that. But like you, Rachel, I do think Mr. Holloway truly cares and has my best interests at heart."

"Might we get back to Serenissima?" asked Catherine.

Thrilled with the turn of conversation, Maureen managed to think again about the mare. "I accept."

Catherine then surprised her by opening the small beaded bag that hung from her waist almost like a jewel. She took out a written check to be drawn from her account in the amount of seven thousand dollars.

Isabelle Garth established separate accounts for each of her daughters with a bank in Richmond. Isabelle also believed that Alexander Hamilton would lead the new nation into solvency and subsequent profit. Never revealing her own financial acumen to anyone other than her husband or her daughters, she had an uncanny sense to know where profits would be made. Among many other abilities, this drew her close to Ewing, and he had rarely made a decision without discussing it with her first.

"Catherine!" Rachel exploded.

Catherine reached over, putting her hand on her sister's forearm. "I am doing the right thing, and don't go running to Father."

"All right," Rachel agreed, quite thrilled at how their plan worked.

No sooner had Maureen placed the paper folded next to her plate than a sheepish Sheba came into the room. "Missus, Lemuel says Hiram Meisner is at the door and should he allow him inside?"

"Send him in." Maureen lifted up her hands, palms inward. "Whatever it is, I want you to hear it."

A humble Hiram entered, standing. "Mrs. Selisse."

"Yes, Hiram."

"On Tuesday morning, Dennis McComb's wife came to me with apologies saying that Dennis would be tracking Moses and would not be back until he captured him. He thought he knew where the killer was fleeing."

"Yes." Maureen did not ask the constable to sit, but he didn't expect it.

"He has not returned and he was riding your gelding. Nor has he sent word."

"I see," she coolly answered. "Did Dennis say where he thought Moses was running and where he heard such a thing?"

Hiram sighed. "He did not tell his wife."

"And?"

"I fear Moses has killed again."

"Oh, Mr. Meisner, I do hope you are wrong," Catherine interjected, keeping the pretense that she thought Moses was the killer.

"I do, too, Mrs. Schuyler, but Dennis would have sent word if he had captured the man. Since I don't know where he went, I don't know how long it would have taken to reach me, but a horse trotting and galloping can cover many miles a day, as you know. I should have heard something."

"Well, I am sorry to hear this," Maureen simply replied.

"The gelding—"

"Don't worry, Hiram."

"Thank you, madam." He bowed and left.

After they heard Lemuel's voice and the door close, the three remained silent.

Finally, Rachel spoke. "At least Moses is away from here."

"But what of the woman, that terrible woman?" Maureen's voice rose.

Catherine calmly said, "If he killed because of her or to steal her, he wouldn't run away and leave her. She must be with him."

Maureen weighed the thought. "True."

Sighing inwardly, Rachel added, "It must be a relief to know they are fleeing."

"It's certainly better than having them here," Maureen agreed. "But I look forward to the day when they are caught and punished."

"It may take some time, but I'm sure they will be." Catherine sounded truthful. "Forgive me for being forward, but, Mrs. Selisse, might you consider hiring a strong fellow or someone you can trust to manage the farm or to simply protect you until things become more clear? You're here with your people, of course, but with no strong protector."

"Mr. Holloway would do it." Rachel sounded all innocence.

"Rachel, that really is enough!" Catherine scolded.

Pretending such an idea was foreign to her, Maureen smiled indulgently at Rachel. "I am most grateful for your concern and most grateful, Catherine, that you will now own Serenissima. I am not a horseman. Well, you know that. I enjoy a ride, but you should have the mare."

"Who will tell Yancy Grant?" Catherine asked.

A smile crossed Maureen's slightly colored lips. "I will."

Driving home, Catherine holding the reins, for she loved anything to do with horses and she was a good whip, the two sisters and Bettina giggled, exchanging stories. Then they considered what might have happened to Dennis McComb.

"Something about him. I couldn't abide him," Rachel said.

"He's dead, I expect, or he'd be back by now," said Catherine. "Either he was set upon by robbers or he met with an accident." She felt the smooth leather in her fingers.

Catherine, Rachel, and Bettina drove, dappling sunlight bouncing off the two horses' hindquarters.

"I think horses enjoy a good carriage ride as much as we do." Rachel noticed King David's pricked ears and alert expression, as well as Solomon's happiness.

"I like the rhythm." Bettina smiled. "Miss Catherine, you got your Serenissima."

"So I did." Catherine grinned, then changed the subject. "Wasn't it odd to be with two murderesses and act as we did?"

"We have no choice," Rachel replied.

"I can bear Miss Selisse more than that two-faced bitch who destroyed Ailee's face." Bettina clipped her words.

"Even if Maureen Selisse hadn't killed Francisco, we wouldn't warm to her. Vain. Arrogant. Possessive." Catherine thought out loud. "Then again, she had endured his philandering under her nose probably for years. Ailee can hardly have been the first."

"I suppose," Rachel agreed.

"It's not so much the loss of love, it's the humiliation," Catherine opined.

"People don't always need a reason to kill," Bettina shrewdly noted, then smiled. "Miss Selisse and Sheba will be yoked together for the rest of their lives. That's punishment enough."

Catherine and Rachel laughed.

Then Catherine asked Bettina, "What did you find out?"

"Mrs. Selisse has commissioned a statue for her husband's tomb and it will take a year to be carved. Sheba says it will rival great statues in Europe. Mrs. Selisse is paying a fortune for it." Bettina rocked sideways a little with the carriage motion. It was an open carriage, so the breeze felt wonderful on her cheeks.

"A statue of what?" Rachel inquired.

"The Avenging Angel, flaming sword in hand," said Bettina, nodding. "You know there is a flaming sword which turns in all directions at the east of Eden to guard the tree of knowledge." Bettina sure knew her Bible.

"So Maureen's put the sword in the hand of an angel," Rachel said. "Or maybe there is such an angel and I don't know much about it."

"Well, we know there is one east of Eden," Catherine declared. "Genesis, chapter six, or is it five? Anyway, it's Genesis," Catherine declared.

"Now, why did Adam eat that apple?" Bettina wondered. "And then we womenfolk get all the blame? Bearing children in pain and working our fingers to the bone. All because of one shiny apple. And we've got acres and acres of them at home. But why did Adam eat that one apple and make such a fuss?"

"Because he was as dumb as a sack of hammers." Catherine let out a peal of laughter.

They laughed, gossiping all the way back home.

32

Wednesday, August 10, 2016

Sam Holloway lay back in his recliner. The ex-governor fell in and out of sleep. Although a lifelong Virginian, and one would think he'd root for the Orioles or the Nationals, but he'd always been a Phillies fan. But even Sam's beloved Phillies couldn't keep him alert, although a double play brightened his outlook, before he fell back asleep.

Outside, the high humidity and a high temperature convinced even the insects to slow down or sleep. Maybe Sam was following suit.

Penny peeked in. His wife knew better than to turn off the TV when a baseball game was on. She also knew better than to say too much about her favorite team, the Kansas City Royals.

For their generation, baseball was the game; football followed second.

Walking back to the air-conditioned sunroom where

she'd been working on a needlepoint pillow, her daughter ducked in. Millicent Grimstead came to the house each day and stayed most of the day to help her mother and cheer her father.

"You've made progress." Millicent dropped in a chair. "Wendell, here."

The dog came over and Millicent gave him a new Wubba.

Penny thought the toy looked strange. "Where did you get that thing?"

"PetSmart. It is strange. But it's supposedly indestructible. PetSmart isn't making that claim for the canvas streamers at the end of the Wubba, but they do say the ball itself is tough."

"I'm sure Wendell will give it a try." Penny smiled as the handsome dog happily took his new toy politely from Millicent's hand, then ran out of the room.

"Where's he going?"

Her mother replied, "Oh, he has a stash. Well, he has a few. Under the bed. Behind the old tack trunk in the mud room. He's good at hiding things."

"How's Dad?"

Penny hesitated. "That ruckus with Eddie took something out of him. He's quieter, withdrawn. And withdrawn is not your father."

"No. Daddy wasn't even that upset when I wrecked the truck when I was seventeen."

Penny dropped her hands in her lap, the needle with the red thread still in her right hand. "He was rather composed over that, but as I recall he stomped around quite a bit for days. I could hear him, *thump, thump, thump.* He'd talk to the insurance agent, *thump, thump, thump.*" She laughed.

"Mother, what's wrong with Eddie? He's not right."

"Ask your sister, who is conveniently in Montana. I called her and reported the fray. She's torn, which is natural. She defends her son, even if she thinks he was in the wrong. She says he's under pressure."

"Who isn't?" Millicent shot back.

"There is that." Penny sighed, picking up her pillow and carefully inserting the needle.

"Mother, how do you have the patience to do needlepoint?"

"I raised you." Penny winked at her eldest daughter. "That's where I learned patience."

Millicent said, "And I raised your granddaughter. Our Susan is one step ahead of a running fit over this country club golf championship, which is only a month away. I think it's a month away, and I should know because Susan is obsessed with this. She's been runner-up two times, finished in the top four for over a decade."

"She wants her name on that huge silver trophy," said Penny. "Mary Pat Janss. Susan wants to be up there with her mentor."

"Another good person gone. Boy, you always knew where you stood with Mary Pat."

Penny laughed out louder than she'd planned. "That woman's speech could rust a cannon. Oh, I do miss her.

I miss so many of my old friends and new ones. It seems to me that so many young people are dying. Cancer. It's always cancer."

"Mother, sixty is young to you."

"What's wrong with that?" Penny pointed a finger at her daughter. "You're sixty-seven."

"Some days I feel it and some days I don't." Millicent heard Wendell throwing his new toy around. "Back to Eddie, I'm embarrassed."

"Ambition is outstripping good sense and good behavior. Your nephew doesn't just want to be senator, he wants power, more power than he has now in the statehouse. Eddie wants to go to the Senate or be tapped for a vice presidential slot in the future. Virginia has become a pivotal state, far more critical than when Sam and I were in the governor's mansion. Virginia was Democratic and that was that." She looked up from her pillow. "Now they call it a purple state. Each party has to fight and fight hard not just every four years but for Senate elections, seats to the statehouse. It's relentless, ruthless, and Eddie wants to be the big dog."

"Mother, he can't hold a candle to Daddy."

"Who can?" Penny then softly added, "Truthfully, Millicent, if your father were young today I don't think he would run for office."

"I'm surprised that that Ned Tucker did," Millicent remarked.

Penny laughed. "Not as surprised as his wife, but don't you think that was a fluke? A seat became available in the House of Delegates and he ran for it almost on a whim."

"Now he's got it, but I must say, he's rather a good public servant and Susan almost flourishes. Within reason, Mother." She smiled slightly at the thought of her daughter.

"I will tell you one thing that disturbed me. Eddie visited Dr. Fishbein, the hematologist, as well as Sam's oncology doctors. He wanted to know all about Sam's condition, the effects of leukemia, and he wanted to know, can it affect the mind? I found that odd. Eddie wanted a prognosis. In other words, he wanted to know how long Sam has to live."

"I hope Dr. Fishbein and the others didn't tell him."

"Of course not. Ethically, they can't. Dr. Fishbein wouldn't anyway. He and the team over there at Martha Jefferson have been wonderful. We all know how this will end. We just don't know when."

"Mother." Millicent hesitated. "How long do you think?"

Penny put down her pillow. "Honey, I don't know. Some days I think we've got three months and other days much less. And until Sam was diagnosed with the final stages of leukemia, I had no idea how painful it can be. He bears it with great fortitude. He doesn't speak of it and he tries hard not to show it. Sometimes I look at him and I see that young, oh so handsome man I married and I can't believe he's leaving us. Back then Sam seemed indestructible. Even during the whole awful segregation mess, the death threats from both directions, he never wavered. He might have been wrong, well, he was wrong, but he never wavered. It breaks my heart that that's what he will be remembered for first. And it breaks my heart to see him weaken."

"Me, too. Daddy could handle anything. Mother, Harry mentioned something when I was over at Susan's. She's been caddying for Susan and they'd come back from the golf course. Anyway, Harry said, 'Who has the most to gain by the governor living and who has the most to lose?' "

"Hmm."

"Harry comes at things sideways and she sees things we don't. I've been thinking about that and thinking about Eddie. Forgive me, but Eddie does stand to gain when Daddy dies. Then he can mourn front and center, if you will, and he can make emotional pledges about continuing Daddy's legacy."

Coolly, Penny appraised this. "He also has a great deal to gain by Sam living. He can ride on his coattails, use the old political machine unless Sam pulls back their support. Oh, yes, Eddie will get a boost when Sam goes, but as long as his grandfather lives he can say he speaks with him daily, et cetera, et cetera. Harry, though, has hit the nail on the head. Eddie is out for himself and only himself. I haven't wanted to face it. Now I must."

A knock on the doorjamb, then Mignon stepped in the room. "I'm sorry to disturb you, but Edward just called me. He asked to read what the governor and I have written so far. He says he wants to help. Maybe we can move it along faster, to finish before—"

With no show of emotion, Penny pulled the thread tighter in the pillow. "Mignon, I'm sure you told him no."

"Yes, Mrs. Holloway, I did. I also told him that to read work in progress without the author's permission is considered bad manners in publishing." She continued, "He said I was as much the author as your husband. He was persistent. I told him while I was working with the governor it was his life, I'm a jumped-up secretary. That ended the conversation."

"I can't speak for my grandson, who seems intent on upsetting everyone, but I am regretful that you had to be discomfited. Thank you for telling me."

"Yes, ma'am." Mignon left, returning to her small office next to the governor's library/office.

Putting down her pillow, Penny walked to the edge of the room and looked down the hallway. "Millicent, come with me. I don't want to shout for Mignon and wake Sam."

Mother and daughter knocked, then entered Mignon's makeshift office.

She rose. "Please sit down. You can have my seat."

"No, dear. Allow me to ask you a question. Has Sam ever discussed his medical condition with you?"

"He has said he has leukemia. Nothing more."

Penny's next question surprised them. "Did Barbara Leader ever discuss it?"

"No. She only confirmed that he needed his medication at specific times. Well, she also confirmed that it is painful and that there's not much more that can be done for him."

"I'm sorry to trouble you," said Penny.

"No trouble but may I make a suggestion?" Mignon pointed to her computer and the papers she had printed. "When I leave each day, I think we should secure the papers."

"We don't have a safe."

"The next best thing would be the freezer. No one would think to look in the refrigerator. And if for some reason, not much of a possibility but should there be a fire, the refrigerator will still be safe," Mignon suggested.

Millicent asked, "What about the computer?"

"I can put it in the trunk of my car, or perhaps somewhere else if you don't want to have it off the premises."

"Mother, why don't I take it with me each evening?" offered Millicent. "Not that your suggestion is improper, Mignon, only that if someone wants to spy on your work they would think you had pages or the computer. At least, I think they would. No one would suspect me."

"Good idea." Penny nodded.

33

Tuesday, October 5, 1784

York Square sent roads off in each direction. Well-built houses, many of them brick, lined these roads along with churches and schools.

More shops surrounded the square itself since travelers from each point, north, south, east, and west, passed through it. About three thousand souls lived in a ten-mile area around York. Filling that ten-mile area were stores, taverns, inns, sawmills, hemp mills, grain mills, two oil mills, and an impressive iron forge.

The activity fed growth. Fifteen boardinghouses, all concerned that they be known as God-fearing domiciles, housed newcomers who would soon enough buy farmland or open a business once they acquired enough cash. Indentured servants, some slaves and some freedmen, plumped up the numbers kept by officials. The good soil, the abundant water, and the industriousness of the inhabitants brought people in like iron filings to a magnet.

The houses in town had mews in the back, and behind those tidy places for horses ran straight alleys, some cobbled. The dream of the city fathers and some mothers, although unelected, was to pave all alleyways, all the main streets. Anything to vanquish the mud.

John, Charles, and Moses had been in York for two days. They stayed in a boardinghouse close to Bartholomew and Mary Graves. John and Charles surprised themselves with the flood of emotion that overcame them when they saw fellow ex-soldier Bartholomew. It was mutual.

Bartholomew showed the men St. John's Episcopal Church, which stood on the ground of York County Academy. Or perhaps the academy was on the church grounds. Built of fieldstone, it was simple but pleasing and it had wonderfully large windows. While Bartholomew taught his classes, the Virginia men walked the town that was truly filled with churches. Christ Lutheran, large, Georgian in design, once a log structure, was harmonious, retrained, beautiful. Charles made drawings of all of them.

John would look over Charles's shoulder while his brother-in-law executed swift strokes, in minutes capturing the subject on paper. Moses said little, but if he saw another person of African descent, they would nod to each other. It wasn't clear who was free and who was not. In Virginia if a slave rode or walked off the estate, he or she usually carried a small brass square or rectangle, indicating they were on an errand for the master.

Often the master's name was engraved on the chit, sometimes a number. As most people knew one another, it may have seemed unnecessary, but rumors abounded of gangs of white men who would steal slaves and freedmen, only to sell them to plantations farther south or in the opening Delta. Sugarcane broke down bodies, especially from the cutting, but the carting and then the burning proved arduous also. Rice, an easier crop in some ways, grew in terrible summer heat that was harder on human bodies than harvesting wheat, corn, or tobacco. A captured man fetched a good price, and many a slave dealer never asked where they came from. That brass chit might save someone and might not, but if the name on the chit was powerful, a thief would think twice.

John and Charles also noticed the ease with which Africans moved throughout York.

In the mews, Martin the horse won Mary's heart. Bartholomew hoisted his wife up on the fellow after he had a day's rest, and Martin, sweet and kind, gave her confidence. She gave him carrots and apples; nothing was too good for Martin. She insisted the farrier see him at once. She raised the ceramic teapot wherein she kept what she called her "mad money," marched out and bought Martin a blanket for winter.

A gregarious person, Mary not only didn't mind cooking for four men, Moses ate with them, and she outdid herself. The former combatants would tell stories about the war. Mary and Moses would listen.

As this was to be John and Charles's last night with the Graveses, Mary wanted it to be especially happy, with food so good the tales would reach Virginia.

The small house had a dining room that barely contained them.

They chattered on that night, and even somber Moses smiled.

"You men," Mary shook her head in admiration, "how quickly you closed in part of the loft for Moses." She turned to Moses. "The horsehair in the walls will help keep you warm and you will have heavy blankets but winters are hard here. You'll be glad to come into the kitchen for breakfast. Sunup."

"Yes, Miss Graves." He nodded.

Bartholomew would chide Mary about her soft heart. Yet when he saw her with Martin or when he heard her with Moses he knew he wouldn't have her any other way. Men could be too harsh. He knew he could.

"Can Virginia pay its bills?" Bartholomew asked John and Charles.

"Our governor says we can't. They argue all the time and the people resist taxes. The memories of the king's taxes are too recent," John replied. "If old King George had sent troops to protect us, engineers to help us, I sometimes think there would have been no rebellion."

Charles shrugged. "Kings think of power, of strutting across the stage. George thinks of Louis in France and wants to outshine him. He doesn't think of his subjects, even in England. As for Ireland, Wales, and Scotland," Charles said, "they exist to send men into troops, to send goods to London."

"As an Irishman, there's not much I can say about the king in a beautiful lady's company," Bartholomew said.

Mary blushed.

"Quite so." Charles beamed at Mary, who delighted them all with her cooking and her unforced warmth.

"Well, Bartholomew, can Pennsylvania pay its bills?" John asked.

"No," came the terse reply.

"Is this not the case with all former colonies?" John posited. "Heavy financial burdens and no effective way to discharge them? Congress is too weak."

Bartholomew laughed. "We had a visitor in the county, Colonel Hartley, who cautioned us for our 'lack of political life,' which is how he put it. We are too busy farming, tending to business, so to speak. But he said something else that struck me. He said that in republics, men ought to *think*, and we are in the infancy of thought. He's right, you know. Where else is there a republic?"

"Rome. Cicero's Rome." Charles laughed.

"Oh, we'll bump along," John added. "We have to, don't we? If we don't, ships will come from Europe and try to pick us off. Not just England, either. I suppose it's like my mother used to say, 'Sink or swim.' "

"Hear, hear," Bartholomew agreed.

• • •

The next morning, John and Charles hitched up Castor and Pollux. Moses came to bid them goodbye. "Thank you. Take care of my Ailee."

"We will," John promised.

Charles added, "You are free now, Moses. The manumission papers I forged look better than legitimate ones. Let Bartholomew keep them safe. Give them a year of labor. Everything is paid for and then do as you please, but don't come back to Virginia."

John put his hands on Moses's shoulders. "It would be death. Truly it would. Dennis's pursuit should have told you that, and you can't expose Ailee to danger."

"Can she not escape as I have?" Moses almost pleaded.

"Perhaps, but it will take time, and she will be fleeing with a baby," Charles stated. "So you would be exposing your love and your child to grave danger."

Tears filled Moses's eyes. "I know. Look after them."

John impulsively grabbed Moses's hand in his. "May God keep you. Trust in Him. He is all we have."

Martin whinnied when his friends left. They took the steeple with them, dropping it off just south of the town where they noticed a new church being built. No one was there, but they managed to lift it off. Charles left no note. Perhaps it would be considered a miracle.

Back in the wagon, they chattered about what they'd seen, heard, and, of course, Bartholomew and Mary, to whom they said farewell in the house.

They had given the Graveses the horse, a fine gift, but

they also left five hundred dollars for the feeding and care of Moses.

October 6 was brisk, promising to be a radiant fall day. York isn't that far from the Maryland line. The two now hoped they might be miles beyond it by nightfall.

"Well, have you thought about what we do when we arrive home?" Charles asked.

"Yes. We say nothing, we do nothing. If Hiram comes to us, we say we didn't see Dennis, and we don't know why he would wish to catch us up."

"True. We don't know who McComb told or what he told them if he did. Best not to say he was after us."

"Do you think Moses will stay in York?" John inquired.

"I don't know. He knows if found in Virginia, he will die. He might lead an intelligent constable to Ailee. He didn't strike me as stupid, only as beaten, saddened, lost."

"Yes." John nodded, then changed the subject. "It's different, killing a civilian, isn't it?"

"I didn't think about it. Kill or be killed." Charles considered what he'd just said. "Perhaps we wouldn't have been killed by McComb, but it would have ruined Ewing and we would have been hauled into court for conveying a murderer and stolen property."

"True, but I think about the Ten Commandments. Thou shalt not kill. But we put on a uniform and we're told to kill someone in a different uniform, someone who has done nothing to earn our enmity, except to fight for another power, a king. But kill we did and it's a sin. How do you know what's right from wrong?"

"You don't." Charles said this with finality. "I served the king with pride. Then he abandoned us in the prisoner-of-war camps. You, my enemy, treated me better than my own king and his council. And my countrymen killed American prisoners of war, jamming them in the holds of ships in Boston harbor, starving them, not tending to their wounds. This gnawed at me. An officer of long-standing, Bartholomew paid me to write false discharge papers and then he escaped. He told me this was a land for young men. If it hadn't been for Piglet"—Charles petted his constant canine friend—"I think I would have felt totally alone. I lived because some of the men under my command were prisoners with me and I was their commanding officer. But in time, John, I questioned everything, and I, too, escaped. So am I traitor to my king?"

"No. Your king abandoned you." John was sure of this. "You had to fend for yourself."

Returning to the subject of Dennis McComb, Charles said, "You and I should agree to the same story, which is we don't know anything."

"Yes."

They rode in silence for an hour, the *clip-clop* of Castor and Pollux soothing. Piglet fell asleep and quietly snored.

John finally spoke. "I never thought life could be so—" He tried to find the word or phrase.

Charles found it for him. "Complicated."

34

Friday, August 12, 2016

"I've put three hundred miles on this car in three weeks. That's the bugger about living out in the country. It's twelve miles to go buy a tomato." Harry looked down at the odometer on her Volvo station wagon, now reading 199,062.

"You don't have to go twelve miles. Walk in the backyard." Cooper noticed the sign for Zion Crossroads as they passed it, heading east on Interstate 64.

"True. I'm so glad you got an unexpected day off and Friday, too. I've been dying to go to Ledbury's and it's one thing after another. Haven't been able to get to it."

In downtown old Richmond, Ledbury's was a relatively new men's clothier, specializing in shirts designed by the owners. Harry wanted to buy a fancy shirt for Fair.

"It's so quiet in the car without the animals," Cooper remarked.

"I fear opening the door when I return home. Revenge." Harry had considerable experience with feline payback.

"Hey, I looked at your new website. That was up fast. What did you think of working with Rae Tait? We watched those video outtakes together, but I never asked you how it was working with Crozet Media."

"Good. I don't have much to compare it to, but I thought she was organized, creative, and careful about the money. She finished early and under budget. Now, there's a rare experience."

"We still have no idea who broke into the office," said Cooper. "Granted, it's not number one on the burner as nothing of value was lifted. Still, it irritates me."

"Maybe it was a couple of kids having a destructive or light-fingered moment," Harry posited. "Remember when every year mailboxes would be smashed by baseball bats? Kids. A couple of them were bored, decide to break in and see what's there."

"Right now it's as good an explanation as any, but I don't know. The good thing, there have been no other break-ins or attempted robberies. None in Crozet. Not Old Trail, either."

"I'd be tempted to break into Over the Moon and steal those beautiful notecards and some books, but I like Anne DeVault too much."

Cooper found driving on I-64 somewhat hypnotic. "Who would have thought a bookstore would succeed?"

Harry defended the little town. "Cooper, Crozet may not be much to look at, but its citizens do read."

"It's the old southern story. The money is out on big estates, while the towns not so much."

"Up until the Industrial Revolution, that was the story everywhere," said Harry, a history buff. "Can you imagine what the country looked like without railroad tracks, paved highways, telephone poles, and electrical poles? Lines hanging overhead. It must have been so beautiful and quiet. I mean, look at this four-lane highway. It could be any four-line highway until you're on the other side of the Mississippi. Looks different then." Harry liked the old roads but you couldn't make good time.

"We live in the twenty-first century. We have no choice but to deal with it," Cooper sensibly replied.

"People leave," said Harry. "They move far into the country or up into the mountains. We don't have to live like this." She paused. "Sometimes I just want to go, like deep into Wyoming or Montana or northern Nevada. Just far away from everything, and then I remember the screen door shutting, Dad walking into the house, or the smell of Mom's fried okra. I look at the mountains, I inhale the air, and I listen to the redtail hawk. I don't know as I could go anywhere else."

"Me, neither. Sometimes I think the opposite of you. I'll find a job on a big-city force and move up the ranks, more money. Every day will be filled with drama, crimes, people needing help. Like you, I look around and think, 'Do I really want to be the first woman police chief of Charlotte, North Carolina, or Philadelphia?' "

"Speaking of crime, anything new regarding Barbara Leader?"

Cooper shifted in her seat. "How new is new?"

"Coop." Harry's voice dropped.

"Yeah, well, a few oddities. Nothing big enough for the media, just oddities."

"And?"

The tall woman shrugged. "Background footwork. Barbara Leader did her undergraduate work at what was then Randolph-Macon College, which you probably knew. Upon graduating, she was accepted at the University of Virginia's nursing school, where she excelled. We questioned a few of her professors. She specialized in blood disorders because her younger brother died of leukemia. Everyone we spoke with mentioned her passion for the field, and that's how she wound up in hematology. Dr. Fishbein also praised her. After fifteen years in the hospital with his blessing and the other doctors', she switched over to home care. Dr. Fishbein said having someone of Barbara's caliber in a home nursing situation was uncommon. Usually it's people who can turn over the patient, give pills or shots, simple stuff like that."

"I forgot about her brother," Harry remarked. "He was still in junior high. How wonderful that she specialized in blood diseases."

"Dr. Fishbein thought Barbara's care prolonged lives.

He said she had an instinct for where the patient was and what he or she needed. And she wasn't afraid to argue with doctors, especially over medication." Cooper added, "She really cared."

Harry remembered her lifeless body in the driver's seat. "I'm sorry I didn't know her better."

"Here's the thing. She checked out thallium chloride from the hospital. Dr. Fishbein swears he did not prescribe it to anyone. Why would he? But Barbara checked it out, using her initials."

"You didn't tell me."

"Why would I? She signed an old logbook, which she placed in a desk drawer. She didn't use the computer to enter the information."

"Coop, that is odd. Maybe she made money selling it."

"To whom? People don't abuse thallium chloride. They want Oxycontin and stuff like that. And if she was selling it, why leave her initials in an old logbook?"

"Maybe she really was contemplating suicide."

"Always a possibility. I can't count the times when we've investigated a suicide and people said, 'They seemed fine.' Some people are obviously distressed. Others hid it. Barbara Leader was murdered."

"What does Rick think?"

"Murdered. The drug results in a swift death. One doesn't shoot up thallium chloride."

By the time they reached the outskirts of Richmond, both were still focused on this strange event.

Harry finally said, "What if Barbara took the drug to kill someone else? Maybe a patient in terrible pain."

"Thought of that, too. She had no record of any suspicious deaths on her watch. Also, her family and friends mentioned she was opposed to assisted suicide. Her husband quoted her as saying 'God gives life and God takes life, not us.' "

"What a moral tangle. Who wants to see someone suffer prolonged intense misery? But it does seem wrong to kill someone. And then I think of battle, especially prior to mechanized warfare, the coup de grace."

"Maybe this was a coup de grace, unlikely as that seems." Cooper flicked her fingernails on the passenger window, making a rapid rattling sound.

"She could have taken the drug to hand over to someone else whose spouse or child was suffering."

"Possible. Either out of compassion or for money."

"Coop, did she need money?"

"No. She and her husband were not rich but living within their means."

"That alone is a miracle," Harry ruefully said. "This is what I think. She lifted the drug. We don't know why but someone else knew. Either it was for them to put them out of misery or for them to kill someone out of mercy. That person, afraid that she might talk if there's suspicion, kills her."

"Possible."

"We need to find out who knew."

"Harry." Cooper raised her voice. "Once we found the

evidence everyone in the hematology department knew, as well as Dr. Fishbein's staff."

"Let me amend that. Who knew she took it who wasn't a medical person?" Harry turned off I-95, which she had switched onto as they approached Richmond. She took the Broad Street exit.

"Why are you taking this exit? Ledbury's is farther downtown on South Fourteenth Street."

"'Cause if I take the Broad Street exit, I know where I am. Richmond used to be easy to drive in. Not anymore," Harry defended her driving. "Another thought. Maybe Barbara taking the thallium chloride has nothing to do with suffering."

"Harry, that's impossible. Why would she or anyone want such a lethal drug?"

"Maybe it is murder, pure and simple."

"So she knew too much? She was too compassionate to kill someone else. Not the type to assist in murder for reasons which we can't fathom. Suffering makes more sense."

"It does, but as you know better than I, murder always makes sense to the murderer. And most murderers believe they will never be caught. Maybe Barbara or her family was threatened. She left evidence that she took the thallium chloride. It wasn't immediately obvious, but she wanted it known for other reasons. Maybe she left a clue because she feared for her own life."

Once at Ledbury's, they opened the door to be greeted by a handsome wire-haired fox terrier.

"Willoughby, where's Daddy?" Harry recognized the fellow, tail vigorously wagging.

"Dazzled by choices." Bill Hall's deep voice rang out.

The two women joined him where he had shirts spread on a table. In good shape, he could wear anything but was stymied by all the choices and colors.

Harry and Cooper knew Bill from his work for the Fur Ball, one of Richmond's coveted fund-raisers, as it was always fun, plus it helped animals.

Pointing to a subtle striped shirt, Harry suggested it "Very Belgravia," mentioning an old, desirable section of London.

"Is," he replied. "And what are you two doing here?"

"A husband run. Wanted to buy Fair something special," Harry said.

"No husband yet," Cooper joked.

"Well, that's both good and bad. Men can be a lot of work." Bill laughed devilishly, then inquired, "How's Governor Sam?"

Bill knew the Albemarle County contingent as they came to the Fur Ball, he knew Susan was Sam Holloway's granddaughter, and he also knew the governor. Bill knew everyone, having served on numerous committees, and he was a real whiz as a fund-raiser.

"Good spirits. Penny's wonderful with him, as is Susan's mother. He's working on his autobiography."

"That will be an important book." Bill meant that.

"Hey, how's O.B.?" Harry changed the subject.

O.B. meant the "other Bill," as Bill Hall's partner had

the same first name. It could get confusing but never to Willoughby because they smelled different. All humans do but they don't seem able to detect it.

"An engine of energy and chat, as always." Bill smiled broadly. "Before I forget, check out Fetch-A-Cure, the comprehensive oncology center. They're doing amazing things that might eventually help people." He paused, then inquired, "The governor has cancer, doesn't he?"

Harry replied, "Leukemia."

"Ah." Bill grimaced.

Cooper added, "The man is really tough."

"You have to be to be the governor of Virginia, especially when people can cite precedent back to 1607." Bill said, "Not the cannibalism, of course."

They all laughed, especially Willoughby who then interjected, *"I could run this state."*

Bill reached down to pet the handsome head. "How can anyone live without a dog? I couldn't get up in the morning without this fellow."

"Some people have no feeling for animals." Cooper had certainly seen enough of that in her work.

"Speaking of that." Bill picked up the striped shirt. "Can you believe Eddie Cunningham using his grandfather like that? Eddie's doing a good job of whipping up the disaffected. I guess they need someone upon whom to blame their troubles."

"It is shocking," Harry agreed. "But, Bill, I suppose these are the times in which we live. It's dog-eat-dog."

"I resent that," Willoughby barked.

35

Wednesday, October 6, 1784

The eastern side of the Blue Ridge Mountains glowed golden, then reddish, as the sun rose. At sunset the displays behind the range varied from a thin silver shine outlining the mountains to explosions of swirling scarlet, pink, lavender, gold, purple. Few people living within sight of these ancient mountains could resist being mesmerized by them. At sunrise, the mountains themselves change color as the sun, rising in the east, touches them.

Not yet nineteen, Jeddie fell under their spell. Sometimes, with a task completed, he'd sit on an upturned box, a hay bale, or the top of a fence and just stare. He thought about the horses, his desire to improve as a rider and a horseman. He was fascinated by breeding. One needed a powerful memory and for the last three years Jeddie studied every horse he saw, on the estate and off. He would recite their pedigrees the way some men recited John Milton. The more fun-loving recited Chaucer.

This morning, he led Serenissima through a heavy dew. She played with him. She'd push him with her nose. He'd correct her. She'd push his shoulder. Then he'd turn her out. She'd fly away, stop abruptly, turn to thunder right toward him. Then she'd stop in front of him and smack her lips. The lip smack meant many things, and "I love you" was one of them.

He'd pull her lower lip, run his hands over her ears; he'd smack his lips, too. She repeated the running away, the return, and finally a big, big kiss as long as he would continue playing with her.

This morning they played for twenty minutes, the lovely early morning light softening everything.

Jeddie didn't hear Catherine walk up behind him until Serenissima flicked her ears.

"Jeddie."

He straightened up. "Yes, Miss Catherine."

"She likes you best."

Pleased, he tilted his head to the side for a second and Serenissima nuzzled his cheek. "I love her, Miss Catherine. I will sleep in her stall if she needs me. I will do anything you ask or she asks." His ear-to-ear grin made Catherine grin back. "I knew you wouldn't let Yancy Grant have her!"

Catherine held out her hand for the mare to sniff. "He knows horses, but he doesn't care about them. It's all money to Yancy."

"Everyone around knows he offered Mrs. Selisse four thousand dollars for her."

"That he did. I offered more and this morning I'm feeling poor." She laughed. "Well, Mother left me some of her money. I expect she thought I would use it as I saw fit. If we breed her with care, I think we will establish one of the finest lines of blooded horses in the country."

"Yes, ma'am."

"Jeddie, there are fine horsemen all over. I find the northern breeders look for a longer angle on the hip. Here, I'll show you." She traced an elongated isosceles triangle on Serenissima's hip. "They want carriage horses. More towns up there, and the estates are smaller. Soils not much in many of those states. A man with exceptional driving horses is a big bug. Here, more riding, running. But wherever breeders are, at least what I have observed, is they aren't systematic."

"Yes, ma'am. That's why I've memorized the bloodlines you told me about."

Catherine smiled at this young man. "Good. Now tell me, how is Crown Prince doing?"

"He can be ornery, but he's quick to learn."

"Queen Esther's bloodline is." She inhaled the air. "Doesn't it smell and taste like fall?"

"Yes, ma'am."

"Here come Binks and Ralston."

The two younger boys reached the paddock.

Catherine teased one of them. "The sun came up, but you didn't."

Binks, twelve, looked stricken. "Miss Catherine, Momma said I had to sweep out the room."

"Binks, that doesn't take that long, but better not to get on the bad side of your momma. Jeddie and I will be back in a little while. But you have time to loosen up Sweet Potato, and Ralston, walk out King David."

"Yes, ma'am." Ralston liked King David, such a powerful fellow.

As Cooper and Jeddie walked toward the row of slave quarters, she said, "You've been wise, keeping quiet about Moses when he and DoRe brought the mare."

"Yes, ma'am."

"If people knew what Moses had asked of me to save Ailee from Francisco, they might think all manner of things. Sometimes, Jeddie, I wonder what goes on in people's heads. Not much that's good, I fear."

"Yes, ma'am. Too much loose talk."

With piles of firewood neatly stacked by the front door, walkways swept, back gardens tended, and colorful flowers by porches, on windowsills, the cabins bore testimony to the artistic impulses of the inhabitants. The slaves didn't have much, but they made the most of what they had. In particular, the women cared about their flowers. Serena grew huge mums. No one else could match her mums. They all tried. Her sight failing, Old Paulette nurtured her white and purple morning glories, which climbed around her porch posts.

Catherine loved the display. She did her best with her mother's garden, but she lacked the touch.

Walking down the straight row of cabins brought back memories of her mother in rapt discussion about their flowers with other ladies, who had also departed. Catherine would stand next to her mother as theories abounded and once she remembered Paulette, straight as a stick then, getting worked up with the late Abby over the merits of acorn squash versus pattypan. Paulette was a pattypan devotee.

They reached the weaving cabin, the last in the row, close to the woodline.

Catherine opened the door, the big loom in the center of the large room.

"I like to hear the *click-clack*." Jeddie noticed the rug on the loom, half finished.

"Me, too. A woman needs good hands and a good eye for this work. One mistake and you've ruined the pattern. Let's go upstairs."

The wooden boards reverberated as they climbed up.

"They finished this in jack time." Jeddie admired the loft.

"Did. I wish they could have tapped into the chimney and built a fireplace up here. Maybe next year. That would take so much reinforcement and time. It's always warmer up top so maybe winter won't be so bad up here. Just go to bed with a well-stoked fire."

"Yes, ma'am."

Catherine looked out the window. The place had real

glass, not an oiled skin pulled up or down. At the back of the cabin, the newly built kitchen jutted out. They realized one couldn't really cook close to the loom and the stored hemp, cotton, linen, and wool, all of which lay on their sides on square shelves downstairs and now upstairs. The large center fireplace in the large cabin also had a mesh screen, a luxury, again to make certain no embers escaped from a downdraft, given the flammable contents of the cabin.

The stairs reverberated again as the two descended. Catherine poked her head in the kitchen. That newly built brick fireplace had on each side huge hearth openings in which to place freshly baked bread. The bread stayed warm next to the flame yet protected from it.

Fireplaces and hearths demanded a careful sense of detail. Those slaves involved in carpentry, masonry, bricklaying, flue building, knew what they were doing. A few had such renown they could be identified by their brickwork or stone work.

Standing in the center of the main room, a cot at one end with a small bureau and table, Jeddie asked, "Is Mr. Ewing gonna make a glassworks?"

"My father resisted spending the money for the glass in this building. Now he thinks he can lure glassblowers here and build a furnace for them. He says if we have our own small forge, we should have our own glassblowers. I asked where he thought he would find them. He said he didn't know but he would find them. That's my father."

Jeddie smiled. "Yes, ma'am." He changed the subject. "When are John and Charles coming home?"

"Soon, I should think. They will be full of stories."

"Yes, ma'am."

As they walked back, the sun higher now, Catherine spoke. "Jeddie, Bumbee will move into the loom cabin. She knows everything about weaving and Bettina said she wasn't getting along with Howard."

Howard was Bumbee's husband, a man with a roving eye. His body roved with it. Bumbee was in her late thirties, and possessed good sense as well as artistic talent. Her rugs, even shirt clothes, had a tight weave or a loose weave, whatever you needed. When asked how she found designs, especially for the rugs, she swore she would dream about them, wake up, and she had it.

The loft also had an outside stairway so one could come and go unnoticed. The woodline would provide cover for Ailee if she left the loft.

"Bumbee threw a pot at Howard yesterday."

"Hit him?"

Jeddie laughed. "No."

"Bet he ran like the devil."

Jeddie laughed. "That man burnt the wind getting away from her."

"I would, too." Catherine laughed as well. "If you should see anything, you know, out of the way, down there, someone you don't know, go up the back stairs and warn them."

"Yes, ma'am."

"And keep the little ones out of there. There's Sweet Potato." Catherine put her hands on her hips. "Well, Binks, she hasn't bucked you off."

"No, Miss Catherine, not yet."

Catherine looked at Jeddie. "Come on. I'll race you to the stable. Let's see who can tack up first."

Jeddie won, but they rode out together, joining Binks and Ralston. Supposedly the four were working horses but really, they reveled in a gorgeous October morning.

That night was fog enshrouded and damp. Bettina and Father Gabe led Ailee out of the cave. Her blind side got scraped with limbs and bushes, but they made it to the loom room.

Father Gabe opened the door. Bumbee wasn't moved in yet. The place, quiet, chilled to the bone. Father Gabe built a fire while Bettina, lighting her lantern now that they were inside, led Ailee up the stairs. Ailee studied the room. It was clean with a bit of color on the floor as Bumbee put down one of her red-and-yellow rugs. A small bed with a horsehair mattress covered in canvas was tucked in the corner. Bettina had made the bed with old sheets and two blankets. A pitcher, bowl, and water stood on the nightstand.

"Ailee, the men will carry up a bureau tomorrow. We'll fill it with clothes. You'll be able to keep warm. All will be well."

Ailee nodded.

"If anyone comes that you don't know, or you see a white man walking down the row and you don't know him, you go out that door, out the stairs, and the woods are right there. There's a narrow path, you can go as far down as you like. No one will see you go out. One of us will come and bring you back when all is safe." Bettina liked the loft, liked being able to look out high. "I will visit you every day and Bumbee will cook until you can. God bless." Bettina kissed her cheek.

Once alone, Ailee walked around, touching everything. Then she lay down on the bed, pulled up a blanket. The left side of her face still hurt.

What a good place this would be to live with Moses. She cried and cried, finally falling asleep.

36

Monday, August 15, 2016

"Cooler down here." Harry welcomed the temperature.

"Remind me why we're down here," Susan grumbled as she followed the narrow deer trail along the creek.

"I knew we should have stayed at home," Pewter complained in chorus with Susan.

Mrs. Murphy sidestepped a tree root. *"We could leave you here."*

"But then we'd have to come back." Tucker leapt over the root.

"I never said anything about coming back." Mrs. Murphy brushed against an increasingly irritated Pewter.

Without a peep, Owen, Tucker's brother, steadfastly followed the two humans.

"You promised your DAR chapter that you'd walk the creek that used to divide the old Garth property down to your grandparents' farm, which was founded shortly before the Revolution. Was the Selisse farm first."

"I did." Susan took a breath. "I never realized how far it was."

"On the topo map, it reads five miles over various terrain."

"My ancestors didn't walk this creek. They used the farm roads. Why am I walking? What was I thinking?" Susan complained louder.

"The old map from the time, the one around the time of the Jefferson-Fry map, shows this creek. Well, it shows all the tributaries into the rivers, of which this was one. Running water changes, so banks change, bends change, and the modern map shows some differences. We are walking to see it and to see if any old foundations are visible," Harry patiently explained, for she was fascinated by natural phenomena. "Remember, back then, many of the poor built right by water so they wouldn't have far to haul it. Digging a well could be expensive."

"Still is." Susan sat on a big stump. "Let me catch my breath."

"Sure." Harry plopped down on an upturned log.

The dogs happily sniffed everything while the cats peered into the creek, searching for guppies, crawdads, anything that moved.

"Can you imagine owning all the land that the Garths owned or the Holloways? And they were so smart they never subdivided over the decades. Even after 1865, they hung on pretty much until World War One, when cars changed things. A bit of money began to creep south of the Mason-Dixon Line."

"It's a flood now." Harry laughed. "But you know, I respect those people who held it together, who didn't want to divide up their land even though they no longer had money."

Susan smiled. "No weed wackers, tractors, or snow-plows. Tough, how tough they were."

"Your people have a wild history. All that talk about Creole blood."

"Harry, it was just talk, because Francisco Selisse and Maureen, the first wife, didn't have children. Well, she didn't. He availed himself of local talent."

"It's kind of like the Cherokees, isn't it? They interbred with the white people and the blacks, and certain last names underline that. Selisse is a name still seen in the phone book and at Junior League."

Susan sniffed. "Oh, when I was in Junior League, Marilyn Selisse always claimed to be descended from Francisco. She had that Creole look. I never paid attention to it."

"Getting snotty, are we?" Harry teased her.

"I couldn't stand her then and I can't stand her now. I will shortly be facing her for the country club championship, and you know she does nothing but play golf. Once she married Leigh T. Roudabush, can't forget the T, she focused exclusively on golf."

Leigh T. Roudabush created and owned a plumbing supply company that expanded as housing expanded. If a fixture was created of marble with gold faucets, he'd find it for you.

"She had what he wanted," Harry remarked.

"Six children later, yes." Susan laughed.

"Speaking of Creoles, today is Napoleon's birthday, 1769, and he married a Creole."

"She must have been a real bombshell." Susan took another deep breath, getting her wind back. "History records her as having bad teeth, being of average intelligence, but a woman who drove men crazy."

"You know, I don't envy any woman that. I just want to drive one man crazy," Harry said thoughtfully.

"I think you do," cracked Susan. "Me, too, but when I was little I used to wonder about the Selisse monument in the graveyard. And I wondered if I had Selisse blood. G-Mom swore no and said G-Pop's grandmother, who was still alive when she married Sam, said the Holloways did not have a drop of Selisse blood. As you know, we've got all the family Bibles, as much as the discharge papers for Mother's family for the men who served. Francisco didn't serve in the war, but he helped pay for it."

"As did Ewing Garth. Those kind of people never get credit."

"No, but they usually thrive in business or run for office. Holloways have been running for office since the time of Monroe. I can't decide if we are anchored by our past or imprisoned by it."

Harry reached down to pet Tucker, who, like the cats,

had given up on the guppies. "We're southerners. We're imprisoned by it."

"You can't say that to a member of the DAR," Susan teased her.

Harry unfolded the new topo map. "What I can say is let's go. We should reach the corner of the Selisse tract in an hour if we keep a steady pace."

Susan was already tired. "Then we have to climb that hill."

"One step at a time," Harry encouraged. "Come on."

"What I look forward to is a big lemonade and Mignon or Mother driving us back to my station wagon. We sure aren't walking back."

"Susan, you walk the golf course when you can," Harry said.

"That's different. Actually, I wish Farmington and Keswick and all the courses would outlaw carts. You're supposed to walk. It's part of the game; plus, you feel great after eighteen holes."

"Money. Jam 'em on the links."

"Hate it," Susan forcefully said, then noticed a rock outcropping. "Look on the map."

They stopped. Harry pulled the map out of her back pocket. "It's here. There are two more back on Garth's. This one's pretty jagged."

Pewter sat down. *"I'm not going in there. Too dark."*

"You can see in the dark," Tucker chirped.

"Doesn't mean I'm sticking my head in there."

Mrs. Murphy dashed in. "*It's teeny. Two people could wedge in. No bears.*"

Pewter was having none of it.

"These rock outcroppings aren't common down here in the Piedmont. More the farther west you go, but I think the rock outcroppings and little caves we do have were formed by the glacier," Harry noted. "Virginia owes the glacier a big thank-you. All that soil that was pushed down and little plants and creatures that don't live elsewhere. We are the true dividing line between a northern climate and a southern one."

"Ned is fascinated by that, too," said Susan. "Once he got on the environmental bandwagon he's made it a priority to study everything unique to Virginia. He knows even more than G-Pop, who made environmental protection a priority when he held office."

"The environment wasn't so important politically then, so he was ahead of his time," Harry remarked. "But these little caves and outcroppings, they were part of the Underground Railroad."

"G-Pop knew that. He was always interested in the war and he told me when I studied history in high school that the Underground Railroad started when some of the northern states outlawed slavery, end of the eighteenth century, more in the nineteenth. Until then there wasn't anywhere to run." Susan found the railroad daring.

"Wouldn't it be great to start a tour company that took you on the different paths of the Underground Railroad?" Harry shaded her eyes. They were close to the corner of the old Selisse tract.

"Would. You'd think someone would have done that."

"Susan, here's the thing. Well, let me back up. Reverend Jones says that the Wests, the people that built St. Luke's, questioned slavery, and their children and their grandchildren became part of the train, so to speak. But no one knows too much about how they did it. Things like just getting food to the runaways without someone smelling you out, literally."

Susan put her hands in her back jeans pockets. "Why would we know about it? If we did, wouldn't it mean they got caught? Or were killed, sent to an early grave?"

"You're right. Never thought about that."

Leaving the cool creek bed, the sound of running water, they climbed the steep hill. The animals panted. Harry and Susan would slip, bend over, go up on all fours. Finally reaching the top, they beheld the Blue Ridge Mountains in the distance. To their left, the gathering of buildings could be seen, the distinctive rooftop of the château easily visible.

Sitting for a few moments under a chinquapin, everyone waited until they weren't breathing heavily.

Back on their feet, they approached the graveyard in fifteen minutes, the Selisse tomb dominating all. The animals ran ahead, the cats leaping onto the carefully laid stone wall about two and a half feet high around the family graveyard, a neat rectangle thirty-five yards by thirty-five yards, planned with enough space for future generations if the deceased were carefully laid out.

"Tucker!" Mrs. Murphy smelled something wrong and hollered. *"Bark!"*

Without questioning, Tucker barked loudly, and Owen followed his sister.

Pewter jumped off the wall, running to the Selisse tomb. She let out a horrendous yowl.

Knowing their animals, Harry and Susan ran toward the graveyard.

"Oh, no!" Susan quickly opened the wrought-iron gate.

Right behind her, Harry rushed to the monument.

Governor Samuel Holloway was sprawled at the foot of the Avenging Angel, the flaming sword aloft. He lay on his side, his feet toward the monument, his body across the tomb for Jeffrey Holloway, his hand on the grave of Holloway's second wife, Marcia West Holloway. Sam had joined his ancestors at last.

37

Monday, August 15, 2016

Fifteen minutes later

Noticing Mignon's car parked in the driveway, Harry put her arm around Susan's waist. "Will you be all right alone here for a minute?"

"Yes." Susan nodded, tears in her eyes.

"Let me check the house just in case." Harry ran toward the governor's house, Mrs. Murphy, Pewter, and Tucker preceding her.

She cautiously opened the front door. Not a sound. Walking down the main hallway, she looked into each room. Tucker sniffed the closets in the rooms containing them.

"*In here!*" Mrs. Murphy meowed.

Hurrying to the call, Harry stepped into Mignon's small office. She was slumped over her desk, her face on the keyboard. Harry immediately rushed to her, took her pulse. She was alive.

Picking up the phone, Harry called 911, calmly gave the location and the situation. It wasn't until she put the phone in the cradle that she realized Mignon's computer was gone.

Harry ran out of the house and back to Susan, who was now sitting on the ground next to her grandfather.

"The sheriff's department will be here in a few moments." Harry sat next to her childhood friend. "I'm sorry."

Owen, wedged next to Susan's leg, gazed up at her with soft brown eyes.

Tucker joined her brother.

Mrs. Murphy and Pewter sat next to Harry.

"I wonder why he came out here?" Mrs. Murphy asked.

Intently studying the freshly mown grass, Pewter said, *"Looks like he crawled for part of it."*

"Poor man. How painful it must have been. He had to have known he was dying." Mrs. Murphy hated to see Susan cry.

Harry put one arm around her dear friend. What could she say?

Susan finally gasped. "He had a good life, didn't he?"

"Yes."

"Sometimes I think of G-Pop in the war, jumping off that sinking ship, staying in the water until he got everyone onto a life raft or anything to hang on to."

"He had incredible courage."

A siren lifted their heads and the animals', too.

Susan wiped her eyes. "That was fast."

"He was our governor. It should be," Harry soothingly said.

"Can you imagine being governor?" Pewter asked, whiskers swept forward, as she noticed the rooster-tail plume of dust from the squad car, an ambulance right behind.

"No," Mrs. Murphy replied.

"You two aren't pack animals, you don't understand." Owen nuzzled Susan. *"Pack animals need a leader."*

"I always thought it was because humans don't have much sense. If someone is your leader you can blame it all on him," Pewter thoughtfully replied.

"And I suppose they always can, because the leader won't have any more sense than the rest of them," Mrs. Murphy responded.

Tucker stood up as the squad car parked in front of the house. *"You all are too independent."*

They left off the subject as Sheriff Shaw and Cooper walked toward the cemetery. Two people from the ambulance unloaded a gurney. The driver stepped out of the vehicle, too. Everyone made their way toward the fallen governor.

Harry called out, "Go into the house first. Miss Skipworth is the third door on the right."

Susan wiped her eyes again. "What's wrong with Mignon?"

"I'm not sure. I think she was hit on the head."

"Harry, why didn't you tell me?"

"There's nothing you could have done and you deserved a quiet moment with your grandfather. I thought it best to leave her. If I'd moved her I might have harmed her more."

"What's wrong?"

"I think she was knocked out." Harry said this loud enough for Rick and Cooper to hear.

Rick left her. "Coop, you stay here. I'll be right back."

Cooper expressed her sympathy to Susan even as she studied the ground with a practiced eye. She noted, as did the animals, the marks on the turf for the last fifteen yards. The governor had struggled with what little strength he had.

"Coop, we walked up from the creek and found him," Harry informed her. "Maybe a half hour ago now. I think he had just passed."

Cooper knelt down, touched his throat where the jugular is, then touched the inside of his wrist. "Yes, I think you're right." She pulled out her cellphone with the camera, expertly taking pictures, including the turf. Then she told the ambulance boys to take his body to the ambulance.

If Susan had thought about it, she would have understood why. The day was hot. Best to take the body to the morgue, wait for Penny's orders on whether to perform an autopsy or take the remains directly to the funeral parlor.

The ambulance driver had gone into the house with Sheriff Shaw, come back out, and pulled another gurney from the back of the ambulance.

As he waited in the house for the other two to join him, Cooper asked a few questions.

"Susan, do you know where your grandmother or your mother are?"

"It's Monday. Mom has been coming over daily to help G-Mom with shopping, little things like that. G-Mom's usual day is Tuesday for shopping, but with G-Pop's increased needs, she goes out more often now. She usually takes Wendell Holmes, the dog, as he has his own special fan in the car. G-Mom doesn't like to be without the dog. I haven't called her. I thought I would wait for you all."

"Would you like me to call her?" Cooper offered.

"No. I'll do it. I'd like to call her now."

"Of course. Let's go into the house or in the shade." Cooper put her hand under Susan's elbow to walk with her while Harry walked on the other side.

Tears ran down Harry's cheeks. She loved Susan and hated to see her in sorrow, and she also loved G-Pop. She'd known the ex-governor all her life as Susan's grandfather, which was how she would always regard him. Fame and success meant little to Harry. Friendship meant everything.

Once in the house, Harry and Cooper walked Susan to the kitchen. She sat down and called her grandmother while Harry opened the fridge to fetch everyone an iced tea.

"*Tuna?*" Pewter stood on her hind legs, patting Harry's knee with her paw.

"Not now." Mrs. Murphy swatted at her.

"This is a terrible time. I need to keep my strength up." Pewter did, however, drop to her four paws.

"G-Mom, is Mother with you?" Susan, hearing an affirmative answer, said, "Come home. G-Pop has passed. Harry and I found him. There's nothing you can do. The ambulance is here and so is the Sheriff and Cooper. But come home."

"Where are they?" Harry asked, when Susan ended the call.

"Down at Barracks Road." Susan named the shopping center.

"I'll wait with you. Let me go out to Rick for a minute."

As Cooper left them, Susan slumped in her chair. "It's not like we didn't expect it, but"—she paused—"I guess you're never ready."

"No. No. Especially for him. He was a force of nature," Harry consoled her.

Susan nodded, then added in a small voice, "That's why it was so hard to see him go down. He fought it hard. He faced death with courage."

Harry reached across the table, taking her hand. "He'd faced death before. He'd seen a lot of it."

Later, back at the farm, Harry jumped when her cell rang. Fair jumped, too.

"Is she all right?" Harry asked Susan.

"They think Mignon suffered a mild concussion. Her sight is blurry in one eye, but she seems clear in her mind. She remembers nothing, doesn't think she heard anything. I wonder if G-Pop heard her get hit over the head, got up and tried to follow whoever did it?"

"I don't know. How's your mother and grandmother?"

"Philosophical. Accepting. They don't know why he went outside, but pretty much G-Pop did what he wanted."

"Do you need anything? Fair and I will zip right over."

"Thank you. Ned's here. The kids will be here tomorrow. If I had to find my grandfather, I'm glad it was with you."

Susan's son and daughter, adults working in big cities, would bolster her. Anytime she saw them, her spirits lifted.

After ending the call, Harry relayed the message to Fair. "I have a funny feeling."

"It doesn't appear simple, does it? And where is the computer?" He wondered at this as well.

Harry called Cooper, home from work now. "Coop, it sure was good to see you today."

"Mignon will be okay. It will take time. Sometimes a person's memory returns."

"Susan called me. I'm calling you because there are four things which don't add up. I'm sure you've thought of them, too. First off, Mignon being hit over the head. Second, her computer is missing. Third, the governor struggling to the graveyard, and four, the marks on the mown grass. He grabbed grass to pull himself along and I fear died in pain."

"Rick and I have talked about that. Mrs. Holloway requested his body be taken directly to the funeral parlor. Pushing her for an autopsy might not be wise."

"Here's what I can't get out of my head. Why did the governor go to the Avenging Angel? He's trying to tell us something."

No one had noticed the small squares scratched onto the base of Francisco Selisse's tomb. Placed there over the centuries, they called down curses. Could it be that a curse, undetected, had haunted the Holloways for more than two hundred years?

38

Sunday, April 17, 1785

Ewing Garth stared into the fire in his large sitting room. "It will be another frost tonight."

Gathered around him, his two daughters and sons-in-law agreed.

John listened to the comforting crackle. "I thought we had harder winters in Massachusetts than here, but maybe I was wrong."

"Most years I plant by now, but this year I am inclined to wait. After the last frost is the time." Ewing sighed. "Charles, what hear you from your brother?"

"Parliament involves him more than he anticipated, though he likes it. Our father weakens but refuses to surrender his rounds of sociability. Nigel reports that France is embroiled in outrages over lavish expenditures by the queen, the nobility. Perhaps it's human nature to shine, to be fashionable in address and dress." He slightly smiled.

"Who spends more, men or women?" Catherine raised her eyebrows, ready for everyone's response.

"Oh, women, indisputably." Ewing placed his folded hands over his abdomen. "The cost of lace alone!"

Rachel laughed. "Father, who had to have a brocade waistcoat?"

"Now, dear, I can't look raggedy when called upon to do business. A man is judged by his appearance."

The sisters laughed, then Rachel replied, "So are women, and even more, Father, men are judged by the appearance of their wives, daughters, even their sisters."

"Well, now—" Ewing tried to find something with which to counter this.

Filled with humor, John said in his deep voice, "I believe the ladies have a point."

"Well, they do, but consider *our* wives, they need no adornment. Jewels pale next to them," Charles added.

Rachel reached over to pinch him. "Very flattering, but jewels do not pale."

"Sweetheart, what is a ruby next to your lips or a sapphire next to your eyes? Naturally, I am proud when we go in public and you wear such bewitching clothes, but I admire both you and your sister. You are not vulgar. Nothing is overdone."

The two sisters liked hearing this but wondered if this would come back to haunt them if they happened to find an alluring bauble.

"He's quite right," said Ewing. "Your mother would wear her silk dress, the dark blue one with the bit of lace." He patted his upper chest. "Her figure was beyond compare."

"She also wore the diamond-and-sapphire necklace and earrings you bought her when I was born." Catherine grinned.

Meekly, he agreed. "Yes. But, well, I don't expect you girls to understand, but I found your mother most beautiful in the morning. She'd sweep up her hair with a ribbon, wear her flowing housedress, and when she walked, the skirt would move just so. Oh, what an apparition."

The two young men nodded, then Ewing changed the subject. "Hiram finally removed the leaflets with the reward for information about Dennis McComb's disappearance. Isn't that odd? Nothing. You'd think someone would have at least found the body. Hiram believes Dennis found Moses, and was then killed by him. That's a good story and certainly serves the purpose of pushing for more constables and at a higher salary."

"He does have much territory to cover," Rachel blandly replied.

"He does, but we must take care of our own problems." Ewing held up his hands, palms outward. "I'm not saying we don't need constables any more than I'm saying we don't need a militia, but who is to pay? It seems every legislature in every state froths at the mouth, always over money."

John and Charles had never told their wives what really happened on the way to York. Nor did they discuss it between them. Had to be done and that was that.

Apart from stories about York, they mentioned that on the return trip they passed the farm wherein they'd spent a night. A beautifully carved sign now hung on a pole: TWILIGHT ACRES. The wives enjoyed that story.

"It is vexing," John agreed, then added, "I know I am in the small numbers, but I believe we need a standing army and a navy. As long as the Europeans fight among themselves, they will leave us alone, but I believe once they realize the natural riches here, they will be back."

Ewing was intrigued. "Do you really?"

Charles stuck by John. "Money is even more of a problem there than here. The British, the French, the Austrians, even the Russians, continue to advance in artillery. The Spanish possess a good navy and they are much closer to us than the others. When they look at the New World, they see riches to plunder, riches so they can build even bigger armies and navies."

"Yes, the Spanish are in the Caribbean and beyond, but we must remember your countrymen also ply the Caribbean. I'm a simple man," said Ewing, who was not. "I believe in trade. Trade brings peace. War disrupts trade, drags people down with heavy expense and taxes. Those countries overrun are despoiled. If I can sit at a table and deal with men different from myself, why can't they? Which reminds me of Francisco Selisse, a hard man, to be sure, but he was tireless in his pursuit of profit and he always made sure something was left on the table."

"Beg pardon?" Charles had not heard of that expression.

"The man was shrewd and difficult to overcome. But if you dealt fairly with him, even though he would get the better of you, he left money on the table so you had something. And he never, ever bragged about winning his hand, so to speak."

"You dealt successfully with him." Catherine said this with warmth.

"Yes. I found it more hospitable to form a few ventures with him than not. We did well on our timber purchases. However, look at the success of the forge at Scottsville. He had a feel for such things."

"He was a brute," Catherine pronounced in judgment.

"He was." Ewing, startled by the loud crack of a log, laughed at himself. "I don't know how you two withstood all that gunfire during the war."

"Harder on the cannoneers," Charles said. "They went deaf."

"The strange thing is, you get used to it," John stated. "The bombardment at Yorktown seemed almost natural after a time."

"Speaking of Francisco, Rachel, I think you will be owing me four embroidered pillowcases."

Rachel, eyes wide, exhaled. "It's not even a year. I thought Maureen would wait a year."

Catherine laughed her silvery laugh. "I didn't. Jeffrey Holloway is too handsome and she is going to snatch at pleasure where and when she can."

This subject enlivened them all. Their laughter was so loud it awoke snoring Piglet.

• • •

While the Garths sat by the fire, the flickering light of another fire played on the ceiling. Ailee had gone into labor. Bettina, Bumbee, Serena, and other women attended to her. As this was the young woman's first birth, she was frightened.

With the exception of Ewing, everyone on the farm knew about and protected Ailee. She had not needed to run onto the outside stairway and into the woods. It helped that it still felt like winter and fewer people were about. The large weaving lodge attracted no attention except for those few women who wove cloth. At night, Ailee would walk, hooded, with other women for a bit of exercise. Within a week of moving into the large loft, she recovered sufficiently to cook. She also learned to repair garments and to darn socks. She never spoke, nor did she smile, but she expressed her gratitude to others. She would take their hand and squeeze it.

The labor lasted six hours, exhausting her, but finally she delivered a healthy girl.

When Bettina held her up to Ailee, the new mother turned her face away. The baby was white. She was not Moses's child.

Wisely, Bettina did not try to force Ailee to hold her baby. "Bumbee, fetch Ruth."

Within minutes, Ruth climbed the stairs, removed her coat, studied the mother.

"Ruth, will you take the baby?" Bettina handed the

tiny perfect little thing to the young woman, who was nursing her own baby.

Ruth couldn't hold any baby, kitten, puppy, bird, without wanting to mother it. The little hands waved in the air. Ruth held the child against her bosom and rocked her. "Look at the face. What a pretty baby."

Bettina, Serena, Bumbee looked at one another and smiled.

"Ruth, I will see that you are rewarded for this. Best go now."

Ruth threw her coat back on, held the baby under the scratchy wool, and left while the other women cleaned up the place, as well as Ailee.

Bumbee sat by Ailee. "You sleep now. I'll be here. I'll stay up here."

Bettina trod downstairs, brought up a pillow and blankets for Serena from her cot. "If you have to lie down, and I would, this will help. It's going to be cold tonight. I'll throw more wood on the fire on my way out."

Bettina and Serena looked at Ailee, then at each other. Bettina put her hand on Bumbee's shoulder and squeezed.

So much sadness and nothing to do for it.

39

Monday, April 18, 1785

Bumbee awoke with a start. She looked to Ailee's cot, but the woman wasn't there. Half asleep, she carried her blanket and walked down the stairs, ready to stir the embers of the fire, throw on some logs to warm up the place. The cold steps on her bare feet roused her. At the bottom she saw Ailee hanging from the top railing of the stairway to the loft. She'd twisted her sheet to make a noose.

Dropping her blanket, barefooted, Bumbee rushed out into the cold. Father Gabe's cabin was the closest. She pounded on his door. Already awake, the old fellow opened it.

"Father, Ailee's dead."

After Bumbee told him what she'd found, Father Gabe gathered a few men. They cut the poor woman down, wrapping her in the sheet with which she'd hung herself just as Bettina and Serena hurried in.

Bettina touched the sheet. "Oh, child, what have you done?"

"Let's bury her now," Father Gabe ordered. "No laying out."

So the straggly group shortly found themselves standing over a deep open grave, into which the wrapped body of Ailee was placed.

The light frost still made digging the grave difficult.

Bettina recited the benediction instead of the service for the dead. "May the Lord bless thee and keep thee, may the Lord make His face shine upon thee and be gracious unto thee."

Bettina stopped at Ruth's cabin, which rested on the north side of the row, closer to the main house. She knocked on the door, opened it to find Ruth nursing the two babies, hers and Ailee's, with a two-year-old at Ruth's feet, the fire warming them all.

"Ruth, the babe's an orphan."

Ruth looked into Bettina's eyes. "Ailee wasn't strong, poor thing."

"She'd seen enough." Bettina dropped into a handmade wooden chair next to Ruth. "I will talk to the Missus."

Ruth nodded. "And I will pray."

Bettina reached over to stroke the newborn's cheek. "So much pain, so much pain." Then she smiled. "But like a little cricket you'll be happy and hop around. All your sadness came early."

"Amen." Ruth patted the baby's cheek, as well.

Shawl wrapped around her, Bettina, always erect, slowly walked to the main house. Serena fell in beside her.

Serena felt dreadful. "If only we'd known how she felt. We could have talked to her."

"Honey chile, if someone has a mind to leave this earth, you can't stop them. They'll find a way. Ailee's with Jesus now, her sins are washed away. She was far more sinned against than sinning."

"But to take your own life." Serena gasped.

"A sin, yes, but she will be forgiven. Christ died for our sins. The Old Missus and I would talk of such things."

"I barely remember her."

"Her girls shine like she did. We will find out just how much today."

"Oh, Bettina, they won't cast out the little one." Serena clasped her hands together as though in prayer.

"No, they won't, but I have an idea." That was all the formidable woman would say.

After making Ewing's breakfast, hearing him prattle on about buckwheat versus old-time red clover, she and Serena washed up the dishes, stoked the kitchen fireplace. Then Bettina walked to the stable, where she knew she'd find Catherine.

"Jeddie, where's the Missus?"

"Back paddock." Jeddie pointed in that direction. "Serenissima's paddock."

Bettina found Catherine leaning over the fence, watching the pregnant mare walk.

"Morning, Bettina."

"Miss Catherine, Ailee had her baby. Will you come with me and see?"

Such an unusual request alerted Catherine. She walked next to Bettina to Ruth's cabin. Bettina said nothing. She knocked on Ruth's door.

" 'Min," Ruth shortened. "Come in."

Seeing Catherine, Ruth stood up, the two cradles in front of her and the two-year-old asleep on his small pallet.

Bettina slightly lifted the patched cradle blanket. "Born last night."

Catherine leaned over. "She's beautiful." Then it struck her, the child was white. Ailee was light-skinned, but the child was white.

"Ailee hung herself this morning," Bettina quietly informed Catherine.

The beautiful woman's hands flew to her heart. "Dear God. Oh, Bettina, how could she? How could she leave this tiny little thing?"

"I don't know." Bettina shook her head. "I reckon when she saw the baby, she knew it was Francisco's and she didn't want it. She hoped it would be Moses's baby."

"Did she ever speak?"

"Never."

Catherine sank into the handmade chair as Bettina sat

on a sturdy bench and Ruth sat also. "Ruth, you are kind to nurse the child."

"She can't help how she came into this world. She will never know her mother's love."

"No, but she can know love. Ruth, I will pay you twenty dollars a month to feed the baby." As this was a large sum, Ruth drew in her breath. "You will have anything you need for her, your baby and son. Don't show her to too many people yet. I need to talk to my sister and to our husbands."

Bettina's eyes focused intently on Catherine. "Missus?"

"Bettina, how do you fight a scandal? If you deny it, nobody believes you. Not that anyone would think who this baby's father is, nor that we harbored the mother. We will never speak of that."

Feeling Catherine's eyes upon them, the two women agreed. It wasn't difficult to agree. That knowledge would be too dangerous.

"You all tell our people never, ever speak of Ailee or Moses," said Catherine. "And we will never tell the baby."

Ruth rocked both cradles with her feet, as her husband built them with rockers on the bottom. "Miss Catherine, what are you going to do?"

"Pull the wool over my father's eyes. I hate to lie to my father, but there's no other way. If I'm successful, I'll tell you how to handle this and him. If I'm not, I don't know exactly what will happen. You see, if I am right, she won't be raised as a slave. She'll be free. She'll pass."

Bettina sat up straight. "Lord, Miss Catherine!"

"What is gained by another woman being a slave? This little baby has a chance." Catherine's eyes shone brightly.

Ruth, smiling, looked down at the sleeping newborn. "Then we must all help her."

One hour later, Catherine and Piglet had herded John into Charles and Rachel's house. Working on his drawings, Charles reluctantly stopped, but he wasn't peevish about it.

Catherine explained everything that had just happened.

A long silence followed.

"What can we do?" Charles was dumbfounded.

"We fight a scandal with a scandal," said Catherine. "First, we tell Father that this is the illegitimate child of a townswoman. We feel we must not reveal her name to protect her, but I rashly promised to take the child."

Rachel smiled at her sister. "Better I do that. You never do anything rash. You're too logical."

"Well, one of us has to do it. All right. All right." Catherine pushed on. "We take the baby up to him, put her in his arms. We all four ask him to protect the child, to allow you two to raise her as your own."

"That's the scandal?" John wondered.

"The beginning. The next time there is a gathering, we take the baby. Naturally, everyone will buzz, and we tell them this is our cousin's child and she was unable to raise it. They won't believe it. They know we haven't had children, but they'll believe we're protecting our cousin with a lie. We do have Mother's cousins down in Charleston. Won't be long before the rumors fly. And yes, people will know she's illegitimate, but we will deny that, hotly deny it."

Piglet barked.

"You, too," Catherine said, breaking the tension.

"Is Ailee in an unmarked grave?" John asked.

Surprised, Catherine answered, "She is."

"That doesn't seem right," he somberly replied.

"It doesn't, but we can't put her name on anything," Catherine said.

"We can place slate over her grave. She's in the servant's graveyard with the others, right?" Rachel asked.

"That's where Bettina said they buried her. We've all promised never to speak of Ailee or Moses or any of this. I know of no other way."

"Well, let's do it, then," Charles resolutely said. "Ewing's had his lunch now and is smoking his second pipe of the day."

Ewing looked up from the broadsheet he was reading. Bettina had been informed when Catherine walked through the back door. Bettina sent Serena to fetch Ruth.

The four sat down with Ewing, who was aghast at the sordid story. Why should they take this baby? The girls pleaded. He thought it highly irregular. Someone else can raise an illegitimate child. They also told him they'll use the cousin tale to protect the townswoman so close to home.

Ruth came in with the girl. She held the baby for Ewing to see, and at that very moment, the baby girl opened her eyes, appearing to look directly into Ewing's. She managed a tiny smile. He smiled back. Then he held out his arms. Ruth put the baby in his arms. Ewing Garth had fallen in love at first sight.

That sundown, Ewing visited his wife's grave. He told her everything.

"I don't know if I did the right thing, but, my love, is not life the most precious thing?"

As he spoke, a great blue heron flew overhead, looked down at him, uttering his croaking call. Ewing believed his wife had answered him.

Within six weeks of Rachel and Charles taking in the baby, Ruth being the wetnurse, Rachel became pregnant. It took Catherine and John a bit longer, but Ewing's dream of having a house filled with grandchildren came true.

Marcia West, as Rachel and Charles named the adopted baby, grew into a unique beauty, famed for her cat eyes. She lived a fabled life, bequeathing to her own offspring two things: high intelligence and a physical weakness impossible to control.

Monday, August 22, 2016

Flags across Virginia flew at half mast. Governor Holloway's funeral cortege started at the statehouse. Various civic worthies praised him. Edward Cunningham delivered a fulsome speech in which he promised to continue the work of his grandfather. Subdued though it was, the whiff of campaign clung to it. His sister Pauline and her husband and children had flown in from Montana, and she, too, gave a short speech with an engaging story about her grandfather teaching her to fish. She caught one, cried when she pulled it out of the water and saw it wiggling. So Sam took the hook out of its mouth and threw it back, saying he hoped the fish was a Democrat. Millicent chose not to speak.

Finally, the motorcade rolled down Monument Avenue as people lined the streets to say goodbye. Some knew him. Others remembered him from their youth, and for others, it was a good excuse to get out of work.

A parade is a parade, even when the lead vehicle is a hearse. The overcast day could have been hotter, but it was hot enough.

Once out on I-64, cars pulled over as the police motorcycles preceded the funeral cortege. Some people honked their horns as a farewell. Most watched, and those who remembered his career felt the breath of time passing.

Two hours later, due to the slower pace, the line of vehicles had thinned out to twenty. The shiny black hearse pulled up to the graveyard. A tent placed by the open grave offered shade. Penny and her children and grandchildren sat under it. As childhood friends of Susan's, Harry and Fair sat in the rear, along with some of Eddie's old friends and Pauline's. Oliver Wendell Holmes sat at Penny's feet.

The graveyard service, the true Episcopal funeral service, was brief and dignified. It seemed a more-than-fitting goodbye to a war hero, a public servant, a man who made his mistakes in public, finally learning from them. Sam was a man who continued to serve, even out of office. Any historical group could depend on him. The Miller Center for Public Affairs benefited from his presence, as did the American Cancer Society, which he and Penny supported fully. Given the many eulogies spoken in Richmond, none were spoken here. The huge spray of lilac-tinged roses, Sam's favorite flower, covered the walnut casket. Bound with gold and white ribbon, it was taken off and the casket lowered into the earth.

"Ashes to ashes, dust to dust—"

A Navy honor guard fired volleys, and then, instead of taps, a bosun blew a ship's whistle, which the governor had requested in his precise funeral instructions. He didn't want eulogies, but given his status, there was no way to avoid that in Richmond.

Millicent Grimstead was on one side of her mother, Pauline Cunningham on the other; the three women walked slowly back to the house, where the parting reception would be held. Susan fell in behind her mother, as did Eddie, the spouses behind what Sam always called "my girls." How alike they looked.

Harry had often noticed this, but it truly struck her at this moment.

When Harry's parents were killed in an auto accident, she came home from Smith to find that Miranda Hogendobber had arranged everything. Susan had also come back from her own college to help. Millicent and Penny stepped in, too. Pauline had already moved out of state.

Looking around, Harry saw so many friends of Susan's, from all over the country. As was the custom, in a time of crisis or sorrow your friends stand by you.

A TV camera rolled at a discreet distance. Sheriff Shaw, Cooper, and others on the force remained on the periphery. Other officers tended to traffic out on Garth Road.

Once inside the house, Harry found Mignon, a hat covering her bandaged head. The new part-time nurse, Rebecca Coleman, was also there. The place was bursting at the seams.

After an hour, Harry asked, "Susan, do you need anything?"

"No," Susan replied. "It's wonderful to see this tribute to G-Pop."

"And G-Mom, too. People love your grandmother."

"Harry, if only I knew why he went out to the Avenging Angel. It haunts me."

"Don't worry about that now." Harry kissed her friend on the cheek. "We can think about it later. Do you think your mother or G-Mom need anything?"

"No. I thought Pauline's tribute exactly what G-Pop would have liked, him throwing back the fish because she cried."

"Yes. Even Eddie behaved," Harry said.

"More or less. He did promise to carry on G-Pop's legacy. He could have concentrated on G-Pop and not said a word about his sorry self."

"Susan, there's no such thing as a politician who cannot talk about himself. It's a form of malaria—once bitten, it forever recurs." She half smiled.

"I used to hate funerals. Now I understand it's the respectful way to say goodbye."

Harry agreed.

As Harry walked down the hall lined with ancestors she noted a grieving Wendell Holmes at the foot of the governor's chair.

Walking in, she knelt down to pet the sad dog. "Wendell, you made him happy."

"He was my poppy," the springer spaniel moaned.

"You have to take care of Penny."

"I will," Wendell promised.

Harry stood up. The door connecting into Mignon's tidy workspace was open. She heard rummaging. Going over and looking in, she saw a focused Mignon opening the long desk drawer, shifting papers inside.

"Mignon."

The young woman, without looking up, said, "I'm remembering things. *Ha!* Got it."

Mignon held up a thumb drive as Harry came over to her. "I put everything on this, including sensitive information which I didn't put on the page. I wanted to talk it over with the governor."

"Let's get this to Cooper right away without calling attention to ourselves if we can." The two women moved through the crowded rooms surreptitiously, until finally locating Cooper.

Mignon took the deputy's hand, placing the thumb drive in it. "Found it. I remember I made it."

Expression unchanged, Cooper slid her hand into her pocket. "Thanks. I hope this tells us what we need to know."

Later that night, sitting on the sofa, cats around her, Tucker at her feet, Fair sitting across from her in the deep club chair, Harry said, "It was a good sendoff, wasn't it?"

"Was. I expected more raking his political career over the coals in the media. I'm glad they didn't. Nothing to be done about it now. It's not like he was Governor George Wallace."

"Governors have to deal with Washington's messes, don't they? I mean, if there are budget restraints, the federal tap is turned off, the states can't print more money. The federal government can print whatever they want. Any Supreme Court decision, the states get it in the neck. No matter what that decision is, there are those for it and those against. To me the biggest difference between the president and a governor is the governor actually has to solve problems, has to look his constituents in the face. Presidents can add another layer of Secret Service people, plus the usual phalanx of flunkies."

"I wouldn't put it that way, but you're not far off, I guess. But the president deals with foreign policy. If there's a wing nut anywhere in the world, he or she deals with it. Well, some don't, but then the next guy is stuck with an even bigger mess."

"Maybe they're all cowards. At least Governor Sam wasn't a coward."

"Honey, I know equine health. Politics, I don't know anything anymore. It all seems crazy to me."

"Crazy, I think that's why I can't settle myself. That man crawled out to the Avenging Angel, the last yards he crawled so he could sprawl over those two tombs. I think he was trying to tell us something."

Fair wrinkled his brow. "I can't imagine what."

"There's something in that cemetery. Why was his nurse Barbara killed? And Mignon hit over the head and her computer stolen? You know, well, you didn't know, that Susan's mother was taking the computer home at night. And why was Crozet Media broken into? Whatever it was, the governor figured it out."

"Then why didn't he just come out with it?"

"Maybe he didn't know until it was too late. Whatever it was, someone else knew. Had to."

"Never thought of that. What could be so dangerous? Fraud? Robbing state funds? Misconduct while in office, bribes, that sort of thing?"

"He may have been wrongheaded, but he wasn't a crook. Samuel Holloway was an old-time politician, you scratch my back and I'll scratch yours, but he wasn't a crook."

Fair thought about that, then replied, "It is hard to imagine him stooping that low."

"Could he be protecting someone else?"

Fair put down his book. "If he would protect anyone, it would be Penny. Even if he caught Eddie with his hand in the till, he'd turn him in."

"Exactly. Eddie has the most to lose. I know Eddie is behind this somehow. If he's been on the take, he's darn good at hiding it. Of course, he could have an offshore bank account."

"That would come out sooner or later. Look at how our government browbeat the Swiss bankers." Fair thought allowing some crime is better than criminalizing many activities.

"Putting money in offshore accounts does not necessarily signal a criminal," Harry replied.

"Honey, are you thinking that the governor did not die a natural death?"

Stroking Mrs. Murphy's cheek, Harry thought for a moment. "Why take the risk? He was close to death and his decline has been sadly apparent. Maybe he was pushed along but not actually killed? The only reason to kill him would be if he were planning to spill the beans before he died, make a clean slate of it. If our killer knew the governor's condition, maybe he provoked his death with overexertion, something like that. He goaded the governor, who would die without a mark on him other than his needle marks from all the shots. It could happen. What I really think is that whatever it was he knew or wanted us to know, maybe he wanted it to come out after he died. Maybe to spare Penny. Fair, something's just beyond reach."

"If it is as you might think, then who is in danger now?"

"No one, I would think, unless someone else knows or has an idea. The computer is gone. Whatever was at Crozet Media might be gone. Barbara Leader is gone."

She thought for a moment. "But Mignon found her

thumb drive. She could be in danger, but only Cooper and I know."

"Then it's medical. If that's your list."

"Huh?"

"The one person killed is the one person with medical knowledge."

"The man was dying of leukemia. How could that affect anyone else?"

"Maybe it was more. Who knows? Maybe he had AIDS. Something like that could be a bombshell. And you know, more and more older people are contracting HIV."

"Now I'm more confused than ever."

"Maybe that's for the best, honey."

Tuesday, August 23, 2016

"I can't ask her that." Susan shook her head. "I know she won't do it."

Harry walked over to Susan's bay window as they retreated inside due to the heat. "It would be terribly upsetting to exhume the governor, but what if he *was* killed?"

"Given his tenuous hold on life, whoever did it would be stupid," Susan countered. "Again, given his deterioration, why kill him?"

"If I knew that, I'd have this figured out. Okay, what if he wasn't directly murdered? But whoever was in the house, whoever knocked Mignon over the head, knew that violent exercise or even a brisk walk, given his state, would hasten his death. I talked about that to Fair, and the more I think about it, the more I think I'm on the right path."

Susan rested her chin in her hand. "Well, given how

quickly he was failing, I'd think any extreme exertion would stop his heart."

"It's possible that G-Pop heard Mignon get hit. Think about it. He tries to protect her, chase down the culprit, but his heart gives out."

"It would be like him to protect her." Susan turned this over. "It might be, but we shouldn't say anything to G-Mom, or my mother, for that matter. They're really feeling the loss. Give them time. I take that back. Until you or I find something, we shut up. They're going through enough."

"But what if your mother and grandmother find out whatever it is that created this mess? Then they're in danger."

"Harry, if they were in danger, we'd know by now," Susan resolutely said.

"Not necessarily. Let's try this. We go through his office."

"Harry, I can't go over there and root around my grandfather's office at a time like this. You expect me to ask G-Mom and Mom? Come on, now, be reasonable."

"She's right," Mrs. Murphy, sitting on the floor with Owen, Pewter, and Tucker, affirmed.

"There is another way. G-Mom and your mother run errands, have lunch, sometimes even play a few holes of golf on Tuesdays. Let's drive by and see if their cars are gone. We go in and see what we can find."

"I don't know about that."

"We aren't stealing anything, we aren't harming anything. We're double-checking in a way that won't disturb them. I'm willing to bet your grandmother wants to keep to her routine. It's consoling."

"And what if they come back while we're there?"

"First, we go to Ivy Nursery, buy a lilac, his favorite bush. If they come, we run out back and begin planting it."

"The lilacs have bloomed."

"So we're planting for next spring. Buy some mums for now. They won't think anything of it, and it's better than flowers from the florist."

Susan smiled. "Have you ever seen so many flowers?"

"Overwhelming, and your grandmother sent them all to cancer wards for both adults and children here and in Richmond." Harry's voice softened. "Here she is losing her partner of—"

"Sixty-eight years." Susan filled in the number.

"Sixty-eight years and she's thinking of others."

"Flowers can be shredded or chewed, but people should have sent more food. Mrs. Holloway would have given some to Harry," Pewter opined.

"Doesn't mean she'd share with you." Tucker raised her eyebrow.

"The kitty-in-distress routine. Works every time," Pewter bragged.

Noticing that Pewter was preparing to flop on her side and utter piteous cries, Owen ordered, *"Don't you dare. Not in my house."*

"Spoilsport," Pewter said and huffed.

"Susan, come on. Let's hit up the nursery. It's ten o'clock, hot, and will get hotter. If we do have to plant because they're in the house, it will be tolerable. If we get to go through his desk and they return, we'll be doing it in a full furnace, but it's worth it." Harry made this decision for Susan.

"Well—"

"Susan, it can't hurt!"

"All right. All right."

Susan complained the entire way to Ivy Nursery and the entire way to Big Rawly.

"They aren't here!" Harry jubilantly remarked. "Let's take the lilac and the mums out back, pull out the shovels, so if they return all we have to do is zip out back."

"Why do I let you talk me into these things?" Susan said, carrying the mums.

"Because you know there is something. I'm right. We just have to figure it out."

"Yeah. Yeah."

They put the lilac and the mums under the shade of a large old poplar, then scurried back inside.

The governor's library office smelled like his cologne with a dash of bourbon. The two cats and two dogs followed them into the office. Wendell had gone with Penny and Millicent.

Harry took charge at the desk. "You cruise the side drawers, I'll pull out the large center drawer."

Susan pulled out a double drawer, two front handles,

but it was one big drawer inside. Down on her knees, she sifted through hanging file folders.

Harry lifted out a blueprint for a new potting shed. Underneath that were car and truck titles.

"He had a truck title going back to 1952!" Harry exclaimed.

"Was it a Ford?"

"Was."

"That was the truck my mother wrecked when she got her driver's license." Susan smiled. "He said it was the best truck he ever owned."

Moving to the other side of the desk, Susan opened the top drawer. "Envelopes, stationery, and what's this?"

Harry took the copper bracelet. "Remember about ten years ago when people wore copper bracelets? Supposed to help the metal balance in your body."

"That's ridiculous. And I never saw G-Pop wear this."

"Doesn't mean he didn't put it on when no one was around. Keep going."

"Pushy," Susan grumbled. "I hate it when you're pushy."

"I do, too," Pewter commiserated.

Pulling open the bottom drawer, Susan carefully pulled out a huge, ancient family Bible. "Wonder why he took this off the shelf and put it in here?"

"Maybe to protect it from dust. It's a little raggedy and very valuable."

Susan opened it to the first page, neatly folded white

papers were lodged there. "Hmm." She began reading the papers. "Diagrams. Look."

Harry replaced the contents of the long, narrow drawer and shut it while Susan placed the Bible in front of Harry with the diagrams.

"G-Pop's mother, pneumonia. G-Pop's father, fatigue, weakness, sudden collapse." Susan read off the first diagram on large paper.

"He's made a diagram of cause of death." Harry pointed to the prior generation, G-Pop's grandparents. "His grandfather was born in 1862 and died in 1930. Cause of death unknown. Suspected heart attack. Grandmother, breast cancer." She looked above to reread the cause of his mother's death. "Pneumonia."

"People have always known what a heart attack is." Susan was also fascinated by this diagram.

"A wide umbrella, you can shove a lot of stuff under it. In the end, everyone's heart gives out. And people knew what cancer was, but I don't know as they realized how many cancers existed. Breast cancer becomes obvious, as do any cancers producing large tumors. Wonder why he did this and how he researched the results."

"Easy." Susan flipped a few front pages in the large Bible, one on the right labeled "Deaths." While not as artistic as an illuminated manuscript, the old Bible's pages were impressive, as was the handwriting of successive generations marking Holloway comings and goings. Having a beautiful handwriting carried weight then. It bespoke years of practice starting when one was about six, and it bespoke education and respect. You had to be able to read and write to execute letters in such a high fashion.

"You're right." Harry noted the brief description of each passing just as she noted the birth weight of each baby, as well as how many did not live to maturity. "We take survival for granted. Look at the notes by these babies. 'Weakened. Died in her sleep.' Or this one, 'Wasting disease, such pain. Age thirteen.' Sad. How did parents go on? Seems like everyone, including your grandfather's grandparents, lost one or two children." Harry read again. " 'Cecil Holloway, born 1860, died 1863. Could take no nourishment.' Your poor great-grandmother. Imagine watching a child starve and no one knows why."

Susan soberly looked at the elegant writing in black ink, surprisingly unfaded. " 'Hortensia Kelly Holloway, born 1842, died 1888. Cause unknown. Died in her sleep.' She lost two children, she lost her husband in the war, but somehow she kept Big Rawly together and she never remarried. Amazing what people live through and still accomplish. Do you think we're as tough as they were?"

"No." Harry continued reading, then pulled over the diagram.

"Some of these names have a red cross by them. His grandfather. The thirteen-year-old who wasted away. Goes all the way back to Marcia West Holloway, and there's a full red line under her name. She died at sixty-six. What's it say in the Bible?"

"Fainted. Never awakened," Susan read.

"What's on the other sheets of paper?"

Susan unfolded two more sheets, her grandfather's upright handwriting very legible. "He wrote out the symptoms of leukemia, when he began to feel tired, headachy. This went on for longer than I knew. Years. He drew squares for when he'd feel poorly then a line up to a plateau."

"You think he knew?"

Susan pointed to the second diagram. "Sure looks like it."

"Look at this third diagram." Susan pulled out another page. It was like the first diagram with the names, births, and deaths of Holloways but this carried forward.

"Your name is on here!" Harry exclaimed.

"It's like play it forward. He has his name, no death date yet, but that red cross by his name. Penny's name then Mom and Pauline, a red cross and question mark, and then a red cross by Edward and Edward's daughter. None for me, and he even cited our children. Look, there's Danny."

" 'Tested.' " Harry puzzled over this notation. "Each of the cousins' children, his great-grandchildren, have 'tested' written by their name and"—she squinted, for the writing was small—" 'negative' by some. Red cross by others."

"What is this?" Susan threw up her hands.

"I have no idea, but your children and their cousins were all born within the last thirty years."

"Right," Susan affirmed. "But so what?"

"These are the only names with 'tested' by them. My guess is that everyone born before those thirty years could not be tested. Maybe that's why he has a question mark by some with a red cross."

"Died from what?" Susan wondered.

"Well, HIV, for one," Harry replied.

Susan pulled up a chair, sat next to Harry, studied the diagrams, looked back over the careful citings in the beautiful family Bible. "None of us have HIV, and if we did, apart from sorrow, how could it affect G-Pop?"

"Maybe he had it?" Harry questioned. "Got it before tests."

"Harry, G-Pop died of leukemia, a blood disorder, and if you go down the list of family deaths, it's possible other ancestors died of it. Weakness, anemia, that sort of thing, could all be attributed to leukemia. They just didn't have a name for it."

Harry leaned back in the big chair.

"Cancer passes, doesn't it?" Tucker questioned.

"Some do." Owen seriously considered this. *"Golden retrievers get a lot of cancer."*

"Susan"—Harry sat upright—"when Danny played football for Western Albemarle High, didn't he have to have tests? Stuff so the coaches would be alert should he become dehydrated, collapse?"

"Yes. We also had to take him for allergy tests," Susan added. "My daughter, too."

"Do you remember the tests?"

"I do. For some parents they caused a problem, especially the HIV test. That sent a few right through the roof. There was a test for a heart murmur, what we always called an athletic heart, a heart that skips a beat. They had to blow in a paper bag. Some kind of lung-capacity thing. The list goes on. I suppose it's for the good."

"More. Tell me more tests."

Susan, picking up on the urgency in Harry's voice, focused intently. "If anyone had a fracture from the past, even early childhood, we had to deliver a current X-ray. I tell you, getting the kids on the teams wasn't cheap."

"More. Or let me put it this way, apart from the HIV test, do you remember anything that surprised you?"

A long, long pause followed this. "Come to think of it, there was one. The kids were screened for sickle-cell anemia and the sickle-cell trait at birth. It was quite hush-hush. Only the parents were informed of the results, but the sickle-cell trait could develop into sickle-cell anemia, which can cause sudden death, say, if a football player is training too vigorously in high heat. That was a test done at birth. So Ned and I copied them and gave them to the coach, who promised secrecy. We didn't care."

"What do you mean?"

"The administration and the coaches believed that if a student was known to carry sickle cell, they might suffer discrimination. They were responsible about it and went to all this trouble because of the recommendations by the National Collegiate Athletic Association."

"Western Albemarle is a high school," Harry responded.

"It might as well be a junior college. It's not like when we went to high school. Those coaches watch these kids with a hawk eye. If anyone looks a tad peaked, they sit them down. They're real bears about concussions. I never worried that my kids would suffer. The coaches were vigilant and so were their teachers. Luckily, my two didn't take drugs and made good grades."

"Much of that due to you and Ned."

"Thanks, Harry, but remember when we were in junior high and high school? It was all our peers. Fall in with the wrong crowd and down you go."

Harry pulled the more recent diagram to her, comparing it with those of the ancestors. "Susan, what if your grandfather was trying to trace a hereditary condition?"

Susan's eyes widened. "Sickle-cell anemia?"

"Exactly. And there is discrimination. Sickle cell was considered a black person's disease. In the old days, if your grandfather had it, they wouldn't tell him. They never told any white person. Doctors always said the white patient had leukemia."

Susan whispered, "Maybe Dr. Fishbein did tell him. It's a different time now."

Harry murmured, "And maybe the governor began to figure it out on his own. Susan, it's a different time for some of us. Plenty of people are trying to hold back the clock."

"Dr. Fishbein only told the family G-Pop had leukemia." Susan now wondered about this. "Harry, this is so upsetting and so confusing. If my grandfather knew he had sickle-cell anemia, I think he would have told us."

"I think he would, too. Maybe he was on the cusp of truly knowing it to be true. Maybe that's why he crawled to the graveyard, to the Avenging Angel. It's in the graves, in the family."

"Dear God." Susan began folding the papers back together.

"For a lot of people it wouldn't matter anymore, but for some, sickle-cell anemia would still be a stigma. If you're African American and you carry the trait, who will marry you? And what if the person you hope to marry has the trait? Big decisions. If a white person has it and being white is really important to you, if you're also carrying that taint of racism, sickle-cell anemia could be considered a disaster."

No sooner was that out of her mouth than Susan blurted out, "Eddie!"

Harry pondered this. "Given his political base, it would create huge problems. And given his ambition, who knows what he would do? I'm trying not to believe it."

Mouth tightening, Susan replied, "What is the old saying? 'Power corrupts and absolute power corrupts absolutely.' Not that Eddie has absolute power, but he is a rising star, he speaks to overflow audiences." She paused. "I don't know. I don't really understand it."

"If we did, I suppose we'd be in politics," Harry realistically said.

"Car!" both Tucker and Owen barked.

Susan hurried down the hall. "It's Eddie! Put everything away!"

Just as Eddie entered the hall, Harry closed the large side drawer of the desk.

The cats and dogs sat with Harry and Susan as they had raced to the sunroom.

Susan and Harry waited for Eddie to find them.

"What are you two doing here?"

"I could ask the same of you," Susan fired back.

"Thought I'd see if G-Mom was here."

"Eddie, you know she runs errands on Tuesday." Susan fought to control her emotions, which worried Harry.

"What's wrong with you? It's not a crime to drop by and it's not a crime to forget her schedule."

"Bull, Eddie. And who are you to talk about crime?"

His eyes narrowed. "Susan, you're off your nut."

"I didn't kill anyone, Eddie. You did." Enraged, Susan had let the cat out of the bag.

Sitting on the back of the sofa, the two cats prepared to fight or flee.

Eddie waved off Susan as though she were a bug. "I don't need to listen to this." He turned to Harry. "I hope you don't believe this nonsense."

"What I believe," Harry calmly stated, "is that your craving for power has warped you. The funny thing is, Eddie, I don't think you believe half the stuff you're saying. You're throwing red meat to the reactionaries. You don't care about women's advancement, gay marriage, abortion, all that social stuff, any more than you care about cleaning up the toxic dumps we have in the state. You just want votes."

His face reddened. "I do care. I care about giving away free money to people who sit on their asses. I care about all of it. And when I'm elected, you'll see."

Susan stood up to face him. "You will never be elected senator. You killed Barbara Leader because she knew G-Pop had sickle-cell anemia, not leukemia, and you have the trait as well."

Shocked, he took a step backward. "How do you know that?"

"Research." Harry stood up next to Susan.

Eddie backed up, reached a large umbrella stand by the sunroom door filled with umbrellas and a few canes. He pulled one out, then advanced on them. The big silver ram's head would be lethal.

"Run!" Harry opened the door for Susan to bolt, then followed.

Eddie charged out the door after them. The two friends had a head start, but he was gaining.

"Susan, run to the cemetery," Harry yelled. "We can dodge around the tombstones."

"I think I can make it to the car."

"If you don't, you'll be clubbed to death. We can keep him busy in the graveyard." Now alongside Susan, Harry said, "He has that club, but it's two against one. All one of us has to do is get behind him."

Trusting Harry just as she trusted her to hand her the right club on the golf course, Susan put on the afterburners. The two women reached the cemetery, put their hands on the low stone wall, and vaulted over it. The cats followed suit. The dogs ran to the wrought-iron gate, where Owen lifted the latch. Just as the two corgis dashed into the supposedly peaceful last resting place, Eddie shot over the stone wall as though it was a high hurdle in track.

Susan and Harry split up. He moved toward Susan, swinging the cane like a maniac. She dodged just out of reach, but sooner or later he'd connect. Harry came back around. Knowing she was behind him, he whirled to swing at her. One close swing forced her to duck, hit the ground, and roll away. He jumped on her. Eddie tried to pin Harry with his left hand while raising his right hand with the cane.

Tucker leapt up, seizing his right arm in her powerful jaws. Owen grabbed his calf.

Screaming, Eddie didn't let go of the cane. Instead, he tried to use it on the dog hanging on him.

Claws at the ready, Mrs. Murphy climbed up his back, ripping Eddie's shirt, biting as she progressed. Pewter latched on to Eddie's leg with Owen.

This gave Harry more time to roll farther away, and Eddie crashed down on the ground with the cane just missing her again. Even though Tucker hung on, Eddie was strong.

Susan, now behind her cousin, was angrier than she'd ever been in her life. She jumped on his bloody back as best she could, wrapped her right hand under his jaw and jerked as hard as she could. She heard his neck pop, but it didn't break.

Harry, scrambling to her feet, ran up to Eddie, put both her hands together in a double fist, and smashed into his mouth. Jagged teeth came out.

Mrs. Murphy had crawled up on his head. She dug her claws in to stay aboard.

The two friends fought with all their strength. Finally, Eddie dropped the cane. Without a second's hesitation, Harry snatched it up and swung over his head and down, straight into his skull. He sagged down. Susan slid off his back.

Yet another motionless body lay at the feet of the Avenging Angel.

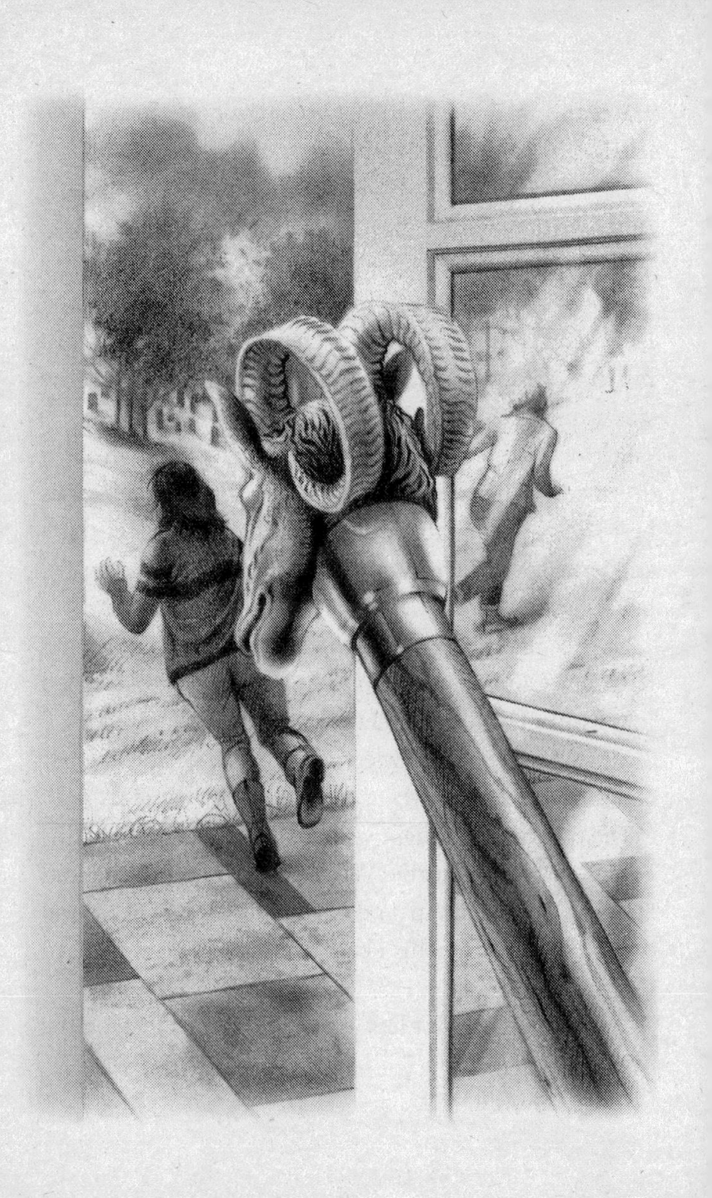

42

Sunday, August 28, 2016

Gathered at Penny Holloway's were Susan; Ned; Susan's mother, Millicent Grimstead; Harry; Fair; Cooper; and the cats and dogs. They sat in the sunroom.

Eddie was hospitalized with a cracked skull and was expected to live. It would take time to know if he would regain normal functions like the power of speech. He had suffered brain damage. There was already a movement to remove him from his state Senate seat.

His wife neither defended nor criticized him. She said nothing because she knew nothing except that his ambition had become ever-consuming. Chris felt that she and the two children had become mere props. She did confirm that Charlene, their daughter, had the sickle-cell-anemia trait. As Charlene was six, she was screened at birth for sickle-cell anemia and the gene. Chris had herself screened so she knew she did not transmit it. Eddie refused to be tested. As both were over thirty, they had never been screened. Anyone under thirty was tested as part of a state mandate. Governor Holloway got his facts right, as he usually did.

Chris told Penny that when Charlene was of age she would tell her, although Penny vehemently protested even thinking about it. To her way of thinking, what good would it do?

"G-Mom, you've been through a terrible time. I wish I could make it better," Susan addressed her grandmother, sitting in her favorite chair, as Penny had recounted Chris's conversation.

"Honey, you take what the Good Lord gives you," Penny quietly replied. "I wish Sam had confided in me, but he probably wanted to sort it out for himself."

"Cooper and I viewed the outtakes for Eddie's website," Harry began.

Penny smiled. "My, that was a day."

"Eddie clearly infuriated his grandfather. I wonder if the governor had been tested for the sickle-cell trait. But whatever was going on between them, Eddie felt threatened."

"I suppose he was. Think what a revelation sickle cell would be. It would undermine Eddie's appeal to his right-wing base."

"As for Sam, he considered his opposition to integration the worst thing he'd ever done. But you all are young, you don't know how we grew up, what we were told. Segregation was a way of life. Most of us questioned it as we matured, then put those questions aside. White people were simply not ready, and it was Sam's fate to be governor when everything exploded. Some people forgave him; others did not. He never forgave himself." Sorrow filled Penny's voice.

Millicent Grimstead quoted a line from the Bible. " 'Judge not lest ye be judged.' "

Feet on a hassock, Ned said, "The Bible is like the Constitution. People pick out what serves their purposes. My dolorous experience in the statehouse is that some elected officials and their constituents live to sit in judgment upon others."

"Hasn't gotten us very far, has it?" Harry remarked.

"What else can they do?" Pewter laughed. *"They can't run fast, they have no fangs or claws, they can't see in the dark. How else can they feel powerful except by judging others to be even weaker and more stupid than themselves?"*

None of the other four-legged souls could answer that, so they didn't.

"Do you think Eddie killed Barbara?" Penny asked.

"I do," Susan resolutely answered. "Somehow he got her to take that drug from the hospital. Eddie must have learned about these things when he worked on drug issues in the House of Delegates. Given that no marks showed up in her autopsy, he found a way to get her to eat it, drink it, or take it as a vitamin. She probably had no idea."

"Such was the medical examiner's conclusion. Our

hope is that if Eddie regains clarity, he will confess. But Barbara, who administered the governor's drugs, had to have a good idea what his true condition was," Cooper said.

"Eddie will never confess," Susan spat. "He'll lie to his dying day. I wouldn't even be surprised if once he becomes operational again he won't go out and present himself as some sort of a conservative martyr."

"Then you and I will be charged with attempted murder." Harry tossed that off nonchalantly. "And we'll have to prove he's a murderer."

"Possible," Susan answered. "But wouldn't it be funny to tell people from the witness stand how he was brought down by two cats, two dogs, two women? The media would have a ball with that."

"And therefore, we all keep our mouths shut." Millicent Grimstead pointed to the two friends. "I trust your report, Officer Cooper, since you were first on the scene, offered no conclusions as to Eddie's attackers."

"Since no one has confessed, all I saw was a man with a split skull, a chewed-up left calf, claw marks on his back. No wild animals were in sight and the call was made by his cousin, who also did not view any intruders." She paused. "But I can now tell you since our computer whiz in the department went through the thumb drive, your husband did know he had sickle-cell anemia. The section of his autobiography, I think that's the correct term, concerning his health traces the symptoms. He uses this as an ironic comment on his former racism. So Mignon also knew. She was lucky Edward suspected her but didn't know for sure."

"This is such a terrible, terrible thing." Millicent's eyes misted.

"Do you think Daddy knew Eddie had killed, Mother?" Millicent Grimstead asked.

Penny replied, "Possibly. The red crosses that Susan and Harry showed us on Sam's diagram, how long he had worked on that. Sam was piecing it together. He must have been researching his own family, as well as the nature of the disease, for months. But yes, I think he knew that Eddie would do anything to cover up that he had the trait. Sam was probably moving toward having Eddie arrested as Barbara's murderer. But he wouldn't do this until he felt the case was airtight. That's the way Sam worked."

"I wonder if that's why he crawled to the graveyard?" Susan would forever remember that sight. "He was telling us the answers lay under the ground, among our forebearers."

"And so they do," Harry said.

Wendell Holmes, next to Penny, said, *"If I'd known, I would have bitten Eddie's throat."*

"We tried," Tucker and Owen remarked.

"My fangs sunk deeper than yours." Pewter puffed up.

"I really thought he was going to kill our human," Mrs. Murphy said.

"It was nip and tuck," Tucker agreed. *"But we prevailed."*

"They'd be dead without us," Pewter boasted.

"Humans are doing the best they can," Mrs. Murphy replied.

"Wouldn't they be better off if we ran the show?" Owen asked.

"They would, we wouldn't." Tucker laughed and the others laughed with her.

Afterword

Sickle-cell anemia occurs most frequently in African Americans and people from the sub-Saharan part of Africa. In the New World those of Caribbean descent have it and it can be found in people from Central or South America. Actually, it shows up now in all ethnicities but the above-mentioned peoples have the highest incidence, especially African Americans.

Francisco Selisse was from the Caribbean and Marcia West Holloway's mother was mixed race, but in the eighteenth century dark enough to be identified as African American. Ailee would have been deemed an octoroon, meaning she was one-eighth African American, her father being white. Those who read history will recall the famously glamorous Octoroon Ball in New Orleans, which was celebrated for decades. As so many have written about it, it must have been one of the best parties in New Orleans, which is saying something.

But both Francisco and Ailee carried the genetic trait, which probably meant that Marcia had full-blown sickle-cell anemia. If two people who carry the trait mate, the numbers, if they have four children, are one without, one with full-blown sickle-cell anemia, and two that carry the trait. It is for this reason that most states now mandate a screening of infants. As adults, they will be able to make informed decisions about whether to have children if they marry someone who also carries the trait or if they have disease as opposed to the trait. If they do go ahead, they can be vigilant about their offsprings' health.

Human beings for centuries, millennia even, could describe illnesses. We often knew which ones were hereditary. Today we have much more information and instead of saying dropsy runs in the family, we can be precise.

What we can do about such diseases when they present themselves is another matter. When you start reading all the literature about cancers, sickle-cell anemia, multiple sclerosis, et cetera, it's a wonder any of us stay upright for long.

Mother Nature will work her will one way or the other.

As for Moses, he more than likely carried the gene as well, given the pains for which his father, DoRe, suffered. When Moses's years of work were up, he remained in York. He'd learned of Ailee's suicide when Charles wrote Bartholomew. He continued to work for the Graves, displaying an aptitude for math. Bartholomew taught him and they worked on many projects together.

Moses married in his forties. He never spoke of Ailee. He doted on his two sons, who also became mathematicians.

Jeffrey and Maureen Holloway lived a good life. If Maureen felt any guilt about killing her first husband, she never showed it. When she died, Jeffrey married the much younger, gorgeous Marcia West. It was a fruitful marriage.

The Schuylers and the Wests became part of the Underground Railroad, although there were no trains then, so the term wasn't used. That's another story.

All our ancestors made decisions that affect us today. It has always been thus. They did the best they could with what they had, and so must we.

Dear Reader,

I am not fat. I have big bones. When I eat, I have good manners. You should see Tucker eat. Furthermore, she'll eat anything. I, at least, display discretion.

Mrs. Murphy and Tucker are either criticizing me or telling me what to do. When I need a second opinion, I'll look in the mirror.

Yours,

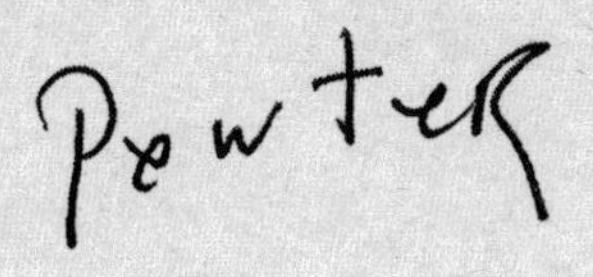

Dear Reader,

Why respond to Pewter's complaints? You couldn't make her happy if you blew a fan on her in Hell.

Now, to this book. Walking along the creek mentioned herein, there are rock outcroppings and small caves. I didn't mention it, but lingering in these old hideouts I could smell ancient tobacco odors, the tang of long-ago fires. Made me think about the cats and dogs who traveled with the fugitives, warning them of danger. I'm sure some of them were tiger cats.

Guess we never will know all of our history, but anything that happened in this country happened to us, too. Still does.

Ever and Always,

Dear Reader,

Virginia harbors many spirits, some even before the English came in 1607. We dogs can feel them, smell them, and sometimes see them. The spirits are human as well as animal, domesticated and wild. But since humans refuse to acknowledge other dimensions, they miss the wisdom these departed souls can impart. Still, humans can often feel spirits even if they won't admit it. Harry feels them at the Avenging Angel tomb.

Pewter denies most of this stuff but she, too, knows we aren't alone. Part of her lack of interest is the departed bring no food.

My mother told me when I was a puppy, "When you drink the water, don't forget those who dug the well." I don't.

I guess the spirits have their realm and we have ours but I have to share mine with Pewter. Not fair.

Your best dog ever,

Tucker

Read on for an exclusive sneak peek
at Rita Mae Brown and Sneaky Pie Brown's
next Mrs. Murphy Mystery

A Hiss Before Dying

Available in hardcover and ebook
from Bantam Books

1

October 17, 2016 Monday

A blood-red sugar maple glowed next to the farm lane as the autumn sun shone through its leaves. Two cats and one dog walked in the pleasant sixty-degree weather toward the barns, the Blue Ridge Mountains at their backs.

The bottom rim of the sun, hovering over the spine of the mountains, would soon dip down, ushering in an explosive sunset followed by a beautiful twilight. The changing seasons specialized in twilights of various blues.

Animals moved about as day gave way to night. Day hunters and feeders headed for home; the night creatures popped their heads out of dens, stuck beaks out of tree hollows, preparing for activity. The deer moved toward their sleeping places, which were usually sheltered from the winds in a thicket. Even the beavers stopped timbering, carrying a few thinner branches toward their lodge. That would be tomorrow's task, trimming the branches.

Mrs. Murphy, the tiger cat, green-eyed Pewter, the overlarge gray cat, and Tucker, the intrepid corgi, relished this time of day. With a few barks from Tucker, the retiring deer enlivened as she chased after them. Deer were so much bigger; to see them scatter away just puffed up the domesticated three. A few harsh words might be exchanged with the fox whose den extended under the roots of an ancient walnut.

The turtles, the salamanders, the fish and crayfish prepared for night. When they sat by the creek, the cats would stare at the freshwater creatures, but in the main they found the fish boring. Birds, on the other hand, squawked, chattered, spit seeds, dropped earthworms on them, cussed the cats unmercifully.

A blue jay looked down from a poplar tree. "*Empty-handed.*"

"*We weren't hunting.*" Pewter detested that bird.

"*You couldn't catch a mouse if your life depended on it. Fat, fat, water rat,*" the handsome bird taunted.

Before Pewter could return the insult, Tucker looked up. She'd heard the sound wind makes through feathers built for speed as opposed to feathers designed for stealth.

Overhead, not too far, a fully grown bald eagle carried bloody flesh in its talons.

The three froze. Even the blue jay shut up.

The eagle tucked its wings close to its body and made a sharp dive toward the three pets, who flattened on the lane. At the last minute, the bird opened its wings, a span seemingly as long as a Cadillac, turned slightly, and with one mighty flap, off he flew.

"*Did you see what he had?*" Mrs. Murphy asked. "*All I saw was bloody flesh.*"

"*A piece of rawhide hung from above his talon.*" The dog looked at the huge bird fast disappearing thanks to his uncommon speed.

"*An eyeball. He carried an eyeball in his talon hanging from the flesh.*" The sharp-eyed blue jay informed them. "*It was swinging. Blue. A blue eyeball. As blue as my feathers.*"

"*Sometimes a horse will have blue eyes,*" Tucker mentioned.

"*Human, a human eyeball. They're easy to identify, really. Somewhere out there is a person with half a face,*" the blue jay proclaimed, opened wide his own wings, then lifted off toward the house.

The three looked at one another, then resumed walking toward the house and the barn.

Tucker, puzzled, wondered, "*Maybe the rawhide held the eagle. You know, he was somebody's pet and he got loose.*"

"*Tucker, a person would have to be crazy to keep a bald eagle. They're ferocious, huge, and wild,*" Mrs. Murphy replied.

"*We were once saber-toothed tigers.*" Pewter puffed out her chest.

"*Yeah, and you sold out for tuna.*" Tucker teased.

"*Better than Milk-Bones. Dogs are really dumb,*" Pewter shot back.

The dog and gray cat argued past the pastures and paddocks. The horses kept eating. They'd heard it all before, including knock-down, drag-out fights in the barn when the two would chase each other, buckets flying, brushes, even halters pulled off their hooks.

Mrs. Murphy generally exhibited more decorum.

They pushed through the animal door at the large screened-in porch, then through the door into the kitchen, which also had an animal door.

In the kitchen, every cabinet door was open, dishes stacked on the counters.

Mary Minor Haristeen, "Harry," stood on a half ladder wiping down the interior of the cabinets with a wet rag. This was to have been a short task. That was three hours ago.

"Don't step on the dishes," she admonished the cats already on the counter.

"*These are old bowls. Throw them out.*" Pewter advised. "*You don't have to keep everything. Look how chipped this stuff is.*"

"*It was her mother's,*" Mrs. Murphy said.

"*Guess what? Her mother isn't here to see it. I am. I don't want to eat out of old bowls. I'm a modern cat.*" Pewter sat close to the stacked bowls, tempted to push them off the counter.

Through the window over the sink, in the light of the setting sun, Pewter saw her blue jay nemesis settle on an overhanging tree branch. The bird turned his head to the right, then to the left to afford a clear view.

"*Fatty!*" he shrieked.

Pewter charged the window, nearly knocking the bowls to the floor, spit loudly, and slammed a paw into the window.

The jay giggled, then hopped up a branch, closer to the window.

"*I will kill him!*" Pewter promised.

"Get off here. You nearly knocked Mom's bowls over," Harry chided.

Harry climbed down the half ladder, put the rag in the sink, wiped her hands. Then she picked up the bowls, climbed back up, and slid them in place. She repeated this until everything she'd put on the counters was back in place.

Just as she finished, the back door opened and her tall neighbor, Cynthia Cooper, a deputy in the Sheriff's department, stepped inside.

"Now you come over. I could have used you to put away this stuff." Harry pointed to the cabinets.

"A cleaning fit." Cooper nodded.

"Fall and spring. Best time." Harry stepped down, folding the ladder.

"You say." Cooper leaned over to pet Tucker.

"Sit down. Hey, look at the sunset before you do."

Cooper walked over to look through the sink window. "Like someone tossed a match into the sky."

"I never get tired of sunsets, or sunrises for that matter. Get off work early?"

"No. It's six-twenty. Tell you what, it's been a long day."

"Accidents?"

"No."

"*Dad's home!*" Tucker rushed outside through the animal doors to greet Fair Haristeen, all six-feet-five inches of him.

"*She's so obsequious.*" Pewter pouted.

Fair stepped inside the screened-in porch, stomped his boots to remove the dust, then opened the kitchen door. "Hi, honey." He kissed Harry on the cheek, then kissed Cooper, too. "Never pass up the chance to kiss a pretty woman."

"You're the worst." Cooper laughed at him even as she enjoyed the attention.

Fair was one of those men people liked, men and women.

"You know, honey, I actually understand that." Harry laughed. "And I'll have you know you've walked into a better organized kitchen. Anyone want a drink? Tea?" Harry offered.

"Too late for tea, but if you have a beer I will indulge. And I owe you a six pack." Cooper promised.

"You do not." Harry pulled out glasses and three beers.

"We saw an eyeball!" Pewter wanted attention so she jumped on Fair's lap. *"It was bloody. A big, blue eyeball."*

"The bald eagle had it." Tucker filled in detail.

Harry, wisely, put down some treats. Pewter liked Fair but dried chicken twists trumped affection.

"How cold is it supposed to get tonight?" Cooper asked. "I haven't had time to check the weather on my phone. Like I said, a long day."

"No frost. We usually get the first frost mid-October but it's warmish right now," Fair replied.

"Which reminds me, time to close in the screened-in porch," Harry noted. "We can do it this weekend and then switch the horses' schedule."

In summer, the horses remained outside at night and inside, out of the sun, during the day. The rotation was reversed in the cold months when fall truly arrived.

"They look good. I noticed driving in how shiny their coats are." Cooper complimented Harry, who took care of them.

"Curry comb. Hair is starting to grow. They're getting ready for the cold. I just brush out the dirt, then brush with a smoother combination, and bingo, they shine like patent leather. Good food helps, too, like some rice bran. Anyway, you said it was a busy day. If it wasn't accidents, robberies?"

Cooper smiled. "No. But I got a call from our dispatcher, telling me to go to Route 250 right at the top of Afton Mountain before it plunges down the east side. Route 250 has a hell of a grade. Drove up there. Nothing urgent, just a call for an extra pair of eyes. Got there and here is this big transport loaded with brand-new Volvos, motor running—everything fine—but no driver. No one in sight. The keys were in the ignition, the emergency brake was on, nothing was damaged. We checked his shipping papers. He was on his way down to Volvo of Charlottesville. Called them. He was due in. No one had heard a thing. We called Louisville, Kentucky, where he'd picked up the freight. Everything was fine when he left. But now: No driver. No cellphone. Only shipping paperwork."

"That's odd," Harry said.

"His wallet was in the truck. Sunglasses. Not a thing touched that we could tell."

"What did you do?" Fair thought it peculiar, too.

"The Volvo dealer sent up three men: one to drive, one as a passenger, and one to follow. Luckily there was someone in the dealership that could handle that big boat. As there was no crime, no report. We thought it best to get the new cars to the dealer," Cooper added. "We looked around for the driver. No sign of him. As a precaution, we dusted the car for fingerprints."

"He could have been carrying contraband." Harry, ever imaginative, thought out loud.

"Well, they go through every new vehicle to prepare it. If something is amiss, I reckon we'll know. But *poof*, just disappeared with that big rig idling by the side of the road."

"Maybe he stopped to go to the bathroom and had a heart attack." Fair offered.

"We'll have bona fide search teams out tomorrow. It's rugged terrain. Really, could be just what you said but that doesn't mean we'll find him easily."

"Coop, someone might have picked him up," Harry, always excited by a mystery no matter how tiny or removed from her own life, said.

"Don't know." Cooper shrugged.

"Just think, what if that had been a Brink's truck, a truck jammed with bags of money?" Harry grinned. "An unlocked truck."

Fair laughed. "I remember when I was in third grade. Dad and I were down on Main Street. We'd walked back to Water Street and a truck full of beer turned over. Cans rolling everywhere. I mean in minutes half the male population of Charlottesville was there scooping up them cans."

"See, there are good accidents." Harry laughed.

"Well, I saw an eyeball. That's not a good accident." A tidbit of dried chicken fell out of the side of Pewter's mouth as she loudly made her points.

"Pewter, they don't care about eyeballs any more than you care about a rig full of new cars." Mrs. Murphy shrugged.

She was right. For now.